Dear Reader,

I'm thrilled to share with you the third book in the Sweetblood series, *Tempted by Blood*, Jackson and Arianna's story. The world is a deadly and seductive one, where a team of vampire Guardians fights to protect humans from Darkbloods—vicious members of their race who kill like their ancestors and sell the blood on the vampire black market. The rarest, called Sweet, commands the highest price.

If you've not read the first two books, don't worry. The Sweetblood world is new to Arianna, too, but as you'll find out, she's not new to it. The owner of Paranormalish, a blog that checks out paranormal happenings, she's learned to ask a lot of questions, dig beneath the surface and take a lot of pictures, which gets her into all sorts of trouble.

And that's where Jackson comes in. He's a charmer and a playboy, but he's hiding a terrible secret. When he's assigned to protect Arianna from Darkbloods, she ignites in him those dark cravings he's been struggling to control. Tempting him as no other could, she awakens what he fears is the real enemy—the one buried deep inside him.

This is a story about secrets—everyone has them. But it's what we do with them that matters…because some are more dangerous than others.

Happy reading!

Laurie

LAURIE LONDON

TEMPTED *by* BLOOD

Recycling programs
for this product may
not exist in your area.

ISBN-13: 978-0-373-77645-0

TEMPTED BY BLOOD

Acknowledgments

Thank you, first of all, to my wonderful readers. A year ago when my first book came out, I was surprised and humbled that so many of you took the time out of your busy lives to contact me. I've loved "meeting" so many of you.

To the fun and sometimes zany online book bloggers and reviewers, thanks for your support and enthusiasm. I'm continually amazed at your creativity, professionalism, dedication and love of the romance genre, particularly you rabid paranormal fans. You make it cool and exciting to be a reader and an author in this digital age.

To Becky, Mandy, Janna, Kandis, Kathy and Shelley, thank you so much. I'd be adrift without you. Thank you to the Cherryplotters for the great ideas and for confirming when I'm on the right track...or not.

Thanks to my friends Julia, Eric and Marc, for tidbits that I twisted for my own evil purposes, and to Kevin, for help with a local urban legend that inspired a few of the details.

Thank you to my wonderful editor, Margo Lipschultz, for all your support and encouragement. You breathe life into my ideas and know just what needs to be done to make them better. Thank you to everyone at HQN Books, including the awesome digital team and art department, for all your behind-the-scenes work. Thanks to my agent, Emmanuelle Morgen, for believing in me.

To my husband, Ted, and my two "babies" who are taller than me, thanks for putting up with crazy. I love you.

TEMPTED
by BLOOD

To Mom, for your endless love and encouragement, and your incredible example.

CHAPTER ONE

WHEN SHE SAW the number of vehicles parked in the second driveway on the left, Arianna Wells tensed and almost turned her car around. She hated having an audience for these things.

With her eyes forward, she drove past the house, then a dozen others in the neighborhood, and parked the old Cadillac under a streetlight around the corner. Out of habit, she scraped the wheel rims against the curb. Her father had loved this car and was so proud of himself when he gave it to her for her sixteenth birthday. Problem was, she'd been nineteen at the time and he'd mixed up her birthday with one of his many ex-girlfriends. Adding a new scratch when she was frustrated or pissed off always made her feel better. She shoved the transmission into Park and it lurched into a rough idle.

She stretched her arm over the seat and peered out the back windshield. Maybe that wasn't the right place. All the houses had the same mirror-image design, painted one of three colors with identical rows of box hedges lining the walkways. Roads to the left and right led to similar cul-de-sacs. Everything was confusingly similar. It'd be easy to turn down the wrong street and knock on the wrong door.

She pulled the address from the front pocket of her jeans and realized she still needed to change her shoes. She'd gone in to work today for an unscheduled meeting and hadn't thought about tonight until she was already at the office. Hopefully, she had a spare pair of boots in the trunk. If they went to the site of the disappearance, traipsing through wet bushes in flip-flops would really suck. From what she'd learned about getting to the Devil's Backbone, even wearing hiking boots, it wouldn't be easy.

She opened the folded scrap of paper: 4112 Maple Grove Avenue.

Yep, that was the right house. The one with all the cars.

She crumpled the scrap into a ball and threw it on the seat. Thanks to rush-hour traffic in Seattle, it had taken an extra hour to get here and she really didn't want to reschedule. The hems of her jeans were damp from running into the office and she was still chilled. She supposed she could've parked in her company's garage today, thus avoiding the rain and the wet sidewalks, but she didn't have a pass and paying forty bucks for a two-hour meeting was just wrong. She could have asked Carter, one of her coworkers, to hack into their building's property-management company and print her a parking pass, but unlike him she had principles. Although on a day like today, she wished she didn't.

She grabbed her phone, hit Redial, and a young man answered on the first ring.

"Look, Blake," she said, not bothering to hide her

irritation. "I told you I don't do this with a bunch of people around."

"Is this Icy Shadows?"

He only knew her by her screen name and Arianna preferred to keep it that way.

"Yes, and don't tell me your mom is hosting her book club."

She heard the low murmur of male voices, a muffled curse, and she was pretty sure someone in the room with Blake said, "Do you see her yet?"

Good thing she'd parked around the corner.

"It's just me and the guys who were with me that night. That's all. I figured you'd want to talk to them, too."

What part of "I want to conduct this interview alone" didn't he understand?

Before agreeing to meet with him, she'd thoroughly checked out Blake's background, as she did with every-one she interviewed in person. He was a seventeen-year-old honor student at Cascadia High School, on the varsity tennis team, vice president of the French club. In a write-up in the local paper about some community service project, his marketing teacher had called him a leader.

Using her internet-sleuthing abilities—some people would call it stalking, but she preferred to call it due diligence—she'd tracked his movements online. She found his social-media pages, followed him to the few blogs he'd read, hers being the only one that didn't in-volve music, and she'd looked at dozens of pictures and videos. The few times he'd posted on her blog, he'd been respectful and articulate. The guy was who he said he was—a decent kid with a very interesting story that she was dying to hear in person.

But she knew nothing about his friends and she had her rules.

"We'll have to do this another time, then. Good-bye—"

"Wait. Wait. I'm really sorry, but they really want to meet *the* Icy Shadows from Paranormalish."

I'll bet.

"Sorry. I'm shy." Not really. Although she did hate crowds, she guarded her online identity with the finesse of someone navigating a minefield. Each movement, each next click could be disastrous.

If Xtark Software found out how she spent her free time, that she lied on her employment application about having a blog, she'd lose her job. The game company was anal when it came to its employees' use of social media, requiring everyone to turn over their computer passwords so company security officials could monitor their online activities. They worried about employees sharing too much and other companies stealing their proprietary secrets—as if someone in the graphics department would know anything about software design. But a blog run by any employee was a huge no-no. As far as she was concerned, however, it was no one's business but her own, and she preferred to keep it that way.

And then there was that business with her ex. When he'd found out about her blog, it had turned her life upside down.

She'd learned long ago that people thought her interest in unexplained phenomena was weird…crazy, even. Sitting on a cold metal chair at the Fremont area police precinct as a five-year-old, having no one believe her had taught her that. They'd tried to explain that shadows don't just come alive and kidnap people; a real person took her mother. They'd given her a stuffed animal to hold—Comfy Carl, they called him. She could still picture the bear with crisscrossed threads for eyes that smelled as if it'd spent months in the damp trunk of a patrol car. But she knew what she'd seen and a toy wasn't about to convince her otherwise.

At a young age, Arianna figured out pretty quickly that if she wanted to be taken seriously and keep a roof over her head, she'd better keep her interests to herself. The blog was her way of exploring topics she couldn't discuss out loud.

No, she couldn't risk Blake's friends finding out anything about her. It could show up later online somewhere, making it easier for Xtark to discover what she was doing. Conducting these sorts of things one-on-one lessened the chances of that happening.

"Okay, okay," Blake said. "I'll make them leave."

Arianna paused, her hand on the ignition, still not convinced she wanted to chance it.

"Pleeease?" His voice cracked midstream and he suddenly sounded younger, more vulnerable.

She knew her readers were dying to hear what happened that night at the Devil's Backbone, complete with pictures and videos. Ever since Blake posted that the captain of the football team never came back after visiting the site and a watered-down version hit the news outlets, her blog readers had been pestering her to interview him. Many of them had never seen pictures of the site of the old sanitarium, which had burned to the ground at the turn of the century. Situated on private property, it was rumored to be haunted, and kids snuck in late at night to party there. Blake claimed the missing boy had been with them when they visited the site that night. He'd posted on her blog that he was too scared to go with them, so he waited in the car. All of the kids returned except for one. Sure, they could've been drinking, but given the fact that it happened at the Devil's Backbone it was enough to pique her interest.

"A guy named George from another website has been emailing me, wanting to know what happened, but I'd rather talk to you."

She winced. "George from OSPRA?" That meant he'd been reading her blog.

The Olympic Society for Paranormal Research and Analysis had been relentlessly pursuing her since she started blogging, pressuring her to join their organization of crazies—vampire hunters, ghost hunters and alien-invasion enthusiasts. After she'd repeatedly turned them down and inadvertently scooped them on a few investigations, they got pissed off and someone tried hacking into her website. If it hadn't been for Carter, who beefed up her security settings, they'd have succeeded.

"Yeah, I think so."

Bastards. That was it. "Okay. I'll be there in fifteen minutes. But if even one of those cars is still parked out front, the interview is canceled. For good. Understand?"

Blake lowered his voice. "Is there any way my younger brother can stay? He was one of the guys with us that night, too, and has a totally different story than I do."

Did no one listen anymore? Was the spoken word that hard to understand? She let out an exasperated sigh and picked at a tear in the vinyl upholstery.

Interviewing one of the others who was there would give a good perspective to the article—make it even more compelling. George wouldn't be able to compete with that.

Blake was quiet on the other end of the line, waiting for her answer. She could almost hear his silent plea for help. Then it dawned on her. Maybe he was seeking validation from her so that his friends would know he wasn't making up the story. That all of this wasn't just a twisted joke or the product of an overactive imagination. Clearly, he had experienced something but no one believed him. A familiar pang tugged at her heart. She knew how it felt to witness something that wasn't possible. To be given a stuffed animal and a pat on the head because no one could figure out how to make you feel better.

She recalled the disapproving looks her great-aunt and -uncle had given her as they'd lamented that this preoccupation of hers was too deeply rooted in the satanic. After a few months, they'd given up and sent her to live with a string of foster families.

"Fine. Your brother can stay. But if I come back and get any inkling, any strange or nagging feeling that you lied to me, and your friends aren't gone—"

"I promise," he said hastily. "Just me and my brother."

"Okay. Fifteen minutes."

Before the line went dead, she heard him yelling at his friends to leave.

JACKSON FOSS DIDN'T PLAY by the rules, and he sure as hell wasn't going to start tonight. Besides, he hated being rushed.

Reluctantly, he raised his head and turned toward the door, feeling his pupils dilate even more than they already were. This was the second time Mitch had interrupted him, and if it happened again, Jackson, swear to God, was going to storm out there and acquaint his knuckles with his partner's face.

Techno music blared from the ceiling speakers. Although it was loud inside the tiny room, its walls upholstered in tufted pink vinyl, he didn't have to raise his voice. His buddy would be able to hear him just fine.

"I said I'll be right out." But he lied—he'd need at least a few more minutes.

He turned his attention back to the woman beneath him. He was aroused but didn't feel like using what the good Lord gave him. That wasn't what he was after. At least not this time.

Soft waves of hair tickled his nose as he settled in again. The too-sweet smell of her drugstore perfume was so concentrated, so overpowering here at the base of her neck that he almost sneezed. He tried like hell to ignore it and placed his hand to her temple anyway.

Technically, Mitch was right. They were on duty

tonight and being on duty didn't involve *this*. He just wasn't a slave to protocol like some people were. Sure, he'd be the first one to admit they shouldn't be at the Pink Salon for more than just a standard walk-through. A drink at the bar? Maybe. Shooting the shit with a few of the regulars? Yeah. But this? Not really.

It wasn't that he wasn't serious about his role as a Guardian—he was. It was just that this was necessary, too.

With a jolt, her energies shot through his palm and up his arm, static electricity popping in his veins, leaving in its wake a warm, numbing sensation.

Heaven.

Inch by inch, his muscles unknotted, the gnawing hunger in his gut subsiding. Clarity settled over him, the clutter in his mind evaporated. Now he'd be able to concentrate on the things a Guardian *should* be doing. Walking the streets. Monitoring the police bands. Hanging out in alleys, searching the shadows for those who lived on the fringe of their secret but civilized society.

For a short time, at least.

Thank God things had been slow lately, so he didn't feel too guilty being here. After the Seattle field team busted a huge Night of Wilding party recently on one of the San Juan Islands, the streets had been pretty quiet. Those who weren't killed during the raid had gone into hiding. Not that there weren't still members of the underground seeking out desirable blood types to sell on the black market—hell, he'd caught one last night stalking a young mother who was holding her child's hand—

but, for the most part, work was slow. Mitch just needed to unknot his tighty-whities and chill out.

Ah, yes, sweetheart, just a little more and I'll be finished.

"You must work out a lot," the woman said, running her hands over Jackson's back.

"Yeah, guess you could say that."

Not wanting to crush her small frame, he shifted his weight slightly and kept his hand against her temple. Evidently the anorexic look was in fashion this winter. The chick he'd been with earlier had been just as skinny.

Having yanked off her own shirt when they got to the room, she now tugged at his clothes, fumbled with his belt. He didn't put distance between the two of them to make it any easier for her.

Lucky for him, she'd had a healthy dose of sun recently—her stored energy levels were higher than most people's in Seattle who lived under a gray blanket during the winter months when the ultraviolet index was low. He was feeling stronger already, much more rejuvenated than if he'd been with someone else.

Had she just been to Hawaii? Cabo, maybe? Yes, Mexico, he decided. When they entered the private room a few minutes ago, he'd asked her to remove her silver rings and bracelets, citing an allergic reaction if his skin came into contact with the metal. Not exactly true, but close enough.

"God, I needed this." Maybe he *would* be able to skip a couple of days.

"Me, too." She managed to slip her hands under the

waistband of his low-slung jeans, reaching, search-ing. Of course, she thought that was why he'd brought her here. It's what he wanted her to think. It's what he wanted everyone to think.

"Ooh, you're commando. Did I tell you I like a man with easy access?"

"You lucked out then because I'm all about easy." He sucked his abs in farther, making more room inside his pants without having to go through the hassle of shoving them down. He'd let her handle him for a few moments while he did his thing. As far as he was con-cerned, it was the perfect combination.

Her fingers brushed the head of his erection and she gasped. "Is that—oh, my God—what I think it is?" She'd found his piercing. Her pulse spiked as he hoped it would.

"It's a little surprise for you."

"No way." She giggled nervously, her voice higher pitched than before. "Does it really, you know, make it better?"

"I'm told it does." That tiny metal stud had seen its fair share of action. With minimal effort on his part, he could easily satisfy any woman. "Like I said, it's your lucky night."

And just like that, her excitement shot into his veins like a pinball ricocheting off the lighted bumpers. He held still and wallowed in the sensation.

She said something else, but he wasn't really listen-ing. This was his favorite part, experiencing the rush of anticipation from a female donor host when she made that discovery. It added an extra spice to the energy.

Fear did the same thing, but he didn't let himself think about that.

She tilted her head, seeking out his mouth.

I don't think so. With his face turned away to keep his fangs hidden from view, he chose not to react to her body language. He ran his free hand down her arm to distract her.

"Kiss me," she ordered.

"Tobacco. Just chewed a wad." The lies easily rolled off his tongue. Only a few more moments, then he was outta here. "Didn't know I'd be hooking up with the hottest girl in the club."

"Really? You think so?"

"Absolutely. If I had, I'd have never taken a dip. I'm addicted, though. Weak. Totally unable to quit. Will you forgive me?" God, he was laying it on thick, but then women liked being with men they thought needed fixing. Men who needed their help.

"Of course." She gave a little laugh that sounded like a cross between a woodpecker and a machine gun. It would've grated on his nerves if he wasn't so mellow right now.

He didn't like to kiss them, if he could help it. Even the pretty ones. Kissing led to feelings, which led to intimacy, which led to talking about the future. Not that he hadn't played house with various women—both human and vampire—over the past century, but whenever they started in with the baby names, the bathroom colors and the mixing of bank accounts, he got itchy. As in the kind of itch that needed someone else to scratch it. After a while, when the charade became too hard to maintain, it just so happened that he'd become a shitty liar, very conveniently forgetting to cover his tracks. He really hated the "sugar, this just isn't working for me any longer" speech, so he gave *them* a reason to break up with *him*.

His last on-again, off-again girlfriend had thrown all his crap on the front lawn when she discovered he'd been with another woman. His leather coat, his Xbox, all his games—ruined in the rain. He didn't blame her for being pissed—he'd expected it. He cringed, though, when he thought about that damn coat. His favorite. It'd smelled musty ever since. Yeah, it was easier for everyone involved to not let things go that far in the first place. It really wasn't worth it.

Dating standards aside, he couldn't kiss this woman anyway, he noted as he ran his tongue over his partially extended fangs. A side effect of being sexually aroused, whether he planned to bite her or not. She sure as hell didn't need that shocking visual. A female screaming at your appearance, if only for a moment before her memory could be wiped, deflated more than just your ego.

With every heartbeat, her energies continued to pulse into him, and her movements became less vigorous. Her nails weren't digging into his ass the way they had been, her ankles no longer clasped behind him. One leg slipped from his hip to dangle bonelessly off the edge of the mattress. Finally, she yawned. With his ear against the side of her face, he heard her jaw pop.

"I'm sorry. I feel so…tired all of a sudden."

"I've worn you out already?" he joked, though he knew it was true.

"Don't worry. I'll totally rally."

When she yawned into his shoulder again, he knew it was time to go. He'd taken enough. He ran his tongue over the tips of his fangs.

But first...maybe just one taste.

With his ring finger, he located and caressed her artery, feeling the steady rhythm of her heart there. He could sink his teeth in and drink. One sip. Although her blood type was common, with all the sun she'd been exposed to, it would have the same stored energy signature.

He'd taken blood from an earlier host, but what would be the harm in another little taste? Or two?

Wait. Stop.

He didn't need more blood. He'd had plenty tonight to sate his physical requirements. This desire was all in his head, he told himself. Completely unnecessary.

Reluctantly, he dragged his hand away. This dark nature of his was a cancer that never fully went away. Coaxing him. Whispering in his ear like a jealous lover who didn't want to be forgotten.

No. He wouldn't give in this time, as he had less than an hour ago. He clenched his teeth, cutting his lip in the process. "Shit."

"Wh-what's wrong?"

He waited a moment, willing his fangs to recede into his gums. "Nothing." With effort, he pushed away from the drowsy woman, forcing himself to look at her as a living, breathing human and not unsuspecting, vulnerable prey.

Neon lights from a neighboring building flashed through the narrow window high on the wall, obscuring her features in garish, almost cartoonlike pink shadows. Her shirt was open, her breasts exposed. They didn't sag much to either side, he noted. Instead, they proudly displayed an unmoving quantity of silicone beneath the taut mounds, too large for her waiflike body.

What would she look like in forty or fifty years? A grandma with Playboy-size implants. He stifled a chuckle and his fangs disappeared completely back into his gums. Humor always had a calming effect on him.

He didn't want to consider that increased cravings for blood and energy were the first signs a vampire was reverting to the uncontrollable blood urges of his ancestors. No, he wasn't a damn revert, nor was he in the beginning stages. He'd never killed a human and he wasn't about to start. He may be a screwup in other ways, but there was no way he was giving in to that. Besides, if anyone suspected a Guardian was reverting, tests would be done and he'd be hauled in front of the Council. The sentencing would be swift, the punishment harsh. Regular members of vampire society got a long stint in rehab. Guardians weren't so lucky.

Even though it happened more than a century ago, every detail about that night in the catacombs beneath Paris stuck in his memory like black ink on a fresh piece of paper. It was there if he chose to think about it. The moist stillness in the air. The sound of water dripping in one of the adjacent passageways. Hushed whispers echoing off the stone walls. The shuffle of feet as they made their way in the darkness to gather around the man held in chains.

Traitor, someone hissed.

A disgrace to your family.

You've endangered all of us.

Then the screams began.

Jackson shuddered. He was a young Guardian in training at the time. But even now, he didn't want to think about what had happened to the agent who'd reverted and killed several humans, so he forced the memory out of his head.

The Governing Council was more civilized, or so they said. But once you witnessed something that brutal, that unforgiving, it was pretty damn hard to forget.

This was just a temporary hiccup. He'd muscle through it and be fine. What he needed right now was a little more yin to go with his yang.

She tugged at his triceps and made a little sound of protest. It wasn't a surprise that she didn't want him to go, but he reached for his coat, anyway. They never wanted him to leave, especially after knowing what his body jewelry could do for them. He enjoyed being someone's addiction, liked to be needed, no matter how temporary or superficial.

"You're not going already, are you? But we haven't—"

"What you need is sleep and a healthy dose of sun tomorrow." *Good luck with that, though.* Chances were, in Seattle at this time of year, that golden orb wouldn't be making an appearance anytime soon.

"The sun? I don't get it."

"Just promise me, okay, sweetheart? Rain or no rain. You'll spend time outdoors." He considered telling her to take a vitamin-D supplement, but decided that'd sound too weird.

"Um, sure."

As soon as his boots hit the floor, he leaned over and brushed four fingers over her forehead. "Sex with me was unlike anything you've experienced before," he said, implanting a memory suggestion. "The only thing you'll remember about me is that I'm an amazing lover and tonight was—" he searched for the appropriate dramatic word "—in-fucking-credible."

Her eyelids fluttered briefly as the thought took hold. When she opened them, her lashes hung over her eyes in that unfocused, just-had-sex look. "God, that was mind-blowing. The best I've ever had. You've got a real monster behind that zipper." Even her voice was thick and raspy.

"Why, thank you." There had to be a special place in hell reserved for guys like him.

Techno music blared even louder as he entered the hallway, the sound waves tangible on his skin.

In the dim light, Mitchell Stryker was leaning against the painted brick, arms folded, mouth pressed into a tight line, but he couldn't hide the flicker of amusement in his eyes. Oh, yeah, he could look as pissed off as he wanted to, but Jackson knew better. The guy had a serious case of envy.

Jackson pulled the door shut behind him. "What?" he asked, feigning innocence.

"Dude, you're on a roll tonight." Mitch brushed a blond forelock from his face.

"What can I say? When you got it, you gotta use it."

Even though vampires were naturally more sexually active than humans, any idol worship of Jackson's sexual habits made things a helluva lot easier. No one suspected he had off-the-chart energy needs and that it wasn't sex he was after—at least not all the time. They simply thought he was always horny. Who was he to argue?

Doing a little shuffle step, Jackson snapped his fingers and pointed at Mitch. "You seriously need to get laid, my friend."

Mitch straightened up and adjusted his leather coat with a quick shrug of his shoulders. "Why do you say that? Not that I'm arguing with you or anything."

"If you have to ask, you're worse than I thought. You're way too uptight, banging on my door and shit. You need to be banging something else and let me do my *thang.*" Jackson elbowed his buddy. "Need some help separating a little filly from the herd out there?"

Mitch shoved him back and laughed. "Don't you worry about me. I can manage just fine, thank you very much. Speaking of managing, looks like your *thang* got a little wild in there." He indicated Jackson's lip.

Jackson flicked his tongue out and tasted blood. Mitch probably assumed it was the woman's but he didn't bother to set the record straight. It wasn't as if a sip now and then was against the law.

"Is that the second or third one tonight?"

Alarm bells went off in his head. He didn't want

Mitch to think he was taking blood every time he had sex. He shrugged, tried to act casual as he rubbed his mouth with the back of his hand.

Not long ago, he could stretch it out for two or three days before the energy cravings got too powerful to ignore or the need was triggered by something he didn't expect. And decades earlier, like most vampires, he'd been able to go for weeks at a time without blood. Something inside him was changing, but he sure as hell didn't want to know why. He'd need to be more careful next time.

"Didn't you get it on with that curvy redheaded chick when we got here?" Mitch continued. "I saw you guys stumble out all lovey-dovey, your hands all over her."

He sauntered down the hallway, an extra spring in his step. Goddamn, that chick's energies felt good. "Couldn't help it. Got a thing for redheads."

Mitch laughed behind him. "And blondes and brunettes."

"Hey, I'm all about equal opportunity. Democracy and shit. I like to spread the wealth evenly among the people. It's only fair."

"Sounds like communism to me. Listen. Dom called. He…um…tried calling you directly, but you didn't pick up. He needs your sweetblood report. Says it's a week late and that you're making him look like a lazy ass to Region unless he gets his numbers in soon."

Jackson stopped and pulled out his cell.

Five missed calls—all from his field team leader. Damn. He must've been more engrossed back in that room than he thought.

"How many sweetbloods do you have on your list?" Mitch asked. "If you want, I can do a few of the drive-bys."

He thought about the latest addition, a young human girl he'd saved at the Night of Wilding party. He'd always thought that keeping tabs on known sweetbloods was a waste of time—Darkbloods or other vampires would get to them eventually. It was a fate most of them suffered, despite the Guardians' best efforts to keep them safe. Their addictive blood was almost impossible to resist and commanded the highest price on the black market. But the girl reminded him of his little sister who'd died many years ago. Old feelings of regret welled up but he quickly tamped them down. There was nothing he could do about Betsy now. "Nah, I can do it, but thanks."

He hustled down the hallway toward the main part of the Pink Salon, his boot heels pounding on the floor. Better return Dom's call from outside and see if he could buy a little more time. Although the guy had mellowed out considerably since marrying Mackenzie and starting a family, Jackson didn't want to chance it. His field team leader had a bitch of a temper if you pissed him off, for which Jackson seemed to have a knack. Plus, he could hold a serious grudge.

Jackson pushed aside the rows of hanging beads and stepped into the alcove at the side of the dance floor. As usual when someone emerged from the entrance to the ultraexclusive salons, dozens of sets of eyes focused in their direction. He ran a hand through his newly high-lighted hair—green and blue streaks this time—and his acute hearing picked up a few female sighs. Yeah, chicks dug the hair. Made picking up women as easy as going through a drive-through.

His eyes locked onto a pretty thing sitting at the bar. He flashed her a smile, making a mental note to head over there on the way out. Clasping forearms with the muscle-bound bouncer who regulated the comings and goings of the salon, Jackson slipped him some green. "Thanks, Rocky. You're my guy."

"You bet, man," the human said, nodding appreciatively at the Benjamin before tucking it away. "Anytime. How was the meeting? Enjoy yourself back there?"

Officially, the Pink Salon referred to them as meeting rooms; Jackson conducted a lot of "business" there. "Always."

Although the guy didn't know Jackson and Mitch were vampires, on some level, he had to have realized there was something special about them. Most humans did. They instinctively reacted by giving them a wide berth or going along with shit. Besides, this place was like a home away from home for Jackson. They played his kind of music, and these were his kind of people— fun-loving, always willing to party and not into heavy conversations.

He waited as Mitch brushed past him into the crowd and moved out of earshot. Then he turned back to the bouncer. "Hey, that gal I was with? Make sure her friends know she's crashed back there."

Rocky nodded. "You wore her out?"

"'Fraid so."

He caught up with Mitch threading his way through the dance floor. "Yo, wait up. What's the hurry."

"Come on. We gotta go."

"I'm not ready to leave yet."

"Seriously, man." Mitch flicked his arm with the back of his hand. "Don't you think you should call Dom first? He's gonna rip you a new one if he doesn't hear from you."

When you know something's inevitable, why rush it? He considered the list of sweetbloods he still needed to do drive-bys on. Two here in town, one up north and one in an Eastside suburb. Then there was the girl. Mitch was right. He didn't have time to do it all if he stayed much longer. He'd probably just lose track of time again.

"Yeah, okay. I'll call him from the road."

CHAPTER TWO

INTERVIEWING BLAKE AND HIS brother had been a colossal waste of time and now Arianna was late picking up her cousin. She should've insisted on meeting Blake at the Devil's Backbone rather than his house. But because the site was difficult to find and was surrounded by private property, you had to know someone to take you in. Instead, she'd spent the evening trying to pry verbal information from a couple of boys who clearly were better at texting than talking in person.

She glanced at the glowing hands of the clock on the Caddy's dashboard. Almost midnight.

"Come on, Krystal," she mumbled to herself as she waited in the car parked outside the apartment building. What kind of teenager studied on a Friday night, anyway?

Warily, she watched the fog advancing off the sound a few blocks away as it searched for low-lying spots in which to settle. In the light from the overhead streetlamps, it took on a gray-green color and, if you blinked once or twice, it was suddenly thicker. There hadn't been a trace of fog over at Blake's house. She worried if she had to wait too much longer, visibility would be so bad that she'd have to drive away inch by inch because her piece-of-crap car didn't have working fog lights.

The two-story apartment building sat at the end of a long narrow driveway less than a mile from where Arianna lived—too far for her cousin to walk home, though she did try to convince Arianna it was no big deal. Maybe Krystal's mother would've been okay with that, but this wasn't a tiny farm town in eastern Washington and Arianna didn't have substance-abuse problems. This was the big city and no one walked home in the dark around here.

Her fingers twitched with the urge to blast the horn, but the neighbors probably wouldn't appreciate that. She definitely wanted to avoid running up to the door— shadows were everywhere. Along the shrubs at the base of the windows, underneath the spindly birch tree in the front yard, next to the minivan parked in the driveway. In an argument repeated for years, her sensible self said this fear was unreasonable, but the memories of her five-year-old self were ingrained too deeply to forget. Most of the time, she was able to push past it—you couldn't exactly be afraid of the dark and run a blog like Paranormalish. But tonight she felt on edge for some reason.

She texted Krystal again: I'm still waiting. Where are you?

Comingggggg.

U said that already. Hurry. I'm tired.

K. Grabbing backpack now.

Yeah, right. Krystal texted that ten minutes ago, too. To kill time, Arianna opened her camera phone and flipped through the pictures she'd taken at Blake's. Two teenage boys sitting on a couch with their grandmother's colorful afghan behind them. Blake looking scared. His brother looking confused. She deleted some, keeping only a few of the best ones to post on her blog. Then she watched part of the video she'd taken. One boy talking. The other boy listening. Arianna asking questions off camera. Boring with a capital *B*. The whole interview was. So much for interesting blog content.

She hit Delete and was about to set the phone down, when she remembered that videos were automatically saved to her cloud account, too. Carter had set it up for her in order to save memory on her phone and make them easier for her to access later. Once, when she'd been having all sorts of technical trouble with her website that she attributed to OSPRA, she took a chance and asked for Carter's help. Since he was always bitching about Xtark—sometimes she wondered why he even stayed on with the company—she'd turned to him, trusting that he wouldn't rat her out to corporate, and he didn't.

"Don't let these bastards dictate your personal life," he'd said. "You need to maintain some sort of control. If you want to keep something private, then you shouldn't have to feel you've got to turn over your passwords or tell them about your blog."

"But I don't want to lose my job."

He'd rolled his eyes. "Please."

"Carter, if they find out, I'm toast. And I kinda need this job. My bank account needs this job."

"Don't worry, you won't lose it."

Then he'd set up something called a proxy account, which supposedly hid her identity from snoops, as well as a cloud account. Thanks to him, she didn't have to worry about running out of memory any longer.

From her phone, she accessed the cloud online and deleted the boring pictures and video there, as well. With that housekeeping done, she settled back in her seat, again wishing they had explored the sanitarium, instead. Although the charred remains of the building were almost completely hidden, supposedly the ravine where they dumped the bodies of residents who had mysteriously died was haunted. Thirteen steps were carved into the side of the hill, leading to the bottom, thus the Devil's Backbone. That place would've given her plenty of interesting images. Local legend said that when you got to the bottom and turned around, you could see straight into hell. Now, *that* would've been something interesting to post. But at the last minute, Blake had freaked out and didn't want to go back.

What did that leave her with? Zilch.

When she met Blake, she couldn't help noticing that he looked a lot like that kid on YouTube who'd signed a big record deal recently. Maybe she could leverage that. Tag the singer's name, or something. She pictured the blog title: Friend of Tai Simmons Look-alike Gone Missing. That'd garner a few hits on an otherwise boring post, wouldn't it?

"Ari," she said to herself, "you're really stretching it this time."

She was about to set the phone down when two sets

of lights blazed in her eyes, illuminating the interior of the Caddy for a moment, virtually blinding her. She held a hand up to block the light. A jacked-up vehicle with its high beams on, including large yellow fog lights, had just turned onto the street. The driver probably had no clue how obnoxious that was. Or maybe he did. Guys who drove rigs like that dug the attention— good and bad. It was swagger on wheels.

Something darted out in front of her car. A cat. It paused in the middle of the road, staring at the oncoming vehicle.

"Move, little kitty."

But it didn't. Not one inch. The poor thing was paralyzed in place, its body a dark silhouette against the lights.

Oh, no, the fog's too thick.

The Jeep probably couldn't see it. She jumped out of the car to shoo the cat away, but before she could, the vehicle seemed to speed up, its engine revving louder. At the last moment, the cat shot into the bushes at the side of the road, narrowly avoiding becoming roadkill.

Anger surged inside her. Clearly, those jerks had seen the cat. What kind of idiot would purposely try to run over an animal? She glared into the windows of the Jeep as it drove past, wishing her eyes were daggers. She expected to see a car full of joyriding losers—hats turned backward, liquor bottles being guzzled, but instead she saw two guys in the front seat wearing sunglasses—what the hell?—and staring straight ahead.

They even looked like assholes. Identical ones. There should be a law against trying to run over someone's pet. She should report them to…to…someone. Remembering the camera phone in her hand, she took a few pictures as the vehicle's red taillights disappeared into the fog. Like that would make any difference.

Assholes Almost Run Over Garfield

Men in Black Attempt Kitty Killing

Making up ridiculous blog titles for imaginary posts always gave her a small sense of power over circumstances beyond her control. In fact, she had a monthly feature where readers would vote for their favorite outlandish blog-post title. Unfortunately, it hadn't won her many friends with the other paranormal bloggers. Seemed OSPRA was always on the list. Hell, she'd make her own list with those ridiculous titles.

She sighed and climbed back into the car. Everything always came back to her blog. Maybe she'd skip a day or rerun an old article. People did that all the time. Other than a little ad revenue, it wasn't as if she was getting paid to do it. She was the boss and if she decided to skip a day, well, then she should be able to do so and not feel guilty.

A slash of light from the apartment building on the other side of the road cut through the darkness. She looked up to see Krystal stepping onto the porch. The teen waved goodbye to her friend, slung her backpack over one shoulder and skipped down the steps.

Finally.

Arianna reached over to unlock the passenger door then opened her camera phone. She couldn't wait to show Krystal that one picture of Blake. Would she think he looked like—

Movement behind Krystal drew her attention. Two shadows she hadn't seen before seemed to separate from the darkness alongside the building. Confused, she scanned the area, but saw no one. Just shadows.

Was the fog playing tricks on her? She blinked rapidly, trying to clear her vision. Then the shadows began to advance. Straight toward her cousin.

Arianna's throat tightened, strangling her airways. She wanted to scream at Krystal, tell her to run, but the sound was stuck in her throat. Just like what happened with her mother twenty-two years ago when the shadows had come alive. But she couldn't move a muscle—she was frozen. Just like that stupid cat in the road.

The dark forms got to the minivan parked in the driveway and split up, with one going around to the other side. Then, at precisely the same time, they took shape. Gone were the shapeless, shadowy figures. These were flesh-and-blood men.

With their hands in their pockets concealing God knows what, they wore long, dark trench coats that grazed the tops of their boots and although the muted light from a streetlamp cast angular shadows on their faces, their identical expressions were devoid of any emotion. A pair of macabre robots on a mission, just like the two who took her mother.

Something inside her snapped, jerking her to action, and Arianna jumped from the car. "Run, Krystal!" Her voice cracked like a prepubescent frog's.

"What are you talking about?" Her cousin had been about to step off the curb, but instead, she skittered sideways, looking at her feet as if expecting to see a snake.

"Those men. Behind you. Come on."

Krystal spun around, dropping her backpack in the process. "What men? Ari, you're freaking me out."

How could she not see them? They were less than twenty feet away, coming toward her from both sides of that van.

Arianna felt helpless again. That same little girl hiding under a skirted table at the street fair.

One of the men spun a finger in the air, signifying a wrap-up, and the other nodded. They'd obviously done this sort of thing before. In a flash, they were on Krystal like a pair of jackals, lifting her off her feet and whisking her down the sidewalk.

Arianna tried to scream—surely someone would hear and come help—but she couldn't catch her breath. It felt as if she'd been punched in the gut. They moved faster than humanly possible, their trench coats billowing behind them. Her cousin struggled, arched her back, but it was no use. A ninety-pound girl was no match against two men.

And neither was a five-year-old girl.

Something stirred inside. She couldn't just stand here and watch her cousin being taken away by the men from shadows the way she had with her mother. "Put her down!"

In unison, they snapped their heads in her direction as if they were just now noticing they had a witness, but it didn't halt their stride. She fumbled with her phone, attempted to dial 911, but the picture app was still displayed on the screen, and she ended up pressing the wrong buttons. *Shit, shit, shit.*

They rounded the corner and disappeared behind a sprawling cedar, its lower branches stretching out across the sidewalk.

Without thinking, she sprinted down her side of the street, past a few parked cars. She thought about going for help, but she didn't want Krystal out of her sight. If she waited for the police to come or banged on the doors of any of the buildings on this block to get help, no one would believe her when she told them what happened, and her cousin would be long gone. Her only hope was to get some photographic evidence of the vehicle and license plate then call for help. When she got to the corner, she saw them trying to stuff Krystal into the back of the Jeep.

Her cousin managed to kick the shorter one in the face. Arianna heard him grunt. Krystal braced both hands on the door frame, but the other one came up behind her and easily pushed her inside.

She couldn't just let them take Krystal away without doing a single thing to stop them. Though she'd taken a few martial-arts classes, she now realized, she'd focused too much on self-defense. She'd never thought she'd need to know how to attack someone.

Standing from her crouched position, she wished she had a gun or something. She cursed herself for being too afraid to even hold one, let alone learn to fire one. If she could, she'd step into the roadway right now and shoot them. Just like in the movies.

Bam, bam, bam!

It was what she'd have done if she had the chance twenty-two years ago. She'd replayed it in her mind hundreds of times. Like a gunfighter, she'd stand unafraid in the middle of the road as the crowd of people scrambled to get away from her. They'd hide behind lampposts, cars. Duck into doorways and shops. She'd jerk the gun from her holster, boldly take aim and fire. Two quick shots that would echo off the buildings and change the course of her future. The shadowy men would crumple to the ground and her mother would be safe.

Instead, as the Jeep's engine fired to life, she aimed her camera and snapped a few quick photos before switching it to video mode. Seeing things through that tiny screen made real life seem a little less real. She stepped out into the road to get a better view of the license plate and was so focused that she almost didn't see the movement to her left.

She snapped her head up just in time to see another man emerge from the shadows.

Ten feet away.

The overhead streetlight illuminated bronze hair that reached to his chin, the top portion held back away from his face by a small ponytail. He was big—much bigger than the other two men. At well over six feet tall, he had linebacker shoulders underneath his leather coat and a formidable presence that seemed to suck the oxygen from the air.

His gaze burned into her before he made a noise that sounded like a growl. He covered the distance between them in two commanding steps.

She wanted to pinch her eyes shut, block out the nightmare, but for some reason, she didn't. Up this close, she noticed that his hair was streaked with green and blue highlights. She was vaguely disturbed that she noticed this innocuous detail about him when the thing that should be first and foremost on her mind was that he'd stepped from the shadows.

Obsidian irises were ringed by an iridescent green color so captivating that if she had any breath left to gasp with, she would have. Her legs could no longer support her weight and she felt herself slip. An energy charge snapped in the air when he steadied her, snaking invisible fingers around her body. She caught the faint smell of alcohol on his breath and noted that his square jaw was peppered with stubble. A small scar interrupted the slash of his dark eyebrow, similar to one she had from hitting her chin on the windowsill as a child.

All very humanlike—yes—but she knew what she'd seen. He'd morphed from a shadow, just like those men in the Jeep and just like the men who took her mother.

She staggered backward and caught herself on the hood of a car, setting off a high-pitched alarm that cut through the night air.

She'd never been so thankful for that shrill sound.

Until he banged once on the hood and the siren quieted.

"Who the hell are you?" he said, staring at his hands before giving her a quick head to toe.

Who am I? My God, that's a question I should be asking him.

She shook off that strange, electric sensation and pointed. "They…those two men took my cousin."

He glanced at the Jeep. "Yes, they did, didn't they. Get back, sweetheart, and try not to look."

She blinked once, twice, zeroing in on the fangs that were hanging from his mouth like twin daggers.

This time she had no trouble screaming.

CHAPTER THREE

Jackson left the woman behind him and sprinted down the street, cursing himself for sending Mitch back to the field office. He could've used the guy's help. This was just supposed to be a routine task that he'd check off his to-do list. Hell, if he thought he'd run into more Darkbloods tonight…

And that woman… Shit. She'd seen him in his shadow form. And what was it with her energy signature, anyway? He'd never felt anything like it, not even from the woman earlier who'd been to Mexico. But maybe he didn't want to know why things felt so different lately. He shoved her out of his mind as he narrowed his focus on what he had to do.

This weather wasn't helping, either. With the fog, shadows weren't as distinct, making it hard to blend in and shadow-move. The Jeep was pulling away with the young girl trapped inside. Damn. He wouldn't make it. If that woman hadn't drawn his attention, he'd have gotten there in time.

Unzipping his coat, he knew he'd have one opportunity to save her, then she'd be gone. Without slowing his stride, he grabbed a half-moon blade from the multitude of weapons strapped to his body. He threw it sidearm at the vehicle, flicking it as it left his fingers and giving it a good spin. The blade hissed like drag-on's breath as it flew through the air.

Pop.

It lodged in a back tire. The rig skidded to the left, slowed.

That was all Jackson needed.

He quickly covered the distance, yanked open the back door and climbed up on the running board.

"Goddamn Guardian pig." With both hands on the wheel, the driver struggled to regain control.

Before the bastard in the passenger seat could level his gun, Jackson was slamming a fist into his jaw. The guy's head jerked sideways and hit the dashboard with a loud crack. Just as Jackson reached for the driver, the Jeep screeched to a complete halt, knocking him slightly off balance. He reached for the guy, grabbing nothing but air, and the asshole jumped out.

Jackson hesitated. Go after him or see to the girl?

The guy in the passenger seat groaned.

Jackson couldn't leave her here, he decided. If this one came to, he'd be weak. His willpower shot. Given that the girl was a sweetblood, there'd be nothing stop-ping him from attacking her in order to regain his strength. With that first taste, it'd all be over. That's what it was like when a vampire tasted Sweet. Jackson had seen it happen enough times to know he wouldn't be able to get the guy off her without potentially rip-ping out her throat. Most likely, he wouldn't be able to stop the guy even if he wanted to.

"Out," he ordered the girl. He'd take care of these

two lowlifes in a minute, once he knew she was away from them.

She huddled in the far corner of the backseat, her eyes almost too big for her face. His stomach tightened. He still couldn't get over how much she resembled Betsy. The shape of her face, her brown Shirley Temple curls, the way her bottom lip quivered as if she was on the verge of crying. Just like she had when he'd rescued her the first time.

In a disgusting display, Darkbloods were going to auction her off to the highest bidder with the winner draining her onstage for all to see. After the Agency's medical staff checked her out and he wiped away the memory of her two-day ordeal, she was returned home. But now, here she was, at the mercy of Darkbloods again. That was the problem with sweetbloods, they attracted trouble like fresh meat to a zombie.

He reached over to help her out, but only when she shrank away from him did he realize his own fangs were fully extended. Rather than wasting precious minutes talking her down gently—this wasn't a time for nice—he grabbed her by the scruff of her jacket and hauled her out.

"Go back to your mom," he said as her feet hit the pavement. DB number one was running down the street. Thank the good Lord for the fog. At least it made shadow-moving hard for all of them.

The girl hesitated, clutched her hands around her middle as if she was about to get sick. A twinge of guilt hit him. All sweetbloods were trouble magnets. He should've kept better tabs on her. Just as he should've with his sister.

"Go," he barked.

Her whole body jerked as if she were awakening from a far-off trance. She blinked and her eyes focused on him again. "She's my cousin, not my mom."

He bit back a smile as he turned to the guy in the Jeep. Human teenagers…vampire youthlings. They were all the same—concerned with things that didn't matter in the long run. Her scent was much stronger inside the rig. Instantly, he felt his pupils dilating and a familiar but deafening beat sounded in his head.

Suddenly, his goal of killing this guy and then catching his friend didn't seem quite so important. Or at least not as important as feeding his immediate needs.

Blood. Energies. Blood. Energies. The words drummed in his head with the rhythm of her heartbeat.

He'd have to wipe their memories, anyway. What was the harm in—

A sound from the front seat cut through his fucked-up logic like a boning knife.

Shit. What the hell was he thinking?

That was the problem. He wasn't. His dark nature was.

He should take care of this loser first, anyway.

Staking a Darkblood would have to be enough to stoke his dark nature—the ancient, violent urges of his ancestors, urges that lived inside every vampire, whether civilized or not.

He pulled out his curved dragon blade just as the DB opened the door.

The similarity between Jackson and the DB was painfully obvious. They both wanted the same thing—blood and energies.

And yet the difference between them was huge. It had to be. He cared about humans and didn't want to lead a life like this loser. Trolling night after night, living like their ancestors did who preyed on innocent victims and killed them. That wasn't him. He didn't want it to be him.

What he wanted was to make a difference. He wanted to matter. Do what was right. Make those around him proud. But none of that would happen if he let his dark side get too powerful and take over. And if it did, if he slipped up and let himself go, not only would his parents' expectations and predictions for him have come true, but he'd lose everything he cared about.

Besides, he thought as he looked at this sorry bastard, he didn't want to end up like this. Smelling like rotten meat because of an all-blood diet, the Darkblood hissed at Jackson and flashed a mouthful of teeth. His irises were completely black, the whites of his eyes a dark gray, and they locked onto the human female like the desperate predator he was.

Jackson would fight with everything he had before that happened. It simply wasn't an alternative.

Jackson struck fast and the silver went deep. The DB let out a cry and lashed out, his hands dual claws on Jackson's forearm, clutching, digging.

"Son of a bitch."

The blade had clearly missed its mark, but the DB

shouldn't be this strong, either. A stab by a knife made from this silver alloy should have this guy flat on his ass.

Unless…he'd had Sweet recently, Jackson realized. Given its healing properties and the high it gave vampires who drank it, that could be the only explanation.

He withdrew the handle and struck again. This time, he twisted the hilt until the blade went where he wanted it to go.

The DB finally crumpled to the ground, and Jackson took a half step backward, watching as the body quickly turned to ash. Sadistic, maybe. But Jackson liked to watch this part. All that was left of the guy were rivets, zippers, glass blood vials and collection needles. His dark nature fed on shit like this. The sicker the better. Sure, he lived life hard—partying, screwing, fighting—but it was for a reason. It fed the evil part of him, kept it at bay, preventing him from spiraling out of control.

"That is so disgusting," Krystal said from behind, "and it stinks."

Having expended all that negative energy, Jackson was feeling better already. Not perfect, but he should be able to manage now. Before he forgot, he retrieved the half-moon blade embedded in the back tire and turned around. Krystal's cousin, the woman with the golden eyes and the long auburn hair, was partially shrouded in the heavy fog. She was holding up something. Her phone.

Was she trying to get a signal? he wondered.

He pulled out his own phone and texted Mitch an

I-need-your-fucking-help-now message. He'd need a cleanup crew to dispose of the vehicle and make sure there were no other witnesses. Someone would have to go after the DB that got away, and the two females would need to be taken home and have their memories wiped.

And then it dawned on him.

Her phone.

The woman had been taking pictures.

WITH A SWIPE OF HIS HAND, the man brushed his hair from his face and came toward them. His strides were long and fluid, like a powerful animal's. Arianna subtly moved Krystal behind her and took a half step backward.

Damn her morbid curiosity that always seemed to get in the way of common sense. Why hadn't they left when they'd had the chance? They could've been back home by now behind locked doors. She'd have out her garlic, her crosses and she'd make sure to tell Krystal not to answer the door. Who knew if any of the vampire myths were correct, but she wouldn't have taken any chances. Too late for that now.

Her mind spun out of control with the incredible event she'd just witnessed. As unbelievable as it sounded, she couldn't deny it. Vampires really did exist in this world. They weren't just made-up stories and fables. They were walking, talking individuals who melted with the shadows and preyed on humans. Thank God, she'd taken pictures and video, otherwise no one would ever believe her. Not even the loyal readers of

Paranormalish. She glanced around desperately, looking for a way out.

"Give it to me." He snapped his fingers.

Her first reaction was to do what he said, and she made a move to hand the phone to him. Wait. What was she doing? This was her only evidence of what she'd seen. There was no way in hell anyone would believe her if she didn't provide proof of what she'd just witnessed. She knew that all too well.

And those knives of his...

When he'd pulled one out and raised it above his head, the reflection of the moonlight had flashed along the curved blade, illuminating it from point to hilt. It was as if it were lit from within, drawing power from the man who held it.

She bristled at his commanding tone and yet she shrank away from him at the same time. "Give what to you?" she asked, quickly finding her courage. She raised the pitch of her voice slightly in an attempt to sound innocent.

She'd been waiting for most of her life not only to see something like this with her own eyes, but also to have undeniable proof that there was something out there beyond the realm of human reason. Shadows did come to life and threaten people. Just as she always knew they did.

"The phone," he growled.

"I don't know what you're talking about."

"Come on, honey, don't bullshit me. Neither of us has time for this."

Honey? Did he just call her *honey?*

She straightened her spine and glared at him. Men who threw around fake endearments like candy, assuming it would make a woman cave, were enough to make her break out in hives. It was something her father did.

"For one thing, I'm not your *honey.* And for another—"

He turned his full attention to her and the words faltered in her throat. Vampire or not, the guy was gorgeous. Probably the hottest guy she'd ever seen in person. Just about anyone could look good, airbrushed in a magazine. He was the real deal.

Amusement flooded his green eyes and one corner of his mouth curved up. It was a look that said he knew exactly how attractive he was and the effect he was having on her. This rough, unpolished sexuality was one hundred percent male and it sent shivers down her spine. He was a vampire, for God's sake.

"I don't know what you're talking about. I don't have a camera."

"You were taking pictures, *honey,*" he said pointedly, drawing out the two syllables. Clearly, he knew it pissed her off and yet he did it, anyway.

Her face heated with anger. "Too bad. You can't have it." As if she would simply—

In a flash of movement, the phone was suddenly gone from her hand and he was pocketing it.

She took a half step back, appalled. "What do you think— You can't just— That's my private property. Give it back to me."

"Well, it's mine now." He snapped his fingers at her cousin. "You, too."

She could suddenly relate to the whole mother-bear thing. Messing with her was one thing, but messing with her fifteen-year-old cousin really chapped her hide.

"Come on, Krystal with a *K*," he said, when her cousin didn't immediately respond. "I don't have all night."

A freight train roared in her head and the little hairs on the back of her neck stood on end.

How did he know that was one of Krystal's pet phrases? Because her name didn't start with a *C,* when she met new people, she'd introduce herself as Krystal with a *K.* What the hell was going on?

Her cousin handed over the phone without complaint or comment, as if the guy was God or something. Most teenagers would at least say something when it involved their phones.

As if in answer to Arianna's unasked question, he said, "Lucky for both of you, Krystal and I have met before. Otherwise, you two would've been toast."

Krystal looked confused. "We—we have?"

Which could only mean one thing. Arianna's legs felt boneless as the weight of his words sank in. "Her disappearance. Last month. That was you?" Her voice came out hoarse and breathless.

"Not her disappearance, no. That happened because of guys like that back there." He pointed his thumb over his shoulder.

"I...I don't understand."

Cursing to himself, he glanced out into the night. She could see the muscles in his jaw working, and she imagined he was mulling things over, trying to figure out what to tell her. When his gaze landed back on Krystal again, his expression softened. Hell, he looked almost protective of her.

"Okay, what in the world is going on?" she prodded.

He sighed and she noticed the resignation in his eyes. "Where's your car?"

"Why?" Her hand went instantly to the keys in her pocket. She was not about to divulge—

And before she knew what had happened, he had her keys, as well.

"What the hell? You seriously need to stop doing that."

"Which car is yours?"

"I'm not telling you that," she fired back.

"You'd better, because I'm driving you home."

"So that you can find us again and kill us next time?" She wrapped her arms protectively around her cousin, who seemed to be in shock.

He rolled his eyes. "I already know where you both live. If I had wanted to kill you, believe me, I could've done it a long time ago."

She blinked, but when she didn't answer right away, he said, "Fine. I'll find it myself." Then he grabbed both of them by the upper arms and marched them up the street.

Arianna tried to dig her heels in despite her flip-flops, but it did nothing to slow him down. He was too strong. "You can't do this to us."

"I'm not *doing* anything to you."

She tried wrenching away from him. "Then what do you call this?"

"Well, I'm not leaving the two of you here, if that's what you mean."

"I'll scream."

"I'd prefer it if you wouldn't," he said gruffly, gripping her arm tighter. "I don't think I need to remind you of what I'm capable of."

No, he didn't. It was burned into her retinas like a red-hot branding iron. The fangs, the weapons, that... that guy folding in on himself were images she'd never forget. And she knew how fast he was. If he wanted to, he could slice her throat open before she'd even feel the press of the blade. She'd go along with what he wanted for now and watch for a chance to escape.

They were only about three cars away from the Caddy when she remembered the statistics: women who get into a car with a stranger have just reduced their chances of survival. Getting driven to another location would be a disaster. For both her and Krystal. He could just be telling them he was taking them home when he might have other plans for them entirely.

She pulled again, tried to wrench herself from his grasp, but he was too strong. His grip was like a handcuff around her upper arm. Glancing around, she knew she'd need someone else's help. Down the street, light from a doorway cut a sudden column of warmth into the darkness.

This was her chance.

So, for the second time tonight, she yelled.

GODDAMN IT, he *was* helping her. Adding another human into the mix would only complicate things further.

"Quiet," he ordered.

But she didn't. He slid his hand down to grasp hers and felt that familiar snap of human energy. But rather than calming him, it was like a triple jolt of caffeine, instantly jacking his heart rate up, just as it had done the first time he touched her.

What the fuck?

First the woman at the club, now this one? Was being hypersensitive to a human's energies and blood just another sign of reverting? Needing more might only be part of the problem. Jesus, he'd have to work fast, otherwise he could really lose control. He grabbed Krystal's hand, as well.

Calm down, he pushed into both of their heads. *I'm only here to help.*

The girl relaxed, but the woman didn't. "Hey, you," she yelled to a guy who was headed to his car parked down the street.

Panic ripped through him. What in the hell was going on? Why hadn't the thought suggestion worked? He couldn't remember that ever happening before. "Stop," he commanded her, jerking her close. "I'm not hurting you, nor do I plan to."

She hit his chest with an *oomph.* "Then let us go."

The girl was staring at both of them, a bewildered look plastered to her face. If he didn't act fast, her memory plant may not hold. He'd have to take more drastic measures.

So he did the only thing he could think of.

He leaned down and kissed the woman.

She gasped as his mouth covered hers, struggled against him at first.

An asshole move for sure, but what choice did he have? It would shut her up as he implanted a thought suggestion. The intimate contact would surely make it take hold this time.

Even though he was prepared, another powerful jolt of electricity charged into his body. His lips tingled, his face heated up, his bones felt as if they were turning to rubber. Fire raced through his body, igniting just about everything. His fingers. His toes. And a few key places in between.

Damn. What the hell is going on with him? Is this what reverting feels like?

If so, no wonder it was so compelling. Her energies were rejuvenating him like a hit of adrenaline or a megadose of caffeine.

The woman's mouth was hot on his and tasted faintly of some Italian spices and… Bubble gum? He'd have guessed she'd be more of a mint-gum person. Soft waves of her auburn hair brushed across his face. It smelled like honey. Or maybe that was her gum. Everything about her was tantalizing.

But he could not—would not—give in to it. Struggling not to get lost in the sensation, he forced himself to think of what he needed to do. He'd wipe her memory, take the two of them home, then get the hell away from her forever. Everything about this woman was way too dangerous.

He no longer cared that Krystal reminded him of his

sister. Like most sweetbloods, she'd probably succumb to an unscrupulous vampire at some point in her life. There was nothing he could do to prevent it. He'd have her name taken off his list and put on another Guardian's. Let someone else keep tabs on her, just as long as it wasn't him. The long-ago guilt he'd harbored about his sister seemed much less important than his survival in the here and now.

"Shh," he whispered against her lips, working his way past her mental barriers. He was vaguely aware that this felt different, as well, but then he couldn't recall doing a mind wipe on a human host during a kiss without putting his hands on her temple. He quickly implanted the thought suggestion.

You have nothing to worry about. You saw a street fight, that's all. I came along and broke it up.

Her body relaxed just a touch, her free hand no longer pressing against his chest in an effort to get away.

Thank God, it appeared to be working. Finally.

He slipped into his usual mode with a woman and let his hand go to the small of her back, just above the curve of her bottom. She didn't push away. If he weren't holding on to the girl, he'd have threaded his fingers through the woman's luxurious curls to caress the back of her neck or cupped her ass to pull her hips closer. But he didn't. Despite his reputation, he did have a few scruples.

And then, because he couldn't help it, *You're kissing me because you're grateful for my assistance. You and your cousin were in terrible danger.*

Only when he stepped away from her was he aware that her arms had gone around his neck at some point during the kiss. She blinked, touched her lips with the tips of her fingers, as if confused by what just happened.

"What—what was that?"

"You tell me," he said, shrugging. "You were the one who kissed me."

Her cheeks colored to a lively shade of pink. "I—I did? But I don't understand…how?"

"How? Well, if you'd like another demonstration, I'd be happy to oblige."

The combination of a cough and a nervous laugh bubbled from her lips. "I'm grateful for your help, but… ah…that's not necessary." It took two tries to get her hair tucked behind her ear. She was clearly unaccustomed to doing what she thought she'd done—willingly kissing a complete stranger.

Thank God the mind wipe took this time. He didn't know what he would've done otherwise. Give him a knife and a Darkblood and he was golden, but anything that needed a careful hand or any kind of finesse wasn't his deal.

After tonight, hell most definitely had a special place waiting for him. They were probably having his name engraved now.

The woman grabbed her cousin and held her close. "Are you okay?" she asked, stroking the girl's hair. "I'm so sorry you had to see that fight. The city usually isn't like this. I promise."

"I'm okay," Krystal said.

Though relieved that the memory implant had taken hold, he was still confused. The woman made it sound as if the girl wasn't from around here. "She's visiting you?"

"No. She moved in with me two months ago."

Right before she'd been kidnapped, he realized. But that didn't surprise him. It wasn't safe for sweetbloods to live in big cities, where vampires were concentrated in order to be close to human hosts, and tonight proved that. She'd be better off way out in the country, where it was less likely she'd run into vampires.

"Where did she live before she moved in with you?"

"In a small farming town in eastern Washington."

Perfect. "Then she needs to move back. The city is no place for a girl like her."

"She can't right now. I'm the only family she's got for the time being."

Apprehension knotted his gut. This sweetblood girl had no other options but to stay in the city.

"I'm Arianna Wells, by the way," she said, holding out her hand.

He pretended not to see it and tucked his hands into his pockets, instead. He really didn't want to experience her energy again. He was barely holding it together as it was. "Jackson Foss. Nice to meet you." Changing the subject, he asked, "How far away do you live?" Although he knew the answer, he still needed to pretend he didn't. She wouldn't remember that he'd already admitted knowing her address.

"About twelve blocks north."

"Good, I'll see you safely home, then."

"*This* is your car?" he asked as they approached a decades-old Cadillac parked half on and half off the sidewalk. Its pale yellow paint was chipping, one of the hubcaps was missing, the back bumper was askew and a dent in the back passenger door made him wonder if it even opened.

"Yeah, why?"

"Well, for one thing, who parked it?"

"You just broke up a gang fight and you're concerned about my parallel parking?"

He laughed. "It's kind of a piece of shit, if you want to know my honest opinion. It isn't what I had expected from you." He hadn't really considered what he *was* expecting, just that it wasn't *this*.

"I actually don't recall asking for your 'honest opinion.'" She cocked an eyebrow. Even though he'd wiped her mind and planted some completely self-serving thoughts, he liked that she stood up to him. "That is, if you want *me* to be honest with *you*."

Okay, she had a point. "Fair enough."

He opened the passenger door and waited for them to climb in.

"You're driving us?" Krystal asked.

"Yes. I'll either come back for my truck on foot or have one of my associates pick me up." He shut the door and jogged around to the driver's side.

Arianna probably loved this old thing because of its sentimental value, he thought as he slid in behind the wheel. Maybe it used to belong to someone she really cared about. Her grandfather? The boat of a car did look like the kind that had belonged to an old duffer who met the boys at the neighborhood coffee shop for an early breakfast before playing eighteen holes. He'd probably kept his clubs in the large trunk and set his hat on the back ledge. No doubt she couldn't bear to part with it. But what did she expect his or anyone else's reaction would be? There was no denying it. The car was a total junker.

"Unfortunately," she said, "what's under the hood runs well. That's all that matters."

He didn't quite follow her. Had he heard correctly? "Why is it unfortunate? I'd think it'd be a good thing that the car runs well, despite what it looks like on the outside." On the seats, he noticed duct tape covering several tears in the vinyl, too.

She looked a little sheepish. "Never mind."

CHAPTER FOUR

ARIANNA'S PENCIL SLIPPED OUT of her hands as she walked past a row of cubicles in the accounting section of the Xtark offices. As she stooped to pick it up, all the files she carried fell to the floor, papers scattering everywhere.

Damn. She was totally discombobulated and distracted today.

Having misplaced her phone somehow, this was turning out to be the worst day ever. Normally she didn't need to come into the office two days in a row, but there was another meeting. One of the new assistants had been let go yesterday. Apparently, she hadn't divulged that she was a writer and she had social-media pages using her pseudonym. They'd fired her without giving her a chance to explain.

"Does anyone else have any secrets they'd like to confess?" the VP in charge of operations had asked in such a patronizing tone that Arianna had wanted to punch him. She was pretty sure that would've gotten her fired.

"Forgive me, Father, for I have sinned," Carter had muttered under his breath.

She'd almost laughed out loud. She was pretty certain that that would have landed her in hot water, too.

And to top things off, she'd slept crappy. She'd tossed and turned, and had some really bizarre dreams—one of them involving the really hot guy she'd met last night. When she awoke, she had a major kink in her neck and muscle aches that were so entrenched that even a strong cup of coffee and two Tylenol hadn't helped.

Where was that damn phone? she wondered as she gathered up the papers. She'd searched her bedroom where she always plugged it in to charge on her night-stand, then the kitchen counters, even all the cracks and crevices in the Caddy. She distinctly remembered having it when she interviewed Blake and when she picked up Krystal, but hell if she could find it now.

Seeing that gang fight must've been more traumatic that she'd thought. She had to have dropped it some-where in all the chaos. After she got out of here, she'd go back to the area to see if she could find it, even if the search did seem futile. If it was there, somebody probably had picked it up by now and was making calls to the Netherlands. Even though it was password pro-tected, hackers had their ways. At least it hadn't rained again last night. Maybe the man who'd broken up the fight had seen it. Could he have picked it up?

Her face heated up at the thought of him. She hadn't really kissed him, had she?

His full lips had been soft yet commanding against hers. His chest strong and muscular under the palm of her flattened hand. She'd even felt the beating of his heart.

She'd planned only to give him a quick peck and

was caught off guard when the kiss turned out to be so much more. He obviously hadn't been surprised by that turn of events because without hesitation, he'd slipped his tongue past the seam of her lips and forced her mouth open. And she'd let him.

What had caused her to do something outrageous like that? It just wasn't like her. Sure, the guy was really hot, but she normally wasn't the swooning type.

Though his hair was tied back, a few multicolored strands had grazed her cheeks as he leaned over her. What kind of guy would color his hair like that? she mused. Sure, it looked great and she was pretty sure he knew that. There was no doubt that he was the kind of guy who liked attention. And he was obviously very practiced when it came to having strange women kiss him, too.

Good looks and charm typically meant nothing to her, thanks to her father. It was a sugar high that left you temporarily elated until reality set back in and you got practical. And Arianna was practical to a fault. So why the hell had she kissed him? She grabbed the pencil she'd dropped and held it so tightly that it snapped.

"Need some help?"

She looked up to see Carter step out of the elevator. He leaned heavily on his cane and approached slowly, as if each next step could cause him to fall.

"Nah, I'm fine," she replied as she picked up the last of the files.

As she got into step beside him, matching his pace,

she noticed his pained expression. "You okay?" He looked a little worse than he had this morning.

He grunted. "Nothing that a medical miracle couldn't take care of."

Although she wasn't privy to all the details, she knew that Carter was suffering from a debilitating disease that only seemed to be getting worse. It had to be really frustrating for him, especially since he used to be really active, running marathons, climbing mountains, kayaking the sound. When she first started at Xtark, she'd seen pictures in his office of the time he and his buddies summited Mount Rainier. He'd looked healthy, vibrant and happy. The past few times she'd been in his office, she didn't see the photos and had wondered if he'd stashed them away. She certainly didn't blame him for not wanting a reminder of what he used to be capable of doing.

"Sorry to hear that," she said, keeping her voice low as they walked past the customer-service department where dozens of CSRs with headsets were answering calls. Xtark might make her mad a lot of the time, but they did put out some very popular games, including the violent and gory Hollow Grave. Plus, they didn't outsource, which she appreciated, though it probably wasn't due to their desire to support the local economy and workers, but because they didn't trust anyone who wasn't directly under their control.

God, she was in a bad mood today. Xtark paid her well and was a pretty decent company to work for...as long as you played by their rules. If she didn't like it, she could walk. One thing was certain—she needed to get a serious attitude adjustment. Maybe that was what she needed. A vacation.

"Don't worry about it. I'm learning to deal with the hand I've been dealt, because when we die, we die alone." He sounded so matter-of-fact; was that what happened when you were faced with no alternatives?

For an instant, she considered her own mortality. How would she live her life if her days were numbered or if she knew her independence would soon be gone? One thing was certain. She sure as hell wouldn't be working for Xtark.

"Are you just coming back from the doctor's office now?" She knew Carter had weekly visits to monitor the progression of the disease. Why wasn't he working remotely, the way she did most of the time? Surely it would be easier for him working from home.

Seeing what life was like for him made her feel pretty lousy for being frustrated about her job. He put up with a lot more on a daily basis than she did. Just getting to work had to be a bitch.

"The very place, yes."

She didn't want to turn into one of those people in the lunchroom who griped about everything. In fact, this morning, one of the CSRs who looked too young to have even graduated college yet had laughed at Carter after he left the room. She'd said it was disgusting how his shirt wasn't long enough to cover his muffin top. Arianna had quickly retrieved her yogurt from the refrigerator and left them to gossip on their own. She wished she'd told the young woman to grow up, that Xtark wasn't like her sorority house where members were chosen simply because they shopped at Nordstrom. Carter was a computer genius who not only was one of the lead designers of Hollow Grave, but also built Xtark's popular online forums. If it weren't for him and what he'd done for the company, that young woman probably wouldn't have a job.

But she hadn't said anything. Seeing him now emphasized how shallow and mean some people could be. And she should've known better. Growing up as the girl who saw shadows move, who tried to tell everyone that monsters did exist, hadn't exactly made her popular. More like an outcast who was made fun of until she'd learned to keep her mouth shut. Carter, however, didn't have that choice. Next time, she vowed to speak up and defend him.

When they got to his office, she hesitated, looked around. "Can I talk to you a sec?"

"Sure." They stepped inside and she closed the door.

"Do you know if there's a way to find a lost phone? You know, some kind of GPS device that can track down its whereabouts?"

"Yes," Carter said as he pulled his desk chair out and sat down with a heavy sigh of relief. "But the app would need to be on the phone before it was lost or stolen."

She cursed under her breath.

"Why? I take it you lost your phone?"

"Yes, and it's driving me crazy not having it. I suppose if it doesn't turn up in the next few days, I'll have to get a new one." She rubbed her neck. Her throbbing muscle aches weren't getting any better, either. "Normally I'm not very forgetful, so it's really frustrating."

Although they were alone in his office, she lowered her voice, anyway. "Hey, I don't know if you've been following Paranormalish lately, but I was interviewing one of the boys involved in the disappearance of the high-school student near the Devil's Backbone."

"Sounds vaguely familiar."

"I know you set up my cloud account, but to be honest with you, I've totally forgotten how to access it via the computer. Although the interview wasn't great, I did take a few photos that I think people will be interested in seeing. Believe it or not, the kid looks just like Tai Simmons. The interview sucked, but I figured I'd post a picture or two and get some good laughs."

"T-Si?" Carter scoffed. "You looking to expand your readership into the teen-girl segment of the population?"

"I know," she said, laughing. "But it's the only hook I can think of, since we didn't go out to the disappearance site. It's not like I've got any appropriately ominous photos to share."

Carter laughed and started scribbling instructions. "So, did you find out any additional information on what happened?"

She cast a quick glance at the door to make sure it was closed tightly. Even though she had been the one to bring up the subject, it still made her nervous talking about Paranormalish at work. And especially after this morning's announcement.

"I didn't learn much more than what I knew before." She rehashed a few of the details with him. "The thing that nags at me, though, is that the boy disappeared on the same night that Krystal went AWOL. I know it sounds far-fetched, but I can't help wondering if there's a connection somehow."

"Krystal?"

Hadn't she told him her cousin was living with her and what had happened? She could've sworn she had. "You know the girl I've written about on the blog, the one who went missing for a few days then mysteriously showed up back home with no recollection of her whereabouts while she was gone?"

"That's Krystal?" He handed her the paper.

"Yep. My cousin. I just couldn't tell readers that. She'd only been staying with me for about a week when she suddenly didn't return home one day. I, like, freaked out. I'm surprised you don't remember. I was a basket case."

"It's not like I haven't had problems of my own," he said tersely.

Although taken aback by his tone, she decided to just ignore it. "I was worried about her, but I didn't know if she was being a wild, irresponsible teenager or if something really bad had happened to her."

"What about her parents?"

Arianna shrugged. "She doesn't know her father, and her mom has some serious substance-abuse problems. That's why she came to live with me in the first place. My aunt was going into rehab and Krystal had nowhere to live for a while. I got a call from the State saying she'd be put into a foster home unless I could take her. She's doing a home study–type high-school program, so she didn't have to quit school to move over here."

"Did you call the police?"

"Yeah, but they figured she was a runaway and would turn up at some point. Still makes me mad thinking about it. I searched everywhere, checked her phone records and computer to see where she last was headed, but everything was a dead end. I had just about given up hope when several days later, she turns up as if nothing had happened." Not exactly. Krystal arrived home, gaunt and exhausted, but at least she was alive. After eating like a horse, she slept for almost a full day.

Carter looked confused. "She doesn't remember anything?"

"Nope. Even now she doesn't. It's like an alien abduction or something, where all this stuff is done to you, then they return you home with no memory of anything ever happening."

Carter was writing on the scratch paper. In addition to various geometric designs and the number ninety-two—the year he graduated from high school, maybe?—he had written Krystal's name in block letters, though he spelled it with a *C*. As he continued to listen, he added rows and rows of stripes to each letter. Who knew he was such a doodler?

"And when I realized that the high-school boy at the Devil's Backbone disappeared on the same night as Krystal, I couldn't help but wonder if the two events were connected somehow."

He stopped writing and let his pen rest on the paper. A large, red ink spot formed under the tip like a spreading bloodstain before he lifted the pen and looked at her. There was something in his expression that she couldn't quite read. "But there's a big difference. She came back. He didn't. If they were connected events, that doesn't make sense. Either they'd both return home or they'd both stay missing."

He could go ahead and think the two events weren't related. It wouldn't do anything to change her opinion that they were. Two kids roughly the same age didn't just go missing on the same night. There had to be something more.

"Yeah, but I still can't shake that feeling. Over the years, I've come to trust my instincts and my instincts tell me there's more to this story than we know. Which leads me back to those pictures."

"Oh, the pictures. I'd offer to pull up the account from here, but—"

"Yeah, I know. Big Brother is watching." She tucked the scrap of paper into a pocket and turned to go. "Thanks, Carter. You're the best."

THE UNMISTAKABLE ODOR of rotten meat wafted through the crowd and Jackson felt a rush of I-told-you-so. Before they got here, Mitch had protested going to the Pink Salon a second night in a row, but Jackson had needed energy on the sly and this was as good a place as any to get it.

He whipped his head in the direction of the smell and held up his fist, signaling silence.

"Darkblood pair. Eleven o'clock." The words, barely audible, hissed out of his throat.

On the far side of the dance floor, past the elevated cages with stripper poles, two figures dressed in matching trench coats rounded the corner in unison and stopped in front of a booth where several youthling couples sat with two obviously clueless human males. Clueless, because if they had any idea about the true nature of their party buddies or the goal of the new arrivals, they'd hoof it out of here.

"Looks like the cockroaches have come out of hiding, after all." Then, slipping into the West Texas accent of his youth, he added, "Let's go have us some fun."

Loosening his coat to make his weapons more accessible, he elbowed his way through the long line of scantily clad drunk people waiting to dance on one of the elevated platforms. The crowd parted for him like the Red Sea. Even those who had their backs to him stepped out of his way. A dozen steps later, he hesitated.

He should probably let Mitch do this. Although the guy had spent years teaching at Council headquarters, he hadn't been in the field much. A club takedown would be a good, real-world experience for him.

He turned to his partner. "Wanna handle this one? I'll ride shotgun."

The guy's baby blues lit up with excitement. "Hell, yeah."

"Know what to do?"

"I'll shove a silvie into their—"

"Whoa. Hold on there, Slick. First of all, do you have a second knife?"

Mitch extended his hand, exposing the tip of a barely

used, Agency-issue blade strapped to the inside of his wrist under his sleeve. "Got a couple of bullet dispensers though, including—" he patted his pocket "—my baby Beretta and a bad boy I'm dying to use in the field."

"Nope. No heat, only silvies. Here, take one of mine." Jackson slipped him a silver alloy stiletto—one of his backup blades, not his good one. No one touched his dragon blade. "And don't use it inside the club. One wrong slip under a rib and they'll charcoal in front of all these witnesses."

Mitch raised an eyebrow. "Can't you scrub them if that happens? Do a mind wipe?"

"I'm good, but I ain't *that* good."

Even newly energized, Jackson wasn't able to do the amount of head-fucking it'd take to wipe the memories of all the club goers. It'd take four or five Guardians at least. Maybe down in one of the UV-intense regions, where human blood and energy tended to make vampires more aggressive and their skills more pronounced, but not in Seattle, where almost every human host was vitamin-D deficient. Mitch hadn't been working in the field all that long and he'd recently spent time in Australia with Dom, so he'd made the assumption that things worked the same here. Not true.

Besides, this wasn't that kind of operation. Although he had to admit, it would be fun in a Wild West shoot-'em-up sort of way.

"If you do have to fork one, go low in the belly or give 'em a kidney shot from behind. Just don't nick a heart. We'll finish them in the alley."

They quickly worked out a plan.

"Okay, let's rock," Jackson said.

Mitch melted into the crowd and Jackson eased around the perimeter of the dance floor toward an exit at the back, never dropping his eyes from the Darkblood pair. He palmed his knife, flicked open the blade with a click and waited in the shadows near the door. Mitch approached the table from the other side and sidled up behind the two DBs. They stiffened. Several long seconds later, they began to shuffle toward Jackson, obviously being herded at the points of Mitch's knives and his persuasive way with words.

Jackson moved deeper into the shadows, trying simply to blend into the darkness, not meld with it. There were too many potential human witnesses around for him to just disappear. But when he stepped backward, he bumped into a young mixed couple making out—a human female wearing a skimpy sequined halter top and thigh-high boots, and a young male vampire in a letterman's jacket.

Jesus, the kid didn't look nearly old enough for the Thirst to have started. But then how was he to tell? At over a century old, he thought any born vampire under the age of thirty looked like a child.

Jackson gave the youthling a two-fingered I'm-watching-you gesture followed by a turn-around-and-get-the-hell-out-of-here look. Both the human and vampire complied.

The bass from a speaker pounded so loudly in his ears he wasn't sure what was the beating of his heart and what was music. He flexed his empty hand. Nothing like a good altercation to sand off the dark, rough edges. Today, he woke up feeling more out of sorts than normal. It had to be the blood of those two women last night. First, the sun-rich blood of the woman in the private salon last night, then Arianna.

Mitch escorted the Darkbloods into the hallway, calmly, quietly.

Niiice. If they could wrap this up quickly, he could go back in and hang out.

The two DBs moved in unison, their black coats swirling around their ankles. Did these losers think a simple pickup awaited them in the alley? That was only for routine reverts, vampires who needed a little reminder about the laws of their kind. Not members of the Darkblood Alliance who didn't abide by Council law, who thought it went against the laws of nature *not* to feed from and kill humans.

No, guys like these two got the special treatment.

The kind that involved a slip of a special blade and some ashes.

But just as Mitch and his two new BFFs approached, all hell broke loose out on the dance floor behind them. Shouting erupted above the music and Jackson heard the sound of breaking glass. A few chairs went flying.

A fight, probably in the cage line—people hated waiting their turn to go on display.

The screech of the DJ's record blasted like squealing tires through the speakers. That was when Mitch glanced away for a split second. It was the only invitation the DBs needed.

Mitch hit the ground, sputtering from an elbow to

the chest, and the two charged the exit, heading straight
for Jackson. They were fast, probably jacked up on
Sweet. Jackson shifted his weight to the balls of his
feet, ready to spring.

Yeah, bitches, bring it on.

Light glittered off something in his peripheral view.
Damn. The human female. Those complicated things.
He flattened himself against the wall and let the DBs
pass him.

One glance at his partner coughing on all fours confirmed the guy just had the wind knocked out of him.

"Your silvie," Mitch managed to say.

What? Darkbloods had his blade? "Goddamn it."

Jackson ran out after the bastards into the alley
behind the club. He wasn't about to let them get away,
otherwise they'd be back to prey on another unsuspecting human some other night. DBs were always on the
prowl for people with the extremely rare sweetblood.
Although their two human male targets inside the club
weren't sweetbloods—Jackson would've been able to
smell that—chances were, one or both of them had a
fairly uncommon blood type. One that the DBs were
after.

Besides, they had his knife. No one messed with his
knives.

In just a few strides, he got to the short one first.
With a roundhouse kick, Jackson's boot landed squarely
on the side of the guy's head, snapping his wraparound
sunglasses and collapsing him to the ground. A well-
placed shove, a little hitch with his blade, and the DB
was already charcoaling.

One down, one to go. Jackson retrieved his weapon from the body.

The other one made it almost to the street by the time Jackson caught up with him next to a Dumpster. He jumped onto the guy's back and clamped him in a choke hold. Was this the one with his knife? He didn't care if the guy had a Darkblood blade; they were poorly made and fairly ineffective. But a nick from Jackson's own blade would be an entirely different story.

The fucker spun around, clutching at Jackson's biceps, but he didn't succeed in loosening them. Damn, he was strong, though. Much stronger than the other one. Probably from the Sweet. Jackson hitched his arms tighter and the guy choked. As with any vampire who lived on an all-blood diet, the air from his lungs reeked, and Jackson tried to keep his head turned away as much as possible. DBs used the stench as a calling card of sorts. If you were looking for a little action, you knew you could score a hit from the guys who smelled like a Texas meat locker with a faulty refrigeration unit.

Being this close, Jackson would need a serious shower after this was over. The DB continued to struggle, but when that didn't work, he fell to the pavement with Jackson's arm still firmly wrapped around his neck.

"Take it down if you can't handle it on your feet," Jackson said mockingly through clenched teeth. What a fool.

Thanks to his black belt in Brazilian jujitsu, Jackson preferred the ground and pound, anyway. At the first opportunity, he wrapped his legs viselike around the guy's torso, locked his ankles in place and squeezed. The loser groaned loudly. Like a boa constrictor taking advantage of every exhale, Jackson's thighs compressed him farther.

With a flick of his wrist, Jackson positioned the tip of his knife on a precise spot between the guy's ribs—he could find it with his eyes closed.

Just as he was about to finish the job, he saw the flash of a blade and felt the sharp sting of silver on his forearm.

Was that from his own knife? The one lifted from Mitch?

Energy began to pour out of his system. Pain instantly radiated outward. He had his answer.

His grip on the guy's throat weakened. With a few more beats of his heart, Jackson knew the effect of the silver would be coursing throughout his body and he wouldn't be able to hang on. Like hell if he'd let this one get away. It'd only be a matter of time before this blood-dealing loser was back to work on the streets of Seattle, enticing vampires to revert. Ply a susceptible vampire with enough blood and the old cravings of their ancestors—the uncontrollable kind, the blood-sucking, energy-slogging kind—would be too strong to ignore.

With a final surge of adrenaline, Jackson gripped the handle with both hands and angled the point upward.

"Eat this, you son of a bitch."

And in one mighty, satisfying jerk, the blade found its mark.

Footsteps pounded on the cobblestones just as Jackson rolled away, trying somewhat unsuccessfully to avoid the charcoaling body. A thin layer of ash covered the toes of his Lucchese ostrich-skin boots and he tried to brush it off. He wasn't picky about a lot of things, but these boots set him back almost a thousand bucks. He'd bought them to impress his parents when he showed up at the ranch wearing them—they were the only kind of boots his father wore—but they hadn't even noticed. Still, he loved them and didn't want them covered with Darkblood stink.

"Holy shit, are you okay, man?"

"Good timing," he growled, ignoring his partner's outstretched hand as he pushed himself to his feet.

"The little one elbowed me right in the gut. Couldn't breathe for a minute. Damn, you worked these guys over fast."

With his back turned, Jackson examined his injury. It was more like a scratch, really. He was weak, yes, but like carb loading before a marathon, all the human energy he'd slogged tonight should prevent the effects of the silver from being too serious. Or at least he hoped it would. The pain had made its way to his shoulder now and he grimaced.

Mitch's eyes widened. "Are you okay? He got you, didn't he?"

"Yeah, with my blade."

"I'm sorry, man. I should've seen it coming. Should've anticipated something like that happening. I heard the noise, saw shit flying, and I must've gotten distracted for a split second."

"Don't worry about it. Darkbloods on Sweet are unpredictable."

Mitch pulled out his cell phone.

"Who the hell are you calling?" Jackson asked, though he was pretty damn sure he knew the answer.

"A medico team."

"No, you're not. This is nothing." He couldn't let the medical staff see him in this weakened state and do any testing. Who knew what the results would show.

Mitch eyed him skeptically. "You don't look so good. Are you sure?"

"Yep. I'm fine."

He tried not to reveal just how much pain he was in as he turned toward the nondescript back door of the club. Mitch already thought he was a stud when it came to women and fighting the bad guys. Might as well make it a hat trick, let him think this didn't hurt like a motherfucker. "Now, come on, let's get inside and take care of those reverts."

"Reverts? You mean those guys at the table with the humans?"

Jackson rolled his eyes. "No, Cinderella and her evil stepsisters."

CHAPTER FIVE

"Do you want more salad?" Arianna asked Krystal as she unplugged the panini maker and grabbed her own plate.

When she got home from work, she'd decided to fix dinner before she tackled her blog post for tomorrow. Now that Krystal was her responsibility, she was trying to set a good example by actually eating meals at a table, rather than in front of her computer or the TV the way she usually did. Besides, she wasn't looking forward to writing the article in the first place, so she welcomed the distraction.

"I'm good," her cousin answered flatly.

Arianna glanced over to the banquette where Krystal was still poking at her salad. Something had to be bothering her—she'd hardly said anything more than a one- or two-word sentence in response to Arianna's questions about how her day was, and she was pretty sure it wasn't the food causing her surliness. The girl had devoured the same salad several nights ago, and the panini wasn't made with anything weird. Arianna picked up her glass of wine and slid in on the opposite side of the table.

"So you want to tell me what's wrong?"

Krystal didn't look up from her plate. She hid behind

those brown curls covering her face as if she didn't care, which Arianna knew was far from the truth.

"Come on. You can talk to me. What's going on?"

The girl still didn't answer, so Arianna continued. "Is it something to do with Sarah or one of your friends back home?"

"No, nothing like that."

Arianna touched her sandwich, but it was still too hot to eat. The melted cheese would scorch the roof of her mouth. She took a bite of the salad, instead. "Is it your mom? Because if it is, you can tell me anything, Krystal. I promise." Ever since Arianna's mother died, Krystal's mom, her mom's twin, had had issues. First it was alcohol then prescription meds. She'd been in and out of rehab for years.

Krystal smashed a piece of feta cheese from the salad with her fork. "No, it's not about Mom, either."

Then what could be bothering her? Arianna had started to lift the glass to take a sip, when she set it back down again. "Listen, I'm not your mom. I'm your cousin. That basically means we're like sisters, only it's *waaaay* cooler. You can tell me anything. What am I going to do, ground you? Well…I guess technically I could, but I'm not going to. Come on, talk to me."

Krystal sighed heavily and dropped her fork with a clank. "It's my phone. The one you just got me. I—I…" When she looked up from her plate, tears glistened in her eyes. "I lost it. I'm sorry, Ari, I didn't mean it. It's like I had it one minute, then the next minute I didn't."

A knot quickly formed in her belly. How could they both lose their phones on the same day? She reached over and gave Krystal what she hoped was a reassuring squeeze. "When did you notice it was gone?" she asked cautiously.

"This morning. After you left for work. I looked everywhere. My backpack. My room. I'm really sorry. I didn't mean to lose it. I know it was expensive and everything. I'll pay you back. I promise."

Arianna's heart melted at the girl's distress over disappointing her. "It's okay, Krystal, things like this happen. I know it wasn't your fault."

"Yeah, but I should've been more careful. I'm not used to having a phone to keep track of."

"If it makes you feel any better, I just lost mine, as well. Can you believe it? Both on the same night." Arianna tried to make it sound as if she thought it was a funny coincidence, but what were the chances of it happening to both of them simultaneously?

Krystal's eyes widened. "Really?"

"Yeah, I've been trying to remember exactly where I was the last time I saw it."

"Me, too!" Looking relieved, the girl turned her attention to her sandwich.

Arianna watched her cousin take a bite and waited for her reaction; it was nice having someone to cook for, she decided. "How's the food?"

"It's good. What's in this one? Cheese, tomato and… what's the green stuff? Spinach?"

"No, basil. It's like the ingredients from a pizza, but without the meat." Arianna wiped her fingers on her napkin and took a sip from her wineglass. Although it was a cheap, peppery merlot from the grocery store, it was actually pretty decent. "Hey, do you remember that street fight we saw last night?"

Krystal frowned, thinking. "Um…yeah, kinda."

"And the guy who broke up the fight and helped us home?"

"Oh, yeah, I remember him."

"Do you remember his name?"

"No, sorry. He had big muscles and a huge tattoo on his arm."

"He did? I don't remember that." She couldn't exactly call the police and ask to speak to the officer with the tattoo. "Wasn't he wearing a leather coat?"

"Not when you were kissing him. The tattoo was right here." Krystal giggled and pointed to her biceps. "It was a colorful snake with fangs and…"

Fangs? Arianna couldn't remember the point she was going to make.

As Krystal continued to talk about the fight and the guy with the tattoo, the kitchen felt as if it were spinning. Arianna pinched her eyes shut and rubbed her forehead. She must have a serious case of vertigo or something. Then, to make matters worse, her stomach began to twist and roll.

Oh, God, she wasn't going to vomit, was she? She grabbed the edge of the table, put a hand over her mouth. What was the deal? She hardly ever got sick. In fact, she couldn't even remember the last time she'd been nauseous.

Krystal had said something about…fangs?

Calm down. I'm not getting sick. I feel perfectly fine.

Just take a few deep breaths in and out and I'll be back to normal.

Then, just as quickly as it came on, the nausea began to subside. But with it came a strange image in her memory. She saw a tall, muscular man—several men, actually—all with fangs. There was a scuffle. No, a fight. A really brutal one involving a body shriveling to dust and a really strange knife. It had a curved blade that flashed in the moonlight like a thousand tiny crystals. She would've liked to have seen it up close. The scene was like recalling a part from a movie you saw a long time ago and yet…that wasn't quite right, either. The men's faces were shadowed, their features indistinguishable, but they definitely had fangs.

Krystal was saying something she didn't quite catch. Her voice was distorted, like it was coming from inside a tin can.

"What?"

"Are you okay? Do you want me to get you a glass of water? Or some crackers?"

Arianna opened her eyes, the sick feeling gone. Clearly, she'd dreamed about some really weird crap after what they'd witnessed last night. She'd always thought it was fascinating how the mind worked like that, trying to resolve problems at the subconscious level. She wondered what it meant that she'd been dreaming about vampires. Maybe all the research she'd done on topics for Paranormalish was catching up with her.

The guy last night was an undercover cop and had broken up a fight between two rival gang members.

He was nice enough to drive them home…after she kissed him. Oh, good God. Her face heated again at the memory. She'd actually freaking kissed him. She quickly shoved the embarrassing image from her thoughts.

Krystal was staring at her, wide-eyed, a mixture of disappointment and resignation on her face. "Water and crackers always helps my mom when she's had too much to drink. That and some Tylenol."

Arianna smiled at her cousin. It had to be tough growing up with an alcoholic parent, where the child took on the role of being the responsible one. "Thanks, but that's not it. I've only had a few sips of wine. Promise." She got up from the table and dumped the wine from her glass down the drain. For good measure, she dumped out the rest of the bottle, too. "There. Just to be on the safe side. That was…weird."

After they did the dishes and Krystal went to her room to do homework, Arianna turned on one of those reality cooking shows, grabbed her laptop, pulled out the scrap of paper from Carter and settled onto the couch. In a few clicks, she was into her cloud account.

As people were yelling at each other on TV, several rows of small picture thumbnails filled her screen. *That's strange.* She didn't remember taking so many photos last night at Blake's house.

She clicked on the first image. She'd seen it before. It was Blake sitting in front of his grandmother's afghan.

She clicked the last image. It was a dark, grainy picture of a sidewalk or road.

Okay. Delete.

She moused over the next one and clicked. Same thing, only this one showed the edge of a car's bumper. A Jeep.

Like pocket-dialing, she must not have realized she was taking pictures. Delete.

These must be from the gang fight. Maybe there were some good ones earlier. She couldn't remember taking any and yet…

She clicked on another one. When it filled the screen, her hands flew to her mouth.

It was the same sort of image she'd recalled at dinner. The photo was grainy because of the dim light and fog, but there was no mistaking the details. There was the man who had helped them home, the undercover cop, with that curved blade held high in the air, poised over another man on the ground. And they both had fangs.

Vampires? That was totally crazy. A chill snaked down her spine and lodged so deeply inside her that she wondered if she'd ever be warm again. But what else could they be? This made it pretty damn obvious.

She remembered now that when she kissed him, he'd seemed out of breath, as if he'd just physically exerted himself. Jesus. Killing someone with a blade would certainly do it you.

With shaky hands, she clicked through the rest of the photos, a dozen or so of them. Along with each one she looked at, her memory seemed to get clearer and clearer. When she got to the last one, her heart just about stopped. There was Krystal, standing next to a Jeep. The man had an urgent expression on his face and was pointing straight at the camera, as if urging her to go to where Arianna was standing.

Then, in one big rush, it came back to her. The shadows coming to life, Krystal being taken by two men, the other guy showing up.

They hadn't witnessed gang members fighting. They were vampires. They had tried to take Krystal, but the other man, the one she had kissed, had saved her. Probably saved them both.

Holding the laptop, she jumped from the couch and headed to Krystal's room, but she hesitated at the door. These photos were very graphic. If her cousin saw them, it might really upset her. As the parent figure in the girl's life now, Arianna had to be conscious of things like that. She closed the computer, tucked it under her arm and knocked.

"Come in," was the reply.

She leaned in the doorway. "Hey, do you remember two guys in a Jeep last night?"

"From the gang fight?"

"Um…yeah."

Krystal scrunched up her brow, thinking. "No, I'm pretty sure I didn't see them."

"Do you remember seeing a Jeep at all?"

"Nope."

Arianna exhaled slowly, trying to get her mind around all this. How could Krystal not remember standing next to the Jeep when Arianna had the proof right here?

"How about some weird shadows that—" she almost

said *materialized from the darkness,* but changed her mind "—that, well…looked weird?"

Krystal shook her head. "Why?"

She pulled up one of the more innocuous pictures. "How about this guy? Does this bring up any strange memories?"

Krystal looked at the computer screen. "That's the guy who broke up that knife fight. The guy you kissed."

"Yeah, I know, but can you remember anything more?"

Krystal thought a moment before answering. "No, not really. Why?"

"No reason. Just curious." She clutched her computer to her chest like a schoolbook. There was no way she'd tell Krystal that she'd survived a vampire attack. Or show her any of the other pictures. There were plenty of others without Krystal that she'd be able to post on her blog. Given all of this, she was *soooo* thankful now that she hadn't told Krystal about Paranormalish. "I think I had one of those strange déjà-vu experiences you sometimes hear about. Must've been a weird dream I had last night. One of those really realistic ones."

Krystal's eyes lit up. "*Ooh,* I love when I remember a cool dream later."

"Yeah, me, too."

NORMALLY, VENTRA CAPELLI had a knack for knowing just the right outfit to wear in any situation. From soccer-mom chic in the suburbs when she faked a flat tire to emaciated hipster at an art gallery wanting a smoke, she knew how she needed to dress in order to throw any humans off guard. When she looked like them and they saw that she needed their help…well, it was like sugar water and flies. Or, now that she lived in the Pacific Northwest, beer and slugs.

But tonight she wasn't sure if this simple black sheath, businesslike yet elegant, with a long strand of freshwater pearls, a few chunky bracelets and diamond studs in her ears would get her what she wanted. For that to happen, those present needed to see her as capable, serious and in control. They needed to trust that she could do the work her predecessor couldn't.

As the elevator descended deeper into the depths of the Prague mountainside, she was thankful she'd thought to bring along hard copies of her documentation. Surrounded by all this rock, she doubted she'd get internet coverage on her tablet, although she'd brought the thing with her, as well.

With a smooth *swoosh,* the doors finally opened up to a large vestibule. She tucked her handbag under her arm and walked out.

She'd heard stories of how beautiful the Darkblood Alliance headquarters were, but nothing had prepared her for this. Her heels clicked on the marble flooring, the sound echoing off the chamber walls, emphasizing the vastness of the space. Various suspended sculptures hung from the frescoed ceiling, not unlike the Chihuly glass pieces in the lobby of the Bellagio in Las Vegas, a hotel she was intimately acquainted with. As she looked closer, however, she realized these weren't glass works of art. They were made from various human bones.

From floor to ceiling, the walls were covered in

human-skull sconces. The lower jaws had been removed, replaced instead by pairs of femur bones, making the skulls appear to be biting them. Unlike jack-o'-lanterns where light shone out the mouth, nasal cavity and eye sockets, each one of these skulls glowed, the bone sheer enough to be illuminated by the candle inside. Hanging down from the coved ceiling was a chandelier made from artfully arranged bones and skulls. The overall effect was a stunning visual representation of the power vampires would always have over humans.

"Lovely, isn't it?" said a silky male voice behind her.

She spun around to see a thin, middle-age vampire standing behind a reception desk. She'd been so distracted by the beauty of this place that she hadn't noticed him. She knew better than that. It wouldn't happen again.

With his dark hair slicked back, he wore a hand-tailored Italian wool suit and a crisply starched white dress shirt. In an obvious display of individuality, a flamboyantly colored silk tie completed the look.

"Rumor has it that a monk in the Middle Ages collected the skeletons of humans who had died of the Black Plague. Forty thousand people, to be exact. Our people did the same. It's quite a masterpiece, wouldn't you agree?"

The Black Plague had changed everything. Until then, vampires had been at the top of the food chain, hunting and feeding from humans as they were meant to do. Humans at least had a small chance of surviving the Black Death, but for vampires, drinking the blood of an infected human was a death sentence. Their population dwindled to just a few pockets of survivors scattered throughout all of Europe—their race had almost been exterminated.

Fear of death had caused a significant philosophical change in vampire culture. As an act of self-preservation, vampires stopped draining and killing humans, learning, instead, that they could survive on much smaller amounts, and feedings could be stretched out over longer periods of time. They took only what they needed and left their human hosts alive. A complete denial of a vampire's true nature, she thought in disgust.

Most of their kind came to believe that humans and vampires could coexist peacefully, which led to the formation of the so-called Governing Council, those watchdog pigs who made her life and the lives of anyone who didn't agree with them hell. Having fangs and needing blood didn't mean you should make friends with your food. The mission of the Darkblood Alliance was to usher the culture back to its roots and live the way they were meant to live.

"Indeed, it is. The whole room is magnificent."

She eyed a macabre piece located in one of the corners. Bones had been wired together to create one large, grotesque figure with three heads, its freakishly long arms and legs jutting out from the torso at odd angles.

"Like it?" the man asked.

"Yes, it's amazing."

"It's interesting, isn't it, though it's not human."

She raised her eyebrows. "It isn't?"

"It's made from the bones of the Master's rivals."

The new leader of the Alliance was obviously ruthless and cutthroat. Important qualities to have.

Apart from the natural aging process, the most common way for a vampire to die was from a stake through the heart, whereby the whole body would disintegrate. So these individuals must've met their end in some other fashion in which the bones had been preserved. Unflinchingly, she read the plaque on the wall, recognizing a paraphrased quote from Cervantes. *A cat, a rat and a coward.* Interesting, indeed.

The man laughed. "The Master does have a sense of humor." Then he continued where he'd left off. "Of course, we've added to the collection over the years. In addition to this piece, there are a few others in the Master's Chambers, which you'll see next, but these are the oldest and most fragile." Swinging his arm wide, he spoke with the passion of a museum curator, not a lowly receptionist, although Ventra understood that sometimes you had to befriend the help in order to get access to those in power.

"Right this way," he said, indicating a corridor leading to the left just past the sculpture. "The Master is expecting you."

She cast one last look over her shoulder, cementing every detail into her memory. When she returned home, hopefully with the title of Seattle Sector Mistress, as well as becoming a voting member on the Xtark Software board of directors, she vowed to put together a room just like this one.

Or maybe a whole house.

GETTING STABBED WITH A SILVIE wasn't the end of the world unless it went into the heart muscle, but it sure as hell hurt like shit.

At the field office, Jackson had just stuffed a sandwich half into his mouth and poured himself another glass of milk, when the door to the kitchen opened. Lily DeGraf, one of the Agency's best tracker agents, waltzed in with a scowl plastered on her face.

Great. What now? As soon as it went full dark, he had planned to head out into the city to get more blood and energies. Sleeping the day away then eating everything in sight just wasn't cutting it. Whatever she wanted had better not require much from him. His pupils were still fully dilated. He didn't want her or anyone else to notice, otherwise he risked being sent to the clinic.

"Dude, what's with the shades? Party too hard last night?"

Perfect, he thought as he adjusted the Ray-Bans. "Yeah, well, now you know."

She laughed. "Why is that not surprising?"

"Because my reputation precedes me."

She wore a pair of spandex workout shorts and a skimpy bra top, and her blond hair was pulled back into a high ponytail. Though recently engaged to Dom's brother, Alfonso, she hadn't changed at all. She was still the same Lily, ready to kick ass at a moment's notice or laugh at a dirty joke. Jackson liked a woman capable of beating the shit out of him, but he sure as hell didn't want to date one. Alfonso was a lucky, but very patient, man, he decided.

"Listen. We need to talk."

Had she figured out that he'd been using the hot tub in the ladies' locker room when no one was around? He couldn't help that he enjoyed the peace and quiet over there sometimes. Plus, he liked the eucalyptus-scented candles. Oh, great. If the other guys found out about it, they'd never let him live it down.

"About what?"

"That normal charming self of yours seems to be in some hot water. Dom's pissed off at you about something. I just passed his office and heard him on the phone with Cordell. Your name and a few choice swearwords were jumbled together into one long, brutal-sounding sentence. For a minute there, I thought I was hearing Santiago."

"That can't be good." The region commander of the Horseshoe Bay region in British Columbia had a way with words—primarily swearwords—ones many people had never heard before. It was an education about the underbelly of the English language when you were around Santiago. But then, Dom wasn't all that different. At least not to Jackson. More often than not, Jackson seemed to get under the guy's skin. He was a great field team leader, and Jackson really respected him for the way he got the job done without micromanaging the people who worked for him. He just tried to stay out of the man's way if he could. Made life much more enjoyable.

"I'm guessing he'll be calling you to his office soon, if he hasn't already," Lily continued.

He glanced as his phone but couldn't see the screen

through the dark lenses. Turning his head slightly away from Lily, he slid the sunglasses down his nose. Nope. Hadn't missed a call.

"What now?" he asked, pushing the glasses back up. He'd filed his sweetblood report shortly after returning to the field office. Sure, he was a little late, as he'd been trying to figure out what to do about the situation with that woman. But he'd taken care of things there and the report was finished. In the past week, he'd done drive-bys on the eight sweetbloods on his list and they were all accounted for.

"Your guess is as good as mine. Want any moral support?"

"Why? You want to see him kick my ass again?"

"Jacks, I'm hurt." She stuck out her bottom lip and put a hand dramatically over her heart. "That's the furthest thing from my mind."

As they headed down the hallway toward Dom's office, the overhead light caught on her ring. "Let me see that," he said, grabbing her hand. The platinum band had an intertwined pattern and three diamonds embedded in the top.

"They represent Alfonso, Zoe and me," she explained, smiling at the reference to her fiancé and their young daughter. "And the woven pattern is our take on a Gordian knot, signifying that our love has no beginning and no end."

"Wow, that's pretty damn romantic, Lil. I didn't know you had it in you."

She shrugged, looked almost a little hurt. Was she

serious or pulling his leg? He'd never thought of her as a romantic, but maybe she'd changed.

"Seriously, it's pretty awesome. I'm glad you've found happiness. Alfonso is a great guy." He dropped her hand and they continued walking. "So, what if you have another kid? There's no room on the ring for another diamond."

"Guess he'd need to buy me a whole new one, then, eh?" she said, smiling. "We have no plans for another child, but if it happens, it happens. I just kind of hope it doesn't. I mean, I'd be excited if it did, but work is keeping me so busy as it is, and I love it. I wouldn't want to give it up to stay home."

Oddly, Lily had never struck him as a traditional role kind of woman. "Stay home? What about Alfonso? I thought he was freelancing for the Agency. Wouldn't his schedule allow him to be more flexible than yours? Couldn't he stay home, instead?"

She knocked him playfully in the arm, sending pain shooting up to his shoulder. "That's exactly what he says, too. Have you guys been talking?"

He tried not to grimace. "I knew I liked the guy. Nope, guess we're both just family men at heart. Can't you just picture yourself with a whole bunch of kids running around? Now *that* to me would be heaven."

Lily stopped.

"What?" He turned around. "Are you coming or not?"

"I'm just surprised, that's all. I've never heard you talk that way before."

He shrugged, then instantly regretted it because of

the pain. Jesus. Was this arm tied to every muscle in his body?

When the union of a vampire couple produced children, it was considered a good one because fertility rates were so low among their kind. He remembered his own parents saying that many times when he and Betsy were growing up. He got that familiar knot in his gut whenever he thought about his sister. "Maybe you don't know me as well as you thought." Shoving his hands into his pockets, he continued toward Dom's office.

"Somebody's broody today. Hey, Alfonso wanted me to ask you if you'd like to come up to the house for a few days next week. We both have time off and Zoe has been asking about you. Wants to make you brownies or something. Xian gave her his recipe."

He liked that they included him in their family. He and Lily's daughter had this competition going as to who could eat the most brownies. Even Xian, the field office manager, participated in their little game. He'd make the brownies—plain for Zoe, with nuts for Jackson—and the two of them would see who could eat their brownies the fastest. Jackson usually let Zoe win just to see the satisfied expression on the youthling's face.

"I'd love to, but I can't. I'm heading down to San Diego tomorrow night. Gibby and I have tickets to some MMA fights." That is, if he felt better. Maybe some of the more potent energies there would more quickly replenish what he'd lost.

"Ah, you and the fights. Don't you ever get sick of

watching them? That's all you've been doing on your time off."

Probably because he had no family to visit. His friends were his family. "Me? Sick of MMA? Never." He'd been a fan of every kind of hand-to-hand combat ever since his friend's father had taken the boys to see the local boxing matches held in an old barn down in West Texas before the turn of the century. Neither boy had gone through their Times of Change yet, so the blood didn't bother them. After they both changed, it'd be another decade or so until he felt comfortable being around blood like that. That's what watching the fights was to him. A connection to friends who had replaced his family.

"So what did you overhear Dom ranting about? Do I need to prepare myself ahead of time?"

She shrugged. "I just heard him talking to Cordell."

Cordell, the field office's technical expert, handled all things computer related. Had Jackson fucked up the TechTran system again? All he'd done last night was log in, make his report and log out. Well, he did play Hollow Grave for a while. The online computer game was used by Darkbloods to attract young vampire males. They communicated the locations of rave-style parties where they sold blood and encouraged them to revert to the old ways of killing humans for food. When plied with blood like that, youthlings were very receptive to all sorts of backward ideas. Agents were encouraged to stay on top of what was going on. Besides, Jackson loved the game. He had reached the

Ghost Hunter level, which opened up all sorts of new weapons and superpowers.

Could he have done something to the Agency system while playing the game? He knew he hadn't compromised his identity. Cordell had set up each agent who wanted to play the game with an untraceable ID. He hadn't messed with any of the settings, not that he'd even know how to do it in the first place.

No, the meeting with Dom couldn't be about Hollow Grave. It had to be something else, but he didn't find that very reassuring. He was glad Lily had come with him. Dom respected her and she had a way of calming him down, getting to the heart of the matter while not inflaming anyone's anger. She was a diplomat, just like her father.

Jackson felt the tension pouring out of Dom's office before he even opened the door. It was as palpable as last night's fog. The field team leader was leaning over his desk, the muscles in his arms bulging as he stared at his computer screen.

Dom looked up as they entered, his brow furrowed, his blue eyes cold and accusing. It was clear that this wasn't a social call. "What the hell is going on with you?"

"You mean at the Pink Salon? I was going to fill out my report—"

Dom stood up to his full six-foot-four height and scrutinized him in such detail that it seemed as though he was looking for the answers on Jackson's clothes, his hair, his shoes.

"What's one of the first directives of a Guardian?"

Not sure if that was a rhetorical question or not, he answered tentatively. "To…ah…uphold the laws of the Governing Council."

"And?"

Jesus. Was he back in grammar school? "Excuse me?"

Dom huffed out a loud breath. "And what are some of those laws?"

This was bordering on patronizing. Jackson stood to his full height, too. Damn if he was going to let Dom intimidate him like this.

"I'm talking about this goddamn blog." With a look that was equal parts disgust and anger, Dom pointed to the computer screen. "What the hell did you do last night?"

A blog? He got called into his boss's office because of a blog? Jackson walked around so that he could see the screen. "Last night? Mitch and I charcoaled a couple of DBs in the alley behind the Pink Salon. It'll be in the report I turn in."

"And the night before?"

"I've already filed that report. I charcoaled two DBs who were after a sweetblood on my list. Is there a problem?"

"There were human witnesses." It was a statement not a question.

"Yes, the girl and her cousin. I verified there weren't others. I made sure they were safe then I wiped their memories." He kept his answer clipped and unemotional, but despite his best efforts, he hadn't been able to stop thinking of her.

Dom didn't say anything for a moment. "You wiped their memories? Impossible."

His boss was calling him a liar? "Believe it, because I did."

"Then how do you explain this?" He pointed to the computer.

On screen was a banner that said *Paranormalish* and beneath it was an article. The title was *Vampire Wars? You Be the Judge.*

"Okay, so, I don't see what this has to do with last night." Humans were always speculating on the existence of vampires. That was nothing new.

Dom stepped back and folded his arms over his chest. "Scroll down and tell me what you see."

Jackson grabbed the mouse. There, in the middle of the blog post, was a picture of him with a blade over his head, getting ready to charcoal that DB. His hands went cold. No way. This was impossible.

"What the hell is this? I don't understand."

"Let me try to explain it to you. You clearly fucked up again. And this time royally. You didn't wipe their memories and you forgot to clear any evidence. What the hell is going on with you? Your witness obviously took pictures and videos of your attack that night and posted them to this blog."

"That's impossible. I confiscated their phones and, like I told you, wiped their memories."

Dom's impassive expression made it obvious he didn't believe Jackson.

"I swear to God. Ask Cordell. He's got the phones

and is deleting all the pictures and videos from that night."

"Well, obviously, she took some with another camera, then."

Jackson stared at the screen and saw the exact picture of himself that he'd seen on the woman's camera the night before last. "It doesn't make sense. I took the phone that had the pictures. To be honest with you, I did consider letting her keep it after I deleted the images, but I decided to let Cordell work his magic on it before I'd return it to her."

Dom pressed a button on his phone and a few minutes later, Cordell walked through the door.

"How could this happen?" Dom asked him. "Jackson says these photos are the same ones on the phone he confiscated. But you have the phone."

Cordell rubbed his thigh as he leaned on the desk. "My guess is that pictures and videos taken by the phone are automatically saved to a cloud account."

"What's that?" Jackson and Dom asked in unison.

"It's an off-site virtual-storage site that can be accessed from anywhere. Your human accessed the account last night and saw the images from the night before."

Jackson ran his hand through his hair. How could this have happened? "What's the gist of the article?" he asked, bracing himself.

"She documents the attack and how you charcoaled the DB right in front of her." Dom tossed a pen onto the desk.

"What was I supposed to do? Tell her to look away while I killed the bastard?"

"You were supposed to wipe her memory."

"I did," he said, pacing to the other side of the office.

"Clearly, you didn't," Dom growled. "If Santiago catches wind of this, not only is your ass on the line, but, by default, so is mine."

"If we've seen it, we need to assume DBs have seen it, too." Lily picked at the red tip of one of her nails. "Or they will. Since the girl is a sweetblood, they'll keep looking for her. This blog has made it easier for them to find her."

Could this nightmare get any worse?

Jackson pulled a sandwich from his pocket. Xian kept a plate of peanut butter and honey sandwiches in the kitchen at all times, knowing eating calmed his nerves. "I'll do what I can from my end," Cordell said. "But without a password, I'm not sure I can get in to the blog and delete it. Correction. I can do it, it'll just take me a little time."

Dom looked angry enough to use the *brindmal,* a bullwhiplike weapon coiled at his hip, woven with strands of silver. He was a master, able to flick the tiniest of objects off a shelf twenty feet away with just a snap of his wrist. And Jackson had witnessed him taking DBs down with that thing almost as easily. Jackson had the sinking feeling that *he* was the enemy right now, so he put a little more distance between them.

"More important," Dom added, "she's exposed us to the human world at large. I don't care how you do it, but you go back to that woman and shut her down."

"Unless," Lily chimed in, "she's one of those rare humans who can't have their memories altered."

He hadn't considered that, but maybe it'd be good for them to think that it was the woman's fault, not his own. The real possibility existed that his ability to do a simple mind wipe, which allowed him to live peacefully among humans, was getting weaker and weaker as his dark urges got stronger and stronger.

"I hadn't thought about that," Dom said. "If that's the case, then we know what needs to happen."

Jackson's gut twisted and the sandwich soured in his stomach. "You wouldn't. That'd be barbaric."

Dom pounded his fist on the table. "And what choice do I have? Do you think I want it to happen? It's written in the old edicts that a human cannot know about us. And if they're immune to the mind wipes, the laws are very clear about that, too. Let's just hope it was you who screwed it up and that it's not her."

The guy was sounding more and more like Santiago.

Jackson knew what the rules were, but that didn't make it any easier to accept. "But she's the sole caretaker for her young cousin, the sweetblood. If she's gone, the girl is alone."

He couldn't let that happen. He'd grown up without a family and the thought of actually causing the same thing to happen to the girl wasn't acceptable. Plus, the woman didn't deserve to die when it was because of him that she even had any evidence in the first place.

"That's not our problem." Dom pressed a couple of keys and the screen flashed to black. With ice-blue eyes that didn't take shit from anyone, he looked pointedly at Jackson and added, "The secrecy issue is what's at stake."

For God's sake, he knew that, Jackson felt like shouting to the field team leader. Since he was on the verge of reverting, maybe that's why the mind wipe didn't take. But there was no way he could admit that to any of them. Not Lily, not Cordell, and certainly not Dom. For his sake, it was best to let them wonder if it was the woman who'd caused the trouble. But that made him decidedly uncomfortable, as well. Either way you looked at it, this was a helluva vicious circle.

"I'll take care of it."

Dom paced to the other side of the room. "You'd better hope you do it right this time. If it turns out she's immune to the mind wipe, then I'll need to alert Region and they'll send out one of the cleanup crews to take care of the situation."

"Fuck the cleanup crew. I said I'd handle it." In addition to making sure evidence of vampires was wiped from a scene, cleanup crews were also tasked with performing on-the-spot executions. The Council might say one of their primary responsibilities was to ensure the safety of humans to satisfy the law-abiding members of their society, but that was bullshit. When it came down to it, all they cared about was keeping their secrets intact.

No, he'd go back to the woman, try the mind wipe again, and pray that it worked. For both their sakes.

Because if it didn't, one of them was screwed.

CHAPTER SIX

"DON'T TELL ME YOU'RE at home."

Arianna knew instantly that the voice on the other end of the line was George Tanaka, the founder of OSPRA. Although she'd never spoken to him in person, she knew what he sounded like. He was the local media darling when it came to anything paranormal. Dressed in black with his fake professor glasses to make him look scholarly, he made appearances on all the morning shows the week before Halloween, talking about local ghost stories and legends.

"To what do I owe this honor?" she said sarcastically. It was the same tone of voice that had earned her many a slap from her great-aunt, but she couldn't help it. She'd made no bones about the fact that she didn't like George's organization or his methods. "And how did you get this number, anyway?"

"I have my ways."

"I'll bet." She'd long suspected George and his team at OSPRA had been hacking into her blog. Every now and then, a blog she'd written would mysteriously disappear, as if someone had the password and deleted it from her account. "Why do you care if I'm home or not?" He didn't need to know that he'd indeed called her home number, not her cell. She still hadn't located the thing.

"Because I'm concerned that if you are home, you'll be getting visitors soon."

"And what's that supposed to mean? You planning on making a house call?"

"Listen, that blog you posted this morning was explosive. The photos, the eyewitness testimony. It's very compelling evidence supporting the theory that vampires do exist. It's a Van Helsing group's wet dream."

She hadn't thought about how the so-called vampire-hunter groups would respond. She knew they'd probably read it because Icy Shadows had a standing invitation to attend the meetings of the local chapter. Due to privacy concerns, she'd always declined. Besides, she'd heard they were an odd bunch who spent all their time talking about knives and stakes in case they ever did encounter a real vampire. Seemed like a waste of time…till now.

"I'm glad you enjoyed it."

"It was you, wasn't it?"

"Excuse me?"

"You were the one who witnessed the attack, am I correct?"

"I'm not going to divulge my sources. And I'm sure as hell not going to divulge them to you. Is that what this is all about? You want to know who took those photos and witnessed the attack so that you can try to capitalize on it?" He probably had media outfits calling him, wanting to interview him, but he had nothing. This was her story.

"Look. I know we've had our differences in the past, but it's obvious from the article and the photos that you're the one who saw it."

It was? How could he be so sure? Mentally, she recalled each photo she posted and could almost recite the short article word for word. Was there something identifying her in the photos? Had she slipped up and referred to herself in the first person rather than third? She'd taken great care not to write anything that could be tied to her directly. Or so she thought. Hell, she didn't even identify the witness as being male or female.

"And because of that post," he continued, "you're in a lot of danger."

"How so?"

"If what you saw is correct, and it looks pretty damn compelling to me, how long do you think it's going to take for either of those two interested parties—the good guys and the bad guys—to track you down?"

"I told you, it wasn't me."

"Okay, fine. Stick with that story if you insist, but they're going to want to know who the witness was and who took those pictures. They'll come to you first in an effort to get to that person."

"And why would they do that?"

"Think about it. You just posted some pretty damning evidence that supports the premise that vampires really do exist. They're not going to be very happy about that. They might plan to pay you a visit to see just what you do know. In fact, I wouldn't be surprised if that blog mysteriously disappears sometime soon."

Things now made perfect sense. She could almost

see George's face, smirking, hoping she'd take the bait. "So that's what this is all about. You're threatening me. If I don't take down that post, you'll hack into my blog and do it for me."

"Don't be absurd. I'm simply trying to warn you."

"Why? Are you upset I scooped you on what is probably one of the biggest stories any of us has ever uncovered? Ghostly orbs and EVPs are nothing compared to this evidence. I doubt anyone's going to be able to debunk these photos."

"I couldn't give a hoot about orbs or electronic voice phenomena, and I'm not talking about debunking anything. Those pictures and your eyewitness account are pretty amazing. So how was it that you even remembered what happened?"

"What do you mean?"

"Surely you've heard the myths surrounding vampires. That they have the ability to somehow put humans into a trance or glamour them or get them to forget what they saw. They can't have existed this long without some sort of ability to hide the truth when it does become known."

She recalled how she had practically thrown herself into that man's arms. Certainly, that wasn't something she normally would've done with a stranger.

Correction: vampire.

Was George right? Could that man have messed with her memory? Done something to her to make her forget? That would certainly explain why she hadn't recalled anything until she saw those pictures. And yet her recollection about what happened still wasn't completely clear. Each of the pictures she'd taken that night sparked memories, but revealed little beyond the margins of the frame.

"And how was it that they didn't realize you'd been taking pictures?" George continued. "I'd have thought they'd have been more careful when they realized you had a camera."

Then it dawned on her. Of course. The man she'd kissed had taken her phone.

Closing her eyes, she visualized herself standing on the side of the road between two parked cars with that man right in front of her. Quicker than humanly possible, he'd snatched the phone out of her hands and made Krystal turn hers over, as well. She hadn't lost it, after all. He'd stolen it from her.

George was still talking. "My advice is to take an extended vacation until this thing blows over."

"Why? So you'll get the media interviews and coverage all to yourself?"

"I'm serious, Arianna. I'm talking about your safety here. Get out of the house while you still can."

EVERYWHERE SHE LOOKED, Ventra Capelli was surrounded by fools.

"I can't believe you let the sweetblood girl slip through your fingers like that." Did she have to do everything around here to ensure things were done correctly? A good manager knew when to do things herself and when to let others do it. Too bad so many Alliance members up here were so incompetent.

Ventra approached the large aquarium on the far

side of the room. She snapped her fingers and someone handed her a water-filled plastic bag with live goldfish. Carefully, she lifted the lid of the tank and dumped in the contents. Instantly, two small sharks darted among the frantic goldfish, their predatory instincts alive and well, despite their being raised in captivity. One came up behind a yellow-and-white-spotted fish and swallowed it in one bite. Watching them feed like this gave her hope for her people. Instincts were never gone. They were only dormant until the right stimuli came along.

"You had her in your vehicle," she continued. "Talk about a captive audience. It doesn't get much more captive than that."

"You don't understand," Ray said. "A Guardian came from out of nowhere. Jumped into the Jeep while we were trying to get away. Killed Vincent and almost got to me. I barely made it out of there alive."

"Pity," she said under her breath.

The ineptitude of these idiots was mind-boggling. They were soft, complacent. Granted, the energies in humans here in the Seattle area weren't nearly as vibrant as they were in the southern regions where the sun's rays were more concentrated, but there still needed to be a basic level of competency, which she just wasn't seeing around here. Individuals like these needed to be micromanaged in order to ensure things would get done the way they were supposed to get done. One thing was certain—the last sector boss clearly hadn't been a good manager.

"So you just ran away."

"What did you expect me to do? Stay and get charcoaled?"

"I expect you to do your job, and your job was to bring that girl in. The others, too." When Guardians had raided the Night of Wilding party, they rescued several sweetbloods. She was determined to get back what was once hers.

"You could let me do it." The squeak from a chair reminded her that she had a visitor waiting for her in the back of the room. She could never remember his name. But then again, he was human, so what did it matter? When he stopped being useful, she'd take care of him herself.

She gave him a cursory glance and laughed. "How does a wannabe like you think you can bring in a sweetblood that Darkbloods couldn't? You don't look capable of wielding a weapon, let alone fighting off Guardians."

The man tensed. "You forget. Guardians aren't always around. Especially during the day. That constraint isn't an issue for me and could be used to our advantage. If you really want her, I can deliver her to you myself."

Want her? Ventra picked at a small chip in her nail, recalling the sting of regret she'd felt, knowing the girl was going to be auctioned off to the highest bidder. Not that she didn't want it to happen—the whole thing had been her idea in the first place—but someone else was going to be the lucky one to drain her dry. During the few days she had the sweetbloods in her possession, she'd become quite attached to them.

Like pets. Almost.

She recalled how the girl's hair hung in ringlets almost to her shoulders. Even though it would've put thousands of dollars into her sector's coffers, she still had fantasized about burying her own fangs into that pretty little neck and sucking till nothing else came out. Then Guardians came and fouled up everything.

But she was a firm believer in fate. Maybe there was a reason that those sweetbloods had survived that night. Maybe Ventra was the one destined to drain one or more of them and not some anonymous wealthy bidder. But then again, some wealthy bidder could make her a hell of a lot of money.

She tossed the empty plastic bag in the trash. "And how do you propose that."

"Do you want her or not?"

Anger flared instantly in her veins at the human's insolence. Was he not afraid of her? Where was the respect? Surely he had to know what she was capable of doing to him. Perhaps he needed a reminder. She stepped closer to him, opening her mouth to let him see her fangs. Slowly, she ran her tongue over one then the other before she continued, "Well, of course I want her."

The man swallowed, flashed a nervous smile. Good. She'd successfully put him back into his place. One of subservience.

"I'll do it, but only under one condition."

Gripping the edge of the table, she leaned close. "And that condition is…?"

Rather than cowering away from her as she would

have expected, he stared her straight in the eye, and with a clear, confident voice said, "Turn me into a changeling. The others before you promised but never delivered."

She should've guessed as much. To a human, becoming a changeling was the equivalent of finding El Dorado and the Fountain of Youth. But changing a human took time. Finesse. And with it came responsibility. She didn't want to be bothered.

If this human wasn't so valuable, she'd have disposed of him right here and now. "That was a deal you made with my predecessor, not me."

"Wasn't this girl one of the ones that got away? Must be frustrating. You don't want to hear how I'd get her?" The man's tone was appallingly condescending.

Before he could take another breath, she crossed the room and had her hand around his neck. "This better be good, human," she said, leaning in close, "because I just realized I haven't had much to eat all day. And I'm famished."

CHAPTER SEVEN

ARIANNA GLANCED AT THE darkening sky as she quickly pushed the shopping cart into the parking lot. If what she knew about vampire lore was true, then she didn't have much time to get back home, pick up Krystal and hit the road. Once it was dark, they could come after her. She cursed how short the days were this time of year.

After speaking with George, she'd thought about what he'd said. Maybe he had been trying to scare her, but he definitely had a point. For such a long time, she'd been used to people not believing her. She hadn't thought about the ramifications if they did.

She debated whether to just delete the post, but the damage had already been done. Besides, she'd started Paranormalish in order to give a voice to those who didn't have one. To report on things that the mainstream media felt was too outrageous and outlandish to investigate. And that's exactly what she'd done.

When she got to the Caddy, she popped the trunk then dumped two bags of ice into the foam cooler she'd just bought and started unloading the groceries.

She planned to take her cousin to the same little motel they'd stayed in on the way back from eastern Washington. It was just over the mountain pass and very isolated. With the exception of Vinny's Kwik Stop, none of the stores stayed open past six o'clock. They probably wouldn't arrive until seven or eight and there was no way she was going to head out after dark for food. Then tomorrow they'd figure out where to go from there.

For a brief moment, she considered heading down the coast, hitting a few of the theme parks in Southern California. A girl Krystal's age would love that. But the thought of being around a lot of people made her really uncomfortable. Ever since her mom disappeared, she didn't like large crowds.

Tonight, in the motel room's kitchenette, she'd fix a quick chicken dish. Tomorrow, it'd be spaghetti. She'd figure out something else if they ended up being gone longer. She'd already called in to work and told them she was taking the week off.

One of the bags tipped over and several lemons rolled out. As she leaned into the trunk to retrieve them, footsteps sounded behind her. Looking under the crook of her arm, she saw a pair of cowboy boots on the pavement. Large snakeskin ones. She jerked herself upright, banging the top of her head on the trunk lid.

"Ouch."

"Careful there." The man's voice was deep and tinged with amusement.

Rubbing the top of her head, she started to ask if she could help him with anything, but as she turned around, the words locked in her throat.

It was the man from the night before last.

Panic tore a hole in her stomach and her fingers and

toes went instantly cold. George was right. They were after her.

Before she could run, he closed the trunk and shoved her into the car. He moved so quickly she hardly knew what was happening until the inside of the passenger door slammed against her shoulder.

"I know what you are."

"Ha. Believe me, I know that."

He flashed her what he probably hoped was a disarming smile. Was that supposed to calm her down? Get her to go along with him? Thank God she didn't see any fangs. "Stop. You can't do this. Where are you taking me?"

"Tell me where Krystal is," he said. He tossed his leather coat on the seat between them, backed the car out of the stall with a screech then jammed it into Drive.

Krystal? Why in the world did he want to know where her cousin was? "Like hell am I going to tell you that."

"If you're smart, you will."

Huddled as far away from him as possible, she glared at him. On his biceps, the colorful snake tattoo—the one Krystal had mentioned—looked coiled and ready to strike. It was even more menacing given the man's large, hulking muscles. Normally the Caddy felt huge, but with his presence soaking up all the available airspace, it felt like a teacup.

"Wh-why? I'm not telling you that. You have me now, so leave her alone. She's an innocent girl."

"If you want to hear why you and your cousin are in

grave danger and what can be done about it, then you'd better tell me."

She would've thought he'd have stopped by the house first. Maybe he had and Krystal wasn't there. Maybe she was at her friend's house. Hope sparked in the pit of her stomach. If only she could get word to her, tell her to stay away, call the authorities. "And why should I trust you? You're a…*vampire.*"

"Because I'm the one who saved you." There was that practiced smile again. "Remember me?"

Like a dope, she recalled the hard plane of his chest pressed against her, his demanding mouth, the feel of his muscular shoulders as she'd wrapped her arms—

"Yeah, I do. You tried to pull some mind-control thing on me and make me forget what I saw. In fact—" His words still rang in her head as he kissed her that night. The rich, lulling tone. Intoxicating her. "In fact, you tried to charm me as you forced yourself on me."

With the sweep of a hand, he brushed his blue-green hair from his face and she noticed it wasn't pulled back like it had been before. "I do not force women. If you had wanted me to stop, all you had to do was step away."

"That's not what I remember. You made me…want you."

He cocked an eyebrow, the one with the tiny scar. "I didn't *make* you do anything. You wrapped your arms around me of your own free will."

"Free will. My ass."

Laughter rumbled from his chest. He gripped the

steering wheel and the snake flexed. If she'd had a black Sharpie right how, she'd have drawn *X*s over its eyes.

"Given the blog you just posted," he continued, "it's no doubt you remember everything else with great accuracy."

"You—you read Paranormalish?"

"I didn't before today, but I can guaran-damn-tee you that I'll be reading it in the future."

Future? So that meant he wasn't planning to kill her? That she'd be around to continue her blog? A huge sense of relief washed over her. But then, they'd obviously kept their existence a secret for centuries, so why would they suddenly let her blog about them. Something in this scenario wasn't quite right—was he lying about the fact that she had a future?

"I've kept my online identity a secret. How did you know it was me?"

"Well, when I see my gorgeous mug on a blog and you're the only one who was taking pictures of me, you do the math."

Last night, when she pressed Enter, uploading the article and photos, she had no idea that this was where it would land her. "So where are you taking me?"

"To your cousin."

What was it with her cousin? "Krystal had nothing to do with this. You have to believe me. She doesn't even know about Paranormalish and doesn't remember anything about that night. She still thinks you broke up a gang fight."

He exhaled slowly, as if he was trying to stay calm.

"You're forgetting about the one that escaped. Plus, there are others."

A shiver snaked down her spine and she pulled her jacket tighter. "Others? Like how many?" When she'd started Paranormalish, she'd imagined a day when some of the things she blogged about were proven true, that people would finally sit up and listen to her. Realize that she wasn't some delusional freak. The skeptical part of her doubted that would ever happen. How could she have guessed that having her dream come true was actually a nightmare?

"Yes, and now that you posted this blog, you made it easier for them to track your cousin down."

"What does my cousin have to do with any of this? Besides, I've been very careful. They can't follow my online footsteps. None of my followers know my real name or where I live."

"Your cousin is a sweetblood, a human with a very rare blood type, which is addictive. It's highly sought after by certain unscrupulous members of our kind who want to profit from it. That's why those men attacked her in the first place, for her blood. Now, because of that blog, you're both targets. Darkbloods looking for her only need to find you. You've basically doubled the chances of them finding her again."

She was floored. Krystal was in trouble because of her. She brought the girl to live with her because she thought she'd have a better life, but what a terrible mistake that had been. "Who or what are Darkbloods?"

"Those two guys who 'morphed from shadow,'" he said, quoting from her blog.

Knowing that he read what she'd written made her face heat for some reason. Which was silly. The blog was public. People she didn't know read it all the time.

He weaved through rush-hour traffic as if the car was half its size. "Is she at your place?"

She debated lying to him, but he'd just head there, anyway. "What are you planning on doing to us?"

"I'm fixing what wasn't done correctly the first time."

Fixing? What did that mean, and did she really want to know? He was a vampire, so it probably involved blood. And his fangs.

"Which is?" Her voice came out a little more high-pitched than normal, making her sound like an infant. Angry with herself, she cleared her voice and repeated the question, more forcefully this time.

He darted a glance sideways. "Wiping both your memories again."

"Stay away from Krystal. She doesn't remember a thing."

"I'll be the judge of that."

"And then what?" She realized she'd subconsciously put her hand up to cover her neck on the side facing him.

He shrugged. "You'll go on with your normal life without any recollection of me or other vampires."

He really wasn't planning to bite them? She kept her hand on her neck, anyway. "And how will that help things? You just said Krystal is a target. If I don't know the danger she faces, how can I protect her?"

"That's the problem with sweetbloods. Most don't live too long."

She slumped against the seat. It had to be worse than contracting a disease or getting hit by a bus. She couldn't imagine Krystal being attacked and killed at some random point in her life by those who'd want her blood. She wouldn't be safe anytime or anywhere. Not knowing the risks in order to prevent them made her sick to her stomach.

"Isn't there anything we can do?"

"Living in the city isn't helping. The vampire population is generally concentrated around larger cities because that's…ah…where the largest food supplies are."

"Then we'll move. I've always wanted to live somewhere sunny and warm. Like Arizona. No, California. I like the ocean breezes."

"That's not going to be any safer, either. In fact, it'll be more dangerous than living here. Because we're unable to process the sun's energy in our bodies, we must get this energy from you. In warmer climates where the UV rays are more intense, the energies in the human population are more volatile."

"What does that mean?"

"It means that vampires who live in warmer regions tend to be more aggressive. Sweetblood humans are better off sticking to northern cities where the UV index is relatively low year-round and staying away from the larger cities."

"Then you can't wipe my memories. I need to make sure she gets out of the city. How will I know all this if I don't remember?"

"That's not my problem," he said flatly.

She balled her fists and wanted to knock an ounce of caring into his thick head. "I get it. This is about saving face, isn't it? You screwed up with me the first time, so now you've come to fix things. Are all of you as concerned about yourselves as you are?"

He took the corner into her neighborhood a little too sharply, running the tire up over the curb.

"And my blog?"

"What about it? We've already deleted the post."

And for the first time since he forced her into the car, Arianna was more angry than scared.

"Where is the girl?" Jackson said as he walked through the garage door into a tiny kitchen and looked around.

"I'm not sure she's home yet." Arianna brushed past him, grabbed a plate and set it in the sink.

"Yes, she is, I can—"

Arianna held up her hand, interrupting him. "Stop. I'm not sure I want to know how you knew that."

"I can smell her," he finished, anyway.

"Great. A bloodhound with a tattoo. And fangs."

He chuckled.

"Who doesn't listen," she added under her breath.

They walked down the hallway to the girl's bedroom, where she was sitting on her bed, reading.

"Krystal, you remember…ah…Jackson, don't you?"

The girl looked up and smiled. "Sure, from the other night out on the street."

He still couldn't believe how much she reminded him

of Betsy. Although her nose and eyes were different, it was the hair. The perfect ringlets. And that smile.

It took less than a minute for him to be sure that she had no memory of him or of vampires. She indeed believed that she'd seen him break up a gang fight, just as he had wanted her to believe.

"Are you here for dinner?" she asked.

Now that he thought about it, he was kind of hungry.

Before he could answer, Arianna piped in. "No, he was just leaving. He…ah…wanted to see how we were doing."

"You should stay for dinner. Ari cooks really good food."

Far be it from him to turn down a home-cooked meal. In fact, now that she mentioned it, he was really hungry. "She does?"

"No, he really has to run." She pushed him out of the bedroom.

Once they were back in the kitchen, Arianna turned to face him. "See, I told you she didn't remember anything. It's just me."

He nodded and couldn't help wondering what she was planning to have for dinner.

"Hold on." She held up a hand and backed away. "Since I know you have the ability to plant a mental suggestion, will you at least leave me with the compulsion to do what I need to do in order to keep her safe? I had planned to take her to a motel for a few days till things blew over. Maybe these…Darkbloods will have forgotten about us by then."

"Not likely."

Wiping Arianna's memory would keep his people's secret safe, but it certainly wouldn't help her or her cousin. He should just do what he needed to do then get out of here, but for some reason, he wasn't quite ready to end the evening. Instead, he brushed past her into the living room.

Jesus, it was like a fishbowl in here with these huge windows. Anyone outside in the darkness could easily see what was going on inside.

He crossed the room in three strides and shut the blinds. Glancing at the front door, he saw that the damn chain wasn't even latched. What in God's name were they thinking? Not that it would pose much of a deterrent to a vampire wanting to break in, but every little obstacle helped. Human or vampire, there were douche bags out there from both races. When he messed with her memory, maybe he'd tell her to keep these damn doors and windows secured.

"What are you doing?" Arianna asked as he checked the dead bolt.

It wasn't locked, either. Angry, he spun around to face her.

She stood, angellike, in the doorway to the kitchen, the light from behind illuminating the edges of her dark auburn hair. It tumbled in loose waves over one shoulder and he found himself wondering how it'd feel to run his fingers through the strands. Would they slide through easily? Or would they get stuck in her messy tangles? If braided, it would probably be thick like a rope. He crossed his arms, cursing his weakness for redheads.

"Just making sure things are secure."

"That's so damn noble of you," she said bitterly.

Definitely not an angel.

"Listen, before you disappear into thin air, I want to know—"

"I don't disappear. I move quickly."

"Okay, whatever. But before you do your thing and *leave,* I want to know how you knew the whole Krystal-with-a-*K* thing."

"And what good will that do? I'm still going to wipe your memory."

"Because I want to know, that's all. I'm curious—I was born curious. Is it so wrong of me to want answers even if I don't get to keep them? That girl down there—" she jutted her chin toward the hallway "—means the world to me. I didn't want her to have the same shitty childhood as I did, so I brought her here. The two of us are the only sane, unmedicated members of our family."

He'd definitely hit a sore subject. What happened to her when she was a kid? It couldn't be half as devastating as what he'd gone through. He doubted she'd been responsible for the death of a sibling, then kicked out of the family as a result.

Guilt tugged at his heart, threatening to unravel him. He supposed it wouldn't hurt to be honest with her, given that she knew a lot already. "Because she said that to me when I rescued her the first time."

Arianna's eyes went wide. "The first time?"

"Yeah, I—"

His stomach growled. Loudly. A laugh burst from

her lips. Startled, he looked over at her. "Well, that was unexpected," he said.

"That better not be because of me, because…well… that'd just be wrong."

He meant that her laughter was unexpected, not his stomach growling—hell, he was always hungry—but this was okay, too. In fact, it was better. It meant she wasn't as frightened of him as he would've thought she'd be. And for reasons he couldn't figure out, he found that to be kind of…nice.

"Tell you what," he said impulsively, not quite ready to walk out of her life just yet. "Fix me a sandwich and I'll tell you the story of how I know."

She looked confused. "You…eat regular food?"

"Last time I checked, yes. In fact, I've been eating food since I was born. I like my steak medium, not rare. I'll only eat salad if it has ranch dressing, no mushrooms or tomatoes. And I can't stand seafood, any kind, but especially the raw shit." He grimaced, put a hand to his throat. "Just the thought of it makes me want to gag."

He thought she was going to laugh again, but she didn't. "So you guys are…born this way? Someone didn't…make you a…?"

"A vampire?"

"Only changelings, kind of like hybrids, are made. The rest of us are born."

"What about…blood?"

"Need that, too, but not very often." Liar. He needed it way too often, as in every day, but she didn't need to know that. The food should hold him over for a little while, at least.

"What's the catch?" she asked, her eyes narrowing.

"I don't understand."

"The catch. You know, there's got to be a reason why you're so willing to talk. Are you planning to… you know…drink my blood or something."

Don't tempt me. If only you knew how much I want it. And your energies.

But then, if she did, she sure as hell wouldn't be talking to him so boldly.

"Nope. I'm just hungry. For food."

"So I won't remember any of this? The attack the other night?"

"Yep."

"But you can't do that. Take away my memories. They're mine and they belong to me."

"This isn't a debate. I'm not going to argue with you. Vampires have been wiping the minds of humans for thousands of years. I can either tell you what you want to know or not. But either way, your memories of us will be gone. If you don't want an explanation, that's fine. The process is fast and painless. I can be out of here in—" he glanced at his sports watch "—two minutes and be eating somewhere else in ten."

She paced to the other side of the room.

He could've sworn her gaze slid over to the fireplace poker leaning up against the bricks. As if she could use that as a weapon to force him into doing something he didn't want to do. Without much effort, he could take that thing from her before she even realized it was out of her hands.

"Fine," she said, obviously realizing that she truly had no other choice. "Since I'm not going anywhere as I had planned, I'll cook dinner and you'll talk."

CHAPTER EIGHT

ARIANNA'S TINY KITCHEN was clean, but cluttered. Almost every flat surface had something on it. Coffeemaker, toaster, canisters, utensils, loaf of bread, covered dish of butter. Painted a cheery yellow, it looked homey and lived in. Not sterile. He had a hard time figuring out where to put the foam cooler he pulled from the trunk until she told him to just set it on the floor next to the sink.

"You can pull a chair in from the dining room if you want. Or—" her gaze skimmed over him from top to bottom "—if that doesn't work, you can just hang out here. It'll only take a few minutes."

Without thinking, he pushed the toaster aside and hopped onto the counter the way he did back at the field office when he shot the shit with Xian. He thought he saw the corner of her mouth turn up as she pulled out items from the grocery bags. "What happened to your arm?"

"A minor work injury," he answered, crossing his boot-clad ankles. It felt comfortable, natural sitting here like this, watching her work. "What are you fixing?"

"You'll see," she said, grabbing a large frying pan.

"Just as long as you don't use that thing on me."

"As long as you start talking, I won't have to."

Warily, he eyed the small jar of little dark green things that she was opening. Those weren't fish eggs, were they? "I'm not really a gourmet kind of guy."

"I know, I figured that out already. But trust me. I think you'll like this."

In a few minutes, chicken was cooking in a pan and Arianna was squeezing lemons into a glass measuring cup.

"Okay," she said, picking out a seed. "So tell me about Krystal with a *K*."

"It happened when—"

"Why are you talking about me?" Krystal walked into the kitchen and smiled at Jackson. "So you stayed after all. What are you making, Ari?"

"Chicken piccata."

"Huh?" Jackson and Krystal said in unison.

"It's basically lemon chicken with capers." Arianna sprinkled a few of them into the sauce.

"What are capers?" Krystal asked, eyeing the pan with a look of disgust on her face. Yeah, he wanted to know, too. They looked…weird. And in his world, *weird* and *food* didn't go together.

"They're these little salty things," she said, shaking the jar. "It's like a flavor explosion in your mouth."

"Don't tell me they're fish eggs," Jackson said, holding up his hands in a mock protest. "Because I can guaran-damn-tee you that I won't be eating them."

"Gross," Krystal said, sticking out her tongue. "I am definitely not eating them."

Arianna rolled her eyes as she grabbed a bottle of ranch dressing from the refrigerator. "You two are pathetic. Technically, they're caper berries, tiny little flower buds that have been brined like pickles. Not fish eggs. It's nothing gross and they add a lot of flavor. But if you don't like them, you can easily pick them out."

Jackson studied them skeptically, then looked at Krystal. "I'll try it if you will."

The girl looked as if she'd just bitten into a lemon. "You will?"

"Yeah, in fact, if you want, I'll try the dish first and let you know how it is. I'll give you the eatability rating."

"Gee, thanks, you two, for the vote of confidence. As if I'd make something inedible."

"It's just that I'm not used to eating fancy sh—stuff," he corrected himself before Arianna had a chance to give him the evil eye for cussing.

"Nice," Krystal said to him. As she left the kitchen, she turned to Arianna and added, "I like how this one thinks."

This one? Jackson stared at Arianna, but she didn't appear to be fazed by Krystal's remark. She was sprinkling the chicken dish with salt now. How often did she cook for other men? Was this a normal thing for her to invite guys she hardly knew into her house then whip up a meal? Well, she didn't exactly invite him…and he wasn't exactly a normal guy. But here he'd been feeling kind of special that she was fixing him dinner, when in fact, he wasn't.

At some point, she'd grabbed her hair and secured most of it into a low ponytail off to one side. Several strands dangled free, brushing her face as she worked.

One of her T-shirt sleeves was partially rolled up, but the other wasn't. Her curve-hugging jeans had several holes that were probably made from wear, not from a machine in a factory. Her nose turned up a little at the end, and if he were a betting man, he'd guess she hated that. He, on the other hand, found it charming, almost impish. He was used to women who fussed over themselves, trying to make every little thing perfect and going under the knife when they could, which was why he found these imperfections of hers strangely compelling.

From this angle, he could see she had a smudge of something on her cheek. Flour, maybe, from the chicken? Without thinking, he reached over and rubbed it off.

There was that powerful zing of electricity rushing up his arm again. He quickly pulled his hand away. "Sh—oops. I'm sorry. It's the energy thing. It's usually not this strong, though." He vowed not to touch her again until it came time to wipe her memory.

"No," she said softly, touching her cheek where his fingers had been. She paused, looked up at him with those whiskey-colored eyes. "It's…nice."

His heart thundered in his chest. Her lashes were so thick and dark that the overhead light cast lash-shaped shadows on her cheeks. He wanted to stroke the pads of his fingers over her skin again, get lost in those eyes, kiss her pouty mouth. He'd seen her sampling the sauce a few times. Would she taste of lemon and herbs?

A sound from Krystal in the other room broke the spell. Arianna cleared her throat and turned back to the stove. Then, before he knew what was happening, he felt a hand on his shoulder and she was holding a fork up to his mouth.

"Can you taste this for me and tell me if it's seasoned enough?"

It didn't even cross his mind to tell her no. He opened his mouth for her and she slipped the bite inside.

"What do you think?" she asked, sliding the fork out. "Is it too bland?"

Wow. She was right. Those little non-fish-egg things did give the dish an explosion of flavor. A very delicious one. "It's not bland at all. I think it's perfect. Don't you think so?"

"I haven't tried the chicken yet. Just the sauce."

Without a word, he took the fork from her, taking care not to touch her skin, and cut a small piece of meat from the pan. As he held it up, she slowly flicked her tongue over her lips, then took the bite from him.

Holy fuck. That little move went straight to his groin. She made a little moan of pleasure as she chewed. His shaft thickened until it strained painfully behind his zipper, but he didn't want to move and spoil the moment.

If they rolled around in the sack together, would she close her eyes like this in ecstasy? Rather than bury his face in her hair as he made that first hard thrust, he'd want to watch just to see if she did or not. Would it be the same as this? No, he decided, he wouldn't want that. This look and that little sound, while very lovely, were much too tame.

If he were to have sex with her, he'd want the sensation to warrant a much stronger reaction from her. Fingers digging into his buttocks. Nails gouging parallel tracks in his back. Words like *Oh, my God* spilling from her lips before he was even completely inside.

What the hell was he thinking? Arianna was not the kind of woman who dated men with metal studs in their johnsons. For that matter, she wasn't the kind of woman who dated vampires, either.

He turned away and grabbed the salad bowl, instead.

She was a human who knew what he was. For a woman to have sex with a man, there had to be a certain element of trust, because in essence, she was inviting him in when she was the most vulnerable. It wasn't that he'd never been with a human female before—he'd been with countless of them—he'd just never been with one who knew what he was.

Besides, she wasn't his type. She wasn't flashy or easy or shallow.

As Arianna watched Jackson drying the dishes, she was struck by how bizarrely ordinary this evening had turned out to be. She'd cooked for him and he'd told stories that had made both her and Krystal laugh. Here in her kitchen, he looked both out of place and—she had to admit—completely gorgeous at the same time.

Which really pissed her off. It meant she was affected by his charming ways. She really should fortify herself, insulate her libido from what she knew was trouble. She knew his type only too well. Next thing she knew, he'd be sweet-talking his way into her pants just to add another check in his yes column.

But damn, he was good. She hadn't asked him for his help. He'd just stepped in and started doing what needed to be done to clean up the mess she'd created.

"Thanks for the good dinner, Ari. I liked those little caper thingies." Krystal tossed the dish towel on the counter and headed back to her room.

"Yes, I agree," Jackson said, putting the last of the glasses away. "It was surprisingly good."

"And I'm surprisingly happy about that."

"Has anyone ever told you that you're a mess when you cook?"

"Artistry in the kitchen shouldn't be constrained by tidiness."

He laughed.

"Besides," she continued, "neatness makes me think that something's as good as it's going to get. I'm a dreamer and believe things can always be better."

"That's an interesting way to look at things. Either that, or a damn good excuse."

"Can I get you another glass of wine? Especially considering that you've still got a lot of talking to do?"

With her cousin at the dinner table, Arianna had silently told him not to say anything. Instead, Jackson had laughed at all of Krystal's crazy antics, much like an attentive older brother would act toward his kid sister, and Krystal had soaked up the attention like a dry sponge. Arianna liked seeing the girl have so much fun. Since she'd moved in, she'd been trying so hard to impress Arianna, wanting to be perfect. It was refreshing to see her relax and be a normal teenager for a change.

"Wine? Um, sure."

She noticed the hesitation. Maybe he didn't care for the stuff and he'd just been polite during dinner. "I've got some Patrón in the cupboard, too. That, and some ginger ale. Or there might be a bottle of margarita mix around here somewhere."

"Definitely the tequila. Straight up."

After he was comfortably situated on the couch, glass in hand, she turned to him. "Third time's a charm."

"Huh?"

"Krystal with a *K*. Remember? I've asked about it three times already and I'm still waiting for an answer."

She knew he wasn't eager to tell her, but this was the deal they'd made.

"Oh…that." He knocked back the tequila in one gulp. "Yes, we did meet before. Six weeks ago I rescued her from Darkbloods."

Coinciding perfectly with Krystal's disappearance.

It felt as if all the oxygen had been sucked from the room. Words and thoughts jumbled in her head, but she didn't know if she'd said anything aloud.

Jackson continued, "She and I talked back then… although she doesn't remember, of course. I've…ah… tried to keep tabs on her since then, but obviously, I didn't watch her closely enough."

"What happened?" she managed to ask.

"Since the beginning is the best place to start, tell me what you know, and I'll help fill in the blanks."

All right. If that's the way he wants it.

Arianna took a deep breath. "Shortly after moving

in with me, Krystal met some other kids who were in the same self-study program she's doing. They decided to get together at the downtown library and study for an upcoming project. Since I was working a little late, anyway, we planned to meet up, get a bite to eat, then head home together. But she never showed. I checked everywhere. The library. The nearby coffee shops. Then I thought that maybe she'd taken the bus back or something, but when I got home, she wasn't here. All my calls and texts went unanswered."

"You must've freaked out." Jackson shifted and his leg almost touched hers.

"Totally. And the police weren't much help. Said she probably ran away, given her unstable home life, maybe got into the drug scene. I put fliers everywhere. Then she showed up a few days later."

"That was me. I brought her back here after everything was over."

"Thank you for that, for bringing my cousin safely back. She said she couldn't remember where she'd been, and part of me wondered if they had been right. It's not like she had the best examples back home. She slept the next day and when she finally got up, she was lightheaded and starving. That's all I know. In a few days, she was back to her old self and things went back to normal…except for me. I couldn't forget."

"Did you report it on your blog?"

"Yes and no. I didn't want people to know that she was my cousin, so I treated her disappearance as if I were covering any other story."

"I never considered the people left behind before and what they…you…must've gone through."

He went on to explain how Darkbloods had kidnapped Krystal for entertainment at a big gathering. "Guardians caught wind of it and stormed the place. That's when I came across a group of sweetblood humans waiting to…ah…go out in front of the crowd. Krystal was one of them. She reminded me so much of my younger sister that night." His eyes had a faraway look.

She wanted to ask him about his sister, but first, Krystal. "The crowd?" Just that made her shiver. "What were they going to do to her? Or do I even want to know?"

"I'd rather leave out the details, but I'll tell you if you want me to."

She was touched by his protective gesture. "These Darkbloods…who are they?"

"There are those among our kind who believe we should go back to the days when our ancestors fed from and killed humans. The Darkblood Alliance is an organized group whose goal is to advance and promote that agenda. They try to get new recruits and sympathizers among the civilized vampire population. The organization I'm involved with tries to make sure that doesn't happen. Krystal's blood would command a high price on the vampire black market, so she's very valuable to them."

"And you're going to make sure I have no memory of the danger she's in, basically leaving her totally vulnerable to Darkbloods again?"

He couldn't meet her gaze. "I'll do what I can to keep tabs on the two of you. We've got her in our database of known sweetbloods in the area."

"Yeah, and look what good that did."

His expression darkened, his jaw muscle ticked. Abruptly, he stood and paced to the far side of the room.

"You mentioned your sister. Where does she live?"

"She died," he said flatly. "A long time ago." His back was to her, so she couldn't see his face.

"I'm...I'm sorry. You said Krystal reminds you of her?"

"Yes."

"How so?" Maybe if she kept prodding, he'd cave. She wanted to know more about this man.

He walked over to a side window and peered out into the darkness. She had the feeling he wasn't really looking at anything in particular...just thinking.

"You know," he said quietly, "you really should put blinds up on this one, too."

She didn't reply, just waited.

Finally, he turned back around and faced her. "My sister, Betsy, was right around Krystal's age when she died. It was my fault. I was two years older than her when it happened."

"How was it your fault? You were just kids."

"It...just was."

She could tell he wanted to talk about it, but he just didn't know where to start, so she tried the tactics that he'd used on her. Starting from the beginning. "How long ago did it happen?"

"Neither of us had gone through our Time of Change yet, so we were still able to go out into the sunlight without it making us sick."

"And when was that?"

"A very long time ago." He stood with his body still partially facing her, his toe angled out, his hands in his back pockets, not crossed in front of his body. He hadn't closed her off yet.

"So, when you were kids, you were together, out in the daylight, when something happened?" she asked, rephrasing what he'd told her to encourage him to continue.

"Yes. We were vacationing at a resort on the edge of a small lake. Our parents forbade us from going out in the rowboats during the daylight hours because if something were to happen to us, they wouldn't be able to help us. But I didn't listen. I wanted to row the boat over to the other side of the lake."

"What was over there?"

"A country store. We'd sneak over there to buy candy."

She nodded for him to continue.

"Betsy pleaded with me not to go and I told her she was being a baby. I don't think she liked that, because just as I was pushing the boat away from the dock, she jumped aboard. Out in the middle of the lake, we were horsing around and before I knew it, Betsy had fallen in. I tried to save her, but I couldn't reach her. She just kept slipping deeper and deeper into the depths of the lake until I couldn't see her any longer. She had expected me to save her. I still remember that look on her face. But I wasn't able to get to her. The current took her away and we never saw her again."

He turned away from her.

"You know it wasn't your fault, don't you? Sometimes bad things just happen, even to the most wonderful people. Ones we can't imagine living without. In fact, if you—"

"Shh." He held up a hand, interrupting her. Then he tilted his head to the side as if he was listening to something.

She couldn't hear anything.

In a flash, he was right next to her, whispering into her ear. "Darkbloods. Circling the house. Two, maybe three of them."

Her heart slammed into her throat.

"Do you have an interior room with no windows?"

"No. Just the closets."

He whisked her toward Krystal's room, thrusting a curved blade into her hand. Her cousin jumped to her feet when they came through the door, but said nothing when she saw his finger up to his lips.

"Both of you, in here," he whispered, pointing to the closet. "If someone tries to come in, you need to use this on them. One stab with this silver blade will weaken them, slow them down at least."

"Then what do we do?" Arianna asked as she opened the closet's louvered door and pointed for Krystal to get inside.

"Run."

CHAPTER NINE

THE TEN OR FIFTEEN MINUTES they spent huddled in the closet seemed like a lifetime. Unsure whether Krystal would stay quiet if she told her the truth about what was happening, Arianna explained that Jackson suspected the gang members from the fight the other night had found them. Her cousin seemed to accept that explanation as well as could be expected, but it was probably just temporarily. If they got out of this alive, she'd need answers.

Footsteps outside. Someone was running.

Then a loud crack. It didn't quite sound like a gun—maybe a tree limb breaking.

Light filtered in through the slats in the closet door and glinted off the curved blade she was holding. Even the carved hilt was slightly curved. Holding Krystal like this boosted Arianna's protective instincts even more. If someone tried to harm her cousin, she wouldn't hesitate to use this blade.

"That's one huge honkin' knife."

"It sure is," she started to say, but her words were cut short by a loud thud that sounded like the front door.

They both jumped.

Then the sound of something being dragged down the hallway, straight toward the bedroom.

Krystal grabbed her arm. "Is that—"

"Shh." Arianna shook her free so that she could use the knife if she had to.

The bedroom door opened. She could hear someone breathing and remembered Jackson saying he could smell that Krystal was a sweetblood.

Her heart was beating so loudly that she hoped the intruder couldn't detect it. Could vampires hear the sound of blood rushing through their victims' veins? If only she could make her heart stop for a moment. She grabbed the hilt of the knife with both hands and watched for a shadow to appear under the door.

She listened but heard no sound for what seemed like a lifetime.

Had the intruder already melded with the darkness? Would she be able to see him if he had? Did the shadows mask sound, as well?

A small shuffle of a shoe on the carpet. Then a grunt and another thud.

Oh, God, he was right outside the closet.

Despite the knife, Krystal grabbed her arm again. A little squeak came from her lips.

"Arianna?" It was a man's voice. It came not from eye level, but from the floor.

Jackson? He didn't sound right. Had he been hurt? She reached up to press open the bifold doors.

"Don't!" Definitely Jackson. "Stay where you are!"

"Why? Are they still out there?"

"No...I...killed them."

"Oh, my God," Krystal gasped.

"Then why can't we come out?"

"I'm cut...by a silvie...I'm weak...will—"

She didn't wait for him to finish.

"Don't move," she ordered Krystal. She burst through the door and shut it quickly behind her.

Jackson lay on the floor at the foot of the bed, clutching his arm. It was covered in blood. "Stay away," he hissed.

She didn't listen to him. Instead, she crossed the room and dropped to her knees at his side. Blood was oozing out from between his fingers. Without thinking, she yanked off her sweatshirt and wrapped it around his arm.

"Don't. You can't. Be. Near me."

That's when she noticed his mouthful of teeth. Fangs that had been hidden earlier were now fully exposed. She knew she should have been scared at the sight, but she was more preoccupied by assessing him for injuries. The thick slashes of his brows were drawn together and his pupils were almost fully dilated. Did he have a concussion, as well? A head injury?

"I'm not going to let you bleed to death. I'm calling 911."

"No." His hand shot out, grabbing hers. "You can't involve humans."

A snap of electricity jolted her and she felt a weird pulling sensation along her arm. It was as if something was flowing out of her and going into him. She could feel herself growing tired, lethargic and she stifled the urge to yawn. His pupils didn't seem quite as wide as they had been a moment ago and his fangs seemed to have shrunk.

What she wouldn't give to lie down next to him and go to sleep.

With an angry yet pained expression on his face, he let go of her and rolled to his side. "Get away before I take too much from you." His voice sounded less strained, a little stronger.

"What can I do? Is there someone I should call?"

"You need to get away from here. Take Krystal and go."

"Without you? I don't understand. Why?"

"Because there are more of them coming and I'm in no shape to protect you now."

Something inside her clicked into gear. "Krystal, honey, run. Get into the car."

"I don't understand," came the reply from the closet.

"You heard me," Arianna barked. "Open that door and run straight from this room. Don't look back. Grab my purse in the kitchen by the door. I'll be right behind you."

Thankfully, the teenager did as she was told.

"Good," Jackson said, his voice strained. "Now, you, too."

"Like hell am I leaving you here. You're coming with us."

"I can't, Arianna. I'm too weak. In the closed space of the car, my defenses will be down and I'll attack her. I need blood and energies. It's my body's natural reaction. I'm liable to attack you, as well."

"I'm not about to leave you here to bleed to death all over Krystal's floor. So get your ass up." She stood and dragged his hulking form up with a groan. Thank

God she'd been doing squats as part of her exercise routine for a while, not that it helped all that much. He was really heavy. At least his legs seemed to be functioning all right.

Despite his protests, she draped his arm around her neck and with the curved knife in her other hand, she shuffled him down the hall, through the kitchen and out into the garage.

He stumbled on the step leading into the garage and something clattered to the floor. A set of handcuffs. They were black around the outside, silver on the inside.

"At least put those on me," he growled.

"The handcuffs?"

"Yes. They're lined…with silver. It'll make me…too weak…to attack Krystal."

"You seem plenty weak enough already."

"If you want me to come with you, it's the only option."

She heard the not-too-distant sound of screeching tires on wet pavement.

Jackson's head jerked up. "They're here."

Without arguing further, she grabbed the cuffs and snapped one side around his wrist. He groaned and would've stumbled had she not steadied him. Noticing Krystal was in the front seat, she yelled at her to get into the back. If Jackson was going to be unpredictable, then she wanted him up front where she could keep an eye on him. Once inside the car, she snapped the handcuff to the passenger-door handle, pressed the garage-door remote and started the engine.

As it slowly rose, she jammed the car into Reverse and twisted around in her seat to back out of the garage.

"Come on. Come on." *Please don't give out on me now.*

The garage door had been giving her problems lately. Just yesterday, she'd had to manually open the thing when it got stuck halfway. She cursed herself for not mentioning it to her landlady, but it hadn't seemed like a big deal until now.

The door finally cleared the back bumper. Inch by inch, she saw the driveway behind her.

Then two sets of feet, then legs, then bodies.

Two men in sunglasses and black trench coats, who looked very similar to the ones who'd tried to kidnap Krystal, stood fifteen feet behind her car.

"Drive!" Jackson yelled.

Despite who they obviously were, the thought of purposely hitting someone with a vehicle made her hesitate.

"Punch it," he commanded. "Trust me. If they don't move and you hit them, they're not going to be dead."

All right. She hit the gas and the Caddy flew out, making a loud scraping noise in the process. She'd scratched the driver's side on the edge of the garage door and broke off the side mirror.

Thunk.

She hit something. That's when she realized she'd pinched her eyes shut. She had no idea if she'd nailed one or both of them.

His window rolled down, Jackson leaned out with

a big-ass gun in his free hand, which, thank God, was his uninjured one.

Where had that thing come from? Given that she hadn't known where he pulled the curved blade from, either, she imagined he must have other weapons strapped to his body, as well. He was a man full of surprises.

As she barreled out of the driveway and onto the road, she heard three quick snaps from his gun and realized it must be the sound of a silencer.

"Got him. One more to go." He sounded as if they were at a shooting range at a carnival and he was on his way to winning a giant stuffed panda.

She jammed the car into Drive and cranked the large steering wheel like the captain of an oil tanker. Thank God for power steering. The back of the Caddy lurched and she heard the sound of metal grinding on metal again.

"He's holding on. You need to crank it. Take the corner up there fast and hard. See if you can lose him."

With the accelerator pressed to the floor, all eight cylinders roared to life. The tires screeched, spinning momentarily until they gripped the pavement. Her neighbors were going to hate this. If they made it out alive, she doubted the Neighborhood Watch would ever forgive her.

The intersection came up fast. She must've clipped the corner more tightly than she had intended, because Mr. Baker's garbage cans went flying, which meant there were probably tire tracks in his petunias, too.

The old guy was going to have a total meltdown

when he went out for the morning paper tomorrow. She could picture it now. Coffee cup in one hand, cigarette in the other, bony knees poking out from under his plaid robe. "Those goddamn good-for-nothing kids."

If only all of this were just a bunch of rowdy teenagers.

"Holy crap, Ari," Krystal said from somewhere in the backseat.

"Yeah, no kidding," Jackson said. "You drive this thing like a tank."

What could she say? It was a piece of shit and they were being chased by a vampire. What was another dent or two?

She swerved around a parked car. "Is he gone?" she asked, looking into the rearview mirror.

Before Jackson could reply, or maybe he did and she just didn't hear him, she got her answer.

A hand, then a head, appeared on the trunk.

Despite the force of the speeding car, the Darkblood was somehow pulling himself up over the bumper. Long razor-sharp teeth hung from his mouth. With the sunglasses gone, his eyes were two black orbs staring at her through the back window. The face of a devil.

"Get down, Krystal," Jackson yelled as he leaned awkwardly out of the passenger window. If only she hadn't handcuffed him to the door. If only he wasn't hurt. She gunned it through a yellow light.

Snap, snap, snap.

Jackson was firing at him.

A quick check in the mirror showed that the man

was still there. One gloved hand reached for the ledge right behind the back window.

"Look out," Krystal yelled.

Not watching where she was going, she turned around just in time to see a huge pothole in the road marked by several orange cones and the blinking lights of a construction project. She slammed on the brakes, tried to swerve, but it was too late.

With a bang, they hit the cones, then the hole.

A loud, grinding noise filled the air as the Caddy bottomed out. She held the steering wheel straight and prayed that they didn't get stuck.

Momentum propelled them back onto the paved road and she floored it, putting the construction zone, with its cones as bowling pins, behind them. She didn't see the guy in the rearview mirror. A quick check into the one side mirror that worked didn't show him, either. He wasn't on the roof, was he? It was vinyl and—

Jackson sat back in his seat, eyes closed, a smile plastered on his face.

"What's so funny?" she demanded, glancing at the roof of the car, expecting to see a knife poke through the vinyl at any moment.

"Your driving and this piece-of-shit car may have just saved us."

"Why? What happened? Where is that guy?"

"When you hit that pothole, your back bumper came off along with our…bumper sticker."

CHAPTER TEN

JACKSON WASN'T USED TO FEELING so helpless. With this silver cuff around his wrist, he couldn't be any less of a threat than if Arianna had had him by the balls.

While Krystal used the facilities at the rest stop, Arianna leaned on the door of the Caddy, his cell phone in her hands. She'd swiped it from him at some point and now she stood just out of his reach.

"Give that back."

"It's a bitch when someone takes your phone without asking. Kind of a violation of your privacy, wouldn't you agree?"

"Okay, I get it. I'll give you your phone back as soon I can. Now…give it…back."

She swiped her finger on the touch screen and started scrolling. "Tell me who to call to get you some help."

"I don't need help."

"Would you like a mirror? You're clearly in bad shape. The wound on your arm needs to be dressed and whatever those handcuffs are doing to you, it isn't good. If you don't want me to start at the top of your contact list and start dialing for dollars, then you'd better give me a name."

He pulled at his wrist, but the silver kept him in

check, sapping his remaining strength. These strong-arm antics of hers were infuriating. She had no clue what kind of fire she was playing with. "I can't get anyone else involved."

"Why? Surely there's someone at this agency you work for who will know what to do. This can't be the first time that something like this has happened. I'm sure guys like you get hurt all the time."

"What do you mean *guys like me?*"

"Guys who put themselves in harm's way in order to protect someone else…someone they don't even know. Guys who don't think about what could happen to themselves if they should fail. They just do it, without hesitation, because it needs to be done." She stopped messing with his phone. "Guys like you, Jackson."

She made it sound as if he was a fucking hero or something. Someone who didn't let innocent people die. She couldn't be further from the truth. "It's my job."

She turned her full attention to him. Although she had a determined set to her jaw, her eyes were soft and full of concern. He looked away. He didn't need the walls around his heart to waver under the scrutiny of this beautiful woman. She'd quite possibly saved his life back there, even though she knew full well what he was. That, to him, was heroic. A group of Darkbloods who came across an injured agent wouldn't have hesitated to stake him.

"What are you afraid of?" she whispered, her eyes soft and full of concern.

"Nothing."

"I know most guys don't like being sick and dependent on other people, is that it?"

If he weren't so tired, he'd turn on his trademark charm, flash her one of his killer smiles to disarm her and get back on an even playing field, but he couldn't. "I'm not sick. I just…need a little time. That's all."

"But the sun will be up in a few hours. I don't know what to do or where to take you. We can't go this alone and neither can you."

It felt as if he'd hit a brick wall, with nowhere to turn. All his friends were with the Agency. They were his family. If he contacted Mitch or Dom for help, not only would they insist on taking him to the clinic, which would be disastrous, but if what he suspected about Arianna was true, that she was immune to mind manips, then she'd be in danger, too.

"Don't you have a friend I can call?"

Gibby in San Diego was too far away. Besides, he sometimes worked on the cleanup crew, which meant he was the last person Jackson would want to take advice from right now.

Then he thought about Lily. She was shrewd, the daughter of a Council member, and would probably ask too many questions. And yet…she was engaged to Alfonso, who'd operated outside the bounds of their society. She'd kept their relationship a secret for years.

"Jackson?"

"Okay, hold on. I'm thinking." Lily might demand answers from him, but she'd also respect his wishes. If he didn't want help, she wouldn't force him to get it. "Let me call Lily."

The line was already ringing when she handed the phone to him then walked to the curb about fifteen feet away, just out of earshot. This surprised him. For a blogger investigating the paranormal, he would've assumed she'd use every opportunity to get information to report back to her readers.

Lily answered on the second ring. "Yo, Jacks, what's up?"

He quickly explained to her about the Darkblood attack. "So, now they know…where the girl lives. She and her cousin aren't…safe in their house…anymore."

There was a slight pause on Lily's end. "You know what Santiago would say about this, don't you?"

That was the problem. He knew exactly what the region commander would say. *Guardians shouldn't get involved in the day-to-day affairs of the ones they're trying to protect. There will always be humans dying at the hands of vampires. We can't be responsible for all of them. We can try to prevent Darkbloods from succeeding, but our primary concern is keeping our secret safe.* The guy gave a version of that speech at almost every briefing.

"Yeah, and Dom would say the same thing. That's why I came to you."

"What do you want me to do?"

He took a deep breath and tried not to sound as if he was in too much pain. "For some reason, Darkbloods seem very focused on finding Krystal. They'll no doubt try to pick up our trail. That's where you come in. I need you to muddy it up. Go to her house and lay some scent-masking crystals to throw them off our track."

"Okay, I can do that, but where are you going to take them, then?"

He leaned back on the headrest and closed his eyes. "Hell if I know."

He didn't have a place of his own and he certainly couldn't take them to the field office. Given that Krystal was a sweetblood, it really limited his options.

"I just want to know that...wherever we go, Darkbloods won't be showing up...a few hours later." Lily was a class A scent tracker and if she said a scent was untraceable, then he believed her.

"Will do." He started to relax, but then she added, "When are you going to tell me what happened to you?"

Damn. Why did she have to be so perceptive? "What are you talking about?"

"Don't bullshit me. It's clear that you're in pain. A trained monkey could figure that out. You sound out of breath and exhausted."

He glanced over at Arianna sitting on the curb then dropped his voice. "And how do you know I wasn't just rolling around in the sack with someone?"

"You're a man whore, Jacks, but I'm not an idiot. Did you take a silvie hit?"

Why had he even bothered? "Just a small one," he said, gingerly holding his arm. "No big deal."

"Has a medic looked at it yet?"

"No," he said a little too quickly. "Like I said, it's not a big deal."

"Given that DBs have gotten their hands on that high-grade silver alloy and are making blades and bullets from it, you really should have your injury checked out. Don't you remember what happened to Kip?"

Kip was her trainee who'd been abducted by Dark-bloods and tortured with silver spikes slipped under his skin. He'd been really messed up. Still was, though most of it was mental now. DBs had really fucked with his head.

"But, hey," she continued. "It's your body. Just don't be bitching to me when you have to go through regen treatment at Mom's clinic."

There was no fucking way he was going up there. Lily's mother was the last person he wanted to see. A well-known tissue-regeneration specialist, she'd been instrumental in helping Alfonso get back full use of his leg after a devastating injury, and she was the one who'd treated Kip. But she would also run tests, take tissue samples and probably a whole bunch of other shit that he wasn't interested in knowing about. The results would show Jackson's abnormal energy and blood needs and then the whole Agency and Council would know he was on the verge of reverting. No, thank you.

"So the woman and her sweetblood cousin. Where are they?"

He thought about lying, but figured she'd just see through him anyway. "They're with me."

"And you didn't slip up?"

"What do you mean? In the past few days I've killed—" He counted quickly. Two at the Pink Salon, one on the street that Arianna saw, two in the woods behind her house, then one in her driveway. "Six DBs. I wouldn't call that slipping up."

"I mean you didn't fuck up and take their blood. Especially that of the sweetblood girl, given that you're low on blood and energies with that injury."

"Hell, no." Then, because he knew she'd ask... "Besides, after I got nicked with the silvie, I had Arianna cuff me to the car door."

"I'm impressed, Jacks. You meet a woman and right away, you're pulling out the handcuffs. I like a man who's not afraid to tell a woman about his kinky sexual needs."

"Screw you."

She laughed.

He could always count on Lily to sex up any conversation.

"If I didn't know you like I do, I'd think you were worried about these two human females. Why don't you just wipe their minds and be on your way?"

She was right. That was what he should do. "I...I am worried about them. I wouldn't feel right about leaving them for other DBs to find. Plus—" He debated whether he should say anything, but then he was pretty sure he could trust Lily not to go running to Region.

"Yes..." she prompted.

He decided to risk it. "It's possible that Arianna is immune to the memory thing, that's all."

The line was silent for a moment. "Shit. Given what she's seen and what she knows, that would not be good. Do you want me to go take care of it for you? Maybe you were just tired and—"

"No," he said. He sure as hell didn't want to arouse suspicion that he wasn't capable of doing it himself, even if he was talking to one of his best friends. If a Guardian even suspected another of being on the verge of reverting, it was their duty to turn in him or her to the authorities. He wouldn't want Lily to feel she had to lie for him. She needed to be responsible and do what was expected of her. She had a family and was getting married soon.

"Have you ever known me to be tired when it involves a woman? Besides, if she is immune, then you'd have no choice but to bring her in."

"Are you saying you wouldn't?"

"Yes…no. Shit. I don't know what I'd do. Maybe I'll lay low with them for a few days until this blows over and Darkbloods have moved on to someone else."

"Then what exactly are you proposing on doing with her if lying low doesn't work?"

"I haven't gotten that far yet. I just know that I can't allow anything to happen to her. It…it wouldn't be right. She's all her cousin has. If something happens to Arianna, then Krystal has no one. And for a sweet-blood teenager, that'd be a disaster." He didn't want to admit that there was another reason for him not wanting anything to happen to her, but he could hardly accept the fact himself.

There was something about Arianna that intrigued him beyond the way her energy affected him, but he wasn't sure what it was. She certainly wasn't like the other women he usually surrounded himself with. He felt…almost normal around her rather than a carica-ture of a man, which was how others tended to see him. Maybe that was the difference with her. She seemed genuinely interested in what he had to say and what his opinions on things were and not just that he had big muscles, a killer smile and was good between the sheets. Hell, she had no idea about that last part, which, he had to admit, was refreshing.

Lily sighed. "I'll handle the scent trail, so don't worry about that, but what about you?"

"What about me?"

"For one thing, are you going to be able to get energies and blood? I mean, with that injury, you'll need a little more than normal to help in the healing process. You're probably on the minus side with all that you've lost."

He'd need more than just a little, given the earlier injury, as well. If only he could stop at a safe house. To cater to the needs of their clientele, they usually had vials of blood available, but he couldn't risk exposing Krystal to other vampires. Besides, most safe-house proprietors weren't keen on human guests.

"I'll be fine."

"You'd better be, Jacks, because if you're not, I'll kill you."

"Wow, that's touching."

She made a kissing sound over the phone and the line went dead.

THE YOUNG WOMAN AT THE front desk leaned forward on her crossed arms, pushing her breasts up. It made her cleavage hard to ignore even for Arianna, though Jackson barely batted an eye. With a starry, fangirl expression plastered on her face, she handed him the room key.

"I hope you find it to your liking. If not, please don't hesitate to call the front desk. My name's Summer." She pointed to her name tag, which said Miss Winters. Arianna stifled a smile, but Miss Check-Out-My-Boobs didn't seem to notice. "I'm working all day and would be happy to assist you." She cast a curious glance in Arianna's direction and Arianna became all too aware of how disheveled she must look. Especially compared to Jackson.

His hair was tousled, not messy like hers, and his leather coat, which was partially zipped, revealed his bare chest, making him look celebrity chic, not back-yard barbecue like her ripped jeans and flour-covered shirt. She'd helped him remove his bloody T-shirt in the car earlier, but maybe that had been a mistake. The women they'd encountered tonight couldn't seem to take their eyes off him.

The first time it happened with the waitress at the all-night diner where they'd stopped for coffee and hot chocolate, Arianna found it mildly amusing. But by the fifth time, it was just plain irritating how women—and even a few of the men—reacted to him. At first, she'd assumed he was playing those little mind tricks on them, but she didn't once see him touch them before they started fawning. Women took one look at him and wanted to get to know him better. One word would be all it'd take for him to arrange a quickie or two back by the bathrooms. A few times he did shake their hands or touch their arms, but Arianna was pretty sure he was just taking their energy. They'd walk away, yawning, and the weariness behind his eyes didn't seem quite so pronounced...for a few minutes, at least.

"I'm sure it'll be perfect," Jackson told Summer, flashing that killer smile of his.

The woman blushed a deep crimson and gave a nervous little schoolgirl laugh. "You know where I am if it's not."

When they stepped into the elevator a few minutes later, Arianna turned to him. "Do you always have that effect on people?"

"What?" he said, looking confused.

Did she have to spell it out for him? Surely he noticed that people treated him differently, didn't he? It was as if he was in a totally different class from everyone else. "The woman at the front desk, the waitress, the man on his way to the restroom..." Counting on her fingers, she listed a few others.

"Yeah," Krystal chimed in, one earbud dangling. "It's like you were a celebrity or something."

His eyes widened. "Really?" He seemed totally clueless, as if he had no idea that others weren't treated the same way he was. Then, without skipping a beat, he added, "What can I say—I'm magnetic."

Normally, she'd have been irritated; that was something her father would say. But Jackson's charm was natural—a part of who he was, like the color of his eyes or the way he walked. It was clear he enjoyed people and liked making them smile. Unlike her father, Jackson's personality wasn't turned on with a switch in order to score. Although, she'd imagine, there'd be plenty of that without him even trying.

The elevator dinged and the doors opened. She cast a sidelong glance at him as they stepped into the hallway and headed toward their room. Dark circles shadowed his eyes and a sheen of sweat covered his forehead, despite the fact that he'd just rubbed it with the back of his hand a minute ago. She hoped that all he needed was to get some rest.

Once inside the junior suite, she waited until Krystal was in the bathroom brushing her teeth. Jackson had asked for three generic toiletry kits when they checked in and Summer was more than happy to oblige.

"How sensitive are you to daylight? I mean, I take it you don't need to sleep in a coffin. At least I hope you don't. Although, I suppose if you did need one, Miss Summer Winters would be able to find one for you. I hear Costco is selling them now." She didn't really think he slept in a coffin—over the course of the evening, he'd dispelled many of the common vampire myths—but being this close to him with a bed right here made her want to make light of the situation.

Coffins: A Vampire's Home Away From Home
Coffin, Tea or Me?

Those people weren't the only ones charmed by Jackson tonight.

He sat on the edge of the bed. "Any sunlight will sap my energy, but the stronger the UV light, the faster it happens."

She examined the window coverings and noticed that the so-called blackout curtains seemed pretty flimsy and ill fitting. Who knew how much light would filter in through the edges? With daybreak less than an hour away, she didn't want to wait and find out. Opening up the closet, she found an extra bedspread on the top shelf along with two more pillows and a blanket. "I want you to sleep in the smaller bedroom because it has a smaller window. I'll secure this over the existing drapes to give you some added protection when daybreak comes."

He started to get up.

"No, I've got it."

The weariness in his eyes seemed more pronounced, but his relief was obvious. "Thanks."

It pleased her to know there was something she could do to help him. He'd sacrificed so much tonight in order for them to be safe like this. Not only did he fight to protect them and get hurt in the process, but based on his expression when he was on the phone with his friend Lily, he was risking even more.

A million questions burned in her head, but she voiced the only one she could manage. "You want me to take a look at your arm?"

"Nope. I'm good."

She hoped sleep was all he needed, though she had a feeling it wasn't.

CHAPTER ELEVEN

THE SMALL POUCH WITH scent-masking crystals hit Kip in the chest.

"You were supposed to catch those," Lily said.

His trainer was trying to joke around with him, but he wasn't amused. Nothing made him laugh anymore. He felt dead inside, trapped in a world not of his own making. Without looking at her, he bent and picked it up from the floorboards of her Porsche.

"Where do you want this shit sprinkled?"

"You're going to tell me," she said as she exited the car.

"Fuck," he said under his breath. He did not want to be here. He didn't want to be doing this.

"I heard that."

No longer did the delicate art of scent tracking appeal to him. Tiptoeing around, trying to pick up on the subtlest of clues. It was a job for someone who cared about the little details, and frankly, he didn't. At one time, he thought he did, thought it was the greatest fucking job in the world. He'd aspired to become a class A tracker like Lily, who was sought after around the region and all the other field offices in North America. He'd thought maybe he'd like to teach one day at the

Tracker Academy, to coach others looking to make a difference.

But not any longer.

Hell. All he wanted to do now was beat the shit out of someone. And if it involved staking a Darkblood, well then, that would make this whole fucking week worthwhile. He could go back to his room at the field office and drink himself into oblivion. Correction: self-medicate was the term his counselor wanted him to use, not fucked-up, shit-faced or wasted.

They'd parked a few blocks from their intended destination so as not to make the neighbors suspicious. Lily's red Panamera didn't exactly blend in with the surroundings. As soon as they got closer, they'd slip in with the shadows and no one would know they were there.

"We're going to start at the house and work our way outward," Lily said. "I don't know the direction Jackson took with the woman and the sweetblood girl, which is good. I'm going to have you tell me which way they went and we'll cover their trail as we go, eh?"

Peachy.

Although it was just past sundown, an old man at the corner house was still out working on his yard. With a headlamp strapped to his forehead, he was planting… flowers.

As they shadow-moved in the darkness at the base of the hedges, Kip had the urge to kick over the garbage cans or rattle the garden tools stacked against the garage. Everything was so mundane and ordinary around here that it would be satisfying to upset the quiet.

Lily gave him a look that said, "Don't you dare."

"What?" he mouthed, pretending to be innocent. The old guy would just think it was the wind.

God, it sucked to have your instructor know you so well.

The fourth house down was small by today's standards. With a decent-size yard in an older, established neighborhood, it was surrounded by many trees and shrubs, which meant more shadows to hide in. Unlike the ultramodern neighborhoods with no trees where the houses were so close you could wipe your ass then pass the roll of toilet paper to your neighbor in his bathroom. If you sneezed in your kitchen, your neighbor would say gesundheit from theirs…and you'd hear it. Then you'd tell them to shut the fuck up.

No, that kind of neighborhood didn't have as many shadows as this one had. Plus, the streets had better lighting. Except for grandpa with his headlamp, this one had none.

"Can you pick up the sweetblood girl's scent yet?" Lily asked as they stepped out of the shadows. They stood near the large Douglas fir in the front yard and faced the house.

How could he not? The air around the house was thick with the smell, bringing back a shitload of memories he'd just as soon forget. "Yes."

"Can you tell me how many people live here?"

His irritation ratcheted up a notch at such rudimentary questions. "Two. Both females." He struggled to sound civil and engaged, like a student eager to learn from the master.

"Good." She slanted him a sideways glance, clearly not fooled by his acting job.

He'd have to do better covering up his bad attitude. He wouldn't put it past Lily to bust his chops if he didn't tone it down at least a little. But then duking it out inside the field office's boxing ring did have a certain appeal, even though she could take him to his knees with just a twist of his pinkie finger. His trainer was a badass, there was no doubt about it.

They made their way around to the back of the house where they could move around a little more freely without being seen.

"Jackson said they were attacked by DBs," she said. "Can you tell how many?"

He let himself morph into a patch of darkness near the back porch. The shadows calmed him, making it easier for him to concentrate. Lately, it was the only time he truly felt as if he belonged inside his own skin. The counselor would say he was just avoiding dealing with what he needed to, that it amounted to hiding from his problems. Which was why he hadn't told her about it.

The night air felt especially cool and refreshing. Seemed he was always hot lately. The sound of crickets chirping in the bushes had a calming effect on him, too. He took a deep breath and let the various scents fill his lungs.

"I'm counting the scent markers of at least five Darkbloods. Two of them are not quite as strong as the others, which leads me to believe that they were the ones who arrived on scene first."

"Exactly. The scent structure has broken down slightly, which means it's older."

"The trail leads out there." He pointed to the woods behind the house. "I'm thinking that they circled the perimeter, then headed out in that direction."

"That must've been when Jackson spotted them from inside and took off after them."

Without waiting for Lily, he jogged across the yard and into the trees. She was right behind him when he reached a small patch next to some blackberry bushes. To a human, it would just look like a sandy shovelful of dirt. But to a vampire, it was unmistakable. As soon as a light breeze kicked up, the remains would be carried away like dust.

"They were both staked right here."

"Yeah, I think you're right," Lily said, bending down to examine the ash. "Jacks sure didn't waste much time. What else?"

He surveyed the underbrush. "Based on the broken branches and disturbed earth there and there," he said, pointing, "it was quite a scuffle. And given those blood splatters, Jackson didn't come out unscathed, either." Which didn't really surprise him. The Guardian was a strong fighter, but he lacked Lily's finesse. Dom's, too, for that matter. Jackson was a shark in a cage, a bull in a china shop. Anyone who got in his way would be toast, and it sure as hell wouldn't be pretty.

Lily was shaking her head as the sound of crickets started up again since they first had entered the woods.

No? Not Jackson's blood? Stooping to examine it more closely, he lifted a leaf frond. It had all the same scent markers the Guardian had. "Am I wrong?"

"It's not that. It's his all right. I'm just thinking about how Jackson told me the injury was no big deal, but that's a hell of a lot of blood to be no big deal."

Kip agreed. That was definitely a major energy-depleting amount of blood to lose. At least he'd still had the strength to kill the two DBs.

Then suddenly, because the memory was never very far from the surface of his thoughts, he was transported back into that shabby cabin in the woods, where he'd been chained to a chair for days. The foul stench of Darkblood breath was as vivid now as it ever was. The bloodstain on the floor beneath him had grown wider and wider with every drip. It was like watching his energy and willpower slip out of his system and not being able to do a damn thing to stop it.

He could still hear the sound of the two girls whimpering just out of his reach. He'd tried not to look at them, but their smell was everywhere. In the air, on his skin, on the chains, in his hair, in his mouth.

Despite all the treatment he'd gone through since then—the conditioning, the desensitization—he could still taste the Sweet lingering on the back of his tongue as if it were yesterday when he killed that girl.

Lily knocked him on the arm, jerking him from this nightmare he called a memory or what his counselor would call an overloaded sensory flashback. Apparently, those who were gifted enough to qualify for

Tracker school were more susceptible to reliving events because of their acute senses.

"Damn, you're good, Kip. I'm impressed. What else you got?"

Despite himself, he did feel good at the compliment. "Before Jackson's scent is mingled with theirs, they had been to the far side of the house."

He continued to track the scent from its origin and Lily followed. It went around the garage and stopped near a maple tree in the side yard. "They waited here for a short time. Probably trying to decide when to make their move."

She nodded as she looked around. "That'd be my guess, as well."

He sniffed the air again. "Then two more showed up later. Their scents are mainly concentrated here in the driveway. One was charcoaled here—" he pointed to the pavement "—and I'm not sure about the other one. His scent is mingled with Jackson's and the two females', and it heads off in that direction." With a tilt of his head, he indicated down the road.

"Jackson told me they had a hitchhiker on the back of their car for a few blocks, so that makes sense." Lily pulled out a pouch of scent crystals and started to reach inside, when Kip stopped her.

"Wait. There were more."

"Seriously?" She cocked her head and sniffed. "God, you're right. There are two other completely different signatures. There were so many of them that I didn't separate them out. Nice work."

The trail led to the open garage door. Just inside on the ground was a torn-off side mirror.

"That's odd," he said. "Rather than following Jackson and the two females, it would appear they went into the house."

"Jackson didn't mention a break-in. Said he saw them outside and gave chase." Lily sniffed the air inside the garage. "But you're absolutely right, Kip. Come on. Let's go see if we can figure out what they were after."

"Hold on. Let me go check something out first." He followed the trail from the house to a spot on the curb three houses down, then he jogged back to Lily.

"They'd been waiting in a vehicle down there, probably hoping their goons were successful in bringing them a sweetblood."

"Which they weren't, but I wonder why they broke into the house after their target was gone. What was the point in that?"

Kip shrugged. "But you want to know what's even stranger than that?"

"What?"

"A male in the car with them was a human."

Lily exhaled slowly, thinking. "With their poor sense of smell, what are the chances of them locating two sweetbloods in one night?"

"This one wasn't sweet."

She jerked her head around. "He wasn't?"

"Nope. Type O-pos. Most common human blood type in the world."

JACKSON COULDN'T BE SURE how long he slept. Two hours? Ten hours? His eyes were sandpaper gritty and he wondered if he'd actually had negative sleep hours. One thing was for sure—his arm hurt like shit. He could barely move it. At least the darkness on the inside of his eyeballs felt good.

Instinctively, he eased his foot over to the other side of the bed. Nothing. He could've sworn there was a warm body lying next to him for at least part of the night. Or did he just dream it? It wasn't often that he slept alone. Maybe that was the problem.

He heard the low drone of the television in the next room and wondered how long Arianna and Krystal had been awake.

Despite his arm, he managed to take a quick shower and was just leaving the bathroom when his phone rang.

"Hey, Lily."

"Jesus, where have you been?"

"Ah, right here. Why?"

"I've been trying to reach you all day. I really didn't want to have to track you down. Listen, I don't have time to explain much, but Kip and I uncovered some disturbing information at Arianna's house last night."

"More disturbing than what we already knew?"

She told him about the apparent human accomplice waiting in the car down the street during the attack.

"Well, that's interesting, isn't it?"

Not that it wasn't unheard of for Darkbloods to enlist the aid of a few humans, but they hadn't seen it up here in the Seattle area much. That sort of behavior was more commonplace in the more aggressive parts of the country. Some people were attracted to those with power and DBs had been known to take advantage of it. They got readily available blood from a live donor—assuming they didn't kill the person first—and someone to handle their business during the daylight hours when they couldn't go out. When Guardians found these people, they wiped their memories and sent them on their way.

"What do you think that's all about? Do they have themselves a turn-junkie?"

In payment for their service, Darkbloods often made promises to turn these people into changelings, a process involving draining the blood and replacing it with the blood of at least two vampires. They'd get some of the advantages of being a vampire—longer life span, heightened senses—but without the strength or ability to shadow-move. They were still able to process UV light and weren't incapacitated by it like a natural-born vampire. Despite the inherent risks of a turning, the lure of becoming a vampire could be very seductive.

"Who knows? It's possible that the human tipped them off as to her location."

"Yes, but it also seems rather convenient, timing-wise."

"What do you mean?"

"She told me she's lived in that house for several years and that her sweetblood cousin moved in two months ago."

"So?"

"That's the same cousin who was one of the surviving sweetbloods from the Night of Wilding massacre, but the girl was not taken from her home. She was taken from downtown. Unless they interrogated her, which I doubt because they didn't plan on having their little party broken up, they had no idea where she lived."

"I still don't follow you."

"What I'm saying is that Darkbloods have had ample time to find them before this. Unless we're talking weird timing, I'm guessing it has to do with that blog post. Someone saw it, figured out that the cousin had to be a sweetblood, and either knew or discovered Arianna's real identity."

There was silence on the other end of the line for a moment. "You have a point, Jacks. We found out another interesting bit of information."

"Which is…?"

"We checked her house and things were a mess, like they were looking for something. Drawers overturned in the kitchen, her office torn apart. However, they didn't take her computer. But that's not all. I came across her company badge."

"And?" he prompted.

"She works for Xtark Software."

"Xtark? You mean the company that makes Hollow Grave?" Jesus. He had to sit down. The majority shareholder was thought to be a dummy corporation set up by the Darkblood Alliance, although Guardians had never been able to prove it or make any headway within the company.

"Yep. The one and only."

Then it was only a matter of time before Darkbloods

found out that one of their employees had a relative who was a sweetblood.

"Listen," Lily said. "Why don't you take them up to the house for a few days? I'm here in the city for the rest of the week, but Alfonso and Zoe are there."

"I can't ask you do to that."

"You're not asking. I'm offering."

"I don't need to remind you that the girl is a sweet-blood. She needs to be kept away from all vampires till we get things sorted out."

"Yes, and Alfonso has had more on-the-job desen-sitivity training than you and me combined. And Zoe is still several years away from her Time of Change, so the cravings haven't started for her yet. They'll be much safer up there compared to…what…some ratty hotel?"

He couldn't put his friend in a position like this. What if Arianna was indeed immune to mind wipes? She'd know all about Lily and her family. It was best if Jackson were the only vampire she knew. "But—"

"I'll let Alfonso know to expect you."

CHAPTER TWELVE

ARIANNA WOKE UP JUST AS the Caddy was coming to a stop. She didn't realize she had even dozed off. The events of the past few days must've finally caught up with her.

"Did you get any rest?" Jackson whispered, even though he didn't need to. Krystal had her headphones in and was still sound asleep.

"Yeah, a little." She noticed he'd covered her with his leather jacket at some point during the drive. She started to pull it off to hand to him, but he shook his head.

"Keep it. It's cold outside. I'll go talk to Alfonso. Make sure everything's set up for the two of you." He held out his hand. "Keys."

"Oh, yeah."

At a rest stop, she'd insisted on unfastening the handcuffs and he returned a few minutes later, looking slightly better. She didn't ask him where he'd been and she didn't argue with him when he said he'd drive, although she did cuff him to the door again and pocket the key. However, as the three of them walked to the entrance of a large Spanish-style house, it looked as if he was in pain.

"Where are we?" Krystal asked.

"Some friends of Jackson's. They've got a daughter and apparently she's really excited to meet you."

Krystal's eyes lit up.

Jackson introduced them to a tall blond man wearing a tool belt and a young girl who looked to be about ten or eleven years old.

"Welcome to Casa en las Colinas," Alfonso said, extending his hand. They were lightly callused, his Carhartts well-worn and faded. He must be doing a home-improvement project. As if reading her thoughts, he added, "Don't mind the mess. Trying to get the house finished before the wedding this summer."

"What a beautiful place to get married," Arianna said, looking around the entryway. "Thanks for taking us in."

"My pleasure."

Zoe was already tugging on Krystal's arm. "Let me show you my room. My dad just finished making a bed for me. It's got a canopy, just like a castle bed, with carved dragons and…"

Krystal threw a wide-eyed smile over her shoulder that said she was both flattered and a little overwhelmed. Arianna laughed. She remembered babysitting girls Zoe's age when she was a teenager. They couldn't wait for you to come over and show you every last thing in their room. You were a captive audience, their playmate slave.

She couldn't get over how regular they looked… like a typical human father and daughter. Not what she would've expected. But then, she'd never really thought about how vampires lived when they only existed in her imagination.

She gave Jackson a sidelong look and noticed the pained expression on his face. When Alfonso turned around to say something, Jackson quickly hid the grimace, replacing it instead with that smile of his and macho swagger. He may think he could hide it from his friend, but he wasn't fooling her.

The top of the stairs opened up to a long hallway leading to the left and the right.

"Down there is the family wing," Alfonso said, pointing. "Lily and I have our quarters there, and where the hallway zigs, you'll find Zoe's room. Krystal can stay there or, if you think she'd be more comfortable near you, I can do that, too, though not all the rooms in this part of the house are finished yet."

"Are you doing all the work yourself?" she asked. That would explain the tool belt.

"Just the finish carpentry. Keeps me out of trouble, right, Jackson?"

The two men laughed.

"But you two are staying down in this wing of the estate," Alfonso continued.

Arianna's cheeks heated up. He wasn't assuming they were a couple, was he? She slanted a glance in Jackson's direction, but his expression was blank. Images of what it would be like to sleep with him filled her thoughts. Was he a confident, demanding lover who took what he wanted and assumed it was what his partner wanted, as well? She had to imagine he was and for some reason, the thought excited her.

Alfonso opened the first door, breaking the spell. "Arianna, here's your room."

She relaxed. Okay, they had separate rooms. The little thrill inside that had caused the butterflies to flutter in her stomach was gone.

Without being overly masculine or feminine, the large room wasn't vanilla, either, with dark, intricately carved moldings framing the warm blue walls. Vintage artwork with turn-of-the-century scenes hung everywhere. Ladies with parasols, men on large-wheeled bicycles, families picnicking. Luxurious pillows covered the four-poster bed, which was probably an antique. Behind it, wallpaper with strange, brocade-looking silhouettes caught her attention. It was the only wall that was papered. Vintage also?

Her curiosity was piqued, so she stepped closer to examine it. Although it was so subtle she could have missed it entirely, the dark blue shapes were actually men and women in various sexual positions. Man on top. Woman on top. Woman on all fours with man behind her. Man with head buried between woman's legs. It was like the *Kama Sutra* depicted on the wall. Arianna's cheeks heated and she tore her gaze away. Zoe must not be allowed in here, or her parents would be subject to some awfully uncomfortable questions. But then again, a casual glance would only reveal a busy brocade pattern.

"And just through there, on the other side of the bathroom, is where you'll be staying, Jackson," Alfonso was saying. "Lily wasn't sure if you guys were bringing toiletries with you or not…she said you left in a hurry…so I made sure the drawers were stocked with various items you may need. If there are things you're missing, let me know. If we don't have it in the house, I'll head to the store later."

Jackson looked confused. "We're sharing a bathroom?"

"Like I said, not all the rooms are finished. If you'd rather sleep on the sofa downstairs…"

"No, this will be fine," he said curtly.

"You okay?" she mouthed. That arm was bothering him a lot. She hadn't seen him move it since they arrived.

He nodded as he wiped a thin sheen of sweat from his brow.

Liar. His condition had to be getting worse. Why was he trying to be so stoic about it? What was the big deal? People in his position were probably always getting hurt. Why wouldn't he just seek treatment? Was he that much of a guy that he thought he could just muscle through it himself?

"Is there a first-aid kit in there?"

Alfonso hesitated and Jackson shot her an angry look.

"I twisted my ankle at some point and I thought I'd better ice it. Maybe even wrap it."

Alfonso looked down at her feet. She was suddenly aware that she was standing squarely on each one.

"Yes," he said. "It's got Tylenol, antiseptic, topical pain reliever, butterfly bandages. The whole works. Just in case you should need those things, as well."

She cast a quick glance at Alfonso, but his expres-

sion was unreadable. She wondered whether he'd figured out that the first-aid kit was not for her.

"Can I get you something to eat?"

"No, thank you," she said, yawning. Despite the nap
in the car, she felt as if she could sleep for days. Must
be some of the energy she'd passed on to Jackson. "We
stopped on the way."

"Okay, then. Sweet dreams."

After checking on Krystal and making sure she was
fine sleeping clear down in Zoe's room, she came back
to hear the water running in the adjoining bathroom.

She'd wait till Jackson was done, then she'd take a
quick shower and hop into bed. With these heavy shut-
ters on the windows to block out any light, it should be
easy to fall asleep.

A crash then a thud sounded from the bathroom.

That didn't sound good. She put her ear up to the
door, but didn't hear anything more. Just the running
water from the shower. "Jackson?"

No answer.

She tried the handle, but the damn thing was locked.
"Are you okay?"

"Stay out," he growled.

"What happened? Do you need help?"

"I'm fine."

She could tell he wasn't. She didn't know anything
about vampire physiology and wasn't sure what she
could do to help him. "Do you want me to get Alfonso?"

"No, keep him out of this."

This? There was a *this* to be kept out of? Obviously

he meant something other than the fact that he was injured.

She didn't care if he thought he didn't need her help.
She sprinted out of her room and into his. Bursting into
the bathroom, she found him sitting on the closed lid
of the toilet, a towel around his waist. Hunched over,
he was cradling his arm in agony.

"Oh, my God, Jackson."

He looked up. His fangs were extended, his pupils
dilated. "Get the fuck out."

She forced herself not to back away, even though all
her instincts were telling her to run. He was the predator and she was his prey, but he'd had plenty of opportunities to kill her if that's what he wanted to do. He
certainly wasn't going to harm her in the house of one
of the only friends he could trust.

"If you don't tell me what's going on, I'll have no
choice but to get Alfonso."

"Goddamn it, Arianna. Leave me alone."

"I have been, but that's obviously not doing you any
good. It's him or me. Which do you choose?"

He hesitated and she could tell he was weighing his
options. Slowly, he lowered his hand from his upper
arm. The gash was an angry red, spanning from one
side of his biceps to the other. The edges appeared to
be knitting together already, but it wasn't neat or clean.

"That silver knife really screwed with you. I'll bet
it hurts like hell." It looked as if the wound was getting
infected, though she couldn't tell how deep it was.

"Arianna, you need to get out of here."

"Why? So you can suffer on your own?" She started opening all the cabinets looking for the first-aid kit.

"I need you too much. That's the problem."

Need? A warmth filled her whole body. "What do you mean? You've not let me do anything for you."

"I'm talking your blood, Arianna. That and your energies."

She tried to conceal her disappointment. Those were generic things he could get from any human, though she wasn't sure why that bothered her. She wasn't special; she just had what he needed. Jackson had a focused look to his expression, almost like a trance as he stared at her. His eyes darkened further, the green of his irises gone. She could've sworn he was looking at her neck.

She snapped her fingers and he blinked, his unholy concentration broken.

"Leave me," he choked out. "I—I was almost gone."

"What do you need? Blood? Energy?" Without waiting for a reply, she took his hand, knowing this was how he absorbed the energy of a human. Her hand, then arm numbed as she felt that flowing sensation again.

He tried to pull away. "Let go. I'll take too much."

"Your lack of energy is probably why you're not doing so well, and you're in no shape to go out and get it." Same probably held true for blood, but she wasn't sure she was ready to offer that up. Giving him a little of her energy was fine, but blood? "Now, come on. Let me get that wound dressed before it gets any more infected."

As he waited, she located a stack of washcloths, a bottle of antiseptic, a small first-aid kit and got to work.

"Does it look like I'll live?" She could tell he was trying to make light of a serious situation.

"Have you ever been injured like this before?"

"Sure, lots of times."

Yeah, she could see all the scars crisscrossing his well-muscled chest.

She opened the bottle of antiseptic and doused a cotton ball. "This will probably sting just a little."

He hissed in a breath as she applied it to the wound.

"Are you okay?"

"Mmm." He'd pinched his eyes shut.

Yeah, it probably hurt like hell.

"How did you get some of these?" she asked in an attempt to take his mind off the pain.

"I've forgotten about most of them."

"How about this one?" She ran her finger over a thin white line that extended across his rib cage. She wasn't sure if it was from a surgery or an old injury.

"That feels nice."

"Your arm?" She'd have thought it'd be painful.

"No, you touching me like that."

"Oh." She pulled her hand away, not realizing she'd been lightly tracing the scar with her fingertips. "That didn't tickle?"

"I'm not ticklish."

"You're not? That's crazy. Is that a vampire thing?"

"I'm pretty sure it's just me."

"So how'd you get the scar?"

"Down in Argentina, I got whacked with a machete. A silver-tipped one."

"Is that what causes the scarring? The silver?"

"Yep."

She pointed to a thick scar in the shape of an X above his heart. "How did you get this one?"

He turned away. "I don't remember."

He was lying, but she decided not to pressure him. He'd have told her about it if he wanted her to know.

She'd cleaned the wound as best she could and was now trying to close it up with a series of butterfly bandages. "Why don't you want to have someone take a look at this? I'm thinking that you need stitches. And probably a tetanus shot. That is, if tetanus is something you guys need to worry about."

"If I go to a medico clinic, they'll do tests on me."

"Yeah, probably, but why is that bad?"

He didn't answer right away and she thought maybe he wasn't going to answer at all. When he did speak, his voice was low and choked with emotion. "I'm afraid of what they'll do when they find out about me."

She stopped what she was doing and rested her hand on his good shoulder. "Find out what?" she whispered.

"That I might be on the verge of reverting to the violent ways of our ancestors."

"How do you know that? You seem pretty normal to me. Well, as normal as I'd imagine a vampire to be. Actually, I take that back. I'd have expected you all to be like those Darkbloods, but you're nothing like them."

"Not for long. My energy and blood needs are much higher than they should be. Most of us can go for weeks at a time without blood. I can last a day, maybe two, before I need more. It's the first sign of reverting. Many Darkbloods or sympathizers started off that way. No longer did the Council's peaceful ways make sense. Their blood instincts became too strong to ignore or control."

"And what happens if the Council finds out?"

"For normal members of our population, it means rehabilitation. But for a Guardian, things aren't that simple."

"Surely this has happened before."

"Yes, it has. And I was there to witness the execution."

Her hands got suddenly weak. Watching someone die had to be awful. "You'd be put to death for something that you can't help?"

"If I kill someone, yes."

"But you haven't killed anyone...have you?" she asked cautiously.

"Not yet, but that could easily change. Being around Krystal is taxing all my willpower."

"Then that's it. She and I are going home."

"No. Darkbloods will come after you there."

"Not if we move."

After she'd bandaged his arm, she helped him to his feet and back into his bedroom. Without ceremony, he dropped his towel and pulled the sheets back, as if it were commonplace for him to strip naked in front of a woman he just met.

His ass was tight with a dimple on either side near the base of his spine. His back and shoulders were heavily muscled, flexing as he moved. It would be worth the tackiness of putting a mirror on the ceiling just to watch his muscles in action during lovemaking, she thought. When he climbed into the bed, she caught a glimpse of the front of him. Not only did his shaft dangle heavily between his legs…and God, was he built…but something down there glinted in the light. Something…metal. He wasn't pierced, was he?

She felt a tightness low in her belly and chill bumps covered her arms. Those kinds of piercings were done to increase a woman's pleasure during sex, weren't they? A man who wore one had to be turned on by the act of pleasuring a woman. How would it feel? Would it rub in such a way that it'd hurt? Would she even like it?

What was she doing thinking about sex at a time like this? She reached over and fluffed his pillows. So the guy was hot and she'd been virtually celibate since she left her ex, when, after finding out about Paranormalish, he laughed at her, told her it was a stupid thing to waste her time on. Shoving those thoughts from her head, she started to tuck the sheets around him and noticed how icy cold his skin was. Could he be going into shock?

Thank goodness the bed had an electric blanket. She found the switch and turned it on. With his eyes closed like that, his dark lashes lying heavily on his cheeks, he looked almost angelic. When she turned to leave, his hand shot out and grasped her wrist.

"Stay with me."

Her heart raced in her chest. Had he realized she'd climbed in next to him last night in the hotel room and shared some of her energy with him? She knew he'd never take it from her otherwise, unless she forced it on him as she'd just done in the bathroom, and he seemed in desperate need. When she saw him after he woke up, even though he still looked like crap, he was in better shape than he had been. Lying next to him as he slept, without any of his defenses up, she could've sworn that some of his energy flowed into her, as well, but she couldn't be sure.

"But I thought you wanted me to leave."

"I changed my mind. Your presence is…comforting. I'd like you to stay."

She rubbed his arm and noticed that the worry lines between his eyes had softened. "Okay. I'll stay."

CHAPTER THIRTEEN

JACKSON WAS FULLY ERECT by the time she climbed under the covers with him. He wasn't intending for anything to happen between the two of them, he only wanted to feel the warmth of her body and sleep with her calming energies next to him. He was ninety-nine percent sure she'd done this the night before in the hotel, at least for a short time, but he hadn't wanted to ask. How stupid would he have felt if he was wrong?

He couldn't deny how attracted he was to her, even in his weakened condition. His ass tucked perfectly into the hollow made by her belly and legs, and although she wore an oversize T-shirt and a pair of leggings, she was soft and curvy in all the right places. Like a little furnace, she warmed him from his heels, along the backs of his calves, his quads, his glutes, his back, all the way to the nape of his neck where her cheek rested against his shoulder blade.

He couldn't really explain it, but her touch both excited him and calmed him at the same time. The pain radiating outward from his arm seemed to have lessened since she'd given him some of her energies. She'd be tired now. He should just let her sleep and yet every fiber of his being wanted to make love to her.

She'd be warm inside, too. Hot, probably. If he

slipped a finger between her legs right now, would he find her wet and ready for him or would he have to press the pad of his thumb to coax her along first? As if she knew what he was thinking, she shifted her hips slightly, which made his erection thicken further and his balls ache for release.

Her arm was tucked awkwardly between her chest and his back. He could feel her trying to get comfortable without brushing against his injury. Without asking, he grabbed her hand and set it on the top of his hip. No need for her to be shy.

Her caresses started innocently enough, like a cat kneading its paws open and closed. He wasn't entirely sure if she even realized what she was doing. But he sure as hell did.

God, she turned him on.

If he shifted slightly, rolled to his back right now, her hand would slip to his shaft where she would then—

Damn. His piercing. How could he have forgotten? Arianna wasn't the kind of woman who would go for that. She'd probably be turned off just knowing he had one, let alone want to make love to him. Men got pierced there for one reason and one reason only. To get laid. A lot.

Ignoring the pain in his arm, he flung back the covers and stormed to the bathroom. Once inside, he caught a glimpse of his reflection. His pupils had dilated with lust, but surprisingly, his fangs hadn't emerged yet, although his gums tingled as they threatened to break through.

Stupid son of a bitch. Don't fuck things up with her. She's not like the others.

Arianna wasn't the type who hung out in clubs, trolling for someone to sleep with. She probably met men in coffee shops, bookstores, or through friends. Not in some Belltown meat market. Besides, she didn't have time for a clubbing lifestyle. She worked hard during the day, then at night on her blog, and now, raising her cousin when no one else would.

No, he wouldn't make love to her with the piercing in, he thought as he carefully removed the metal stud. She deserved better than that. He opened a drawer and set it on a folded washcloth.

Besides, he realized, he wouldn't want to rush things with her. He'd want her pleasure to build slowly, deliciously, and he'd want to savor her reaction. He would take his time with her and do it right.

But when he returned to the bedroom, she was gone.

ARIANNA TIPTOED DOWN THE DARK hallway back to her room, though she wasn't sure why she was trying to be so quiet. The girls and Alfonso were in a totally different wing of the house.

She wasn't sure what had happened back in Jackson's room. She could've sworn he had wanted to make love to her—why else would he have invited her into his bed? But when he tensed as she touched him then jumped up as if he couldn't get away from her fast enough, things became pretty clear. He'd obviously had a change of heart. Maybe he'd been genuinely grateful for the care she'd given him, but things had progressed in a way he hadn't wanted or expected.

Rather than wait for him to emerge and then endure all sorts of awkwardness when he asked her to leave, she'd decided to save him the trouble.

She stared at her bare feet as she walked, noting in the back of her mind that she was badly in need of a pedicure. Maybe Lily had polish in the house. If not, she'd see about running to the store. It'd give herself something to do tomorrow, since she was without her computer.

A cold draft ruffled her hair as she rounded the corner. Good. The chill would help her hormones cool down and her head to clear.

"Where do you think you're going?"

She snapped her head up to find Jackson leaning against her door with his arms crossed, essentially barring her from entering. How had he gotten here before she had?

The breeze. Of course. He'd shadow-moved.

"In there," she said, pointing.

"No, you're not. You're coming back with me." From his tone, it was clear he didn't expect her to argue. He grabbed her hand and without waiting for an answer, he led her back down the hallway.

"But I thought—"

"What? That I had changed my mind?"

"The thought had occurred to me when you got up suddenly like you did."

"Don't leave my bed again."

What the— "You're ordering me back to your bed?"

The kind of women he slept with must respond to this sort of thing. Well, she wasn't one of them.

She dug her heels in to pull out of his grasp, but instead of holding her arm tighter, he let her go, shocking the hell out of her. The tiny worry lines on his forehead were back and his eyes were apologetic. Had she read his tone wrong?

"I…sleep better with you there," he admitted. "I want you with me."

She glanced down the hallway at her door, then back at him, aware of the fact that she had a choice to make. If she left and went to her room, they'd both wake up later and things would be relatively the same. Was that what she wanted? Because sex had a way of changing the status quo, adding expectations to a relationship where none existed before.

In his haste, he had thrown on a pair of boxer briefs that accentuated the size of his powerful thighs, as well as other muscle groups. A large one that seemed to grow in size as she watched. She quickly averted her gaze and tried not to be influenced by how devastatingly attractive he was.

She'd never been one to believe that things happened for a reason. In fact, she hated that philosophy. It pissed her off. Was it supposed to give you comfort to know that a terrible awful thing happened because of some higher purpose? That something else was more important than a little girl needing her mother?

Oh, sorry. Your husband was hit and killed by a bus. Guess it was just meant to be.

Your mother was taken away by the shadows who

happen to be killer vampires. She suffered and died because God needed her more than you did.

Well, that was bullshit. Always had been and always would be.

And yet as she stood before Jackson with a choice to make, she found herself thinking along these lines. If he hadn't gotten up and she hadn't left, they'd probably be making love right now. Neither of them would have intended for that to happen, but it would've. But now that each of them had been given a choice with time to ponder both sides, she wondered about the significance of her decision. Could this be one of those watershed moments? Say no and your life goes one way. Say yes and it goes another. Had the fates decided that this was a big enough event in her life that she should make a conscious decision? As she stared at him, she had a feeling it was.

She didn't know much about this man except for his actions. He was bold, unapologetic and yet he was kind. Plus, he'd saved her life. Twice.

Not to mention that her hormones were screaming at her to say yes.

In the end, the choice that would affect her life so profoundly wasn't a difficult one to make after all.

THAT BUSINESS ABOUT TAKING things slowly, while good in theory, flew out the window when Arianna put her hand in his. He almost forgot about the pain in his arm when he ushered her back to his bed.

In moments, her cotton leggings and T-shirt were a heap on the floor along with his boxer briefs. He pushed her onto the bed until she was lying back on the pillows, her dark red hair fanned out around her.

"Have I told you how much I love zebra print?" he asked as he stripped off her black-and-white panties then spread her knees.

Her short pink nails dug into his forearms, urging him to hurry. "I'll try to remember that."

He'd planned to slip a finger inside, play with her for a moment to ensure she was ready, then put on a condom. Even though vampires couldn't get a human pregnant or transmit anything, he wasn't used to having his sexual partners know his true nature, so he always wore one. But when he saw the glistening pink of her sex with a thin strip of dark red curls above it, his plans changed.

Without warning, he dropped his head, tracing his lips along the delicate softness of her inner thigh. She let out a little gasp, closing her legs slightly before relaxing them open for him again.

"Ah, yes, there you go." He felt her fingers slide encouragingly against his scalp.

And then his mouth was on her, tasting her, exploring her folds, silky and hot with desire. Her musky fragrance shot straight to his groin. If he wasn't careful, he could easily find himself spilling his seed right here on the sheets. On his hands and knees like this, his balls dangled heavy and loose between his legs, his shaft hard and pointing in the direction it wanted to go. Right into her.

Soon. But first things first.

His tongue easily found that little ball of flesh at her

center. She hissed, grabbing fistfuls of his hair. He'd been considering cutting it shorter but was glad now that he hadn't. Keeping his mouth on her, he slipped a finger into her warmth and began moving it in and out. God, she was just as silky inside as he had hoped she'd be. Maybe even more so. As well endowed as he was, he knew how important that readiness would be for her comfort. She bucked her hips, bettering the angle for him. He answered her unspoken demand by adding another finger.

"Oh, my God."

Her thighs trembled as her internal muscles tightened around his fingers. It took all his willpower not to climb on top of her and push his painfully stiff erection inside her, instead. She'd be a damn tight fit, but with all this silky heat, he had no doubt that he'd slip right in. However, there'd be time for that in a moment. Right now, he was focused on her pleasure, not his.

"Jackson," she said breathlessly.

She was so close. He could feel it.

Come on, honey. You're right there.

He concentrated on moving his fingers in and out, rubbing his tongue on her in the same fluid, erotic rhythm.

"Jackson," she repeated, this time tapping his shoulder.

Bewildered, he lifted his head. Did she not like this? He could've sworn that she was right on the edge.

"Come up and swing your leg over me."

He liked that she wasn't afraid to say what she

needed from him, but he didn't know exactly what she wanted him to do.

"Keep going, though," she added. "I don't want you to stop."

"What?" He still didn't understand, and then his eyes went wide. Did she really mean—

If he'd thought she was hot before, good God, he was ready to get down on his knees and worship her after what she said next.

"Hurry." Her voice was raspy, breathless and sexy as hell. "I'm close, but I want you in my mouth when I come."

ARIANNA HAD NEVER BEEN BROUGHT to climax with just a man's mouth and fingers before. It hadn't ever felt complete enough. Until now. Holy crap.

With him lying over the top of her like this, his hair tickling her inner thighs, she gripped the base of his shaft and sucked on its broad head as wave after wave of toe-curling pleasure washed over her. If she could form words, she'd be saying, "Oh, my God. I'm having another one. And another." As it was, all she could do was moan.

Trying to take in as much of him as she could, she kept expecting him to climax, as well. But he didn't.

Was she not doing it right? Didn't all guys love oral sex? Especially like this?

He swung his leg over her as if he was dismounting, and then, before she knew what was happening, he was between her thighs again, but this time, the rounded tip of his penis was at her core.

"Did you not like what I was doing to you?" she asked.

Maybe she'd been too aggressive and forward with him. He probably preferred his women demure and wanted them to follow his lead, rather than the other way around. Normally, she wasn't quite this bold. What the hell had come over her?

"Are you kidding?" He lifted his head and the green of his eyes seemed to glow with a light from within. "You're exquisite. Your mouth on me. The taste of you on my tongue. Call me old-fashioned, but I must take you this way first."

First?

She didn't have time to contemplate what he meant because he instantly grabbed her hips and thrust. All the way to the hilt. Had she cried out again? She was pretty sure she had. Rational thought flew out of her head as this man consumed her.

He stretched her, filled her so completely that she imagined she could feel him in her throat again. But this time, from the other side.

His buttocks flexed under her fingertips and the sinewy tendons in his neck bulged as he pistoned into her. Strands of blue-and-green hair had loosened from the half ponytail he wore and hung into his eyes, but he didn't seem to notice or care. He was rough. He was wild. And if he hadn't already brought her to climax several times before, she was certain that this would be borderline painful, rather than incredibly pleasurable.

She matched his frenzied rhythm and was soon on the brink again. His mouth came down heavily over hers, his tongue thrusting, invading, claiming her like this, as well. The taste of her on him served as a reminder of what they'd just done.

An electric energy tingled along her skin, igniting nerve endings she didn't know she had. Deep inside, he pulsed, his shaft thickened. In response, her inner walls clamped even tighter around him.

"Oh, dear God, woman," he groaned, arching his back.

He said a few other things, too, but she was so caught up in wave after wave of mind-blowing climax that it could've been some foreign language for all she knew. This man trapped between her legs and contained within her body was truly magnificent.

Breathing hard, he collapsed on top of her, his forearms bearing the majority of his weight despite his injury.

"You were... This was... Wow." She struggled to find the words to adequately describe what she'd just experienced.

It was obvious that he was a very practiced and skilled lover, familiar with how to coax the most from a woman's body. She didn't want to think about him between the legs of other women, doing things that he'd just done to her. This had been special to her, and in her own little fantasy world, she'd like to think it was special to him.

Her fingers grazed over the muscles in his back and shoulders. He was so broad that she could hardly reach the channel of his spine.

"That pleases me." His lips were hot against her neck.

She tensed. Was this the part where he was going to bite her? She was so completely and utterly enthralled by him that she hadn't thought about it ahead of time, but the man was a vampire. At least she could've mentally prepared herself. Would it hurt? Would he—

"Shh, little minx. I will not hurt you."

"You…you won't?"

He stroked a finger along her throat. Her pulse quickened in response as if encouraging him to drink from her.

"As much as I want this from you, I will not take anything that you don't freely give to me." He hesitated and it felt as if he was going to say something more. She held her breath, but he stayed silent.

He wouldn't bite her unless she told him he could. Slowly, she relaxed.

"There we go," he murmured. "That's it."

She half expected his erection would soften and slip out and that he would soon be snoring. But she was dead wrong. In fact, he was just as hard now as when they first began. She barely had a chance to catch her breath when he rolled them over as one entity and she was astride him.

"I like this view," he said huskily, staring at her breasts.

In this dominant position, with her hands positioned on either side of his broad shoulders, she had all the control now. Or at least, theoretically. He was under her, his dark eyes glossy and expectant.

Callused hands slid over her hips and waist to cup her breasts. Practiced fingers gently twisted her nipples until they peaked and tingled with need. By the time he lifted his head to pull one into his mouth, damn if she didn't feel another climax rushing at her as he suckled.

An hour later, when they finally collapsed on a heap of sheets, she wondered if he had the same wallpaper in his room as she did. She could've sworn they'd tried out each one of the sexual positions showcased on her bedroom wall.

CHAPTER FOURTEEN

ARIANNA WATCHED AS LILY palmed the small knife, then she tried to duplicate the grip with the one she was holding.

"That way, regardless of whether you're attacked from the front or the back, you'll be able to slash and incapacitate your attacker. And when it comes to mean, hungry vampires, that move can come in handy."

Lily took aim at the target and threw the knife. The blade landed dead center with a *thunk*.

"Oh, God, I could never do that."

"Sure you can. All it takes is a little practice."

"Yeah, like years and years." Besides, the thought of knives really freaked her out.

"Not necessarily. I was consistently throwing blades like this after only several months. I was hoping to get accepted into Tracker Academy and knife skills are on the test. Every morning, I did twenty throws and every evening, I did twenty more. Every day, without fail. Consistency is the key. You can't train your muscles without practice." Lily slapped a hand on her own butt for emphasis then laughed.

With her honey-blond hair and perfect figure, it'd be easy not to like Lily if she hadn't been so welcoming to Arianna and Krystal. Even her red-tipped nails were perfect.

"Would you happen to have any nail polish around here that I can borrow?" Arianna asked, remembering the sad state of her own pedicure.

"Nail polish? Hell, I've got a minisalon upstairs."

"I really appreciate you teaching self-defense techniques to Krystal and me. I've taken classes before, but nothing like this."

"Promise me that when she's old enough you'll have her attend classes on fighting with knives. I'll make sure to give you a silver-tipped knife that's fitted to a small woman's hand before you leave."

Arianna's chest tightened. Sure, she knew that day would come, but for now, she wanted to pretend it wouldn't. She could deal with the todays of the world because Jackson was here; it was the tomorrows she didn't want to think about.

"But how will I know that I need to carry it in order to protect us? Normal people just don't carry around knives like these. I know you've got the ability to implant a thought suggestion. Is that what Jackson will do?"

Lily sighed. "In theory, yes."

Arianna held the blade by the tip, aiming at the target when she hesitated. "What do you mean 'in theory'?"

"Hasn't Jackson told you?"

"Told me what?"

"He believes you to be immune from thought suggestions."

"Why? It worked on me once, it just didn't stick."

"Exactly. Why else do you think your memories came back after you saw those photos you'd taken the night before?"

"You mean, that wouldn't happen to anyone?"

"Nope. Memory manips have been done on humans for years. That's why we've been able to keep our existence a secret for so long. It's very rare to run across someone who's actually immune. And Jackson tells me you can see us shadow-move?"

She nodded.

"I can't tell you the number of times Alfonso and I hooked up for a quickie in the shadows. If we'd waited to get a room, we wouldn't have had half the fun. Can you imagine if a human saw that right out in public?" She laughed. "But then, on second thought, I like the idea of having an audience. Kind of kinky, eh?"

Images of what she and Jackson had done last night popped into her mind. Normally, she was a missionary position–type gal. The traditional route was usually, but not always, sufficient. But unlike Jackson, she hadn't had a lot of partners. She'd had a few steady boyfriends over the years, and the sex was decent, although, looking back, it had also been very vanilla. "Um, yeah."

While the girls watched movies, Lily continued to drill Arianna on the finer points of knife fighting.

By the time they were finished, Arianna was dripping with sweat. She took a long soak in the tub before she found herself in Lily's bathroom looking at a large assortment of nail colors. She had more to choose from than most nail salons. Arianna picked out a sparkly blue-green called Azure Like It that reminded her of the streaks in Jackson's hair.

"So, you've known Jackson for a long time, right?"

"Yep. Going on several decades now." Lily leaned in toward the mirror to apply some lip color. "Razzle-Dazzle Me," she explained, holding up the tube. "Alfonso loves red. I'm going to use nail polish in the same shade." Then, without skipping a beat, she said, "How much has Jackson told you about vampires' sexual habits?"

Arianna almost dropped the nail-polish bottle. Was Lily always this bold? Looking at her skimpy workout top, which was essentially just a red bra, and her form-fitting bicycle shorts, Arianna had a feeling she wasn't shy about sex. "I know that vampires tend to be more active than humans because it's a more socially acceptable way to work off aggression than killing."

Lily laughed. "True. I think it's also because our fertility rates are much lower than a human's. We can try for years to conceive and never have any luck. Our increased sexual desires are nature's way of upping the odds. The more sex you have, the greater the chances."

It reminded Arianna of a former coworker who'd been trying for years to get pregnant. Her doctor shot her full of hormones, then sent her home with strict instructions to have a lot of sex.

Lily continued, "Which is why you'll rarely find older couples complaining about lack of intimacy. Having sex several times a day isn't uncommon among our kind even when you've been together a long time."

Several times a day? Wouldn't you be sore? How would you get anything else done with all that sheet time?

Lily handed her a bottle of base coat and those little thingies that went between her toes, then propped her own foot on the counter and began painting her nails a gorgeous shimmery red.

"I like the color you're using. What's the name of that?"

Lily stared at her for a moment, one perfectly shaped brow lifted. "RazzleDazzle Me."

"Cute name." Arianna went back to her own nails as Lily smiled broadly. Must be an inside joke or something.

"Do you know that our saliva has healing properties, as well as acting as a mild pain reliever?" Lily said, pressing the tips of her pointer finger and middle finger on her neck to demonstrate. "You know, to hide any evidence that we were there. It comes in handy with other minor…abrasions, as well."

Arianna could feel her cheeks heating up. "I'll keep that in mind."

"So, as I was saying, when you're not in a relationship, having friends with benefits can be a good thing. Which leads me to something else."

"What? That the two of you have slept together? He already told me that." Jackson had explained everything on the long drive here, while Krystal slept. She liked that he'd felt the need to be honest with her.

Lily looked relieved. "Oh, good. I just didn't want you to find out later and feel uncomfortable. I'm madly in love with Alfonso. What Jackson and I had years ago was purely physical. Sex only. None of this up here." She tapped her forehead with a red-tipped nail. "That's when the magic really happens."

"So, how did you and Jackson meet?"

"We both started with the Agency about the same time. He was working on a missing-sweetblood case. It was my first assignment."

"But I thought that you only kept tabs on sweet-bloods, that you didn't necessarily track them down if they go missing."

"This case was special. It involved a young girl. Jackson wouldn't drop the case after the trail ran cold. Said she's someone's daughter or sister and that we needed to find out what happened to her."

"And did you?"

"Yeah, we sure did, all right." She looked at all the rows of fingernail polish, but Arianna had a feeling she wasn't really looking at them.

"We wiped her memory then took her back to her parents', where she miraculously turned up after being missing for days. Alien abduction is how some people explain why that happens. Others say it was a kidnapper with a change of heart." Lily capped the bottle and shook it again.

This was just like what happened with Krystal. "I get the feeling that it didn't go well."

"It didn't. Three weeks after we wiped her mind and returned her to her home, her body turned up in a local storm sewer. A whole new set of Darkbloods had tracked her down that time."

Arianna gasped. "What—what did they do to her?"

Lily shook her head. "I don't think you want to know."

"Please." Her voice came out as a whisper. It could've been what had been done to her mother and what could've been done to Krystal if Jackson hadn't come along when he had.

"Generally, victims are taken to one of the Darkblood dens where they're strapped to a gurney and their blood drained. It's then put into vials and sold on the black market."

Arianna felt as if she was going to get sick.

"Oh, God, I knew I shouldn't have told you this much. Darkbloods are vicious and ruthless, which is why Jackson and I do what we do. To prevent things like that from happening and weaken the Alliance's power structure. The less organized they are, the more slipshod their efforts."

"What do they do with the people when they're... done?"

Lily cast a sidelong glance to the left, and Arianna got the distinct impression that what she was about to say wouldn't be the full truth. "Sometimes they're buried, sometimes they're dumped, and other times, the bodies are never found. They waste no time with niceties when there's blood that needs to be sold."

CHAPTER FIFTEEN

ALTHOUGH SHE WASN'T A neat freak by a long shot, Arianna felt the need to do something to keep herself busy until nightfall, especially since she didn't have use of a computer or phone. As she gathered up the wet towels in the bathroom, she thought about the conversation she and Jackson had before he went to work out in Alfonso's weight room, his arm looking a lot better.

"After all that's happened, you still don't trust me," she'd said to him. "Do you really think I'd post anything to jeopardize your secret after all you've done—that *all* of you have done for me and Krystal?"

"Sorry. Dom's orders."

She'd wanted to punch something. Or someone. Preferably this Dom character.

"Jackson, I've got thousands of readers who depend on me each morning. They count on the fact that they can drink their first cup of coffee and read Paranormalish. I need access to a computer."

"Impossible."

What could she say to convince him, get him to change his mind? "This isn't just a little hobby of mine. I have regular blog features, comments that need answering, emails, story leads, none of which I can do from here without my laptop. I have two ad spots, which need to be changed out no later than tomorrow."

He'd run a hand through his hair and she'd watched as the green and blue streaks settled back in place. It was clear he didn't trust her, but she didn't know what else she could say to convince him otherwise. "Please. This is really important to me."

"Arianna, I can't. End of discussion."

"No. It's not." She didn't care who or what he was, no one dismissed her like that. "Although the fact that vampires exist would normally be something I'd continue to write about and explore on Paranormalish, there are many other areas within the paranormal realm that I can cover. If I don't make a post in the next day or so, people are going to wonder what's going on. Especially if they read that last post before you guys took it down."

He'd exhaled heavily. "Jesus."

"You can Big Brother me. Watch to make sure I don't post anything I shouldn't. You can be the blog police, for all I care. Just give me access so I can do what I need to do."

He stared at her as if trying to decide.

"If it makes you happy, I'll run everything past you first. It's not like I have a desire to expose the people who—who saved my life. Jackson, this is really important to me."

"Part of the problem is that your computer isn't secure by Agency standards."

"Is there a different computer I can use?"

"I could maybe arrange that."

She'd felt a huge sense of relief, but unfortunately it wasn't enough. That'd just barely keep things afloat. "That's a start, I suppose."

"A start?" He'd spun to face her, his eyes blazing.

"I really need to finish reporting on that boy missing from the Devil's Backbone. Photos and videos from the site—that kind of thing. That's what I would have done already if this mess hadn't happened. My readers are expecting it. Plus, I heard on the radio that another person went missing from the same vicinity. I can't help but wonder if it's from the same place. I want to go there, check things out myself."

"You're not going anywhere." All the warmth and understanding had gone from his eyes.

Did she dare push him for more? He looked about as unbendable as anyone she'd ever seen. But she had to. "Will you take me?"

He'd cursed under his breath and stormed out the door an hour ago.

Well, at least she'd gotten him to cave about the computer, she told herself as she opened a drawer, looking for something to wipe down the bathroom counters. A small metal stud sat on a pile of washcloths. She picked it up, thinking maybe it was a piece of hardware from one of the drawers. Given that Alfonso was still working on the house, she wondered if it was a screw that needed to go somewhere. But it wasn't a screw.

It was several centimeters long with a small ball on each end. She twisted it. One of the ends could be unscrewed. Wait. Was this what she thought it was? Did Jackson have a piercing after all? When they made love, she was pretty sure she'd have felt it if he'd had it in, which was why she'd assumed her eyes had been playing tricks on her. If this was his, why had he removed it?

A sound in the bedroom drew her attention. Jackson must be back from working out. He'd be coming in to take a shower any moment. While she waited for him to open the door, she sat on the counter, crossed her legs to look coy and held out her hand with the metal stud displayed prominently.

He kicked the door open as he was peeling off his shirt. Her stomach did a couple of backflips when she saw his well-defined abs.

"Jesus, Arianna, I didn't know you were in here," he said, pulling the shirt over his head and tossing it into the corner. When he looked down to see what she had in her outstretched hand, a shadow darkened his features. "What are you doing?"

"This looks like body jewelry of some sort."

Without answering, he turned abruptly away from her and started the water in the shower.

"Is it?"

"It doesn't concern you," he growled.

"I just want to know if it is or not. No big deal."

"Yes, goddamn it. It is." He angrily stripped off his shorts and climbed into the shower stall. "Fuuuck," he said from inside. She guessed the water was either too hot or too cold.

"Why aren't you wearing it?"

She heard him fumbling for the shampoo bottle. Then another curse.

"Jackson?"

"I don't feel like it."

"Why not? If it's because—"

He yanked the door open, but was careful to keep his business hidden. The sight of him standing there with rivulets of soapy water snaking down his torso and over the thigh of the one leg she could see made the words catch in her throat.

"It's not a belly-button ring, Arianna," he snapped. "It's a genital piercing."

"Yeah, I—I know."

His jaw ticked. He looked ready to explode. His gaze darted from her hand up to her face before he closed the door again and stepped back inside. She could see his silhouette behind the rippled glass. He wasn't moving, just standing under the water.

Why was he pissed that she'd found it? And why had he removed it in the first place? Except for earrings, body jewelry stayed in place most of the time.

Then she remembered when he'd stormed out of bed on the first night they slept together. Had he removed it then? He had to have. He must not have wanted her to know about it.

She quietly peeled off her clothes and opened the shower door. With both hands pressed to the tile, he stood under the showerhead, letting the water spray his back. He didn't bother to look up when she stepped inside. "Go away."

"If you took it off for me," she said quietly, resting a hand on the small of his back, right over his twin dimples, "you needn't have."

He scoffed.

"I'm serious, Jackson. I'm—I'm game for a lot of things with you, if you hadn't already figured that out. You should put it back in." She tentatively reached around between his legs. She started to cup him when he grabbed her wrist and shoved her hand away.

"You don't get it, do you? It's not a fashion statement, like earrings or a nose ring or a belly-button ring. 'Oh, I think I'll wear the blue one today. It'll go with my shirt.' The main reason guys pierce their dick is to get more sex. To please a variety of partners."

"If that's the case, then why did you take it off before we slept together?"

He didn't answer right away. The water continued to spray him. Then, when finally he spoke, his voice was so low she strained to hear it over the sound of the shower. "I—I didn't want you to have that be your impression of me the first time we made love. I wanted to be…different for you."

"Different?" Did he think guys with piercings like that were commonplace in her world?

"Normal," he added.

Her chest felt suddenly tight and her knees went all rubbery. He cared about what she thought of him and considered her different from other women he'd been with. "You're a vampire," she whispered. "I'm a human. Nothing about you is normal to me. And with or without that in, I'm still desperately attracted to you."

This time when she reached for him, he didn't shove her hand away.

Sweet Mother Mary, he was hard. Rock hard. Her

fingers could barely fit all the way around his shaft. Before she knew what was happening, he'd grabbed her by the hips, lifted her up, and in the blink of an eye, she was sliding down over the top of him.

His hands were everywhere. Spanning her rib cage. Kneading her buttocks. Holding her hip bones for leverage. Twisting first one nipple then the other one just hard enough that it almost hurt. The muscles in his shoulders and arms flexed under her hands with every movement. Guess his arm really was better.

With her legs around his waist and her back pressed against the tiles, he pounded into her over and over, leaving her breathless and aware of nothing else in this world but him, unsure of when one climax was over and the next one started.

When he grabbed the back of her hair, she tilted her head back and laughed. She couldn't help herself. He felt so amazing, so good.

His shaft seemed to thicken then, the tip going infinitesimally deeper inside, as her body opened up farther to him. Oh, God, he was on the verge just as was she.

"I'm having another one," she said, grabbing at his shoulders. "I want you to have one with me." She caught a glimpse of fang before he quickly turned his head away. She found it darkly erotic that he wanted that from her, too.

She grabbed his face and turned it back to hers. His fangs were fully extended, the green of his irises a thin ring around his dilated pupils. He was a powerful, deadly male and for a fleeting instant he belonged to her. "That, too," she said breathlessly as wave after wave of pleasure pulsed through her again. "Take that, too."

Needing no more encouragement, he struck quickly. The sharpness of the pain surprised her as his teeth sank into her flesh. But before she could gasp or cry out, it was gone, followed instead by a warm, almost calming sensation. With his lips hot against her throat, water cascading over them, he swallowed what she gave to him as his seed pumped into her body.

THEY LAY IN A TANGLE of sheets, Arianna's leg draped carelessly over his torso. Jackson seriously hadn't felt this good in ages. Not only was he sexually sated, but he felt unusually calm and clearheaded. Two emotions he hadn't felt in a long time.

"You still never told me why you have this pierced." She had reached down and was fondling him.

That was something he had for *those* women, not Arianna. That part of his life, though necessary, wasn't something he was proud of. He enjoyed and found useful the attention that his reputation afforded him, but she didn't belong in that world.

So, why am I pulling her into it?

"I know you said it's to get more sex, but seriously, Jackson, that can hardly be an issue with you."

"What do you mean?" Although he had a damn good idea what she meant, he was just vain enough to want to hear her say it.

"Because you're hot, that's why. And that's the best damn sex I've ever had. I can't imagine you'd ever have trouble finding a willing partner."

A mixture of satisfaction and pride swelled his chest. This woman, whom he couldn't seem to get enough of, apparently felt the same way about him. He felt himself growing harder yet again. Her fingertips were cool on the base of his shaft and he loved how she seemed as interested in his balls as he was with her nipples. If she kept touching him like this, he was going to cave in to those urges once more.

He found it so incredible that she'd actually offered him her blood back in the shower. She'd seen the very worst of his kind and he'd have thought that the blood thing would've freaked her out, but it obviously hadn't. Its coppery sweetness still lingered on the back of his tongue.

"I mean, not that I'm against the body art," she continued, "but your logic seems flawed."

"I've told you my concerns about reverting. Part of the reason I suspect it's happening is that my blood and energy needs have skyrocketed. Most of us can go for weeks at a time without taking either, but not me."

He wondered how long Arianna's blood and energy would last in his system before he'd need to go out looking for more. At least his arm seemed to be doing better now. In fact, as he rubbed a hand over the fresh bandage, the injury didn't hurt at all. Good. It meant that he'd have an easier time going out later than if it still bothered him.

She sat up and looked at him, her messy hair cascading over her shoulders and partially covering her ample breasts. He brushed her hair away with a flick so that he could play with a dusty-rose nipple.

"So you make your friends and associates think you're having a lot of sex, when you're actually doing it for the energy."

He rolled the delicate flesh between his finger and thumb, then watched as it peaked.

She poked him in the side and he jumped. "Answer me."

"Okay, fine," he said, still staring at her breasts.

What he really wanted was to bury his face between them and feel the creamy softness of her skin against his cheeks. She made a little sound of frustration, then lifted his chin and forced him to look at her face. God, she was beautiful with those pouty lips, crimson-stained cheeks and a few freckles sprinkled across her nose.

He lifted an eyebrow. "I'm no saint."

"Yeah, tell me about it," she said flatly.

"I admit it, I do have a lot of sex…just not as much as everyone thinks." He decided to be honest with her. "The piercing, and my resulting reputation, have made me very popular in a number of clubs throughout the city. I don't have to spend much time chitchatting in order to get what I need. I go in and, *snap,* I have it."

Her face lit up with an expression that was both incredulous and disbelieving at the same time. "So you mean you could enter a club and be going at it with some chick in what…ten minutes?"

"Or less."

She knocked him in the arm. His bad one. And it didn't even hurt. "That is so… You are such a man whore. What if that were me and I were the one trolling the bars looking for men to hook up with?"

"Well, I would hope you were doing it because you wanted to and not because you felt it was the only way you could survive."

Her gaze was blisteringly hot on his face for a moment. What? Did she not believe him? If he weren't so paranoid that he was reverting and that people would find out, he wouldn't be nearly such a man whore. Oh, he'd be no saint, but things wouldn't have gone as far as they had.

Then she flipped her hair decisively over one shoulder and straddled his body. She reached back roughly and his erection jerked when she grabbed it. She lifted her bottom, positioning the tip between her folds.

Oh, God, this was going to be so good, he thought, his toes curling with anticipation. She was marginally pissed off and in charge.

Grasping her buttocks, he rolled his hips upward, hoping to push in farther, but she lifted herself up just enough that the tip was the only part of him inside.

He couldn't concentrate. What was he thinking about before? Every nerve ending along his shaft tingled with anticipation and demanded attention. His need was as raw now as when she first climbed into the shower with him. She may be the one in control here, but that didn't mean he couldn't coax her along. He ran his hands along the smooth skin of her back, feeling her lean muscles, then over the swell of her buttocks until his fingertips touched where their bodies were joined.

Come on, just a little bit more. Please.

"Damn you, Jackson. You're everything I ran from all my life, and yet, you're everything I seem to need."

With an arm on either side of his head, she eased herself down and he slid into heaven. Soft moans and a few loud ones filled the room. It wasn't until they finished making love that he realized he'd forgotten all about his rules and had kissed her over and over.

CHAPTER SIXTEEN

THE NO TRESPASSING SIGN LOOMED up ahead and Jackson pulled his truck to the side of the road, careful not to get too close to the bushes. If he'd known there was nowhere decent to park his nice rig out here in the sticks, he'd have suggested they take her piece-of-shit Caddy.

"Are you sure this is it?" Dense forest surrounded them on both sides and he couldn't see even a pathway in anywhere.

She opened the glove box for the light and checked her notepad. "Yep. According to Blake, the boy whose friend went missing, they parked just ahead of that sign. There's an indentation in the bushes that leads to a path, but it's really overgrown and easy to miss unless you're really looking for it. He said to look for some trash at the trailhead. Beer bottles, fast-food wrappers, cigarette butts. The kind of litter that high-school kids would leave when they all come out to a place like this to scare the crap out of themselves."

"Condoms? Pop-can bongs?"

She threw him a sidelong glance. "Do a bunch of partying as a kid?"

"Some, but I've broken up my fair share of parties lately. Vampire, human. Youthlings are all the same."

"Do you have the flashlight?" She grabbed the camera and video recorder.

He flicked it on and pointed it under his chin, illuminating his face. "I need you," he said in a fake monster voice.

She laughed. "Stop that. You're freaking me out. Besides, I've heard that the people who live in the houses surrounding the Devil's Backbone have guns and threaten trespassers."

He laughed. "What? Are you going tell me next that they're not afraid to use them?"

"I know, it sounds ridiculous, like something from a movie, but that's the rumor. I heard it from more than one person on Paranormalish."

"Do you believe everything you read online? But hey, if I lived in one of these houses and kids were traipsing through my yard all the time to get to that old sanitarium, I'd be pissed, too."

"So you'd use a gun?"

"No, but I wouldn't do anything to stop that rumor."

Since there were no streetlights and the moon was behind heavy cloud cover, he could've easily shadow-moved in the darkness and gotten to the location in a fraction of the time—but they weren't in a hurry. He enjoyed walking with her.

"Oh, there's the blue house that Gary425 was talking about," she said, pointing. "If we pass that, we've gone too far."

He laughed. "Who's Gary425? I thought you were talking about Blake?"

"He's this really sweet guy who follows my blog."

"Gary425? Why not just Gary?"

"That's how I've always known him," she said matter-of-factly. "It's his screen name."

"And you trust guys you meet online?"

"It's not like I'm meeting him face-to-face. Besides, I've gotten to know him pretty well over the years and he's a good guy."

"How do you know he's not lying to you, giving you some fake story about who he is?"

She shrugged. "I suppose that's possible. It's not like I cyberstalk everyone who posts on my blog. But you get a feel for people when you've been doing this for as long as I have. You can sense the ones with a good heart, those who care about what you've written and comment thoughtfully. Even though you've never met in person, you develop a sense of trust, respect, even, but it's not something that happens overnight. It's not like someone emails me and, *boom*, I'm accepting an invitation for coffee."

"Someone could be using a fake picture, make you think they look like some hot guy when, in fact, they're a dirty old man. Who is this Gary guy, anyway?"

"Please." She rolled her eyes. "Everyone uses fake pictures. Hell, for a while, my profile picture was a shirtless Alexander Skarsgard. People don't actually think ASkars is Icy Shadows who runs Paranormalish. It's just what everyone does online."

"ASkars?" Jackson laughed so hard that his stomach hurt and his eyes were watering.

"Shut up," she said, giggling. "You're totally going to

wake the neighbors. Oh, look. You were right. Condom wrappers. This must be it."

They stepped around a large pile of grass clippings, probably put there by neighbors to cover up the path, and trekked through the woods.

"So, what's Gary's story?" Jackson asked skeptically. "Why is he so interested in the paranormal?"

She shrugged. "Why are any of my followers? Why am I? We find the subject matter fascinating, entertaining, a little scary, maybe. Like the kids who come to the Devil's Backbone. People are curious about the unknown. And I suppose that some of us are simply looking for answers."

"You know, you've never told me why you started the blog in the first place."

She pulled her video camera from its case and looped the strap around her wrist. "I've told you about what happened to my mom, right?"

He nodded.

"Well, I knew what I saw, but no one believed me, no matter how hard I tried. My great-aunt told me I was lying, that I couldn't have possibly seen those shadows come alive and take my mom. But I wouldn't back down. I was adamant. It got so bad between the two of us that one day, she even accused me of being in cahoots with the devil. Ha. Maybe I'll see him at the bottom of the Devil's Backbone."

He held a branch to the side, allowing Arianna to pass.

She continued, "I started the blog as a way to search for the truth, as well as to prove to myself that I wasn't crazy. That there were other people out there who believed me, who maybe had stories of their own to tell. Turns out there are plenty. Some have had their own experiences, some of them just like talking about it. Paranormalish isn't some fun little hobby of mine. It's helped me validate myself and know that I'm not a freak, unlike what relatives had been telling me over the years."

He'd never really thought about how profoundly the actions of his kind affected humans. Sure, he felt badly when Guardians failed to save someone, but he hadn't considered much beyond that, never put a face to the pain, till now. It was bad enough that Arianna grew up without a mother because of Darkbloods, but then to be treated the way she was, which had damaging effects on her self-image and self-identity… Well, it pissed him off.

"I can see why you started Paranormalish. I'm glad you found people you could connect with."

She squeezed his hand. "It means a lot to me that you understand. Not everyone does. That's why I guard my identity so carefully. In addition to my aunt and uncle, I've had friends tease me, a boyfriend ridicule me and employers not take me seriously."

Instantly he was on edge. "A boyfriend?"

"Yeah, several years ago, back before I started Paranormalish, I blogged under my real name. I wasn't secretive about what I did. One day, he and his friends got drunk and used my computer to access my account. That's what's scary about the internet. With one click of that enter button, things that took months to create were destroyed in an instant."

"What did he do?"

"He posted pictures of me that I never knew he'd taken. Naked...embarrassing pictures."

An icy-hot anger flared inside Jackson. There was no excuse for a betrayal like that, especially from someone she clearly had trusted at one time. Maybe the guy needed a midnight visit from a real-life bogeyman.

"My reputation never recovered after that. It got to the point that I finally had enough and shut the blog down. I didn't go online for ages, and when I did, I had to reinvent myself. That's when I started Paranormal-ish. I vowed never to tell anyone who I was again. Hell, Xtark would fire my ass if they knew I was blogging and didn't tell them, but that's just too bad."

He bristled at the mention of Xtark. They were much more than just bastards.

"Does knowing what happened to your mom and realizing you didn't imagine things change anything now?" He stepped over a downed log then turned around to help her over.

She swiped at a strand of hair that had come loose from her braid. "Well, I do have answers, which is why I started the blog in the first place. It confirms what I knew for years to be the truth, and then some. Oh, look," she said, grabbing his arm. "Is that it?"

The charred remains of a building sat in the middle of a clearing, its brick foundation crumbling and gaping like an old, unhealed wound. Just beyond it, the land seemed to slope away sharply. The ravine she'd heard about?

She pulled out her camera. "Can you take some pictures for me?"

He took it from her and lifted it up to look through the viewfinder.

"Wait. Not right this sec. The flash could alert the neighbors that someone's here. I'm going to shoot some video first, get some of the sounds of the woods at night on camera. If you can aim the flashlight low onto some of the headstones, I'll start taping. But remember, if you hear anyone coming, we need to ditch the light and run."

He smiled at how she had it all planned out. He didn't tell her that if a neighbor even so much as opened up a door, he'd hear them. But Arianna took lots of footage and photos, and not a single neighbor yelled at them for trespassing.

"I guess it is just an urban legend," she said, pocketing the camera. "No ghosts, no demons, no thirteen steps leading into the ravine, where you could see the mouth of hell."

"Yes, but that boy still went missing from here."

"Do you think it could've been vampires?"

When she reached for his hand almost involuntarily, he smiled to himself. He liked that she instinctively considered him someone who'd protect her.

"It's possible, yes."

"Would you…you know…be able to smell them if it was?"

"Depends on how long ago it happened. Scents deteriorate quickly, especially in the rain, but then, I'm no tracker, either. I haven't picked up on any lingering Darkblood scent around here, if that's what you mean."

"According to Blake's brother, who still claims that the missing boy hadn't been with them—"

"Their minds could've been wiped by the Dark-bloods who took the boy."

"Yes, that's exactly what I'm thinking." She glanced around nervously and pointed. "They were exploring the far side of the ravine over there."

"When did the boy go missing?"

"Around the time Krystal did. I remember because I was so distracted by what had happened to Krystal that I didn't answer Blake's email about his missing friend until a week after she turned up."

"So, that means both disappearances happened around the same time?"

"A little too coincidental, wouldn't you say?"

"Yep," he agreed. "I'll bet it was the same ones who took Krystal…or at least they were taken for the same purpose."

Her eyes went wide. "You mean that party?"

He remembered a young victim, forced to dress up in a fireman's costume. They'd gotten to him too late. Could that have been Blake's friend? "Unfortunately, there were several sweetbloods we were unable to save that night."

She was quiet for a while as they walked back down the path, their footsteps, night insects and the faraway howl of a coyote the only sounds they heard. "Well, at least you caught the ones responsible."

Most, but not all, he almost said.

Once inside the truck, he turned to face her. "Does it seem less necessary to you now? The blog?" She looked confused, so he added, "You know, now that you know what happened to your mom and that it wasn't your imagination, do you think you'll stop blogging?"

He hoped her answer would be yes. Since he was part of the world her blog was trying to expose, he didn't know how he could keep seeing her if she said no. Maybe now that she had answers, the blog wasn't as important to her as it once was. She'd wrap up a few loose ends and then close it.

Although human and vampire relationships weren't common, he knew of several couples, including Dom and Mackenzie, where things had worked out well. They met, fell in love. She became a changeling and made Dom a father. If only he could get this reverting shit under control, then a future was definitely possible with Arianna. Or at least he hoped it was. He had a pretty good idea Arianna felt the same way about him. He certainly had never been happier, more satisfied since the night she came crashing into his world. She complicated his life in the best way possible and he didn't want things to end.

"While it helps to know the truth, it doesn't change things. Paranormalish has become a part of me.... And I love it. Like I said, those people depend on me and I... well, I depend on them, too. They accepted me when no one would. Which is why I'm so grateful to you for helping me tonight. It means the absolute world to me. I hope you know that."

With their fingers intertwined, he stroked his thumb over hers as an ache formed low in his gut. She was dedicated to the blog and he understood why—it fed her soul when nothing else would—but it made a future between them impossible.

ARIANNA CUT THE LAST OF THE three sandwiches on the diagonal and slid the plate over to Jackson.

"Are you like a bottomless pit, or what?"

"Yeah, pretty much," he said, stuffing the first one into his mouth. He had a high metabolism for everything. Blood, sex, energy and food. He did nothing half-assed, and that included eating.

"I got a message from Krystal's mom." Arianna put the peanut butter back into the pantry. "She gets out of rehab soon and wants me to bring her back over to eastern Washington."

"Is she ready to resume being a mother?" Jackson asked skeptically, licking the honey from his fingers.

"I sure hope so. Krystal really misses her."

"How do you know she's not going to slip up again?"

"I don't think anyone can predict that. But you know, I really don't blame her. I wasn't the only one who had a tough time after my mom disappeared. My aunt wasn't the same, either. They were fraternal twins, you know, and were very close. She was on all sorts of antidepressants and soon began to self-medicate. That's when things got out of control."

Another human life destroyed due to the actions of Darkbloods. He crumpled his napkin into a tight ball.

"Do you think Krystal will be safe over there?" Worry lines creased Arianna's forehead.

"I'll tell you what," he said. "Kip owes me a favor. A big one. I'll send him over to see if he can detect any evidence of Darkblood scent in her little town."

"What do you mean, he owes you a favor?" Lily asked, striding through the door. "What did you do for him?"

Shit. The woman didn't need to know everything. "Nothing."

"Excuse me. Hello. I'm his trainer."

"Yeah, and that doesn't make you his mother, either."

"Hmmph." She wrenched open the refrigerator and stuck her head inside.

"It was man-stuff, Lil. Nothing you need to concern yourself with." He stuffed another sandwich half into his mouth and turned back to Arianna. "If Kip comes back with an all clear, it should be fairly safe over there. Darkbloods don't usually bother with small towns because they're too far away from the majority of their revenue sources."

He swallowed the last bite and chased it down with a swig of milk. "At least until we can figure out a better solution."

At sundown, Jackson and Lily had left Casa en las Colinas and headed to the field office. His shift tonight was uneventful.

"Dom wants to talk to you in the computer lab," Lily said as Jackson was finishing up his report.

He never turned them in like he was supposed to

after being on duty, but since he wanted to get back up to Arianna, he decided not to procrastinate the way he usually did. Lily would be shocked to learn he wasn't waiting for days to do a bunch of reports at the same time.

"Great. I can't wait." He pressed Enter and logged out of TechTran. The screen went black for a moment before the Guardian logo materialized pixel by pixel and started rotating.

Lily propped herself on the edge of the workstation next to him, leaned on the half wall and lowered her voice. "Hey, I wanted to tell you that I tried a little experiment on Arianna."

"You did?"

"Yeah. I knew you were worried about her being immune from mind manips."

He glanced around nervously, making sure no one was within earshot. Several other Guardians had just left and Mitch was on the other side of the room, out of earshot if they spoke quietly. "And...?"

"Well, she's not immune."

He stared at her a moment. "She isn't? How do you know?"

She explained how they'd been painting their nails together. "I specifically told her the color I was using."

"Yeah, so?"

"Well, I reached over, did a quick mind wipe, telling her that she never heard what color I was using. A moment later she's asking me what color it was that I was painting my toes with." She wiggled her fingers and kicked a foot out, revealing the red polish. "Raz-zleDazzle Me, love."

"That doesn't mean anything. When I did a manip on her that one night, it worked at first. It wasn't until the next day when her memory was jarred that it all came back to her."

"I know that. Which is why I planted the thought that she and I hadn't done our nails together, that we hadn't even been in my bathroom, that the conversation we had during that time had occurred in the workout room where we'd just come from."

"And…?"

"And I asked her about her nails the next day. She couldn't remember when she'd had them done."

"That doesn't prove anything. It wasn't a traumatic event. Those tend to stick with a person, not the color of someone's nail polish."

Lily shrugged. "I don't think that matters. I tried to trigger it and got no response." She crossed her arms on the top of the workstation and rested her chin. "I think the problem is that she may be immune to you."

When they arrived in the computer room, Jackson could hardly focus. He blindly put one foot in front of the other, not paying attention to a word Lily was saying as they walked down the corridor. The fact that Arianna was immune to him could only mean one thing. He was losing one of the most important abili-ties a vampire needed in order to live among humans in secret.

He was reverting. And Lily knew it.

Dom and Cordell were sitting in front of a bank of monitors when he and Lily entered the room.

"What have you been able to glean from that woman?" Dom asked.

"Gleaning?" Mitch asked. "Who's gleaning? I want to glean, too."

Jackson glared at all of them, hardly able to control his anger. He could feel his pupils dilating and, goddamn it, his fangs were starting to emerge.

Dude, chill. Calm down. It'll be all over if you attack anyone.

"I'm not *gleaning* anything from her," he said through clenched teeth. "I'm making sure things are safe for her and her cousin, that's all."

He held his hand up when he saw the field team leader was about to say something more about it. Probably a wisecrack about his sexual habits.

"I don't want to hear it, Dom. I'm not sending them back to that house totally unprepared. That girl is a sweetblood, and Darkbloods know where she lives. If I wiped their minds and sent them back home, you and I both know DBs would be there as soon as sundown arrived."

"Jesus, you're sensitive. I was talking about Xtark. If she's got a thing for you, maybe she'd be willing to be our eyes on the inside. God knows, we could use it."

Use Arianna? A wildfire of anger surged instantly inside him. His pupils stretched, his gums ached.

He hated that she worked for Xtark in the first place, so there was no way on God's green earth he'd go along with this.

"Fuck, no. She is not going to be a mole for the Agency."

Dom was saying something else, but Jackson wasn't listening. He felt a sudden restless detachment from his surroundings and his ears began to ring. He wanted to break something. Rip something or someone apart. Instead, he pounded a fist on the table. It felt so good that he did it again. One of the table legs collapsed, and a printer crashed to the floor.

Cordell jumped to his feet.

"What the hell is wrong with you, Foss?" Dom said, picking up the state-of-the-art printer that probably cost the Agency some coin.

Lily had her hands on her hips. "I'd say someone's got some anger-management issues that need to be addressed."

Like he didn't know that. He stormed to the far side of the room and leaned against the wet bar.

He seriously needed to get a grip. This uncontrollable anger wasn't good. Maybe he should take a leave of absence to get things sorted out. A part of him knew he couldn't keep hiding and yet he couldn't tell them what was going on, either.

When he heard laughing, he glanced through the fronds of a large potted plant. They'd righted the table and the printer and the three of them were staring into one of Cordell's curved monitors. What were they looking at? A funny picture? A comic? A video? He listened to the murmur of their voices, Cordell chuckling with that deep voice of his and Dom doing some good-natured cursing. Were they laughing at his outburst?

He felt like a damn outsider with this secret. Too nervous to be around them. Too nervous to let them close. It was as though he wasn't a part of the club any longer. He stared down at his hands; they were going blurry.

Fuck. He turned around and pinched his eyes shut. What the hell was he going to do? He couldn't go on this way, but what choice did he have?

He felt hot and sticky all of a sudden. Almost queasy. The feeling of detachment was getting stronger and stronger.

Lily's voice got a little louder. He heard footsteps.

"I don't know where he went."

Jesus H. I'm right-the-fuck here.

Using every effort to control himself, Jackson white-knuckled the edge of the counter.

"What?" he snapped then immediately felt guilty about it. Lily didn't deserve to be talked to like this. She was a good friend who'd done a lot for him. This was his problem, not hers.

Her eyebrows were raised, one slightly more than the other. "Sorry, I didn't see you back here. I—I thought you had left."

"Well, I didn't," he growled, turning on the faucet and splashing his face with water.

Hell, Lily was perceptive enough that even if he'd smiled, if he made himself sound all sugary sweet, she'd have read right through his fakeness. He was a fraud, a loser, and he wasn't going to be able to hide it for much longer. He was a heartbeat away from becoming the very enemy they pursued.

It'd be better for everyone if he just finished up here at the field office and left before any of them started asking the kinds of questions he didn't want to answer.

CHAPTER SEVENTEEN

THE MOMENT VENTRA WALKED into the entryway of the old house, she stopped listening to a word the Realtor was saying. One look at the vaulted ceilings, the coved moldings and the marble floors, and she knew this was the place. Not only did it remind her of the haunted house depicted in the first level of Hollow Grave, but every room had a heavy, expectant atmosphere, ripe with promise.

"Draw up the papers." With a flick of her hand, she dismissed the man and peered into what probably once was a kitchen.

"Given the water damage, the condition of the roof, the remote location, we should offer them—"

"There is no *we* here. I want this house. I don't care how you make it happen."

With a little work, this place would be fitting for a Seattle sector mistress and member of the Xtark Software board of directors. Her meeting with the Alliance had gone as well as she'd hoped. Better, in fact. Not only had they officially made her the new leader here in Seattle and assured her a place on the board, but they wanted to hear her ideas about the members-only clubs for those who wanted Sweet straight from the source.

Although the Night of Wilding party had been discovered by Guardians, and broken up before it really had started, the Alliance was intrigued with the concept she'd come up with.

She'd told them her vision of opening an exclusive, invite-only club for vampires in the Seattle area and that she'd help other sectors open up similar ones in their areas. She thought about telling them of her plans to offer this exclusively, one-on-one, to her best clients, but had decided against it. She didn't want to show her hand all at once. Better to hold something back. You never knew when you'd need to play that wild card.

How long would it take to collect the bones she'd need for a chandelier? she wondered as she looked up at the two-story entry. Months? Years? But hers would be different than the one at the Alliance headquarters. Hers would be made entirely from the bones of sweetbloods.

And she knew just who the first ones would be. She'd start with those who'd gotten away from her already.

"You mean, you want me to draw up an offer right now? I don't think that's wise."

Stunned by how the man continued to question her wishes, Ventra had a hard time believing he was one of the most successful Realtors in the area. Oh, sure, he looked the part with his Brooks Brothers suit, handmade Italian shoes and platinum Rolex, but he needed to realize that the customer's needs and desires came first. And she wanted this damn house.

"Do you not have the documents with you?" She

took a step closer and heard his heart rate speed up exponentially.

She honestly tried not to smile—coming from her, she knew it wasn't a warm or welcoming expression—but she couldn't help herself. This man was almost a foot taller than she was and probably outweighed her by a hundred pounds, and yet he instinctively sensed the danger. The power she had over humans never failed to thrill her. It emphasized the vampire race's superiority and that humans were simply here to serve them.

The pulse under his jaw drew her attention like a beacon, calling to her, and her fangs broke through her gums. His blood scent reminded her that, next to Sweet, it was one of her favorite types. Not particularly rare, but still a good one. And laced with fear, it'd be even better.

A flicker of unease crossed his face and he glanced at the closed door. "Yes—yes, I have them. It's just that—"

She struck fast, slamming him against the wall, and sank her fangs into his flesh. Given the height difference, she clung to him with her legs wrapped around his waist. One of her shoes clattered to the floor.

"Oh, my God." He tried to peel her off, fingers clawed desperately at her arms, but it was futile. She was much stronger than he was.

She grabbed his wrists and immobilized him as she fed, but he continued to struggle and groan. They always did. Although she had the ability to implant a thought suggestion to calm them down, she never used it. Blood tasted so much better this way and adrenaline-laced energy had an extra zip.

After several mouthfuls, she reluctantly withdrew and sealed the puncture wounds. Unlike her normal feeding habits of draining the host dry, she still needed this human's services. Unwinding her legs from his waist, she dropped to the ground.

His eyes were wild and he clamped a hand to his neck. "What did you just do to me? What are you?"

Not bothering to answer him, she calmly smoothed down her skirt and tried to drown out the high-pitched, piglike sound of his voice. Then, as she secured a loose bobby pin in her chignon, she slipped her foot back into her shoe.

Enough with the sobbing.

With lightning quickness, she pulled the handkerchief from his lapel and dabbed at his face. His expression softened ever so slightly as if he wanted to believe that she was capable of showing compassion. In reality, however, she didn't want to come up with an excuse as to why tears and snot were running down his face.

She reached up and her fingertips grazed his temple. "You'll remember none of this. Only that you will be drawing up the purchase documents. But just know that I'll be back later to finish what I started." Then she turned away to lick the blood from her lips.

ARIANNA SAT CROSS-LEGGED on Jackson's bed and scrolled through the comments on her Weird Wednesday feature. "Oh, wow, this is not good." Jackson had brought a laptop from the field office and somehow got the okay for her to access the internet. She wasn't sure what he'd had to do to get them to agree to that, but she wasn't arguing. She didn't, however, have free rein. Everything outgoing was routed through their servers and approved first. But at least it was better than nothing.

Jackson looked up from the table where several guns were laid out for cleaning. "Why? What's wrong?"

"I have a regular feature on Wednesdays where readers can post strange things they've heard about or seen. I've got…let's see…three—no, four—comments about missing people."

"From around the country? People go missing all the time."

"No. They're all from around here. Let's see. One happened at Big Daddy's, a sports bar downtown. Ever heard of it?"

"Yep, been there a time or two."

She read the next one. "Another went out for cigarettes and never came back. This one was—wow—missing from her bedroom. Crap. She's just a few years older than Krystal. And this one…whoa."

Jackson put down the gun he had just disassembled and looked up. "What is it?"

"This last one happened near the Devil's Backbone. Shit. The night after we were there. Guy was a teenager, just like Blake's friend. Do you think the disappearances are linked somehow?"

"Hard to tell. Can you write up a brief summary on each one? Names, ages, date missing, location. We'll send it to Cordell to see if it matches any known Darkblood activities that other Guardians are aware of."

After compiling the list, she went back to working on her post about their visit to the Devil's Backbone. The pictures were good and the account was decent enough, but she couldn't seem to shake the feeling that it was all for nothing. She sighed, wishing she could exhale her frustrations in one big breath.

"How's the article coming along? I'll be interested to read it. The place looked like an overgrown forest to me and not the mouth to hell."

"Yeah, well, that's what an urban legend is. Could be real. Could be fake. But either way it's supposed to be interesting."

"I get the sense that you don't think it is."

"No, it's not that. I'm pretty sure my readers will be interested."

"What, then? Is the computer not working out? I can ask if Cordell can configure things differently." A blue lock of hair slipped forward into his eyes.

"The computer and everything are great," she said, turning back to the screen. "Much better than my old laptop, actually. No, as I wrote this post, I kept thinking that I know what happened to this boy and where it happened, but there's nothing I can do about it. I just don't like feeling so helpless."

"You said yesterday that your blog was much more than finding answers. It's entertaining, it's—"

"But it's not right to be entertained when a boy has died. I don't want to be an ambulance chaser, Jackson. I don't want to capitalize on someone's misfortune. That's not what this is all about."

"You're hardly an ambulance chaser, Arianna. Blake

would not have had a voice if it hadn't been for your blog. Just like you, no one believed him until he found Paranormalish. Now, at least he knows he's not crazy."

"Maybe so, but Darkbloods are out there preying on people, and there's nothing I can do about it."

"Listen. After yesterday, I've thought a lot about your blog and what it means to you and your readers. I do believe you provide a valuable service. What do you call what you just noticed with those missing people?"

She shrugged it off. "It's nothing that someone reading the news wouldn't be able to figure out."

"Maybe not, but Guardians can't be everywhere at once. In fact, up here in the Seattle field office, our agents are spread thin. Darkbloods have been fairly quiet lately, but I have a feeling it's because they're regrouping, rebuilding their power base after the Night of Wilding debacle."

He leaned back and clasped his fingers behind his head. "We caught a lot of the underlings and a blood assassin, but the mastermind eluded capture. Word on the street is that even though the party was broken up before it got started, the Alliance brass is very interested in the concept. Guardians in all the North American field offices are keeping their eyes open for any similar activities starting up in their areas. If your blog can help alert us to potential problems, well, then, I'd say it's providing a pretty damn good service."

CHAPTER EIGHTEEN

"WHERE THE HELL have you been?" Carter barked through the phone. "I've left you dozens of voice-mail messages."

Stunned, Arianna left the media room where the girls were playing video games and leaned against the wall in the hallway. She'd never heard him like this before. Something must be wrong at work, but then, with Xtark, everything was an emergency. Employees weren't expected to have private lives. It was just odd that Carter seemed to be caught up in it. He wasn't what you'd call a corporate shill. "Yeah, well, I lost my phone, remember?"

"I know you're taking vacation, but I need you to come into the office and take a look at the new configuration we're considering for the user forums. One of the VPs in your department is on my ass to get this out by Monday and I didn't want to make any drastic changes without running them past you."

Me? When had anyone ever asked for her input? In addition to doing graphics in the ad department, she merely helped out with the forums. Xtark made changes and she was one of the people who made sure everything kept running smoothly from the user side. But they'd never consulted her first. They just did shit and expected her to make it work.

"I'm on vacation right now. Why don't you talk to Steve or Candy?"

"But you're still around, right?"

Had she told him she was in the area? "Um, yeah."

"It shouldn't take very long. And you can bring Krystal in, too. We're play-testing the new version and want feedback from a variety of gamers. Our in-house testers can't find all the bugs that actual users uncover. We've got groups coming in every night this week."

"I'm not sure she's ever played the game before. Besides, it's kind of gory and violent."

"That's okay. We need feedback from all levels. Beginners to advanced players. We're picking people up in limos and ordering pizza."

She knew they had beta-testing parties, but she'd never heard that they picked people up in limos. Guess Xtark could be nice when they wanted something from you.

"I'm…ah…probably not going to be here much longer," he said. "I'll be taking a medical leave of absence soon and I need to get this stuff taken care of before I go."

She felt suddenly guilty for missing all his calls even though there wasn't much she could've done about it.

Carter's last doctor's appointment must not have gone well. "I'm so sorry to hear that."

"Yeah, well, that's life. I can get Krystal on the list. Can I send someone by your place and pick you up? That is, if you're home."

"I'm staying with some friends right now because my house got broken into. I'm probably going to be moving and I'm not sure how much longer Krystal will be with me, but I'll think about it and get back to you."

She could hear him breathing on the other end of the line. "She'd really— Okay, let me know ASAP."

The call ended. She stared at the phone for a moment before tucking it into the back pocket of her jeans. He was so caught up in his own problems that it failed to register with him that other people had problems, too.

But if what Jackson had told her was right, there was no way in hell she was bringing Krystal into the Xtark offices. She'd go in alone.

JACKSON FELT AS IF HIS HEAD was going to split open. First that crap at the field office, now this.

"Absolutely not. It's too dangerous."

He strode to the closet, where he tossed his leather coat aside and peeled off all his gear, stowing his guns and knives away. Not one to forget any little detail, Alfonso had built a weapons locker in each room, complete with padlock, black-felt lining and an ornate carving on the lid of a warrior riding into battle on a warhorse. Zoe loved horses, which was why Alfonso was always carving them.

"I'm not sure how long he's going to keep working," Arianna called from the bedroom. He could hear her plunking away on the keyboard. "If I don't go soon, I don't know when I'll see him again. It doesn't sound like he's doing very well."

"Taking Krystal there is like throwing a guinea

pig into a pit of pythons. Have I mentioned how much snakes love guinea pigs? One strike and it's all over."

He'd explained to Arianna before that Guardians had been investigating Xtark for months, suspecting the company of trying to attract law-abiding vampires over to the dark side using Hollow Grave as an enticement, as a sort of gateway back to their violent past.

"Who knows if vampires, even Darkbloods, will be there? I won't allow you to take that risk."

There was a knock at the partially opened door. Lily and Alfonso walked in.

"We came to see if you wanted to come downstairs and make homemade pizzas. It's a Friday-night tradition when I come home after my ten-day shift at the field office." Lily's eyes narrowed. "But if you're busy…"

"Who's going to take a risk?" asked Alfonso skeptically.

Jackson told them of Arianna's plan.

Lily confirmed what they suspected about Xtark. "We don't know exactly the involvement Darkbloods play in the company. All we know is that they're involved somehow."

"Okay…" Arianna sighed. "Thank God I never brought Krystal to the office before. I can leave her here for the evening. That is, if you two don't mind."

"Of course," Alfonso said. "She and Zoe have become quite close. I've hardly seen my daughter since you came."

"I don't like the idea of you going there, either," Jackson said.

"Jackson is right." Alfonso adjusted the tool belt hanging from his hips. "When I worked undercover within the Alliance, I heard they were using the game somehow, but I was never privy to any of those details. You could be walking into a den of Darkbloods for all we know."

As far as she was concerned, they were getting too worked up about this. "I work there. I'm in the offices all the time. If I were in danger, something would've happened to me a long time ago. My friend needs me to look over one of the last projects he's in charge of before he takes a medical leave of absence. Since I'm not sure when I'll be back, if ever, it's the least I can do. He's—he's done a lot for me. Lily, help me out here."

"I think you're doing pretty well on your own."

"What do you mean *if ever?*" It had such a final ring to it.

"We can't stay here forever, Jackson. And the city isn't safe for Krystal. You said so yourself. I've been thinking a lot about it. Her mom's getting out of rehab soon and I might just move nearby to keep an eye on them. Oh, I know you're planning to take away my memories of all this, but I'd ask that I keep my desire to be diligent about Krystal's safety and to keep her away from the big cities. Oh, and we both need to be taking self-defense courses. You know, the kind when you learn how to really kick someone's ass. Oh, and while you're at it, can you suggest that I lay off the whole-milk lattes. I really should switch to skinny ones, but I can't seem to make myself. And running. I've never liked it, but I wish I did."

Lily burst out laughing and Alfonso coughed to avoid doing the same. Jackson glared at both of them.

Arianna continued. "I know you can implant suggestions. That's all I'm asking."

"But what about your job?" He couldn't believe he was protesting the move. He should be happy. Or at least relieved.

"I disliked Xtark before, but knowing what I do now, I can't work there anymore."

It felt as if someone had kicked him right in the gut, sucking all the air out of his lungs. This was the first time *she'd* talked about leaving. It wasn't supposed to go like this. *He* was always the one who left in a relationship. Either that or he did something to make it happen—like sleep with someone else then let himself get caught. That would've been on his terms. This wasn't.

He didn't like not having the upper hand. Not one bit.

Before he could think of anything to say, Lily walked past him, giving him a let-me-handle-this pat on the back. She knew that he always sabotaged his relationships and that, for the first time, things were going sour without his doing. They'd been friends for a long time and she knew him well.

"Then you won't go alone," Lily said. "We'll send someone with you."

Jackson shot her a daggerlike glance. What the fuck was she talking about? She was supposed to be on his side, his wingman, but she was actually agreeing with Arianna and not him.

"Alfonso?" Jackson looked to the man for support, but the guy just shrugged his shoulders. Once Lily had an idea in her head, it was hard to change her mind.

The three of them were talking, but Jackson wasn't listening. They were supposed to keep Arianna out of their world, not bring her in as a willing participant.

"Oh, my God," Arianna said, responding to something Lily had said. "Of course I'll help you out. Just tell me what you want me to do."

CHAPTER NINETEEN

ARIANNA, JACKSON AND LILY left for Seattle at nightfall, while Alfonso stayed with the girls. Having worked undercover with Darkbloods for so long, too many people on the inside knew him. Plus, Arianna got the sense that he enjoyed not being involved with the Agency, focusing his attention on the house and playing daddy. Lily had told her that he was trying to make up for lost time with Zoe and that he tried not to leave her if he didn't have to.

Thanks to Lily's insane driving and her trusty radar detector that alerted them to a couple of speed traps, they arrived in the city before it was fully dark.

Because she was considered an unauthorized human and couldn't know the location of the field office, Arianna was blindfolded for the latter part of the trip—never mind that her memories would be wiped later, anyway. She hung on to Jackson's arm as he led her through what seemed like a parking garage into an elevator that, if she wasn't mistaken, was going down rather than up. Then they went through several security checkpoints, three sets of doors, and walked down what felt like miles of corridors before they finally arrived at their destination.

"Okay, you can take that off now," Jackson said.

They were standing in a state-of-the-art computer lab. A bank of televisions were mounted on one wall and tuned into the various cable news outlets, though one, she noted, was freeze-framed on her favorite soap. There were several workstations along the perimeter, a wet bar, a conference table with chairs and two leather couches. In the center of it all was a multitiered desk with three large curved monitors and several people crowded around.

Jackson began the introductions. "Arianna, this is Dom, the field office team leader."

"And Alfonso's brother," Lily piped in.

Except for his hair, which was dark and pulled back into a ponytail, it was clear that Dom was related to Alfonso. He had the same crystal-blue eyes and intense, take-no-shit stare. She shook his hand, half expecting to feel that same charge of energy she felt with Jackson, but it was just a regular handshake.

"Very nice to meet you," Dom said in a slightly accented voice. "We really appreciate your helping us out."

"Well, we'll see how much help I can give you."

"Jackson tells me you've had quite the scare with Darkbloods."

"Uh, yeah, we have."

"Well, I hope he's been taking good care of you in the aftermath."

She chewed the inside of her lip, wondering just how much Jackson had told his team leader about their relationship. "Yes. Very."

Jackson was trying not to smile as he continued his

introductions. "This is Cordell, our resident computer genius."

The man behind the keyboard smiled. "I don't know about that, but I try." He was NBA tall, with long arms and legs that dwarfed the office chair he was sitting in. He unfolded himself like a praying mantis and stood up to shake her hand. Again, no zing, just a regular handshake.

"And this is my partner, Mitch. Not my *partner* partner, but my partner in crime."

Mitch laughed. She turned to a guy with messy blond hair and golden skin. He looked like a surfer, fresh from the beach, not a vampire warrior with guns and knives likely strapped beneath his clothes.

She caught him darting a knowing glance at Jackson. So this was who Jackson partied with at the clubs. These two had to make quite the pair when they went out carousing. She had to imagine that neither man ever failed to get lucky.

She had to force herself not to ball her hands into fists when she thought about Jackson getting it on with random women. Although she had no claim to him, she stepped closer anyway and placed a possessive hand on his snake tattoo. If having a lot of sex helped stave off the cravings, well, then, she'd see to it that he got what he needed. From her. He would not be doing it with some bimbo at a club.

"Yeah, thanks for the clarification," Mitch said. "Don't want Arianna thinking you'll be slipping into my room later to cuddle." He made quote marks with his fingers.

"Only in your dreams, stud," Jackson countered.

"Cordell," Dom said, "tell Arianna what you need and we'll come up with a course of action."

"Sure," the guy said, clearing his throat. "Since Mitch here is the only one who's played Hollow Grave who wouldn't be recognized by potential Darkbloods who may be there, he'll be the one going in with you."

"Whoa, whoa, whoa," Jackson said, holding up both hands. "What the hell are you talking about?"

Dom crossed his arms. "Except for Kip, he's the newest guy in the office, which means he has the least chance of having Darkbloods recognize him. You'll still be going. You just won't be going in with her."

"Fuuuck."

"It's okay," Arianna said. "Let's hear the rest of the plan. It's not like I've never been in to the office before."

From the top of his desk, Cordell held up a small black device that she'd assumed was his cell phone. "This is a portable hard drive. Mitch will need to get access to one of the game designer's workstations. It doesn't matter which one as all of them should have access to the downloadable content."

He went on to explain that the Agency no longer felt that Darkbloods were using the forums to communicate with the vampires they were trying to reach.

She was confused. "The forums? But I'm one of the moderators. How is it possible for that stuff to happen and I'm not in on it?"

"Maybe you don't have access to the whole thing. Just the parts they want you to see."

She thought about the huge forum. They'd put her in charge of the Watercooler, the section where gamers chatted about nongaming topics like movies, TV shows, books. Pretty much everything, though they drew the line at politics and religion. She'd never ventured into any of the other threads. "Well, it would be like Xtark to do something like that."

"How long have you been moderating the forums?"

"Six or eight weeks now."

Cordell leaned back in his chair. "That could explain why you didn't notice anything strange. After the Night of Wilding party, they figured out we were onto them, because we haven't seen a lot of chatter since then. We've been trolling the forums, but haven't noticed anything suspicious for a while."

"Maybe they stopped using the game," she said.

"That's possible, but we doubt it. It was working well for them since many of their target market—young vampire males—are fans of the game."

"If it's not through the forums, then how are they communicating with them now?" she asked.

Cordell's fingers flew over his keyboard. "For the past few months, we've noticed they've had a lot of downloadable content available on their website each week. Most software companies make DLC available every few months. Game add-ons, patches, fixes, little updates that they do in between new versions. But we noticed that Xtark is doing this every week. We think they're hiding codes or phone numbers or locations in part of the game and that they're communicating it each week with these patches. As long as you know what to look for, you'll find what it is that they're trying to tell you."

She glanced at Jackson. Both his and Dom's eyes looked glazed over from all these technical details. She was following what Cordell was saying, but barely.

"You mean, as you're playing the game, you'd do something like rattle the door handle, kill the third zombie first, open the nightstand drawer and you'd find out who's selling what blood where. Why don't you just have someone play the game and figure out these tricks?"

"Well, for one," Dom said, "we don't have the manpower to devote to having someone play the game 24/7."

Cordell pulled up Xtark's URL on his screen and pointed to the New This Week tab. "See? They're releasing this stuff piece by piece on a need-to-know basis or just to tease and create anticipation. We want to know what they're planning up front, not just follow along week by week."

"If we wait, it could be too late to do anything. We fear they're cooking up something big," Dom said. "We just don't know what it is yet."

"So what will I do besides get Mitch in as a playtester?" Arianna asked. "I work in the graphics department, designing print ads. I don't have access to any of the programs."

Cordell swiveled his chair to face her. "We've got a few ideas. Is there anyone in the office that you know doesn't lock up their computer every time they walk away?"

"You mean, like one of the programmers?"

"Yeah, someone who has access to game content."

She went through the list of people in her head. "Well, the guy in charge of the play-testers, Tony, is probably the worst offender. One time he left his station and someone accessed his computer. They sent an email from him that went out to all employees saying that he liked to wear My Little Pony underpants. I remember being shocked that Xtark didn't fire him, but he's one of the best game designers and they evidently looked the other way."

Lily barked out a laugh. "Either that or he's the guy who's behind it all and doesn't feel he has to follow the rules like the rest of the employees do."

Tony? A vampire? "Wow, I hadn't thought of that." On the surface, the guy seemed nice enough, but who was to say what was really under that smile? There could be fangs.

A sudden thought hit her. If they were able to blend into human society and wipe memories, could someone have taken her blood before and she just didn't remember it happening? She rubbed her neck, recalling how Jackson had taken hers. It had been so…amazing with him…sexy. But he'd told her it wasn't always like that. The act of taking blood from a human host, instead of a vial, happened quickly and wasn't often sexual in nature. Could someone at Xtark have done that to her? The thought made her queasy.

But then, Tony seemed so…normal. She glanced around at the vampires surrounding her and she realized that they did, too. How many other vampires had she encountered on a day-to-day basis? They ate food, drove cars, had families, jobs. Although Jackson had told her that their population was just a fraction of the human population, it was possible that she'd seen or talked to other vampires before but just had no idea who they really were.

"No. Wait," she said. "He couldn't be a vampire. While we do have a number of people who work at night, he's one of the ones who comes in during the day."

"Unless he's a changeling," Jackson said. "They're not as susceptible to UV light as born vampires."

"True," said Cordell, flashing a knowing smile. "I can vouch for that. Sunlight does bother me, but it's not nearly as debilitating as it is for these guys."

She'd started to pencil a diagram of Xtark's office layout when the door to the computer lab opened. A black-haired man walked in carrying a large platter of food.

"Thought you all might be hungry," he said.

Guardians wasted no time crowding around him like kids to the ice-cream man. Although she wouldn't consider him small, maybe five-ten or five-eleven, the men dwarfed him. Was he human?

"Xi, you're the man." Jackson grabbed a few sandwich halves. "How did you know I was starving?"

"When are you *not* hungry?" The man went out into the hallway and returned a moment later with another tray.

"Arianna, this is Xian, our office manager," Jackson said. "He's the one who holds everything together around here for Dom."

"I try," Xian said. "Some days are easier than others."

"Like making peanut butter and honey sandwiches." Jackson held up the one he'd just taken a bite from. "What could be easier than that?"

Lily pointed with a piece of celery to Arianna's diagram, refocusing them on the task at hand. "Are you sure this Tony fellow still leaves his station unattended? Maybe it was a one-time thing."

Arianna stood apart from the others, watching the men troll for food. Jackson had already inhaled one sandwich and was reaching for a frosted brownie. He met her glance, wordlessly asking if she wanted one. She shook her head. When she was nervous, she always had a hard time eating.

She turned back to Lily. "From what I can recall, he rarely logs out when he's still in the building. With the beta-testing going on for the next two weeks, chances are, at some point during that time he'll leave his desk and won't log out."

"Okay, that's perfect." Cordell wiped his mouth with a napkin. "Keep working on that diagram. Mitch, here's what you're going to need to do."

"Why Mitch?" Jackson growled. "I play Hollow Grave, too. I'm not comfortable sending Arianna in without me. No offense," he said to his partner.

"None taken."

Lily bit into her celery. "We need finesse, Jacks, not muscle."

His expression darkened and Arianna saw that a tiny

muscle in his jaw was ticking. He drained his beer and spent an inordinately long time lining it up on the table with the other empties.

Normally a fun-loving charmer with an easy laugh, Jackson seemed to withdraw just a little as he sat down. He didn't check anyone's reactions to see how others were receiving this, nor did he challenge Lily. Arianna got the distinct impression that he didn't like being written off as a weapon without a brain. How many times had he been marginalized like this? Pigeonholed for only one purpose. It probably wasn't the first time it had happened, otherwise he would've spoken up.

Lily didn't seem to notice. "Since that business last year when they were trying to find a tracker agent, both Kip and I are recognizable to them." She listed off a few other Guardians who, for various reasons, couldn't do it, either. "That only leaves Mitch."

Jackson's knuckles went white on the armrest.

"While I can understand your wanting to go in with her," Dom said to Jackson, "given the number of DB kills you have under your belt, they probably know you. Your reputation could hinder your ability to operate un-detected. Since Mitch is fairly new to the field office, even if there are other vampires around, they'll just think he's there to play the game. They won't recognize him as an agent."

Maybe Dom had seen Jackson's reaction as Arianna had. The Seattle field team leader was a good guy, she decided.

Dom eased back in his chair and she noticed a coiled whip affixed to his hip. Did all of them have favorite weapons? She knew Jackson's was that dragon blade with the curved handle. It looked ancient, the hilt burnished smooth. When she'd asked him about the weapon, he confirmed that it was centuries old, but that was all he said. She had a feeling there was more to the story.

Lily's was a butterfly blade that snapped open and closed with the flick of a wrist, much like a switchblade. It made a really cool *click-clacking* sound when she did it. Alfonso's was a set of small kunai throwing knives.

They all had their pet weapons. If she were a part of the group, what would hers be? she wondered. She didn't like guns, so that was out. The bullwhip thing wasn't her. She suddenly remembered a line from an old Don Knotts movie where he did a karate-chop move and said that his whole body was a weapon. Smiling to herself, she decided that maybe self-defense techniques were the way to go.

Jackson seemed to relax a little as Dom's explanation sank in, and yet his eyes remained ice-cold, unblinking.

"So help me God, Mitch, if something happens to her, I'm going to take you apart piece by piece and shove each one down your throat."

"Eat myself? Hmm. That could be interesting."

Before her brain had even registered that he'd moved, Jackson flew out of his chair and had Mitch in a choke hold. A chair toppled over and papers on the desk scattered everywhere.

"Jesus Christ," someone said.

Fangs inches from the guy's ear, he seethed, "This is not a fucking joke. You are dead, Stryker, dead, if anything happens to her." His arm muscles flexed around the guy's neck, making the snake tattoo grow bigger. He must've had it inked there precisely for that purpose, because it looked as menacing as hell.

"Easy there, big guy," Lily said, trying to calm him down, but it didn't seem to have much of an effect.

"Jackson," Dom said. "Let him go."

"Do you fucking hear me?" Jackson choked harder.

Mitch tried grabbing the arm crushing his esophagus, but it wasn't budging. Jackson was too strong.

"I'll be fine," Arianna said softly, though her heart was racing. "I'm in the office all the time. I know everyone. A lot of good people work there, and just like me, they have no idea that it's run by vampires." She rubbed her fingers over his snake tattoo and felt that little snap of electricity.

He relaxed his hold on Mitch, but he still didn't release him.

"You can wait for me out in the parking garage of my building," she added, encouraged that he seemed to be responding to her. "I'll give you a pass code so you can get in if I don't come out at the agreed-upon time."

He turned to her and she noted that the intense, I'm-gonna-kill-you expression had softened a little.

Something inside her stirred. Tiny gears seemed to click into place as her heart continued to pound. She'd never, ever had a man go to bat for her like this. Holy crap, it seriously looked like he was ready to kill for her. And not only that, it was amongst his colleagues who were intelligent, completely sober individuals whom he respected, not a drunk at a bar somewhere who decided to get a little touchy-feely. Or one of his Darkblood enemies.

She realized she'd been holding her breath, so she exhaled slowly. "I'll text you the whole time we're inside so that you know everything is going as scheduled. Would that help?"

He paused a moment and the whole room grew silent, everyone hanging on how he would respond. Then, with a grunt, he shoved Mitch aside, grabbed the chair that had tipped over and jerked it upright. Stabbing a finger in his partner's direction, he said, "That candy-ass dimple of yours might work on the ladies, but if you fail tomorrow night, I can guaran-damn-tee that you won't be smiling for long."

CHAPTER TWENTY

THE DOOR TO JACKSON'S quarters at the field office had hardly closed behind him when he felt Arianna's hands slipping up his arms.

"I'll be fine tomorrow night," she said. "I promise. I'm in the office several days a week, anyway. This is no different."

He pushed her arms away and headed toward the closet, ignoring the hurt expression on her face. Okay, so he should have pulled her close, buried his nose in her hair and told her how worried he was about her going into the office with this mission. Who knew what danger awaited her there? For all he knew, Xtark's employees might all be vampires. Sending Arianna in with this mission would be like throwing her into a den of wolves. And if they caught on to what she was doing...

He didn't want to feel protective of her. He didn't want to care so much. Given all his problems, a life with her would be impossible. Without her, all he'd have to worry about was himself and that sure as hell gave him plenty to keep him busy.

Besides, what did she see in him, anyway? He was a self-absorbed playboy with commitment issues and a helluva future ahead of him. Not really good boyfriend material.

He unstrapped his weapons and stowed them in the upright locker, not bothering to put them into their individual slots.

But she seemed to *get* him. Truly understand what made him tick and what kind of person he was on the inside. And he wasn't used to it. Not at all. He was used to the admiration because of his sexual exploits, his crazy antics, but not...*this*.

He stripped off his shirt and jeans and tossed them in the corner of the closet then changed into black shorts, a black muscle T-shirt and a pair of running shoes. He'd log some time on the treadmill before he had to go out tonight. He wasn't on duty, but it had been too long since he'd taken blood and energies from someone other than Arianna. His needs were razor thin and would only get worse if he didn't do something about it now.

Maybe that was the problem. Her blood had muddled his mind. Made it so that he wasn't thinking clearly. He needed a new infusion. Something different. Change things up.

From inside the walk-in closet, he could hear her rustling around in the bedroom, getting ready for bed. Her wake schedule wasn't nocturnal the way his was, so she was probably tired. She padded into the attached bathroom and he heard the water running.

Why didn't she try to follow him in here when he walked away from her? Tug on his arm. Protest. Coax him to change his mind.

Well, of course, fuckhead, you hurt her feelings. What did you expect?

But…but…he'd have thought she'd try to get him to warm up to her again. That's what his former girlfriends would've done.

"Aw, don't be mad at me, baby," they'd say. "Come to bed."

And it'd usually work. He'd let them drag him to bed and then they'd have make-up sex.

But Arianna didn't. She was…different. She seemed to operate on her own agenda—one that may or may not include him. He wasn't sure if he liked it or not, but the more he thought about it, he was pretty sure he didn't.

Fine. While she was occupied in the bathroom, he'd go ahead and slip out the door. He needed to be alone, anyway.

He grabbed a change of clothes so that he wouldn't have to come back when he finished his workout. Answering a bunch of questions about where he was going and when he'd be back wasn't his deal. He'd shower in the locker room, then leave from there.

Thankfully, the bathroom door was closed…well, partially closed. He could just see her leaning over the tub, probably testing the water. Was she already undressed?

He closed his eyes for a moment and breathed deeply, telling himself that he didn't need her. Didn't want her. He was simply going to walk out that door, get a quick workout in, then head to the Pink Salon.

As he walked across the room to leave, he made the mistake of darting a glance toward the bathroom again, hoping for a glimpse of a tight ass or maybe a breast.

But she wasn't naked. At least she wasn't, yet. She was sitting on the edge of the tub, wearing a shirt that hung to midthigh.

Shit. One of *his shirts.* One of his goddamn shirts was sliding itself over her skin.

From this angle, he couldn't see all of her, but what he could see was her leg stretched out as she leaned over the tub. Her toes, with their blue sparkly polish, gripped the tile floor for purchase. How had he not noticed before that she wore an ankle bracelet? It looked like it was made from braided hemp or some kind of cording, maybe with a bead or two. Was that a toe ring, as well?

He could feel himself growing hard. Without underwear, his erection easily tented the thin fabric of his shorts. He had the sudden urge to kiss his way down those shapely legs and nibble on her toes. Would she laugh and try to kick him away? Could he get them to curl with pleasure? Maybe if he reached underneath that shirt to the juncture of her thighs.

He recalled that little sound she made when he'd pushed into her last night. A cross between a moan and a gasp. It made him smile just thinking of it.

That simple sound had told him what a million words couldn't. He was doing things right and she liked what he was doing. As her body had tightened around him, squeezing, pulsing, urging him to join her, he'd reached around and touched where he went into her. Where he stopped and she started. Her silky heat coated his shaft a little more with each thrust he made until he could hardly stand it. The pressure inside him exploded into her and he was pretty sure it was his turn to make some noise. God, he'd even bitten her neck again.

The sound of rippling water and her faint exhale as she slipped into the tub jerked him back to the present. How easy would it be for him to walk in there right now, take off his clothes and join her? In minutes they could be doing what they'd done last night.

No. No. And no.

Succumbing to her charms would be a mistake. What was wrong with him? He shouldn't have to remind himself of all the reasons why Jackson plus Arianna equaled trouble. He lost control around her. He wasn't himself around her. He longed for a future with her that involved more than just a few nights. He wanted to wake up looking at her face tomorrow. Next year. Ten years. Fifty years. The kind of future that *did* involve painting bathrooms and mixing bank accounts. But that was delusional. Impossible. Reverts didn't have a future. So he might as well fucking forget about it.

The downtown clubs would be closing before too long and if he didn't replenish what he needed, he'd be in real trouble come tomorrow.

While he still held on to a shred of sanity and before he could change his mind, he stormed out the door and down to the gym, his change of clothes tucked under his arm. He hoped to God he didn't see anyone else down there. He didn't need their questions, spoken or not, when they realized he was heading to the clubs downtown while Arianna was tucked into his bed.

Good thing he had the reputation he did. Being considered an asshole jerk was much better than the suspicion of being a revert.

An hour later, after a ten-mile run logged on a treadmill and a quick shower, Jackson stopped in the field office's large kitchen to grab a sandwich for the road. Even if Xian wasn't around, he usually made up a few, knowing Jackson inhaled them at all hours.

"Where do you think you're going?"

Jackson spun around to see Dom coming through the door. His son, Miguel, was snuggled into his dad's shoulder with a thumb in his mouth. For a guy who could snap his *brindmal* around the neck of their enemy before anyone blinked, he sure was a natural holding his kid. A mighty warrior tamed by something so small and vulnerable. He had to admit, it was a damn cool contrast.

Dom knew he wasn't planning to play a wholesome game of hopscotch, but Jackson tried to sound innocent, anyway. "What do you mean?"

"I'm not an idiot. You're going out, aren't you?"

Jackson shrugged, stuffed a sandwich half into his mouth. "So what if I am?"

"If you do, you might as well kiss that gorgeous woman of yours goodbye."

"Who said I'm going out carousing?" As soon as he said it, he realized he hadn't protested the reference to Arianna being his woman.

That gorgeous woman of mine?

Mine?

He…he liked the sound of that.

"Let me repeat myself," Dom said. "I'm not an idiot.

With those urban-cowboy boots you have on and that hint of cologne, it looks to me like you're on your way to the Pink Salon. And that can only mean one thing."

Jackson reached into the refrigerator, grabbed the milk and took a swig out of the carton. "I can't get all my blood and energies from Arianna. My needs…" He had to be careful how he worded this. "Well, they're a little more than what I'm comfortable taking from her. She's too new to all this. And, for your information, these are not fake wannabe boots. They're the real deal." His Luccheses were so comfortable, he could sleep in them.

"So you're going to f—" Dom caught himself, shifting his son to his other arm. "Be with some stranger at the club? You think that's going to help?"

"Well, I…"

"Listen." He covered Miguel's tiny ears as if a kid that age understood what adults were saying. "Don't fuck things up with Arianna. Women like her come around once in a man's life. If you're worried about the fact that she's human, well, you don't have to look any further than Mackenzie and me."

Not that *that* was a relevant comparison any longer since Mackenzie was now a changeling. No, he hadn't dared to think that far ahead in their relationship because they had no future. What was the point in thinking about shit like that? You get your hopes up for nothing. Till reality kicks you in the teeth again, reminds you that you have no future and tells you to smarten up or you'll be sorry.

He could still hear the shrill tone of his mother's

voice. It'd been several months since his sister's death and he had just passed his Time of Change. After being out with his buddies one night, he'd come home to find a single suitcase sitting near the door.

"What's this?" he'd asked.

His mother stood in the kitchen, arms folded, no flicker of love in her eyes for her only son. Just cold, hard resignation. She looked old that day, he remembered. Much older than he'd ever seen her. But then sadness and disappointment tended to do that to a woman. "Your things."

His things? Were they kicking him out? Wide-eyed, he turned to his father for support. "Dad?"

He father wouldn't look up. Just kept cleaning that pipe of his. "You heard your mother, son."

"But I don't understand."

His mother flicked a dish towel over her shoulder and pointed at him with an accusatory finger. "You may be able to enjoy your life, Jackson. Go out with friends, carry on like nothing has happened, but we can't. We've done our duty as parents, and you're old enough to be on your own. That day you let your sister die was the day we stopped being a family. So go on. Get out of here. Go ruin someone else's life, now that you've ruined ours."

Usually he was pretty good about locking up those memories in a far-off compartment of his heart. He shouldn't have been thinking of them in the first place. Didn't do him a damn bit of good. He took another swig from the milk container and shoved those depressing thoughts from his head, focusing, instead, on the present…and the fact that he wasn't going to let himself have feelings for Arianna.

"I've seen how she looks at you and—"

"Yeah, yeah," Jackson interrupted. He didn't want to hear it. There was no way he was talking to Dom about why it could never work out between Arianna and him. Once the field team leader heard the word *revert,* things would be all over, and it'd be bye-bye-Jackson time.

"But more important," Dom continued, "I've noticed how you look at her. I've never seen you like this, Jacks." He kissed the top of his son's head and Jackson was struck by how easily Dom had taken to being a father. He held the boy as if he'd been doing it all his life rather than just the past few months.

"Sorry. Don't know what you're talking about."

Dom rolled his eyes. "You remind me of myself when I first met Mackenzie. Confused and unsure of the feelings you're having. Willing to rip someone's head off if you think they're either moving on your woman or not respecting her. I know I'm hard on you sometimes, but I do that because I expect more from you. I know what you're capable of handling and I know that I can count on you. Shit. You're one of the most loyal guys I've ever worked with. Unreliable sometimes? Yes. But I've never questioned your loyalty. That little redhead seems to know what makes you tick, inside and out, and I think that deep down, you know it, too. You're just too scared to admit it."

Scared? Dom had no fucking idea. "I am not." Damn. The only way he could sound more childish was if he'd said, *You're not the boss of me,* but then again, the guy was. He looked at the carton of milk in his hand and put it away.

"Oh, and before I forget, that list she sent us of those missing young people? Well, Cordell cross-referenced it and two of them were on our list of known sweetbloods. They were from that group we saved at the Night of Wilding party. I'd wager a bet that the others are Sangre Dulce, too." Dom often used the old-world term, having grown up in the Cantabrian Mountains in Spain.

"Four sweetblood humans missing at the same time? Are you thinking what I'm thinking?"

"Yep, Darkbloods are cooking up something. Lily and Kip are going out at nightfall to the Devil's Backbone to see if they can pick up the scent trail. If we can track their location, maybe we can save them."

"Arianna will be thrilled to know this."

"Yeah, so think about what you're getting ready to do. I get the sense that she's very different from most of the women you've been with. She's not going to take any kind of bull from you. Once you blow it with her, it'll be over. She'll see it in your eyes, smell it in your kiss, sense it in your touch, and she'll leave your sorry ass. If that's what your intention is—to get her to break things off with you—then don't let me stop you. But frankly, she doesn't deserve that. If it's blood and energies you're after, you can easily take it from a stranger in an alley. You don't need to be fucking around to get it."

"I'd appreciate it if you didn't teach our son to curse before he even says *mama.*"

Both men snapped their heads around to see Dom's wife, Mackenzie, entering the kitchen. She must've been working in her studio, because she wore an old shirt—probably one of Dom's—with rolled-up sleeves, her jeans were spattered with paint, and she had a smear of orange on her cheek. Evidently, Dom hadn't known she was there, either, because he had a guilty-as-hell look plastered to his mug. Miguel turned when he heard his mom's voice and broke into a toothless grin.

"Yeah, it's real funny, isn't it, mister?" she said to Miguel, smiling. "But your daddy has a potty mouth and Mommy isn't happy." She pointed a finger at Dom. "If he says the f-word before he says, 'Mama, Dada, I love you,' I'm going to kick your…behind."

Jackson started to laugh, until she added, "And that goes for you, too."

ARIANNA FELT JACKSON SLIDE into bed next to her but she stayed curled on her side, the down comforter pulled up to her neck. She was surprised that he'd rebuffed her when they got to the room after everything that had happened in the computer room with all the other Guardians. But this was his issue, she told herself. Not hers. He needed time and space to figure things out on his own. He didn't need her input.

But that didn't mean he hadn't hurt her feelings. He'd gone from fierce protector to stay-away-from-me in a matter of minutes. Determined not to cry with him around, a skill she'd learned when dealing with her father, she held it together until she heard the door close when he left. She allowed herself a few tears before she wiped them away and toughened up again.

After soaking in the tub until the water went tepid, she'd searched his bookshelf for something interesting to read. She'd found several epic fantasy novels mixed among the military nonfiction books, memoirs and the stacks of DVDs. Assuming the most dog-eared book had to be his favorite, she'd climbed into bed and read for almost an hour before she fell asleep, when she'd dreamed of realms, kingdoms and quests.

The sheets rustled and she felt his hot breath on the back of her neck. Was he going to kiss her? She smelled alcohol and the faint scent of sandalwood cologne. Had he gone out?

He lay there a minute, not saying or doing anything. She could almost hear the wheels in his head turning as he was trying to figure out what to do. Would he touch her as she so desperately wanted him to do or would he roll over and go to sleep? She kept her breathing regular and slow.

"I'm sorry." He whispered so softly that she had to strain to hear him. "I was an ass and…and you didn't deserve to be treated like that."

When she didn't respond, the bed shifted again as he rolled over. He must think she was sleeping.

"You matter to me, Arianna. So much. That's what scares me."

Then, so quietly that she almost wasn't sure it was him and not the whispers of a dream, he said, "I love you. Now, what the fuck am I going to do?"

CHAPTER TWENTY-ONE

THE XTARK OFFICES WERE ABUZZ with activity. Pizzas from one of Mitch's favorite restaurants sat on a long table in the center of the room. Coolers were filled with cans of soda and bottles of water. Bite-size candy bars were scattered on all the tables. From the napkins to the paper plates, notepads, pencils and key chains, everything was emblazoned with the Xtark logo.

A man with a broken leg hobbled up in front of the group of about twenty people and started talking. Pointing to the computer stations set up around the room, he explained that if tonight was the only time you could come in, that'd be fine. But if you could come every night for the next week to beta-test, that'd be even better. The goal was for them to try to break the game now, so that the code could be fixed before it became available to consumers for purchase. As the guy continued to talk, Mitch slanted a glance to Arianna. She dipped her chin slightly in response to his unanswered question. This was *the* Tony whose unsecured computer was the one Mitch was going to use.

After Tony finished explaining how things worked, he added, "And feel free to grab a Hollow Grave T-shirt either right now or on your way out when you leave."

As the other testers were helping themselves to the

food and picking out their shirts, Arianna motioned Mitch over to where she was standing with a tall, thin man.

"Carter, this is my friend Mitch," she said. "He's a friend I met at the gym. I knew he played Hollow Grave so I brought him along."

This was the guy who was taking a medical leave of absence? He'd obviously been an athletic man at one point in his life, so his condition must be difficult to accept. Mitch started to say, "It's a pleasure to meet you," but Carter just gave him a quick head-to-toe glance and kept talking.

"Where's your cousin? I thought you were bringing her in with you." He ignored Mitch's outstretched hand, so Mitch stuck it back in his pocket and his fingers closed around the hilt of his blade.

He didn't like the guy. Not one damn bit.

"She couldn't make it." Arianna waved to someone and strolled to the other side of the room.

Oh, sure, he had the sympathy vote, but he gave off an air that rubbed Mitch the wrong way. The faint look of desperation behind his eyes that said he'd be willing to do anything if the price was right. Like the suburban husband who embezzled money in order to keep his house from being foreclosed. These guys didn't intend to make bad decisions, but life got in the way and forced their hand.

Mitch had learned from experience to trust his gut instincts. When he ignored them, bad shit happened.

He did a quick scan of the room. No vampires… wait. There were two youthlings on the other side. Good thing Arianna hadn't brought her cousin in. Mitch gave them a quick nod of recognition and the look on their faces said they knew he was one of them. Vampires had been living among humans for centuries and the *look* was one they all were used to giving each other. It said, *Greetings, but keep your mouth shut.*

"I take it we're testing the game's multiplayer modes?" Mitch said, noting that most of the computers were clustered together in groups of two or four.

"They are, but you're not. You'll be playing in here." Carter pointed at a small room Mitch hadn't noticed before. It was outfitted with a video camera on a tripod and a two-way mirror.

"Our research people like to watch the reactions of those playing the game. We'd like to hook you up to a heart monitor, as well to assess your excitement level as you play."

Mitch thought about all the weapons he had hidden under his clothes and politely declined.

"You know, testers are brought in for specific reasons. You should be grateful you get to see the version early and do what we need you to do."

What an asshole. "Do you want me to leave, then?" he challenged.

Carter stared at him before pointing to an empty station. "Very well, then."

Remembering his promise not to let Arianna out of his sight, Mitch glanced over to where she stood, talking with one of the other employees. All the Xtark employees were wearing matching black T-shirts with the Xtark logo, except her. Were they required to wear such shirts all the time or was this something they did when they hosted these beta-testing parties?

He turned his attention back to Carter.

Mitch finally put his finger on what it was about this man that was strange. Despite his failing body, his eyes were bright with awareness. The kind of awareness that said he knew that Mitch was a vampire. But how was that possible? The guy was a human. The only thing he could think of was that when they'd first come in, the man had been talking to two security officials. Mitch hadn't looked closely enough at them, but it was possible they were vampires. Had they seen that Mitch was one of them and alerted Carter?

Maybe, maybe not. Most humans instinctively gave vampires a wide berth, but this guy didn't. It was as if he was used to being around members of the race.

In one of the classes Mitch once taught, a student had coined the term *vay-dar,* meaning vampire radar. Some humans had it, some humans didn't. This Carter dude certainly seemed to have it.

As he took his seat in front of the computer, he glanced at the video cameras mounted in all the corners. He'd have loved to have touched his wire and told Jackson about this interesting development, but he didn't dare do it now.

As soon as Carter left, Mitch hastily picked the first avatar on the screen and loaded the weapon. Arianna and Carter were now sitting down at one of the empty tables near the pizza. Tony was answering a question from the guy behind him.

So far, nothing out of the ordinary, but as soon as he

was able to take a break, he'd make an excuse to use the restroom.

Mitch turned back to the game. Oh, great. For an avatar, he'd accidentally selected some blonde chick with huge tits wearing a skimpy black catsuit and stiletto boots. This should be interesting.

Mitch had just made it to the second level when Tony came over.

"Got any questions so far?"

"No, but the graphics are awesome."

"Glad you like it." The man laughed. "I see you picked Sylvia."

"What?" He was distracted, looking at the two goons by the door who were definitely vampires escorting people to the bathrooms. They weren't Darkbloods in that they didn't have the same smell, but they weren't twin Goldilocks, either.

"She's one of my characters. I designed her."

Mitch nodded. "She's crazy hot. That's why I picked her."

Tony took it as a compliment and clapped him on the back before he left. Mitch played another level for good measure then headed to the pizza table. He had eaten half a slice, when he suddenly realized Arianna wasn't in the room. Had Carter taken her somewhere? He glanced around. Carter was gone, too.

One quick sniff of the air told him that she was nearby, he just couldn't see her. But he'd made the promise to Jackson, so he set off after her only to be stopped by one of the guards at the door.

"Sorry, no unauthorized personnel beyond this point."

"But my friend went that way."

"Like I said, no unauthorized personnel, which means, no guests."

Mitch turned around and texted Arianna. She instantly texted him back. She was heading to Carter's office and everything was fine. He asked her if she could distract the guard at the door so he could slip through.

Sure, she texted. I'll see what I can do.

Soon the guard was gone and Mitch easily slipped through the door.

ARIANNA TRIED TO BE PATIENT as she watched Carter shuffle the papers on his desk for the second time. Was he going to get to the point? She'd followed him into his office because he wanted to show her his ideas for the forums, but all he'd done was move a coffee mug to the other side of his keyboard, straighten a few files and wipe his monitor with a dust cloth.

"I thought you were bringing your niece, not your boyfriend."

"First of all, she's my cousin and second of all, he's not my boyfriend."

She'd already told him this twice. Was the guy preoccupied or what? When they'd first headed to his office, she'd noticed that he'd really slowed down since she'd last seen him. His limp was much more pronounced. And now that he was sitting in his desk chair, he didn't seem much more comfortable.

Maybe it was a good decision that he was taking a leave of absence now. He appeared to be having a hard time concentrating and remembering even the most basic details.

"Given the fact that he's male and under that age of thirty-five—" at least he appeared to be "—I'd think he'd be closer to the target demographic than my cousin."

Especially since he's a vampire.

"Yes, of course, you're absolutely right."

Carter spent the next few minutes going through his ideas about the forum, which didn't seem so monumentally different from what it was now and it certainly didn't warrant her coming in on her vacation, but whatever.

"Here," he said, thrusting a stack of papers into her hands. "These are my notes. You can review them and let me know what you think."

Just as she took them, an alarm sounded in the distance, as though it was coming from another floor in the building. She stiffened. It wasn't because of something Mitch did, was it?

As if in answer to her question, her phone vibrated. One look at the screen and a noose of panic squeezed around her insides. Her mouth went dry and she suddenly had to pee.

911.

Jackson's code for get the hell out of there.

"What now?" she said, trying to sound mildly irritated as she edged toward the door. "Did someone pull the fire alarm?" All she wanted to do was get out of the building before they found out she was involved. Were Darkbloods here? Did something happen to Mitch?

Carter pushed himself to his feet. "It's the security alarm, not the fire alarm. Someone went somewhere they shouldn't have."

Mitch. If they caught him, that meant they'd be coming for her.

"Probably one of the beta-testers," she said. "Don't bother getting up. I'll go check it out and let you know."

Making sure her employee badge was clearly visible on her belt loop but flipped to the nonpicture side, she strode as quickly as she could without running, past the security guard stationed near the elevators, and headed toward the stairs. Jackson had told her that in the event of an emergency she shouldn't take the elevator. The stairs took her straight to the parking garage, whereas the elevator dumped you in the lobby first. If she and Mitch got separated, she was not to wait for him. She was to get out of the building and let Guardians handle things.

But when she opened the door to the stairs, another shrill alarm sounded.

"Miss, you can't go down that way."

She heard shouting in the distance coming from the direction of the beta-testers then saw the security guys on the far side of the section of cubicle walls. They were pointing to her.

Like hell I can't.

She charged through the door and bounded down the stairs.

Ever since a friend had told her how much extra exercise you could get each day, she'd been taking the stairs. Those four thousand extra steps a day really added up. And she was about to add another five hundred. Nowadays, she rarely took the elevator, so it wasn't much of a stretch to do it now. She could easily do these sixteen stories in heels. In sneakers, it was a no-brainer.

With a hand on the railing, she took the steps three at a time, getting to each landing and spinning around the corner to take the next set of stairs. With her gaze focused on the next step in front of her, she ran at a blistering pace until three flights down, the steps seemed to blur together. She missed the next tread, slipped forward and would've fallen on her face if she didn't have her hand on the railing. One reason she always *walked* stairs, never *ran* them.

Damn. She'd have to slow down.

A door far above her slammed, the sound echoing ominously through the stairwell like the chop of a guillotine.

One, two, thud. Heavy footsteps touched one or two of the steps before they got to each landing.

Or maybe she wouldn't slow down. She picked up her pace again, trying to concentrate on the steps in front of her, but not too hard. That was when she always messed up.

The guy behind her was close enough that she heard him grunt when he hit that last landing. He couldn't be more than six or seven floors above her. Oh, God, she still had four more to go. She'd have to go faster and hope—

The metal door on the landing below her flew open. Even though she wanted to stop, her momentum kept propelling her downward.

What had Lily taught her to do if she was grabbed from the front? Hitchhiker thumbs to break away from a wrist hold? But what if he grabbed her by the upper arms or—

No one came through the yawning opening and the door slammed shut.

It was like when she was a kid and the front door would suddenly blow open. Her mother would laughingly say it was the ghost again. Of course, it was just because the door hadn't been closed tightly enough and the wind blew it open. However, in this case, it was an interior fire door, too heavy for the wind to impact. Had someone on the other side shoved it open then changed their mind?

The sound of footsteps above reminded her to keep going. Her pursuer was gaining on her. Not watching where she was going, she stumbled as she reached the landing.

Something that felt like a hand caught her elbow, steadying her.

"Keep going to the garage level. You'll see the Caddy." It was Jackson's voice, whispering on the wind, moving past her.

She craned her neck looking for him, but all she saw were stairs and concrete. "Where—where are you?"

"Go!" His voice was now coming from the landing half a flight up.

She spun around. Other than a fluorescent lightbulb flickering and buzzing, nothing was there.

Jackson couldn't be shadow-moving. Not only would she be able to see him, but there wasn't enough darkness in the stairwell for him to meld with the shadows, just harsh, industrial lighting. It was as if she was talking to the air. Or a ghost.

The footsteps of her pursuer were getting louder. She guessed he was only two floors above her now. Shit. He was practically there.

The metallic clang of a blade being withdrawn from its sheath cut through the atmosphere. She squinted, blinked, but still, she saw nothing. Not anywhere. This had to be a vampire trick she didn't know about.

"Give me one minute," his voice hissed. "If I don't come out by then, leave without me."

THE DARKBLOOD WHO'D been pursuing Arianna didn't know what killed him, even after Jackson stabbed him with the dragon blade and stood over his body for a moment to make sure he was charcoaling.

"Yep. You're toast."

Jackson's skin tingled with energy as he spun on his heel and continued running up to the sixteenth floor, where he shoved open the door. It banged on the wall behind it. No need for subtleties when no one could see you. Being invisible did have its perks.

How long can I sustain this?

Hopefully, long enough. He ran down the center aisles of cubicles. Papers fluttered on desktops and the leaves on a large palm waved as he sped past them.

He first noticed it with Lily in the field office, though he hadn't been sure. When he'd looked down at his hands, they were semitransparent, but she hadn't seen him. And when he had Mitch by the throat, it almost happened again. He felt the same strange sensation. He was pretty sure he would've gone see-through except Arianna's presence seemed to ground him in place, calm his spirit. The invisibility seemed to happen when he lost control. It had to be a reverting thing. Seeing Mitch's text that he'd been compromised made Jackson go ballistic.

It didn't take long for him to locate his partner. Two Darkbloods had him cuffed and were leading him to a bank of elevators. Would his invisibility last long enough to take these guys out? Glancing at his hands, he noticed his transparency seemed to be fading.

Shit. At least he still had the element of surprise. Would that be enough? Were there others lurking around?

The shorter one clicked his earpiece. "Yes, ma'am. I've got the intruder. Bringing him down now." Pause. "Yes, Karl should have her by now."

Arianna. Anger heated his veins again and he felt the energy zing along his skin.

Sorry to break it to you, dickwads, but Karl is a pile of ash in the stairwell.

A quick glance around revealed that no one was watching. The beta-testing must be going on in a different part of the floor.

He withdrew his blade and in seconds, the two DBs were charcoaling at his feet.

"What the fuck?" Mitch, though clearly exhausted from the silver around his wrists, looked around wildly.

"It's me. Jackson."

"But—"

"Shut it. I'm frickin' invisible." He grabbed the keys from one of the partially charcoaled bodies and quickly uncuffed his partner, taking care not to touch the silver. No telling what even the smallest energy drain would do to him in this state. "Did you download the data yet?"

Mitch's eyes went wide. "You're…an Unseen?"

"Yeah, can you fucking believe it? What about the hard drive?"

"They discovered me…right after I hooked it up to that guy's computer. The portable hard drive…is probably still there."

"Good," Jackson whispered. "Get out to the parking garage and take Arianna back to the field office. I'll meet up with you there."

"How is all this even possible?"

"Don't say anything about the Unseen thing, okay? I'll explain later."

CHAPTER TWENTY-TWO

LESS THAN AN HOUR LATER, with the hard drive in his pocket, Jackson entered the field office. Before coming here, he'd stopped off in Pioneer Square and took blood and energies from two random humans, but he still felt like a zombie, as if he hadn't slept in days. Turned out, being invisible was almost as big an energy drain as getting exposed to silver. He needed more blood, more energy, and he wanted to sleep for a year.

He hated trusting other people with a secret like this, but it wasn't as if he had much of a choice. He just hoped Mitch was true to his promise and wouldn't say anything for a while, giving him a chance to get his shit together and leave. Which meant saying goodbye to Arianna, as well. When he'd gotten back to the parking garage, he'd texted Arianna, who was already back at the field office. Safe.

At the security checkpoint, he deposited the last of his weapons into the portal and watched as the conveyor belt moved it along. Putting his arms up, he heard a low humming sound, then a swoosh of air.

"All clear," the guard said.

The fact that he'd somehow manifested the ancient ability to become invisible told him the reversion process was definitely under way. No more wondering if this shit was happening or wasn't. It was pretty god-damn obvious. It was rumored that the Old Ones had special abilities that today's vampires didn't have. Except for Alfonso, who'd recently discovered he had a few latent abilities, Jackson didn't know of anyone else. But Alfonso's situation was different. He'd spent much of his life inside the Alliance and had actually been addicted to Sweet. But he got that under control decades ago. Jackson was addicted to all blood and energies. Its hold on him never waned.

"Step forward and put your toes on that red line," the guard said.

He mindlessly did as he was told, noticing a box affixed to the wall in front of him. It hadn't been there the last time he went through security.

Ever since a member of the Alliance's elite assassination team, the Order of the Red Sword, breached the field-office perimeter, security around the place had quadrupled. A guard had been killed and Lily's old apartment in the attached residential tower had been compromised. But rather than abandon the field offices, which were centrally located in a forgotten part of Underground Seattle, they'd stepped up security to almost epic proportions. Even people who had a legitimate reason to be here had a hard time getting in.

"What's that?"

"It's a retinal scan," Tomas said from the guard's station on the other side of the bulletproof glass. "Lean in, put your forehead against the padding and look straight ahead without blinking."

Jackson did so, expecting to hear the sound of a buzzer letting him through the door. He waited. Waited.

"Um, there seems to be a problem."

The last sandwich Jackson ate turned to acid in his gut. "There is?"

Of course, the eyes. They must look different. It was how you could tell a vampire was controlled by his cravings. The pupils never retracted fully. And later on, after consuming only blood, the whites turned gray. He tried to remain calm. He still ate food, his whites were, well, white, but it was his damn pupils. They felt stretched even now. Or maybe his eyes looked different because of this invisibility thing.

"It seems we don't have a retina pattern on file for you yet, Mr. Foss. A memo went out last week to all agents about this. Sorry if you didn't get it."

He rarely read his email or checked voice mail—that was the problem. But he was only marginally relieved.

"It's one of the new security protocols we just implemented. When you get a chance, you'll need to stop by the clinic to get that taken care of, but for now, I'll go ahead and buzz you in. It doesn't officially go into effect until next week."

Voluntarily go to the clinic? He could guaran-damn-tee that wouldn't be happening.

The field office was hopping when he finally stepped through security and collected all his gear from the conveyor belt. Several Guardians had found a den of Darkbloods on the Eastside, another pair had been spotted inside one of the clubs trolling for victims, and now this business with Xtark.

"Nice work, man." Dom clamped him on the shoulder.

"I can't wait to see what's on this thing," Cordell said, taking the hard drive from him.

Jackson didn't stay for the unveiling. Instead, he went in search of Mitch, finding him at the juice bar in the gym. The guy was so predictable, it was pathetic. No doubt, he'd be drinking something green and nasty. When he pulled Mitch into a nearby conference room, he got a whiff of grass or hay from the paper cup in the guy's hand. Yep, the green healthy stuff. The only thing green Jackson put in his mouth was lettuce with ranch dressing, and even then, he had to force himself.

Jackson closed the door and turned around. "I really appreciate you burying this for a while."

"Dude, how'd you do it? It was epic how you came in and took those guys out. They had no idea what was happening. Something hits each of them, and they begin turning to ash. Freaked me out. I thought I was next in line to fry."

God, how he wished it was as cool as Mitch thought it was. "I wouldn't get your undies all in a knot. It means I'm reverting. That's why I've asked you to hold off making your report on TechTran until I'm gone."

"Reverting?" Mitch's gaze darted around the room. He suddenly looked uncomfortable. Yeah, everyone knew how serious that was. "How do you know?"

Jackson ran a hand through his hair when all he wanted to do was to pound a hole in the wall. "I've suspected it for some time now. The fact that I was able to make myself invisible proves my suspicions are correct. I'm losing control, Mitch. My blood and energy needs are insatiable and you know what that means."

"What are you going to do?"

Jackson shrugged. "What can I do? I've got to leave the Agency."

Mitch pinched the bridge of his nose. "You can't. I mean, what will the office do without you?" He was an academic functioning in the real world now. Sometimes what you wanted to have happen on paper didn't work in real-world situations. "But where will you go? What about Arianna? She's back in your room, waiting for you."

"For the first time in my life, I'm going to think of someone else for a change, rather than myself."

He strode to the wet bar and poured himself a shot of tequila. It burned going down, but he hardly noticed it. Then he poured himself another and tried to ignore his shaking hands.

He supposed that was what love was. Caring about someone else so much that you'd put their needs above yours. He'd been searching for love all his life, to be accepted for who he was and not judged by the failures of his youth, but now that he'd found it, he needed to let her go. Once the reversion process was complete, it wouldn't be safe for her to be around him. That was what happened to the young man he saw executed. Rumor had it that he not only drained his human girlfriend, but killed her sister, too. There'd been warning signs, but he'd ignored them.

"That's bullshit, Jackson. There's got to be something you can do."

"Yeah, a silver bullet to the brain is one option."

"I'm serious."

"Options are only available to non-Guardians. Think about it, Mitch. How many Guardians have you known who've reverted…and lived to talk about it?"

"I've never known any personally, but I've heard of a few."

"And what happened to them? Any of them in the rehab centers?"

"I assume so."

"No, it doesn't happen. A warrant goes out to bring in the individual. Those requests are handled by the local field office. That's you guys. You'd all be tasked with bringing me in. Then, at that point, a writ of execution is drawn up. Petitions, if any, are heard. Though why they bother with that formality is beyond me. I've never heard of the Council being swayed on the matter. Then the order is carried out swiftly and without mercy."

Now it was Mitch's turn to look like he was going to punch a wall. "But that's bullshit."

"It's life."

"So you're going away? Leaving the Agency? Leaving Arianna?"

"What choice do I have? Better that than risking her life." Mitch started to protest, but Jackson interrupted. "Tell me now, how many Darkbloods do you know who are on friendly terms with humans? They use them until their purpose runs out and at that point, they drain them. They don't care that they're killing. They don't care that their needs are ending someone's life. At least I know the cravings are coming and can do something now to prevent the unthinkable from happening. I appreciate that you're willing to hold off that report until I've had a chance to leave."

"Man, I'm really sorry, Jackson. If you ever need anything—"

He held up his hands and shook his head. "Yeah, right. You've done enough for me already. If they find out you aided a Guardian who had reverted, you'd be in hot water. No, my friend, once I leave, I won't be seeing you again."

Mitch exhaled slowly. "What will you do? Where will you go?"

He shrugged. The Guardians had been his family for so long that he had no place he could automatically turn to. After his parents threw him out all those years ago, he'd been on his own, making his own way in the world. "Hell if I know. I haven't gotten that far yet. I just want to get away from today. I'll worry about tomorrow when it comes."

When he got to his room, all the lights were out. He planned to slip in undetected, grab his things, then sleep on a couch somewhere.

He closed the door quietly. As he turned around to head to the closet, he heard a rustle of movement and all of a sudden Arianna was in his arms. Because the events of the night had depleted everything he had, he was so weak that he fell to his knees, then to the floor.

"Oh, my God, Jackson. What was that back there?" With her arms and legs caging him, she kissed his cheeks, his lips, his jaw, his eyelids, his hair. "I didn't know you could do that."

"I didn't, either." A growl rumbled deep in his chest. He wouldn't be able to contain himself much longer.

"But you want to know something? I knew you'd come, that I wouldn't be on my own. I knew in my heart that if I just kept moving, you'd be there. God, Jackson, you were totally amazing."

Forget these little pixie kisses, he needed to be inside her, claiming her. A sudden surge of strength rippled through him. His lips crushed hers as he unzipped his pants and rolled over on top. Shoving up her nightshirt—his shirt—to her waist, he saw that she didn't have panties on. Good. He'd have just ripped them off, anyway.

He shouldn't be here. He shouldn't be doing this. But considering that this might be the last night they'd be together, he told himself to shut the hell up.

She clutched at the shirt he wore, managing to rip it open, buttons flying everywhere. He started to unstrap his weapons, but she stopped him.

"Leave it," she said throatily, her fingers digging into his lower back, keeping him focused, and another growl left his throat.

Needing no more encouragement from her, the tip of his shaft easily found her center. Then, in one swift and commanding thrust, he took her as his own. Over and over, he pounded into her heat, leather squeaking, weapons clanging, until he was on the verge of exploding. Though she was small, hardly a wisp beneath him, everything about her made him feel powerful and invincible. Stronger than he'd ever been before. He could slay a million dragons, walk through a desert at noon, climb the tallest mountains, simply because she believed in him.

If she was hoping for slow and gentle, she wasn't getting it. The floor of his bedroom was for fucking and that was what this was.

Raw and demanding.

Domineering.

She'd even grabbed the leg of the bedpost to keep from sliding along the hardwood floor as he drove into her. She tasted like strawberries, smelled like lavender, and he wasn't going to stop until he'd had his fill.

JACKSON'S LOVEMAKING TONIGHT had been manic. Crazy wild, then calm and controlled.

On the floor, he'd been driven by something primitive that excited everything that was feminine inside her. Then later, in the bed, he'd been slower and gentler, as if he was holding back, trying not to let himself go. On the floor, there was no time for talking, but in the bed, he hadn't wanted to talk. Just put his fingers to her lips to silence her before he poised himself over her. He stared at her, the green of his eyes as dark as the inner forest, melancholy, searching, as he eased his body into hers. It was if he was memorizing every detail of this experience. Under other circumstances, she would've liked it, but she couldn't seem to shake the feeling that something was wrong. His tender kisses and long, slow movements made her ache deep inside.

Arianna trailed her fingers over his chest and belly,

tracing circles and figure eights and swirly patterns lightly with her nails. "You had no idea before tonight that you had the ability to go invisible?"

"No, not really."

"I know I said this before, but you were totally amazing back there. Seriously. A mere whisper on the wind. If you hadn't come along when you did, I don't want to know what could've happened."

He cursed under his breath.

"What?"

"We should've never gotten you involved. It was too fucking dangerous for you. It makes me pissed off to think that I actually allowed it."

"Allowed it?" She propped herself up on an elbow. "Jackson, I volunteered. I went into it knowing what the risks were. Darkbloods at Xtark are responsible for what happened to my cousin. I'm not sure if it's a few bad apples who have hijacked the game or if it's directed from the top, but I wanted to help you guys figure out what's going on. I know it's a Guardian's job to take them down, but this was my way to make sure that happened. It wasn't like I was being led into it without knowing what I was facing."

"You don't know what could've happened back there, but I do. I know what Darkbloods are capable of doing. Just because you've been told a thing doesn't give it the same impact as if you'd seen it actually happen. I have seen it. The broken bodies, tossed aside when they're done. The terrified looks on the faces of those we've been able to save. Krystal included. I've seen these things too many times to count. You haven't."

"You're wrong. I do know. Remember what happened to my mother?"

"Yes, but—"

"Shh. You got what you needed and I'm no worse for wear. That's the main thing. Although I can tell you, I'm going to see if Lily will train me some more. I saw her take down a Darkblood in the parking garage with an elbow to the windpipe. I was standing there, totally amazed when Mitch came through that door. I'm not into the whole guns and knives thing like you guys are, but if I could take a man to his knees with just a well-placed punch, I'd be thrilled."

"I'd say you've already mastered that skill."

She laughed, then changed the subject. "Have there been signs before this?"

"A few but I didn't think it was possible. That it was just my imagination."

"Why?"

"It's an ancient power that a few of our ancestors were rumored to have. They were called the Unseen."

There was a sadness behind his eyes that she didn't understand. "I'd think that'd be good, so why do I get the feeling that it's not?"

"The Unseen were always the most violent. They led small groups of vampires—'families,' they called themselves. They terrorized villages, killing off innocent people for the fun of it. There are historical records of this happening. Inns full of travelers—dead. Hamlets and little burgs—dead. They just weren't attributed to vampires. At least not most of the time."

"Like thrill killers?"

He hesitated, closed his eyes for a moment. "Yes."

She waited for him to continue, but he didn't. "So you worry that you'll become like them? Unable to control your cravings?"

"Yes." It came out as a half choke, half whisper.

It wasn't true. She'd never believe he was capable of something so heinous. This man had dedicated his life to saving people, not killing them.

"Well, I don't believe that for a minute." She grabbed his face and looked him right in the eye. "Not for one goddamn minute. Krystal's a sweetblood. You've had ample opportunity to let your cravings take over, but you didn't. Not when you came upon us that first day, not when you were hurt and not when we were staying up at Lily and Alfonso's. You've got more control over yourself than you think you do. Well…except for tonight on the floor. But then, that was hot. And I liked it. A lot."

He paused, his gaze focused on the ceiling. "But you're not me. You don't know what it's like to worry. Every minute of every day I struggle with it."

"In what way?"

"I've got off-the-chart energy and blood needs. It's gotten so bad that I need infusions daily."

"How do you know that's what you need?"

"If I don't get it, it's like there's a giant cork holding back all the rage and anger of a lifetime. I know it's going to explode someday soon. Tonight at Xtark was just the beginning of the end."

"Then why is it that this ability just manifested itself in you now? You've said it seems to happen when you're angry or stressed. I'd imagine that you've been stressed and angry a lot."

"The lack of energy brings it on. Ever heard of how dickwadish a guy can get when he's hungry? Multiply that by a thousand and give him the ability to kill you with a set of fangs and you'd be worried, too."

She kissed him, letting her hair slip from behind her shoulder, making a barrier between them and their surroundings. She looked into his face and saw only him. "Sorry, but despite what you say, I don't believe you're reverting, Jackson. I just don't." She caressed his lower lip with her thumb. "You're a passionate man with passionate needs, and now suddenly you have this amazing ability."

"But—"

"Shh. Let me talk. I'll tell you what I do know. You're a good man, Jackson. I know that I love you and that I'll do anything to keep you. If what you say is true, which I doubt, then we'll fight it together. It's as simple as that."

"But that's irresponsible, Arianna. Krystal is a sweetblood. It'll be too hard for me to resist her blood if I really am reverting. If you have to make a choice, your place is with her, not with me."

"Krystal will be moving back in with her mom soon. So when was the last time you took blood?"

He looked away. "Tonight. After the mess at Xtark. I went downtown and found a couple of guys heading to one of the clubs."

She wasn't sure what she thought about him taking blood from someone else. "Okay, fair enough. But turning invisible must take a lot of energy. That's not proof in and of itself. What about before that? How long had it been since you'd had both blood and energy?"

He thought about it for a moment. "Since we've been together, I've only had yours."

She couldn't begin to explain how relieved that made her feel. "I don't see that that's a problem. Except for that first time, you've only taken a sip or two from me. And in talking to both Lily and Mackenzie—"

"You met Dom's wife?"

"Yes, she's great. I love her."

"Oh, God, what kind of advice did you get from those two women?"

"Just that it's normal to take blood when you make love. It doesn't mean you're reverting."

CHAPTER TWENTY-THREE

ARIANNA PULLED INTO THE driveway of her house and shoved the Caddy into Park.

Please let my computer still be there.

She remembered Lily saying that it appeared nothing had been stolen when Darkbloods broke in, particularly because her computer sat, untouched, in her office.

She unlocked the front door and dashed down the hallway. It felt strange to be in her house after what had happened the last time she'd been here. How many Darkbloods had walked in these rooms after she'd gone into hiding with Krystal?

Two? Three? Ten? It made her skin crawl thinking about them here around all her things and she wished that the old myths about vampires needing to be invited into your home were true.

The laptop sat right where she'd left it, on top of her desk in the spare bedroom. Breathing a huge sigh of relief, she flipped it open and was soon accessing Paranormalish.

Jackson had been called in to a debriefing in the field office and had said he might be a while. If she wanted to head back up north to Krystal, he'd leave as soon as it got dark. After being escorted out by security so she wouldn't know the exact location of the offices, she stopped by a coffee shop to get a latte for the road. The line was long, so she'd absently checked her email on her phone. Having recently posted about the Devil's Backbone, she wanted to see if people had any new comments or if there were any new missing-person reports.

But the first message that popped up wasn't from someone commenting on either of those posts. It was George from OSPRA commenting on a blog from…

Wait. Today? She hadn't blogged today. Oh, God, she was getting a really bad feeling about this.

When she clicked through and saw the article, she nearly dropped her phone. One by one the pictures from the first vampire attack popped up in all their glory. The Jeep. The Darkbloods. Jackson.

How did this happen? The Agency had deleted this post. Cordell had hacked in—she was so pissed that people kept accessing her private shit—and the whole article was gone. And she certainly hadn't posted *this*.

She called Jackson in a panic, but it went straight to voice mail. What the hell was Lily's number or Cordell's? She was pretty sure she couldn't call information and be routed to the Agency's switchboard, she thought ruefully.

She tried deleting the post from her phone, but couldn't get into that part of the system.

Mobile app needs updating. Password not recognized. URL doesn't exist.

Frustrated and wanting to scream, she pounded her fist on the coffee bar, rattling the silverware and almost tipping over a carafe with half-and-half. A couple of the other people waiting in line looked at her as if she was nuts.

Yeah, she wanted to say. *Call me crazy, but I'm in love with a vampire and now everything's screwed.*

Instead, she mumbled, "Stupid phone," and left without getting her drink.

Thankfully, the traffic gods were with her, because in ten minutes, she was pulling into her driveway.

Sitting at her desk now, she pulled up the Paranormalish URL.

Come on. Come on. Please don't have a different password.

She didn't know what she'd do if OSPRA had changed her password. She typed it in and—thank God!—it worked.

Fingers flying over the keyboard, she quickly accessed the admin area of her blog. The first thing she saw was that this wasn't her original post. Back at the coffee shop, she'd been so freaked out that she hadn't noticed. Sure, these were her pictures, but it wasn't her deleted article. In fact, it was part two of the article she'd written that first night, but never published.

A chill settled over her bones. "That son of a bitch."

Someone—George or one of his cohorts—had hacked into her blog, saw this unpublished article sitting there and decided to post it for everyone to see.

She quickly deleted the post herself, but the damage had already been done.

Those were her words, her damning words. Soon Jackson and the rest of the Guardians at the Agency would know about this—if they didn't know already—

and assume she'd betrayed their trust. How would she ever be able to prove that she hadn't done this?

She could picture it now. *Sure, these are my words. These are my pictures. But, no, I didn't do this. You've got to believe me.*

Riiight. The evidence was clear. She was guilty as sin unless she could prove herself innocent.

Trust was a huge issue for Jackson. She'd promised not to say anything to anyone about him being one of the Unseen. If there was even an inkling of doubt on his part whether she'd keep that promise, he could never trust her enough to be with her. Although it was remote, any chance of her being able to stay with him to not have her memory wiped, would be gone. So for him to think she was capable of something like this would be disastrous.

Would the Guardians give her a chance to explain herself? Could she convince them that it wasn't her, that someone had hacked into her account? She'd have one shot to prove her innocence and if they didn't believe her, she had no doubt that they'd waste no time messing with her head. Jackson would be gone from her memories…and her future.

And without knowing about the dangers Krystal faced as a sweetblood in a world where vampires existed in secret around them, it would only be a matter of time until her cousin was dead. Just like Arianna's mom.

Her only hope for all their sakes would be to get definitive proof that she hadn't betrayed them before she saw Jackson again.

She sent him a quick text and then made a phone call. A few minutes later, with her laptop tucked under her arm, she was heading back out the door.

"ARIANNA WOULD NEVER DO something like this," Jackson said as he looked at the front page of Paranormalish. The byline was hers, the pictures were hers, and as he quickly scanned the article, he saw that the writing was hers.

He just couldn't believe that she'd betray him. Betray all of them. It was part two of the post she'd done when she originally witnessed him taking down the Darkbloods, complete with new photos that hadn't been posted originally.

"I don't know what to say," Cordell said, shaking his head. "It's all here in black and white."

"I know what it looks like, but I'm telling you, she wouldn't do something like this. Can you delete it?"

Cordell's fingers flew across the keys then paused. "Hmm. That's strange."

"What?"

"It's already been deleted. As in…six minutes ago."

Jackson pointed to one of the screens. The red-and-gray Paranormalish logo was right there along with the title of the article: *Vampire Wars? You Be the Judge, Part 2.* "I don't get it. What are we looking at if it's been deleted?"

"The webpage is saved in my computer's cache. But it's been deleted off the server. Well, technically. Nothing deleted online rarely ever disappears completely.

Did I tell you about the time when I was in charge of computer forensics for—"

"I'm sure it's fascinating, but can you tell me when the blog article was first posted? Is that even possible?"

"Ha. Is it possible?" Cordell said. "We've known each other for how long and you still doubt me?"

"I don't doubt you, I just—"

"Give me a minute. There isn't much I can't find out." Despite the man's large hands, his fingers were nimble and flying so fast that they were a blur over his keyboards. "That post went live just over an hour ago…"

Cordell kept talking, but Jackson wasn't listening. "It couldn't have been her then. She was with me."

"Sorry to burst your bubble, but she could've had it scheduled to post at any time. It would've been automatic."

And just like that, his hopes were in the toilet again. He thought about the last time they were together. She'd told him that she loved him and he remembered feeling that if he could only get these urges under control, he'd be the happiest man on earth. He had believed with her help, her encouragement, he may have had a chance to overcome what had been plaguing him for so long.

Either she was an amazing actress and he was a poor judge of character, or she didn't post that article.

He went through the scenarios in his head. Arianna might be a temptress, capable of getting him to do all sorts of things he'd never considered before. Until her, he'd felt he was a confirmed bachelor and had been happy with that. The effort it took to coddle relationships had seemed like a waste of energy, until she came into his life.

No, she wasn't an actress. Hell, she was a horrible liar. She'd gotten under his skin like no one else ever had been able to do before. He recalled the times he'd seen her interacting with Krystal and talking to Lily. She really cared about people. Even those from her blog. Arianna had shown such strength of character. She made him want to do the right thing, make the right decisions, which wasn't something he'd always had the urge to do… Until he met her. He'd struggled with his dark nature, but maybe he could get it under control if they had a lot of sex.

But one thing was for sure. He'd always trusted his gut when it came to people. Which meant she didn't make that post.

CHAPTER TWENTY-FOUR

THE DOOR TO CARTER'S APARTMENT was ajar. She gave a quick little knock and pushed it open.

"Hello," she called out.

"We're in here." It was a woman's voice, instead.

Carter hadn't told her he had guests. His mom? No. She remembered him saying once that his mother had passed away a few years ago from the same ailment he was suffering now. He'd taken care of her at the end and had seen how she'd suffered. Girlfriend? Neighbor?

She stepped through the doorway, walked down a short hallway and peered into the living room.

A woman with white-blond hair sat on a leather sofa. She smiled the kind of smile that didn't reach her eyes. Lips only, like she'd forgotten to tell the rest of her face. In her forties or early fifties, she looked a little too old to be Carter's girlfriend, though. One arm was stretched out comfortably on the seat back, her legs crossed. She wore a black pantsuit, four-inch black heels, and a dark blue blouse with ruffles around the neckline. Her throat, wrist and ears sparkled with blue crystals. Sapphires, maybe? The one in her necklace was a statement piece. Alone on a black cord, the gem was at least three inches in diameter. Two burly guys who looked surprisingly like bodyguards stood behind her with their arms crossed. Where in the hell was Carter?

"Uh, hi, I'm Arianna. I came to see—"

"Yes, I know who you are," the woman said impatiently with a wave of her hand.

This was awkward. She didn't look at all familiar. "You do?"

She paused to give the woman a chance to introduce herself, but she didn't. She just continued to stare with a strangely detached expression on her face. Interested and yet...not. Arianna felt as if the woman was examining her like an object that she was contemplating buying. An ominous feeling settled over her and the hairs on the back of her neck prickled.

Tamping down nervous laughter, she took an involuntary half step backward. "Is...ah...Carter here?"

Something passed between the two men and suddenly they were behind her. She'd have angled herself toward the door, but burly guy number one was right there. They'd moved so fast, they had to be vampires. But not the good ones. What had happened to Carter?

"Are you alone?" the woman said flatly.

She heard herself answering nervously. "I'm here to see Carter. I called a few minutes ago and he said to come over. We're friends. We work together. He's going to help me with my computer. But if now isn't a good time, I'll touch base with him another time."

"Isn't that lovely of him? Carter is such a helpful person, willing to do just about anything. No matter what the cost is to him. Wouldn't you agree?"

"Um, ah, yes. For sure." The woman was definitely

alluding to something. Problem was, Arianna had no idea what. She hated people who skirted around what they really wanted to say. This passive-aggressive stuff was for the birds. But then, she had a feeling she wouldn't like the straight truth, either.

"Carter, you were right," the woman called, looking past Arianna. "She came. Very well done. You can come out now."

Come out now? Like he's hiding or something?

Arianna's heart rate cranked up so high it had to be unhealthy. She could hear the blood pounding behind her eardrums. The room had a very strange, very uncomfortable vibe that made her skin crawl. She'd have backed away toward the door, but the bodyguards were two immovable pillars behind her.

A tiny noise. A shuffling sound from the kitchen. Slippers on a hardwood floor, maybe. Thank God. Carter.

She turned and what she saw shocked her. Even though she'd seen Carter less than twenty-four hours ago, his condition had clearly deteriorated a lot. His eyes were sullen and hollow, his skin was crepey and hung from his bones like loose fabric. Had they hurt him?

She started to ask what had happened but Carter interrupted her.

"Where's your cousin, Arianna?" he said, his voice higher pitched than normal. "The one you were supposed to bring with you to Xtark?"

Why would he care about Krystal? He hadn't even— Then it dawned on her. Everything suddenly became so clear that she almost gasped with the realization. She reached for her cell phone to call Jackson, but one of the men snatched it away.

Lily had told her about changelings, humans who'd been turned into vampires. Their physical ailments healed—Mackenzie being able to have children when she wasn't able to have them as a human, Cordell being able to walk again after spending years in a wheelchair.

Carter didn't want Krystal for himself, the woman did. He wanted the promise of a better life. And what better way to ensure that than to give the woman what she wanted?

Arianna darted a glance over at the woman on Carter's couch, looking for confirmation. The blonde smiled and that's when Arianna saw the tip of her fangs. Self-defense training would've come in real handy right about now. Hell, she'd even take a gun or a knife. Screw her aversion to weapons. She'd shoot these two goons and the woman in a heartbeat. As for Carter...

"How can you do this, Carter? Do you know who they are? Do you understand what they do to people?"

He put his hands up to his ears, not wanting to hear more. "Yes, I know. I know. But I've been waiting a long time to be changed. To trade this useless body in for a new version of myself. Others I met at Xtark told me they would, but Ventra is the first one whose promise seemed genuine, not just 'Oh, we'll do it someday.' I deliver Krystal and she makes me a changeling. Done deal."

She suddenly couldn't breathe, as if she'd been punched in the stomach.

Ventra stood and walked toward Arianna. "You won't give up your cousin even if it means you'll suffer or die if you don't?"

"I know what you are," Arianna said pointedly. "What you all are. And I know why you want Krystal, which is why I'm never telling you where she is."

Ventra darted a glance at Carter before turning her attention back to Arianna. "I thought humans had a higher self-preservation instinct than this. That when it came down to it, you'd care more about your own life than someone else's."

"That may be true for some, but not all of us."

Ventra narrowed her eyes. "Interesting."

Arianna got the sense that she really was fascinated by the concept. "When I was a child, I saw shadows come to life and take my mother. No one believed me. It was only recently that I learned those shadows had to have been Darkblood vampires who prey on humans. People like you took my mother, drained her blood and sold it on the vampire black market. There was nothing I could've done to stop them from taking her then, but there sure as hell is something I can do now. I will never, not in a million years, tell you how to get Krystal."

Ventra snapped her head up. "You saw vampires moving as shadows?"

"Yes," she said cautiously. She'd have thought Ventra would have continued to press her about Krystal.

The woman walked in a tight circle around her and she again felt as if she was an object being examined for possible purchase. Stopping in front of her, she grabbed Arianna's chin and looked directly into her eyes. Ventra's irises were completely black, her whites a dark gray. Although terrified, her instincts telling her to do whatever she could to get away, Arianna didn't drop her gaze. All she had now was her strength and her determination, and damn this woman if she thought she could strip those from her with just a look.

"A Dark Seer," Ventra said softly. "Is it even possible?"

"A what?"

"A human who can see vampires in shadow form." She turned Arianna's face from side to side. "I didn't know that it was more than just a story."

Arianna tried to jerk herself free, but the woman held her tight. There would definitely be bruises later if she lived long enough for there to be a later.

Jackson had never called it being a Dark Seer. What kind of story was she talking about? "What if I can see vampires in shadow form? Are you worried that you're not as undetectable to humans as you'd thought?"

Ventra laughed and the sapphires at her ears sparkled. "Hardly. I'm not worried at all. It's been said that one of our ancestors kept a Dark Seer as a blood slave. Believed it gave him special powers."

Her use of the word *it* in reference to a person was not lost on Arianna. "But I'm not a sweetblood."

Ventra gave her a pointed look. "Oh, believe me, I know you're not. If you were a sweetblood, I'd have very different plans for you." Then, almost to herself, she continued, "He kept her, without making her a changeling for he feared that the transformation process would modify the way her blood reacted with his.

When she died, he was distraught. He searched all of Europe, decimated whole villages and towns, looking for another just like her, but he never found one."

It sounded like one of those macabre nursery rhymes that romanticized death, killing, disease and torture.

Ventra continued, "It's said that all of us have a perfect blood match out there. A human whose blood will transform us into something even greater. But rarely, if ever, do we find it."

A perfect blood match. Could this be what she was to Jackson? Was it her blood fueling this ability of his to be Unseen and not because he was reverting? If what she was saying was true, there'd be no way Arianna's blood would do the same thing to Ventra as it did to Jackson. "What? Like a fated mate?"

Ventra laughed. "I'm not talking mating here." She brought Arianna's wrist up to her nose and sniffed. "Far from it. But you may have just bought yourself a little more time. I'm very much interested in finding out what a Dark Seer's blood will do to me." She straightened up but didn't release her hold. Instead, she squeezed it tighter and Arianna wondered how much more pressure she'd be able to withstand until the bone snapped. "Now, first things first. I have a collection of sweetbloods that needs to be completed. Text your Guardian boyfriend and tell him to bring Krystal to your house."

"Never." Remembering the helicopter thumbs self-defense technique Lily had taught her, she twisted her wrist and succeeded in yanking out of Ventra's grasp.

Before she could turn to make a run for the door, strong arms gripped her from behind. Bastards.

"Why did I think you'd say that?" The woman nodded her head. In a flash, one of the burly guys who'd grabbed Arianna's phone handed it over to Ventra.

Jesus. If she got out of this in one piece, she was *sooo* going to chain that phone to a belt loop or something.

Ventra sat down again, crossed her legs. "Oh, look here. Three missed calls. Want to bet that they're all from him?"

Okay. Think. If Ventra had Arianna talk to Jackson, what could she tell him about where she was? Could she say something in code? Could she mention Carter's name quickly enough before they took the phone from her? She didn't know where they planned to take her, that was the problem. Code or no code, she wouldn't be able to relay that information. She seriously doubted they were staying here much longer.

"Damn nails," Ventra said. "Sure makes texting a bitch."

Well, then that answered that. She wouldn't be talking to Jackson after all. "What are you telling him?" She hoped to God he wouldn't agree to a switch. If only she could warn him that Ventra had no plans to let Arianna go—with or without Krystal.

The woman kept hunting and pecking. "You'll find out soon enough."

Arianna glanced at Carter, who was sitting on a bar stool at the kitchen counter. He appeared to be ready to topple over. In another time or place, she would've felt badly for him, asked if there was something she could get to make him more comfortable, but now, she felt nothing for him, except contempt.

Ventra looked up from the phone. "There. Done." Turning to burly guy number one she said, "Elan, take a few of your people and go to Miss Wells's house. If this Guardian boyfriend of hers shows up but doesn't leave the girl, then you know what to do."

Elan took a gun from beneath his jacket, checked the chamber, then reholstered it. "Yes, ma'am."

Arianna closed her eyes and said a silent prayer. No doubt the bullets were silver.

THE ANGER IN JACKSON'S VEINS had reached the boiling point. If one person here at the field office even looked at him cross-eyed, he was likely to rip their head off. And to make matters worse, Santiago had showed up, unannounced. It was a good three-hour drive across the border from British Columbia. He couldn't have called at some point to let them know he was on his way down?

"What the fuck is going on around here?" The guy wasn't known for being subtle or diplomatic. "I'm hearing rumors you're seeing a human female who is immune to thought suggestions and now she's gone and done what?"

He closed his eyes and counted to ten, trying to keep his dark nature in check when all he wanted to do was sink his teeth into Santiago's neck and rip.

"Arianna isn't immune and she wouldn't betray us like this," he said, looking at Paranormalish pulled up on Cordell's screen. "She's long suspected that another organization has been hacking into her blog. She texted me that someone posted an article from her account. She'd forgotten it was saved in her archives until someone hacked in and published it."

"And you bought her phony story? Of course she's going to say that."

Fuck that Santiago was the region commander. Jackson took a menacing step forward before Dom cleared his throat in an obvious attempt to derail him. His field team leader gave him an imperceptible shake of the head.

"I'm inclined to side with Jackson on this," Dom said. "We've all gotten to know Arianna and I have a hard time believing she'd do this. There'd be no point to it. She has nothing to gain and everything to lose."

It meant a lot to Jackson to have his team leader stick up for Arianna like this.

"Hello? She's got a blog," Santiago said sarcastically as if they were all idiots in the Seattle field office. "And what do blogs need to survive? Readers. Need I remind you that some people thrive on shit like this?"

Dom looked pissed. "If it weren't for her, we wouldn't know how Darkbloods were planning to use Hollow Grave. As it turns out, they're embedding hidden messages in the game with instructions and directions to upcoming blood-rave parties. We're fairly certain that they don't know we have this information because just this morning, they uploaded more downloadable content to their website that matches what we stole from them with Arianna's help. This intel is invaluable and it's all because of her."

Santiago still looked skeptical. "Are you any closer to finding out who's masterminding things at Xtark?"

"Not yet, but we—"

"Hey, can you all come over here?" Cordell's fingers were click-clacking away on his keyboard. Images were popping up on all three of his big-ass monitors.

Jackson, Santiago and Dom gathered around his chair.

"I think Jackson and Dom might be right. Check this out." He pointed to a bunch of code on his screen.

It made no sense to Jackson. He glanced at Dom and Santiago. They had on their game faces, but he'd be willing to bet they were as clueless as he was.

"From what I can tell," Cordell was saying, "it does appear that someone hacked into her blog and posted the article."

"How can you be so sure that she didn't do it herself?" Santiago snapped.

"Well, look. Because of the different IP addresses here and here." He pointed to two strings of numbers. "Except for the post she did from our servers—the one about the missing people from which I've been cross-checking names—this latest one came from a different address than all the rest. It's a static IP address, which means—"

Dom held up his hand. "Layman's terms, okay?"

"Basically, it means that unless she made this one post using a network she's never used before, it wasn't her. I'm guessing someone else got access to her account."

Jackson's phone vibrated. A text from Arianna. Good. She could explain what the hell was going on.

Can you bring Crystal to my house? Plan to visit her mother tomorrow.

He read the message twice to make sure he was seeing it correctly. What the hell happened to Krystal with a *K?* He tried calling her back but it went straight to voice mail.

A dull roar filled his ears, blocking out what everyone around him was saying. Arianna would never spell Krystal's name like that. Was this a sign from her that something was wrong? He recalled seeing an old photo from the cold war, where a hostage subtly held up his middle finger to indicate he was being held against his will.

Was this Arianna's way of saying she was in trouble? Or was this message meant to look like it was coming from her? Either way, something was wrong.

Where the hell was she? He glanced at the time. She should've been halfway to Lily and Alfonso's house by now. Had she gotten into trouble on the way or had it happened before she left the city? All sorts of scenarios flashed through his mind, none of them good ones. Santiago was saying something to him. It was like the guy's lips were moving but no sound was coming out.

"Where's Lily?" With her tracking skills, she'd be able to find Arianna faster than Jackson could.

"She went into the locker room a few minutes ago," Dom said. "Why? What's wrong?"

"Arianna's in trouble."

It took him less than a minute until he was storming through the doors of the women's locker room, unannounced. Past the towel station, past a row of lockers where a few of the female agents gasped, and straight to the back where the showers were located. Lily was leaning toward the mirror, her hair in a towel, a pair of tweezers in her hand.

"What the hell are you doing here?" she said, turning to face him. "You guys are not supposed—"

"Darkbloods have Arianna and they want Krystal."

"But I just talked to Alfonso. Krystal left with her mom. Arianna told him it was okay."

"I don't think they have her. They *want* her and they're using Arianna to get to her."

Leaning on the edge of the sink, he could feel his pupils dilating with anger, with determination, with the burning need to get her back. She was the center of his world and now that she was gone, everything about him was off-kilter.

Lily had a strange look on her face. She was saying something, but as before, with Santiago, he couldn't hear her.

He didn't care what he had to do or where he had to go, but whoever had Arianna was going to die. That thought was the only thing keeping him on his feet right now.

How could he have been such a fool to have missed this? Why the hell hadn't he seen it coming? Darkbloods clearly were desperate to get Krystal. First the Night of Wilding party, then on the street, then at

Arianna's house. When all of those efforts failed, of course they'd look for Arianna in order to get to her sweetblood cousin. Just as he'd told her when that blog was posted. What a damn fool he'd been not to have watched over her better.

But why did they want Krystal so badly? He would've expected DBs to have moved on by now, focusing their efforts on finding other sweetbloods when the leads ran out on this one. What was so special about the girl?

He recalled that night on the island, when he peered into the room where all the sweetbloods were being kept. Krystal was dressed in a flowing white dress, ribbons in her dark curls.

The woman in charge had been holding a chain around Krystal's neck, as though the girl was her possession. She'd walked up and down the line like a drill sergeant, inspecting the other sweetbloods who were in costume while Krystal followed behind. After Guardians broke up the blood rave, the woman had escaped the island. Her cohort was captured and killed, but she got away.

Several humans had died that night, but the rest of the captives had been saved, their memories wiped before they were returned to their lives. With Cordell's discovery that two of the other living four sweetbloods that night had gone missing again, it could only mean one thing.

This woman was involved. She was the one after Krystal. She must be obsessed with finding that which had been taken from her.

"Meet me in five," he barked to Lily as he headed to the weapons room. "And be prepared to do some scent tracking."

CHAPTER TWENTY-FIVE

ARIANNA KNEW SOMETHING was wrong before she opened her eyes. The side of her face felt as if something had exploded next to it. Her shoulder, hip and knee throbbed. She moved a few muscles and moaned. By slightly re-arranging her limbs, she was relieved to discover that she didn't feel the sharp pain of a broken bone, just lots of abrasions. Something hard was clamped around her ankle. A shackle? She didn't dare move another muscle until she could figure out where she was.

An acrid, bitter taste lingered on the back of her tongue. The musty-smelling air was unmoving and quiet, pressing in on her as she lay on this hard surface. Stone, maybe? Concrete? The atmosphere felt charged, as if it were holding its breath, waiting for her to fully awaken. She didn't want to open her eyes. She had a feeling she wasn't going to like what she saw. Besides, if someone was watching her, it'd be best to get her wits about her before they knew she was awake.

As she lay here in the darkness, she was thankful that Krystal was far away. She would not tell them where her cousin was; she would not give her up to save herself. They would not be strapping Krystal to a metal gurney to drain her blood. Arianna hadn't been able to do anything to save her mother twenty-two years ago, but she sure as hell could save Krystal now.

Holding her breath to silence the sound of her breathing, she strained to hear something. A far-off tapping of metal. Rhythmic. Like a heartbeat. Then a rumbling in the distance. A motorized vehicle of some sort.

She heard nothing nearby. Not the faint stirring of the air to indicate someone else was with her or breathing or any sounds of life. Just the ringing sound of silence between her ears. How many times had she wished to be out of a crowd of people? Now she felt completely alone and would've given anything to have someone nearby so that she knew that she wasn't alone.

Opening her eyes slightly, she looked through her lashes and surveyed her surroundings. Although the light was dim, she could tell she was in a narrow holding cell of some sort, with a wall of stone at her back and not more than two feet above where she lay. The area was about the size of a twin bed...or a crypt.

When we die, we die alone.

Isn't that what Carter had told her back in the Xtark offices before he betrayed her? She rolled to her side and looked over the edge into a long, narrow tunnel. Lanterns hung from the walls, their light biting into the darkness. Rows and rows of slots lined the walls, just like the one she was in. She estimated about twenty or thirty.

She noticed a set of railroad tracks running through the center and wooden support beams along the top. Could she be inside a mine shaft? If so, that meant there was only one way in and one way out.

She heard a slight stirring coming from across the way. Were there others hidden in the other slots just as she was? She strained to see and thought she sensed movement in the one directly across from her.

"Hello?" she whispered. "Is anyone there?"

She heard something rustle.

"Shh," said a voice to her left. "They'll hear you. And if they do, they'll send in the rats."

Rats? A sudden chill ran down her spine. Like a horde? A river of them running down the middle? They couldn't get up here on the walls, could they? They'd climb in and she'd have nowhere to escape. Their hairless tails would brush up against her legs, her wrists, her neck. Oh, God, did she hear the faint shuffling of something near her feet? She yelped and scooted as far away as the shackle around her ankle would allow.

Several others shushed her. "We haven't seen them, but they've threatened that they have hundreds of them."

"How many people are here?" she asked.

"I'm not sure," one of the voices said. "Five or six, though last week there were more like ten. Once they take you away, you may or may not come back."

"Have they taken you before?"

"Yes, twice."

"Where did they take you? What did they do?" Part of her didn't want to know and the other part wanted to be prepared.

"I wish I knew, but I honestly don't remember."

Could these people be sweetbloods? Why else would they all be here like this? Then she thought about her

Weird Wednesday comments and the report she made for Cordell. "Are any of you named Kevin, Julia, Chad or Eric?"

"I'm Eric," a male voice answered. "Julia was here, but they took her a few days ago and she hasn't come back."

Oh, my God, Jackson was right. She hated to admit it, but she'd had her doubts that her blog was even useful, but he had assured her it was. He suddenly believed in her crazy old blog, even when she didn't. She wished she could reach out to wherever he was right now and tell him how much she loved him. Thank him for believing in the things he knew she cared about even when she claimed they were meaningless. He seemed to know her better than she knew herself.

Oh, Jackson. I wish I could tell you how much I love you and thank you for loving me.

"How did you know?" Eric whispered.

She thought about her long-standing rule not to reveal her online identity and promptly abandoned her need to keep secrets. "I run a blog that reports on weird happenings. Eric, your roommate posted that you'd gone missing after you went out for a pack of smokes."

"My God, that's exactly what happened. He posted on your blog? That's so cool. So people have been looking for me?"

"Yes. And a classmate of Julia's posted that she disappeared from her bedroom one night last week."

"That's true," another voice piped in. A young female voice this time. "She told me she woke up to find two people leaning over her bed. They were wearing sunglasses despite the fact that it was the middle of the night."

"Me and…ah… We've been investigating the disappearances and wondered if they were linked. I guess I have my answer now."

"Why us? Do you have any idea? I mean, we know that they're vampires— God, that sounds so crazy. But why would they be keeping us here?"

Arianna thought about feigning ignorance but decided the truth was best, so she told them they were probably sweetbloods. What she didn't tell them was that Darkbloods had captured some of them before. The girl sniffled and that was when Arianna realized tears had dampened her cheeks, as well.

"Julia said that the two men who came into her room kept talking about keeping her all to themselves. That apparently they'd done it before. But then the one guy reminded the other that they almost got busted the last time, so they brought her here, instead."

The Darkbloods' boldness stunned her. Were they always this single-minded in their pursuit of sweetbloods? She had a feeling they were. If she remembered correctly, Julia was about the same age as Krystal.

"Quiet," someone said. "Here they come."

She strained but couldn't hear anything except her heartbeat pounding against her eardrums. Maybe it was true that when one of your senses was deprived or gone, the other ones became stronger. How long had these people been here, anyway? Did they even know, since they may have had their memory altered?

It took another few moments until she finally heard

the noise, too. Footsteps echoed off the walls and seemed to be getting louder. How many were coming? One? Maybe two? Then she heard voices.

"Take the one from the lower right," a female said.

In the low light, Arianna could just make out two dark figures stopped on the opposite side of the tracks.

A set of keys jangled, then a man said, "Hold on. I thought we took that one yesterday."

"Nope. It was the one above her."

"I could've sworn— Oh, well. You're probably right. The Mistress really should have these numbered so that we can keep track of whose turn it is next."

Arianna heard the sound of keys *and* chains this time, then someone whimpered.

"Come on," the man said, snapping his fingers. "We don't have all night."

"Please, don't," a young female voice said. "I—I don't want to go back there."

Arianna heard a zip then a rip.

"Here," the woman said. "Tape her."

A moment later, the young female's whimpering became muffled.

"I think she plans to number the holding slots when the bars get installed," the woman said, continuing their earlier conversation without skipping a beat.

"That will be nice for them," he said. "They'll be more comfortable without the leg shackles."

The woman laughed as they moved down to the next column. "Not that these tiny slots will ever be comfortable."

She heard them remove another person.

Arianna was stunned. These two Darkbloods were talking as if their human prisoners couldn't understand them. Much like people talking to each other about horses in a barn, dogs in a kennel, hamsters in a cage. Obviously, that was all they were to them. Pets.

"Here, take him," the man said. "Do they plan to work on the UV platform at the same time as these modifications?"

"UV platform? What's that?"

"It's designed to hold three or four humans at a time and expose them to real honest-to-goodness sunlight, not the fake-and-bake stuff. I mean, that works, but natural is so much better."

"I hear you," the woman agreed.

"Then, at the end of the day, after the donors have been exposed to the sun and are UV-rich, the platform is lowered. The blood will test out better and go for a higher price."

Arianna's head was reeling and she was feeling light-headed. Sun platforms? UV-rich blood? Price? Were Darkbloods planning to sell the people chained up in these slots the way they were going to at the Night of Wilding party or were they planning to sell just their blood? It was all so…commercial…with humans, not as pets, but as commodities. She wondered if everyone was a sweetblood except for her.

"Since UV-rich blood isn't as plentiful up here as it is in other parts of the country," the man was saying, "she's doing what she can to improve the quality of what we do have. So even if they aren't sweetbloods, there will be a higher demand for it than if it came straight from the street."

"It's the same concept as force-feeding ducks for foie gras. The Mistress is taking something mediocre and turning it into something great," the woman said.

"And valuable."

JACKSON STOOD WITH THE small group of Guardians and looked over the water into the inky darkness.

"Are you sure she's out there?" he asked Lily, although he really didn't need to. Arianna's nearby presence sizzled in his veins. Once they got within several miles of her, he knew Lily's tracking abilities hadn't failed him.

"Positive. It's cloaked."

"Are they on a goddamn boat or what?" Santiago asked.

"Either that or a small island," Lily said. "There are many in the San Juan Islands. Some are no more than rocky atolls covered with fir trees."

Dom pulled up a map of the area on his phone. "It's going to take several hours to get a boat up to this remote location. And without knowing what it is they're cloaking, we can't send Finn in with the helicopter."

"Too loud," Jackson said. "For Arianna's sake, they can't know we're here."

"Then we'll commandeer a boat from one of the locals," Santiago said. "Surely there are people living somewhere around here."

"I don't know. Most of this is government or tribal land."

"Without knowing what we're heading toward, they might hear us before we see them," Lily warned.

"And if that happens, Arianna and any of the sweet-bloods they have could be in even more danger." Jackson's gut churned.

"If they're even alive," said Santiago.

Lily rolled her eyes, echoing Jackson's thoughts. The guy could be a serious pessimist sometimes.

"Oh, Arianna's alive, all right. I can feel her energy signature. In fact... Hold on." Jackson jumped off the rocky outcropping and shadow-moved to the edge of the surf. The other Guardians followed him. He was positive she wasn't far away. Not more than a few hundred yards offshore at most. He'd be willing to bet that if she was on an island, he'd be able to walk to it if there was minus tide.

"Listen," Mitch said, pointing. "I hear a boat coming from that direction. Do you see it?"

They all turned and Jackson could just make out light bobbing up and down in the surf. It got closer and closer and then suddenly disappeared about two hundred yards offshore, though they could still hear the motor. "It went through the cloaking perimeter."

A moment later the motor cut.

"We still don't know if it's a damn island or not," said Santiago.

"I'm guessing island," said Dom.

Jackson turned to Lily. "Can you tell if it's Dark-bloods on the boat?"

Lily turned to face the direction of the sound. "Can't tell. The wind is blowing in the wrong direction. Good thing Darkbloods have a shitty sense of smell, otherwise they might pick up *our* scent as it's blowing straight at them."

"Hey, Kip," Mitch said. "How good are you at detecting human scent?"

Kip shrugged. "Decent, I guess. Why?"

"Let's you and me go see if we can find a boat nearby. Motorboat, rowboat, kayak. Doesn't matter. If it's motorized, we'll row the damn thing in." In a flash, they were gone, leaving Jackson, Lily, Dom and Santiago on the shoreline.

Jackson yanked off his boots.

"What are you doing?" Dom asked.

"I'm swimming out there." He unbuckled his guns and handed them to Lily, leaving his knives strapped to his body. "If they find a boat, bring them to me when you come ashore. I don't want them submerged in the salt water."

"But you don't know what you're getting into," Dom said.

"It's better than waiting around for Kip and Mitch to come back with a dinghy the size of a postage stamp. I can't stand the thought that they have her and that she's so close. I'll swim out there and you join me when they come back with something. If I can, I'll disable the cloaking device."

Dom started to say something else, but Jackson didn't hear him as he dove into the surf, nor did his brain register that the water was frigid. With strong, even strokes, he cut through the water and in a few minutes he felt the electrical snap of the cloaking device, then was pulling himself up a steep cliff face.

Lily was right, he thought as he peered up over the top of the rock. This appeared to be a small island just off the coast. He looked behind him and noticed two boats anchored in a small cove. From the pull of Arianna's blood, he could tell she was somewhere inland, not out there.

He hoisted himself up over the rock as he caught a whiff of Darkblood scent. Unsheathing his dragon blade, he crept toward the smell and saw a figure leaning against a tree, holding a pair of binoculars.

Shit. If he'd come up twenty feet to the left of where he did, this asshole would've seen him for sure. As it was, the guy didn't know what hit him.

Jackson turned to look into the thick tree-covered interior of the island, not sure which way to go. "Arianna, I'm here," he whispered into the salt air. "I'm coming for you."

Something stirred deep inside his chest, a sudden realization that hadn't been there before, as if a part of himself had reached out and found what it was looking for.

Jackson? Oh, please, let this be a sign that you're near.

Her voice was as clear in his head as if she were right here, whispering in his ear. "Arianna? Can you hear me?"

Jackson?

Yes, it's me!

Please, God, is my hopeful imagination conjuring

his presence or could he really be here? I can feel him in my bones. Don't let this be a hallucination.

Arianna?

Nothing.

He repeated her name in his head and still didn't get a response. Could he be hearing her thoughts but she couldn't hear his? He stretched out his mental senses, imagining tiny sparks fanning out in all directions looking for her. A warm energy enveloped him.

Jackson? Is that...is that you? I'm not delusional, am I? It's like I'm feeling the heat from a fire I can't see.

Arianna, yes, it's me. He pushed out to her again, more powerfully this time.

Oh, my God, I...I feel it. It is you. Then, as if she was talking to herself, she said, *I just knew he'd come, that he'd find me.*

Holy shit. It seemed as if he was hearing a mixture of messages meant for him as well as internal dialogue with herself. How was this even possible? Sure, he could feel her presence because of all her blood in his system, but her thoughts, too? Something nagged at the back of his head, like he'd heard of this happening before, but he didn't have time to wonder.

He knew she probably couldn't hear him, since she'd never had any of his blood, but if "Tell me where you are" and "What do you know?" could be put into his stretched mental senses, he did his best to convey the messages.

I knew in my heart of hearts you'd find me and that— Oh, a question? Okay, I'm guessing you want

*to know what the Darkbloods are planning and where
I'm being held.*

She hesitated.

As hard as he could, he pushed out, *Yes!*

*Holy shit, Jackson! That was intense. My arms are
all goose bumpy. Okay, here's what I know.* He listened to her thoughts as she told him about the sweetbloods being held with her and described their location
as being underground, maybe a mine shaft, with tracks
down the center.

Was there an old mine somewhere around here? A
rail line? It certainly made sense that there was. In the
1800s, many of the islands were mined for limestone
and coal, and timber harvested.

Surely, a rail line would be easy to spot. He shadow-
moved toward the cliff face again. Whatever it was they
mined here, it would've been taken out on railcars and
transported down to waiting ships. He guessed that the
cove where the two boats were anchored was the only
viable harbor on this tiny island. Sure enough, he spotted a gaping hole in the cliff supported by old timbers
with a set of rails coming out of it.

Would the cloaking-device panel be nearby? It made
sense that it would be. He jogged along an overgrown
path and when he rounded a corner, he came face-to-
face with a Darkblood.

How could he be so careless? And the guy was even
talking on his phone. Jackson sidearmed the blade. It
hurled through the air and landed with a thunk in the
guy's neck. In a flash, Jackson was on him. He grabbed

the guy's phone right before he buried the blade of another knife hilt deep in his chest.

Had the lookout got off a warning to whomever he was talking to?

"Ray, are you there? Ray? I didn't catch what you said about—"

He ended the call and quickly dialed Dom's number. Mitch and Kip had returned with a small rowboat a few minutes after Jackson had left and the Guardians were already on their way out to the island. He told him what little he knew about the island's layout, warning them about the two boats anchored in the cove.

After working out a plan, he struck off again in search of Arianna, despite the fact that Dom had wanted him to wait.

CHAPTER TWENTY-SIX

ARIANNA WAS FLOORED that she'd been able to communicate with Jackson telepathically. Or at least she was fairly certain she was. This must be another strange vampire trick that he hadn't told her about.

She was about to tell the others not to give up hope, that maybe they would get out of this place, when she heard the scuffle of footsteps somewhere in the darkness. It came from a different direction than the two earlier Darkbloods had.

Jackson?

She waited, hoping she'd sense him drawing closer. Nothing. A stab of panic shot through her. Could she have been hallucinating? Imagining Jackson's warm presence and that he was coming to get them out of here? Why wasn't he answering her? If this wasn't Jackson, then it had to be another Darkblood. What did they want now? More sweetbloods? Were they returning the ones they took or were they coming for her?

"Arianna? Where are you?"

"Carter?" She craned her head around to see him ducking under the support timbers at the edge of the chamber.

She wasn't sure whether to be happy or leery. He seemed a little more agile than before, but, as she watched the slow, deliberate way he walked, she guessed he hadn't been through the transformation process yet. But maybe this was a first step. Did the change not happen instantly? Maybe it happened over time.

"Congrats on being able to ditch the cane," she said drily when he stopped in front of her holding cell. "Looks like things paid off for you, didn't they? I hope to hell it was worth it."

"Listen, Arianna, I'm sorry. I didn't mean for all this to happen." He wrung his hands together and kept glancing behind him like he wasn't supposed to be here.

"Suddenly have a come-to-Jesus moment and feel guilty? What do you mean you didn't mean for this to happen? It was an accident that you turned your friend over to bloodthirsty vampires, huh? That post to my blog was just a terrible mistake. You didn't mean to flush me out, knowing I'd come to you for help."

Give me a stinking break.

"Arianna, I—"

"Or does this mean you only planned for *some* of it to happen? That you thought they'd just have one little sip of my blood, send me on my way and I'd be none the wiser? Did you think they just wanted a taste of Krystal's sweetblood and then they'd let us go?"

"This isn't a game, Arianna. None of it was. I was desperate and didn't think about anyone but myself, and for that, I'm sorry."

What a fool she'd been to listen to him over what George had been telling her. Carter was the real enemy. Not George. She clearly was a poor judge of character to have been fooled by him for so long.

"What happened, Carter? Why'd you do it? I thought we were friends. And the last time I checked, friends don't turn other friends over to vampires for them to be killed."

"You saw what was happening to me," he said, grabbing a large skeleton key from his pocket and unlocking the cuff around her ankle. "My body was betraying me. I was a prisoner inside my own flesh."

Even in this low light, she could see that the dark circles under his eyes didn't seem so pronounced and he was definitely more dexterous than when she'd last seen him. Before this, it would've taken him twice as long to put a key into a lock. "You're looking better now."

"I've had a little of their blood, not enough to be anything but temporary. I won't be completely healed until I go through the actual transformation process."

He spoke about it with the same kind of attitude as someone having cosmetic surgery. A little nip here, a little tuck there and you'll be as good as new. Don't mind your friends who died in the process. It was worth it because you're better.

"So did you come here to beg for my forgiveness before they kill me?"

He couldn't look her in the eye. "I'd been working at Xtark for several years, developing HG and designing the forums. They wanted me to code some weird crap into the game and that's when I found out what they were. In exchange for my expertise, they promised to make me a changeling. The process heals the human body of many of its imperfections, so it was my only hope of a normal life again. But they kept coming up with excuses why they couldn't do it. The day you saw me come off the elevators, I'd just been told that I didn't have much more time as an able-bodied person. Soon, I'd have been confined to a bed, with tubes coming out of every orifice. I wouldn't be able to piss or shit on my own."

He paused for her reaction. If he was looking for sympathy, he sure as hell wasn't going to get it from her.

"I couldn't bear to think about that happening to me," he continued. "I used to be so active, so in shape." He patted his rounded midsection, which didn't look all that different from that of many men his age. "Now look at me. I can barely walk the length of this room without stopping to catch my breath, wondering if my legs will collapse before I get to the other side. And that's on a good day."

"While I sympathize with you, it doesn't justify what you've done."

"I didn't ask for this, Arianna."

"Neither did I."

He held out a hand, offering to help her out of her compartment.

Ignoring it, she jumped down on her own. When she hit the stone floor, her knees almost buckled with the sudden weight and she caught herself on the wall just in time.

"Give me the keys, Carter."

"But—"

"If you think I'm leaving without the rest of these people, then you're crazier than I thought."

"But you have to hurry. They have Krystal, and I'm not sure how long they'll be here."

She suddenly couldn't breathe and stumbled backward. That ruthless woman had Krystal?

"That's impossible. She—she wasn't around here. Are you sure?"

"Positive. I heard the Mistress say it was her. Dark hair, ringlets?"

"How—how did they find her?"

Arianna had been so careful with her cousin after finding out she was a sweetblood, and when her mother called, saying she was ready to have Krystal come back, Arianna didn't hesitate. She was eager to get the girl out of the city.

"When you didn't tell Ventra where your cousin was, she sent Darkbloods to stake out your house."

"My house?" When Arianna was at the field office, Aunt Sue and Krystal decided to go to the house to pick up her things before heading over the mountains to the eastern part of the state.

"Yes, and Ventra was very pleased. Let Elan give me a little of his blood. But, God, Arianna. Your cousin is so young. I had no idea."

"Ha. You think her age would've really made a difference had you known? I seriously doubt it, Carter, but you go ahead and tell yourself it would've if it makes you sleep easier at night."

He shrugged. "Come on. There isn't much time."

"Why? What's…going on?" She couldn't verbalize

what she knew they'd be doing to Krystal, let alone imagine the terror the girl had to be experiencing.

"Guardians found us and Darkbloods are occupied with trying to keep them at bay on the other side of the compound. That's why I was able to come here in the first place. Follow me. I'll show you where there's a rowboat you can take back to shore."

She hesitated, aghast. "I can't leave without Krystal... or these people."

"You have to leave her. You can't fight them on your own. Let the Guardians handle things. Besides, if they know I aided you, they may never change me. Unless..."

She didn't like the sound of that. "Unless what?"

"Do you think your Guardian friends would transform me in exchange for helping you escape?"

"So again, it's all about you, isn't it?" she asked, unlocking the last captive. "Which way is out?"

"I'll show you."

"No, you'll show them. I'm going to get my cousin." She blocked out how tired every bone in her body was and focused, instead, on Krystal.

"She's not down here. They brought her by boat and they're anchored just offshore."

Arianna wasn't sure whether to be relieved or not. The mine shaft was freaky, but being anchored out on a boat with no way out had to be almost as stifling.

Carter led the way out into the dimly lit mine shaft. Good thing he was leading them. With all the passageways, this place was confusing, and she had no doubt she'd have gotten lost.

He leaned up against the stone wall, exhausted, and pointed up ahead. "Around the next bend, you'll see the exit." The rest of them ran past, leaving her with Carter.

"Okay, tell me where the boat is. Have you been on it? Is there a dinghy on the shore somewhere that I can use to get out there?"

"Once you get outside, it's anchored in a cove just north of here, down a steep incline. The stairs are pretty treacherous, so be careful. There's a dinghy…if you don't mind killing a couple of Darkbloods to get to it."

Was Jackson close enough to help her out?

Shouts came from a passageway that branched off just behind them.

Carter's eyes were wide with panic. If he was discovered now, Darkbloods would know he was the one to set their prisoners free. He wouldn't be able to bullshit his way out of it and claim Guardians had rescued them.

"Stay here. Wait. Go back."

She started to protest. There was no way she was going back, only forward. A streak of movement came from the left and Carter fell flat on his ass. A Darkblood with a knife blade stuck in his back—oh, God, it was Jackson's curved dragon blade—bit into Carter's throat. Arianna plastered herself to the wall of stone behind her, praying the guy wouldn't notice her. Jackson had to be close.

Jackson, I'm here.

With the deafening sound of her own heart ringing in her ears, she held her breath and tried to concentrate. Maybe she was too stressed out to feel the nuances of his presence, because she felt nothing. However, this dragon blade was proof that he was here in the tunnels somewhere. If only she could stay alive long enough to get to him.

Hunched over Carter and blocking the way out, the Darkblood made disgusting slurping noises as he fed. She glanced around for something to use as a weapon and spotted a stack of lumber piled near one of the support posts behind her. It would take her two, maybe three steps backward to reach them.

She must've made a noise because the vampire suddenly snapped his head up. His eyes were black, his mouth smeared with blood. Red, torn flesh covered the spot that used to be Carter's neck.

Carter mouthed something to her that she couldn't make out then pointed a finger in the direction they'd been heading, giving her a thumbs-up.

He was telling her to run.

Well, she would if she could, but she had the slight problem of getting past this bloodthirsty vampire first. An odd pang of gratitude settled in her gut for this man who was both her betrayer and her rescuer.

"Pull this out of me, bitch," the Darkblood hissed.

The silver…it was keeping him weak. Which meant he was extremely desperate.

She took a few steps backward and her leg brushed up against the stacked wood. The Darkblood went back to what he was doing, replenishing his depleted blood and energies from Carter until that supply ran out. Jackson had said that silver poisoning leaches a vampire's energy like the sun, but at a much higher rate. Clearly, this Darkblood didn't consider her to be much of a threat, as he did nothing to restrain her. No doubt he'd turn to her next, as soon as he was done.

Slowly, she reached down and her hand closed around a two-by-four. With the Darkblood in this weakened state, all she needed to do was knock the guy to the side and run past him. If Carter wasn't dead already, he soon would be. Her first priority was getting to Krystal.

She lifted the board above her head and swung down hard. Right as she did, the Darkblood lifted his head. With a loud *thunk,* it hit him square in the forehead and his body slumped to the side.

Yes!

Tossing down the wood, she made a move to sprint past him. A hand shot out, closed around her ankle, and she went down.

"Fucking bitch."

With blood streaming down into his face, the Darkblood crawled over Carter's prone body as she kicked and scrambled to get away.

"Aren't you a clever one? When I'm finished with him, I had planned to have you for dessert."

Carter groaned. She glanced over to see his fingers pulling at his pant leg, exposing a thin dagger strapped to his ankle.

"But I changed my mind. I'm having my dessert now."

The Darkblood lunged. She rolled and reached for Carter's blade. Her movement must've caught the guy off guard because momentum brought him crashing down in the space she'd just occupied. She pulled the knife from Carter's holster, twisted her body and plunged the blade into the guy's back.

He writhed, arched his back like a coyote howling to the moon. Had she pierced the heart muscle? Then, remembering something Lily had told her, she gave the hilt a good twist and felt a little pop as the blade went deeper.

Almost immediately, smoke started coming off his clothes and the top of his head. Bingo. She must have hit it. He rolled away and his body started to shrivel in on itself. It had to be the most disgusting thing Arianna had ever seen. The pile of ashes lay next to her along with a couple of zippers, a gun, another knife and some items she didn't want to know about.

Trying not to inhale as she pushed herself to her feet, she thought about lemons, Pine-Sol and the smell of spring showers rather than the stench filling her nostrils. It made her want to snort bleach when she got out of here.

The back of her neck prickled. Jackson's concern was clamoring inside her head.

I'm—I'm fine. Carter let me go and I just killed my first Darkblood. You should've warned me about the smell.

She was pretty sure she could sense him laughing.

JACKSON SPOTTED ARIANNA COMING out of the mine-shaft opening. In an instant, he shadow-moved to her and she was in his arms.

"Thank God you're all right," he mumbled into her

hair. "I don't know what I would've done if something had happened to you."

"It's a good thing I can see you move like that, otherwise I'd be a little freaked out right now."

He held her out at arm's length to drink her in. Her hair was a mess. There was dirt on her face. Her jeans were ripped in both knees and her flimsy T-shirt was stretched tight over her breasts. She was the most beautiful woman he'd ever seen.

"What? I smell like Darkblood?"

"You're gorgeous," he said. "Let's get you out of here."

She squeezed his hand. "While I want nothing more than to get away from here, Darkbloods have Krystal. She's on a boat anchored nearby. Or at least she was."

She quickly relayed what Carter had told her. Using a phone she didn't recognize, Jackson fired off a text to both teams as they headed toward the cove.

"Dom, Lily and Kip are securing the east entrance, but Santiago and Mitch will meet us on the beach."

"Oh, I found something of yours." She handed him his dragon blade.

"How did you—?"

"Shh. I'll tell you later."

Several minutes later, they were standing with the region commander and Mitch behind a large rock outcropping. A large yacht was anchored in the moonlit cove with guards positioned at the helm and the stern. A dinghy had been pulled ashore and was also being watched by a Darkblood.

"I can go get our little boat. It's tied up around the

corner. Take me ten minutes or so to row it over," Mitch said.

Arianna pointed behind them. "We don't have time, there's Ventra."

A woman in a white flowing dress was coming down the rickety stairs, followed by three men. The boat's engines roared to life.

"They're leaving the island," Mitch said.

Santiago palmed a knife. "Let's go."

Jackson grabbed the man's arm. "No, if we attack them onshore and those goons on the boat see us, they'll leave with Krystal. We need to get to her first."

"And how do you propose that? We sneak on board their little dinghy?"

He closed his eyes for a brief moment. He had no other choice if he wanted to ensure they'd get Krystal back alive. Once Santiago saw him go invisible, there'd be no getting around the fact that he was reverting.

"That's precisely what I'm going to do." He turned to Arianna and brought her hands to his lips. "I want you to know that you're the best thing that ever happened to me. And no matter what happens, I'll always love you."

He dropped her hands and stripped off his shirt, jeans and boots, thanking the good Lord that he'd decided to wear underwear today.

"What the hell are you doing?" Santiago asked. "You'll never be able to swim out there before their dinghy gets there."

Focusing his energies inward, he felt electricity sparking along his skin, and when he checked his hand, it had that blurry, underwater look again. "I'm not swimming."

"Dude, that's so intense," Mitch murmured.

Santiago chimed in. "You're fucking kidding me. You're going invisible? That's impossible."

"I wish it were impossible, but it's true. I'm going to use it to save Krystal."

"Be careful, Jackson," Arianna said softly.

"I will."

He jumped off the rock and sprinted across the beach toward the dinghy. The only visible sign that he was there were the footprints his feet made in the sand.

One of the Darkbloods was just launching the small boat when Jackson arrived. He waited till the man climbed in before he waded into the water and grabbed onto the back. The water was cold, but he clenched his teeth and hardly noticed it.

There'd be no turning back now. Santiago had seen the evidence with his own eyes. There would be no question that Jackson was reverting. His only hope would be to give them Krystal then disappear forever. Given this special ability, he might be able to resist being captured by Guardians. He'd go see-through and they'd never be able to find him to take him in and prosecute him. But it was the end of his life as he knew it. No more hanging with his buddies, shooting the shit with Dom, teasing Lily about her potty mouth. And Xian. Fuck. The guy was like his own personal manager, keeping him in line and fed.

But most of all, he'd miss Arianna. The one woman who'd been able to see through his mask and uncover the real him. She'd fallen in love with the real him, not the caricature. He'd let down all his walls and she still loved him. Hell, she knew him better than he knew himself.

When the dinghy drew close to the yacht, he let go and swam noiselessly to the other side. He held on to the swim platform while the woman and three men climbed aboard. He counted to ten then pulled himself up.

If there was any doubt whether or not Krystal was on board, one whiff was all it took to know that she was. He peered up over the deck into the cabin to see her standing awkwardly next to a table while the others were sitting. After glancing at his hand to make sure it still had that fuzzy, underwater look, he readjusted his leather weapons strap and climbed onto the deck.

Not having to come up with an element of surprise, he walked right up to the guard on duty, thrust a blade through his chest then tossed him overboard.

He waited for a gust of wind, then opened the cabin door and walked right in. Four vampire males sat at the table. Two wore sunglasses and were clearly Darkblood thugs, but he wasn't sure about the other two. In business suits, they looked like corporate types. Very wealthy corporate types. The woman sat on the edge of the banquette. He recognized her instantly from the Night of Wilding party.

She glanced over and scowled, lifted her nose and sniffed. He held his breath, hoping she hadn't picked up his scent.

"Elan, close that thing. And make sure it latches this time." She turned back to her guests.

Jackson stepped aside, careful not to make any noise, as Elan closed the door. He could take this one out right now, it'd be an easy stake through the heart, but Krystal was too close to the woman. If only he could separate her from the herd, then he'd have free access to do what he needed to the others.

"Ma'am, Fitch is not at his post."

"Well, then, go out and check on him. My orders were for him to keep watch at the stern until we're under way. He'd better not be up top talking to the captain like he was before. If he is, stake him."

"Yes, ma'am."

Good. One less idiot to deal with. Then a mechanical sound came from the belly of the boat. Shit. They were pulling anchor. He didn't have much time.

"So, gentlemen, as I was saying, I appreciate your patience with what happened back there. Raids by Guardians, while annoying, are par for the course sometimes, but it happens far less up here than in the hotter regions. I've had several of these little soirees that have gone on without a hitch."

Guardians had missed other sweetblood killing parties in the area? How many? Where were they? Had there been signs, but they'd missed following up on them? It had to be Hollow Grave.

"That's why your sectors, like mine, are ripe for this business opportunity. Not only is the Guardian presence very thin in our areas, but the humans our people are used to feeding from aren't as energy rich as in the southern sectors. Besides, most have never had Sweet from a live host. So our clientele wants the product we're selling as well as the experience. And many are willing to pay top dollar. This, my friends, is a business opportunity that I can help you get started."

Ventra had to be in charge of the area's Darkblood operations. Alfonso had come to the field office and given a presentation about how the Alliance was structured, but Jackson hadn't been paying attention. She must be the head honcho here and these men had to be leaders of other sectors somewhere.

"Tell us more," one of the men prompted.

The woman continued to talk sales numbers, franchise percentages and start-up fees. Jackson was astounded. She was fucking making a business out of killing humans. Capitalizing on most modern vampires' reluctance to do so, yet knowing the dark nature lurked inside all of them. It just needed to be coaxed out.

Santiago and Dom would be very interested in hearing all this.

"As a gesture of goodwill," the woman was saying, "I'll let you have the girl and you can experience it for yourself, firsthand. Then you be the judge on whether the vampires in your areas would be interested in paying for such an experience themselves."

A sob escaped Krystal's lips and she took a step away from the table. The two men looked at her, their eyes reflecting their hunger.

"Come on, *ma belle fille*," the woman crooned. "It'll all be over soon."

Now was his chance before the other Darkblood goon came back.

He shoved Krystal backward. With a knife in each hand, he charged, stabbing the remaining Darkblood and one of the sector leaders. They didn't know what hit them.

The other man climbed over the table to the other side of the banquette, wildly searching for the cause. The boat lurched just as Jackson threw two blades. The first hit the man square in the chest, but the second one only nicked the woman's arm.

She hissed in pain. "An Unseen. You must be Jackson."

What the fuck? How did she know his name?

He hesitated a fraction too long. Before he drew another weapon, the woman had Krystal by the throat, her fangs fully extended.

"Your human woman has told me all about you. So lovely to make your acquaintance."

"Jackson?" Krystal's eyes widened as the woman pulled her out onto the deck.

"I'm here, honey." He moved away from where he'd spoken.

With the woman's teeth at the girl's throat, he had to be careful how he did this. One wrong move and she'd slice into the girl's artery. If that happened, he could easily dispatch the woman, but with Krystal's sweetblood and him barely able to control his urges, he wouldn't be able to seal the wound without draining her. One wrong move and he'd turn into the monster he'd been fearing all these months.

"Does this make you nervous, Jackson? Is that why you haven't attacked me yet? You afraid of a little sweetblood? It's delicious. You really should try it." Her tongue darted out and she licked the girl's neck.

The temperature of his blood ratcheted up.

"You must've heard the old stories about the Unseen. Violent, even by modern Darkblood standards. Is that you? Are you afraid you're reverting into one of them? Unable to control your natural instincts? Must be awfully difficult for a Guardian to know he's turning into the very enemy he's sworn to fight."

The boat shifted and Jackson steadied himself; he hated boats and hadn't been on one since Betsy died.

"What would happen if you smelled a little of this?" She scraped her fangs on the girl's neck, drawing blood.

Its sweet smell permeated the air, like an invisible finger pulling him closer.

"Stop!" He'd been around Krystal but never in his Unseen form when he felt at his most raw and ragged.

"I was right. You are scared." The woman plunged her teeth into the girl's neck.

Oh, God. His mouth watered as his fangs elongated from his gums. He couldn't fucking do this.

Krystal screamed, tried to hang on to the railing, but the woman pushed her overboard.

"Jackson, help! I can't swim."

With Krystal's blood on her mouth, the woman looked pleased with herself. "So, do you dive in to save her and risk biting her yourself? She is rather tasty, I must say. Or do you stay with me. We'd make a good team, the two of us. With those special powers of yours, there's not much we couldn't accomplish."

Elan came up behind her, a gun leveled in the vicinity of where Jackson was standing. He heard Krystal splashing as the boat continued pulling away. He could stay and fight or go save her, but he couldn't do both. He glanced into the inky depths and remembered his sister. He'd made bad choices that day, which had led to her death. He would not do it again.

"I will never join you."

He dove in and prayed his willpower would hold just long enough to get her to shore.

Santiago watched as Jackson walked through the surf with the girl in his arms and handed her to his woman.

What the fuck?

Two puncture wounds were clearly visible on her neck.

"Dom, can you help?" Jackson was out of breath from the long swim to shore. "The woman bit her and threw her overboard. I didn't think I could stop if I tried healing the wounds."

Dom leaned over the girl and soon her wounds were healing.

Jackson turned to Santiago. Several pieces of seaweed clung to his skin and pretty-boy hair, the girl's blood on his arms. "I know that Guardians who revert must be turned over to the authorities."

"Yes, that's true," Santiago agreed.

"But in consideration of the years I've been with the Agency, I'd like to offer up my resignation, so you're not obligated to bring me in. I've not killed a human yet. I'll check in at a treatment facility and see what they can do."

"No. I can't do that."

Arianna rushed to Jackson's side and positioned herself slightly in front of him. Her eyes blazed with indignation. "How can you say that? He had every opportunity to kill my cousin, not only in the water but for the past few weeks when we stayed together at Lily and Alfonso's house. Are you so cold and heartless and rigid about those rules of yours that you can't see what a big mistake you'll be making? He's clearly not a threat. Hell, I'd say with this ability of his, he's even more of an asset to your cause than he was before. You saw what he did. He'd have killed Krystal if he were reverting."

He was impressed by this human woman's passion and unwavering support of one of his people. "I'm saying, no, I won't accept his resignation because I want him to stay on as a Guardian."

Jackson snapped his head up. "What? But I'm an Unseen. I thought—"

"You're not reverting, Jackson. Dom just informed me that an ancient dormant power has been awakened in him, too, but it has nothing to do with reverting. It's activated by the blood of someone with whom you share a special bond." It royally pissed him off that he was just finding out about this now. Had he known that one of his field team leaders had the power to *vapor,* he'd have taken advantage of it. He could think of many opportunities to put that ability to good use.

"*Enlazado por la Sangre.* Bonded by blood." Dom looked up from where he was holding Krystal's hand. "He's right. As long as I have ample amounts of Mackenzie's blood in my system, I'm able to vapor. Turn myself into mist. It can come in pretty handy sometimes."

"Yes, it has." Lily looked as if she was about to say something else, but when she glanced at Santiago, she changed her mind and snapped her mouth shut.

Jesus, Mary and Joseph. There was obviously something going on between these guys that Santiago didn't know about. They all worked so closely together, it was as if they had their own little goddamn club. Did they pass around notes and tell secrets, too? Play with Barbies and have sleepovers? Thank God he was up at Region most of the time. He didn't have the time or patience for bullshit like this.

Jackson took the clothes Arianna held out to him and got dressed. "But my cravings. My over-the-chart energy needs. How do you explain that?"

Santiago folded his hands over his chest. "I'm not saying you weren't on the road to reverting. You certainly may have been. But your actions tonight prove you're not. No revert would've been able to resist sweetblood. Hell, not many law-abiding vampires could've, either. Whether you've gained control over your dark nature yourself or the blood of your woman has something to do with it, I don't know. All I know is that you're a damn good agent and I'm not about to agree to your resignation."

CHAPTER TWENTY-SEVEN

"I'D REALLY LIKE TO TRY IT sometime." Arianna dipped the peanut butter and honey sandwich into the egg mixture and set it on the griddle.

Jackson peered over her shoulder. He'd never eaten something like this, but since it involved his favorite food, he was game. Plus, Arianna was a great cook. She'd made him try things he never thought he'd like. The sizzling sound made his mouth water. "No."

"But why? Haven't I demonstrated to you that it might be something that I'd be into?"

He laughed and sat up on the counter where he could watch. "I like the fact that you like me for me. That you don't need...extra stuff to be...happy."

"*You* make me happy, but whatever. I'll wear you down eventually."

She could try to talk him into it, but he wasn't going to cave. That was the old him and he'd like to keep it that way. Thank God, Lily walked in, ending the conversation.

"Alfonso thinks he found the perfect location for the proposed safe house and wants the two of you to check it out tonight."

During the debriefing after the island, Jackson had told Santiago about the Sector Mistress's plans for sweetbloods. Since Krystal had been victimized several times already and was Arianna's cousin, he agreed for them to look into some long-term options. He wasn't completely sold on the idea—a Guardian's responsibility wasn't to get involved in human affairs—but he was willing to listen. Which for a close-minded son of a bitch like Santiago was a huge concession.

"I can't wait to see it." Arianna put the sandwich on a plate. "Careful, it's hot. Do you want one, Lily?"

With a perplexed look on her face, Lily watched as Jackson took a bite.

"It's really good," he managed to say with his mouth full. "The peanut butter's all melty."

"Sure. Why not? Looks interesting."

Dom, Mitch and Cordell entered the kitchen and Arianna ended up fixing each of them a toasted sandwich, as well.

"I'm glad you're all here," she said. "I got a call from a friend who worked with me at Xtark. Says I quit just in time. With Carter, the lead game designer, mysteriously gone, the company is making all employees take a mandatory, nonpaid two-week vacation. Sounds like they're scrambling to regroup."

"We hamstringed Darkblood efforts again." Jackson gave Mitch a high five and they clinked milk glasses.

"They didn't have a backup plan in case he left?" Dom took a small sample bite of his sandwich then followed it up with a larger bite.

"Remember, they had always planned to turn him. They probably didn't think they'd need a contingency plan." Lily waved a bite on the end of her fork. "Next time you're up, Arianna, can you make these for Zoe? She'd love this."

"Yeah, sure." After fixing Jackson a second one, Arianna joined them at the center island, plate and fork in hand.

Lily continued, "They must've figured they'd string him along for a while, keep this hanging over his head to get him to do what they wanted with the game."

Jackson noticed Arianna staring at her plate for a moment. He reached over and rubbed her back.

Even though Carter had betrayed her, she still felt badly about the circumstances that had forced him to do something so terrible. She didn't think she'd ever make a choice like he had, but you never knew until you walked a mile in someone else's shoes.

She flashed him a tiny smile.

After finishing the first sandwich, he wasted no time starting in on the second one. "Yeah, they basically had him by the nuts and he couldn't do a damn thing. Hey, where's Xian? I want him to try this."

"He's got a date," answered Cordell.

"Niiice," said Jackson. "I'm going to wait up to see his walk of shame."

"I doubt there's going to be a walk of shame," Mitch said. "Xian is too much of a gentleman, unlike some people I know. Not everyone expects a first date to involve sheet time."

"You are so wrong about me," Jackson said. "Arianna, tell them. We didn't roll around on the first date."

"Uh, technically, we've never even had a date."

"What do you call that night when you fixed dinner

for me at your house? We had wine. We talked. And we most certainly didn't have sex."

Arianna laughed. "That was my attempt to get information from you and to keep you from biting my neck. It wasn't really my idea of a date."

"DON'T PEEK," JACKSON SAID to her as he led her outside. Arianna carefully picked her way down the front steps of Casa en las Colinas.

"How can I with your hands over my eyes?"

"Because you're a cheater and I don't trust you."

She knocked him playfully with her elbow. "What? When have I ever cheated?"

"Do the words Texas Hold'em mean anything to you?"

"Last night? That wasn't cheating. Lily said she saw you peeking at my cards, so I was just evening the score. Ask Mackenzie. She saw it, too."

"I wasn't looking at your cards."

"Then what were you looking at?"

He hesitated.

"See? Busted. You *were* trying to look at my cards. My cheating was canceled out because you did it first."

"Okay. Fine. But it wasn't your cards I was trying to catch a glimpse of. It was your breasts."

"You're so full of crap," she said, laughing.

"I'm serious. When it comes to you and your body, I'm a weak man, Arianna. A very weak man. I resort to all sorts of bad things when it comes to you."

After about twenty steps on the gravel driveway, he stopped her. Night had fallen not long ago and the crickets were just starting up in the forest. He still hadn't dropped his hands from her eyes.

"What is this all about? Where are we going?"

If the empathic connection worked equally both ways, she'd have tried to read his thoughts, but all she got from him was his excitement. Mackenzie had said she was able to hear Dom's thoughts, but then, they'd shared a lot of blood, too. Arianna hadn't had any of Jackson's. Yet. While Mackenzie and the other changelings she'd met didn't seem to be drawn to sweetbloods like other vampires were, she wanted to make sure it wouldn't adversely affect her ability to be around them and run the sweet home before she went through the transformation process. Although Jackson was eager for her to be a changeling, he understood that the home, as well as her blog, were very important to her. And for that, she loved him even more.

"I'm taking you out on our first date."

Her heart swelled. He'd remembered that offhand comment of hers. "You are?"

"Do you recall when we first met and I made fun of your car?"

"Yeah. You said it was a junker and a piece of shit."

"Well, that piece of shit saved our lives," he said, removing his hands. "I had it repaired.... And then some."

She blinked once, twice, hardly believing what she saw.

There, parked in the driveway, was her Caddy, painted her favorite shade of green.

"Oh, my God." She ran up to it and walked all the

way around. It looked like a totally new car. All the dents were gone, the bumper reattached, the wheels rechromed. She opened the back door. Even the seats inside were new. The car had been completely restored.

"You…you did this for me?" Tears stung her eyes as she turned toward him.

"Yes. You like it?"

"Looking at it now, I feel guilty about how badly I've treated it over the years. It's…it's gorgeous."

"I had thought you were just being careless, but it was on purpose?"

She told him the story of how her father had given it to her years ago, thinking it was her birthday, when it really was the birthday of one of his girlfriends. She'd mistreated it all these years because of him.

His expression darkened. "I'm…sorry. I should've asked you first. It was wrong of me to assume you'd like it fixed up."

Her heart felt like a huge, unwieldy lump in her throat. How long had he been planning this? Parts for such an old vehicle couldn't have been easy to find. She grabbed his chin, forcing him to look at her. "I totally love it, Jackson. It's the most thoughtful thing anyone has ever done for me." She reached up on tiptoe and kissed him. "Thank you."

"I didn't know what it meant to you. What it represented. If you'd rather not drive it, I'll understand completely."

She stood on the doorjamb so that she could look squarely into his eyes. "I can't run from my past, Jackson. And you know what? I don't want to. Are there things I wish had never happened? Absolutely. But my past is what made me what I am today and without it, I wouldn't have you. This car—then and now—represents how I've changed since you came into my life. You've provided me answers that I'd been searching for over a lifetime. You filled a void inside that I didn't think could be filled. And like this car, I feel like a better me. I'm happy... I'm fulfilled... I have answers. And it's all because of you. God, I love you so much, it hurts."

His lips were crushing hers before her brain had even registered that he'd moved. In a flash, he shoved her into the backseat of the car and was on top of her.

She laughed. "What if someone looks out and sees us?"

"This won't take long," he grunted.

Powerful muscles bulged under her hands as he shoved her skirt up to her waist. He unzipped his jeans and his thick erection sprang free. When he gripped the base of it to guide it into her body, her breath hitched.

There, on the ridge of the tip, was that small metal stud.

A thrill of excitement ran the length of her spine and curled itself deliciously low in her abdomen. Her thong rubbed against the sudden heat between her legs. She reached down and pulled the fabric aside. Had he forgotten he had it in? No way was she going to say anything, in case he stopped and removed it.

When he slipped the tip into her folds, the warm metal pressed against her sensitive bud. Oh, my God, this was going to be amazing. She tilted her hips, eager to take him in, but he hesitated.

"Will you tell me if it bothers you?" he whispered into her hair. "I'll go slow so it doesn't freak you out."

So he did remember. "It's not going to freak me out," she replied, digging her nails into his buttocks, urging him to continue. The heat between her legs was almost unbearable. Her body ached with a need so powerful that she was certain she'd shatter into a million pieces if he wasn't soon inside her.

This man was everything to her. He owned her heart and soul.

As he slowly slid past her folds, the stud rubbed along her sensitive flesh, demanding her full attention. A surge of pleasure hit her so hard that she was certain she must've screamed.

Not all the way inside yet, he stopped, a worried expression plastered on his face. "Are you okay? Do you need me to—"

"Shh." She brushed aside a strand of his hair that had loosened from his half ponytail and kissed him. "I've never had it happen so fast before."

Apparently satisfied by her response, he pushed his tongue into her mouth, claiming her, as he thrust himself the rest of the way in. She gasped against his lips, her inner muscles stretching just enough to accommodate his size. And then he began to move inside her.

Over and over he thrust as animalistic male sounds rumbled in his chest. That metal stud rubbed against parts deep inside her that, until now, were foreign to her. A wave of pleasure so intense that it bordered on pain swept relentlessly over her again. She clasped her legs around his hips and hung on. Then, with one final push, he stopped, holding himself deep inside. He filled her unlike any man had ever done before.

"Oh, my God, Arianna. Oh, my God."

Then his whole body shuddered as he released into her.

CHAPTER TWENTY-EIGHT

Three months later

THE CROWD AT THE RIBBON-CUTTING ceremony was larger than Arianna expected. It seemed as though everyone who worked at Region or any of the field offices had brought a guest or two. The small theater was packed. They all wanted to see the Agency's new sweetblood house, officially called a sweet home, even if it was all handled virtually. No one except a few authorized personnel was allowed to know the actual location.

She looked around expectantly but didn't see the people she'd invited. They'd promised they were coming, but she didn't expect them to be true to their word. If they showed up, great. If not, it wasn't like she had her heart set on it.

A warm hand covered her shoulder. "How are you doing with the crowd? Hanging in there?"

Touched by how considerate Jackson always was, she placed her hand over his. Her nervousness about large groups of people hadn't come up much, so the fact that he remembered meant a lot to her. Even without the empathic connection, she'd bet he would've noticed.

"To tell you the truth, I hadn't really thought about it. I'm nervous, but it's because of my speech. Many of these people don't know me yet and this is the first impression they're going to have. Not just of me but the entire sweet-home idea."

"Just talk about it like you're explaining it to a friend. You're passionate about this concept, Arianna. They're going to see that and see this project for what it's worth. All the regions have struggled with how to protect the sweetbloods in their areas. This might very well be the solution they've been looking for."

Someone tapped on a wineglass and pretty soon the whole room was a cacophony of tinkling wineglasses.

Dom walked up to the podium and adjusted the microphone for his height. "A few months ago when I first met Arianna, I was immediately impressed by her intelligence, her loyalty and her courage."

Arianna's face heated and she didn't hear much of the rest of his introduction. When everyone began to clap, she knew it was her cue.

Dom gave her a quick hug. "I meant every word."

"Thanks," she said, trying not to sound too sheepish.

She pulled the microphone down and looked out into the crowd. Amidst a sea of unfamiliar faces, she spotted Lily and Alfonso near the stage. Good. She planned to point him out as the genius behind the design of the home and its extensive safety features.

Kip, Mitch and a few of the other Guardians stood clustered together. Cordell stood alone and slightly away from them. His wife, Shannon, had been sick. She hoped it was nothing serious. She made a note to ask Jackson about it later. Since she was going to be working closely with Cordell, not only as the sweet-home administrator, but also because he'd agreed to be the new IT guy for Paranormalish, she wanted to be sensitive to what was going on in his personal life.

She wished that Finn, a helicopter pilot for Region, and his fiancée, Brenna, could've come. A former Army Ranger, Finn was in charge of security at the house, but since he was a sweetblood, Santiago thought it best if he wasn't around this large group of vampires.

In the second row were a few of the Council members she'd met already. Their presence would've made her the most nervous, but she'd already been introduced to Trace, one of the newest Council members in the area. He'd said he was one hundred percent behind her and that a solution like this was long overdue. A beautiful woman with chin-length dark hair sat next to him. Mackenzie had told her that Trace's woman had recently gone through the changeling process, so Arianna was eager to meet her and find out exactly what her experience had been like—though apparently it had been done to save her life.

Dom and Mackenzie sat at a nearby table, their son squirming in her lap. Dom was being particularly attentive, stroking her arm, whispering in her ear. Men could be so obvious when it came to wanting sex later.

Arianna explained how the sweet-home concept worked and fielded a few questions. All in all, everyone seemed really excited to finally have options when they ran across sweetbloods in their fields. It wouldn't be a solution for everyone, but in cases like Krystal's, it would give her a chance to grow up and learn the skills she'd need to survive. She looked out into the crowd and still didn't see the two that she had invited. She'd drawn out her portion long enough. She couldn't stall any longer. Which was too bad. They should've been on hand for this next part.

"And with that, I turn it over to Region Commander Tristan Santiago."

She soon made her way back to her seat.

"Nice job," Jackson whispered. "I can't believe I get to sleep with someone as beautiful and intelligent as you every night."

She gave him a quick peck. How did she get so lucky, to have a man like Jackson feel this way about her? "Thank you."

Another quick glance around the room revealed that the people she'd invited still hadn't come. At least she hadn't told Jackson. It'd be better that he never knew about it.

Santiago nodded to someone offstage. Wearing a sundress and patent-leather shoes, Zoe trumped onstage and handed him a large wooden sign. A few people in the audience chuckled. With her chin cocked just so, Zoe glared at them and marched off.

Santiago looked over at Arianna first then addressed the crowd. "Arianna doesn't know this yet, but we took a vote on what the first sweet home should be named. I'd like to present to you the Kristine Wells Home."

The audience erupted in applause. Tears welled up in her eyes and threatened to overflow. Jackson squeezed her shoulder and kissed her.

"Surprised?"

She nodded, not trusting herself to speak. They'd named the sweet home after her mother. Her heart swelled at the kindness and overwhelming support these people had given her. All of this meant so much.

"But that's not all," Santiago said in that gruff, gravelly voice of his. "I have one more important announcement to make."

She started to turn around to give Santiago her undivided attention again when the back door opened and a distinguished older couple walked in. With light brown hair piled high on her head, the woman had her arm looped through the elbow of a man with a ramrod-straight spine and emerald-green eyes.

A lump of emotion formed in her throat, making it hard to swallow. It had to be them. Jackson followed her line of vision and his shoulders stiffened.

Oh, no, was he upset?

"Did you invite my parents?" His eyes glistened as he continued to stare in their direction.

She nodded. "I'm sorry. I thought they'd want to see this."

His nostrils flared slightly. "I'm stunned they came. They've never shown an interest in anything I've done before. What did you have to promise them to get them to come?"

"Nothing. I told them a little about what you'd done and how much I loved you. When your mother asked a little about me, I told her. Everything. I think the part about growing up without a mother really had an impact on her. She said she'd talk it over with your father and try to see about coming up for this."

A war of emotion flashed across his expression and he turned back around to face the stage. God, she hoped she hadn't made a mistake.

Zoe tromped to the podium again, this time, carrying something wrapped in cloth. A few more people laughed as she handed it to Santiago. She grinned and didn't seem fazed. When she didn't exit the stage right away, Lily waggled her fingers at her, but Zoe pretended not to notice, choosing instead to bask in the attention.

"Pssst." Alfonso, who was seated next to Lily, held out his arms. Zoe brightened, skipped off the stage and sat in her father's lap.

Lily elbowed him playfully and he shrugged. "What can I say?" he mouthed to her. "She's Daddy's girl."

"Jackson, would you come up here, please?" Santiago motioned him onstage.

His head snapped up. "What's this all about?" he whispered to Arianna.

She smiled. "You'll see."

Jackson walked down the center aisle and climbed up onto the stage. Because she knew him so well, she could tell he was a little uncomfortable, but she doubted anyone else noticed. God, he looked great in that suit. It stretched broadly over his shoulders and was perfectly tailored so that you could see his trim waist and thick thighs. She couldn't get him to wear dress shoes, though. He'd insisted on those cowboy boots. But that was fine. He looked really hot in them, too.

Santiago cleared his throat, and his voice boomed into the microphone once more, commanding everyone's attention. Even Zoe seemed to be listening.

"While I can't tell you many of the specific details," he said, placing his hand on Jackson's shoulder, "it is because of this man's selfless act of heroism in the face of terrible personal danger to himself that I'm awarding him with one of the Agency's highest honors for an active agent. On behalf of the Governing Council, I'm pleased to award Jackson Foss with the prestigious Night Brethren Award."

For the second time tonight, the crowd erupted in applause.

Santiago whispered to Jackson and he nodded, taking the microphone. He glanced out into the crowd. "Mom, Dad, thank you for coming. It means the world to me that you made the trip up here." Not normally an emotional man, he pulled out a linen handkerchief and mopped his eyes.

Arianna's heart soared. Maybe inviting them hadn't been a mistake, after all.

After saying a few words of thanks, he hesitated but didn't let go of the microphone. "I was going to wait to do this later, but this seems like the perfect time. Arianna, would you stand up again?"

Me? If she could read his thoughts, she knew he'd be saying, *No, the other Arianna in the room.*

She stood and smoothed down her knee-length wool skirt.

What's this all about?

He gave an imperceptible shrug that said wait and see.

"The first time I laid eyes on you, I knew you were an incredible woman. Not only were you the most beautiful thing I'd ever seen with a spirit and determination that I'd never experienced before, but also you saw something worthwhile in me that was hidden under all my flaws and imperfections. You believed in me when no one else would. Hell, you believed in me when I didn't even believe in myself. The best part of me is you, Arianna, and I can't bear to live my life without you."

The theater was quiet as the hundred or so audience members held their breath. Even little Miguel had stopped squirming.

Jackson stepped off the stage, reached into the inside pocket of his suit and got down on one knee. A roaring, rushing sound filled her head. She forced herself to concentrate so that she could relive every word, every nuance of this moment for the rest of her life.

"So, in front of all these people, including my mother and father, I want to ask you something very important." He opened the box, revealing a platinum ring with diamonds and emeralds nestled inside.

She gasped. It was gorgeous.

"If the good Lord is willing, I want to make a life with you. I want to grow old with you. Have a home. And if the union is a good one...babies." A couple of sniffles could be heard in the audience.

Oh, Jackson. I love you.

He smiled and she was pretty sure her cheeks were wet with tears now, too.

"I love you, Arianna Katherine Wells. Will you make me the happiest man in the world and...marry me?"

She reached down, tucked a strand of hair behind his ear and said yes.

* * * * *

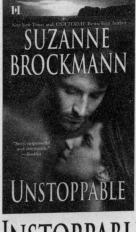

REQUEST YOUR FREE BOOKS!

2 FREE NOVELS FROM THE PARANORMAL ROMANCE COLLECTION PLUS 2 FREE GIFTS!

YES! Please send me 2 FREE novels from the Paranormal Romance Collection and my 2 FREE gifts (gifts are worth about $10). After receiving them, if I don't wish to receive any more books, I can return the shipping statement marked "cancel." If I don't cancel, I will receive 4 brand-new novels every month and be billed just $21.42 in the U.S. or $23.46 in Canada. That's a saving of at least 21% off the cover price of all 4 books. It's quite a bargain! Shipping and handling is just 50¢ per book in the U.S. and 75¢ per book in Canada.* I understand that accepting the 2 free books and gifts places me under no obligation to buy anything. I can always return a shipment and cancel at any time. Even if I never buy another book, the two free books and gifts are mine to keep forever.

237/337 HDN FEL2

Name _____ (PLEASE PRINT) _____

Address _____ Apt. # _____

City _____ State/Prov. _____ Zip/Postal Code _____

Signature (if under 18, a parent or guardian must sign)

Mail to the **Reader Service:**
IN U.S.A.: P.O. Box 1867, Buffalo, NY 14240-1867
IN CANADA: P.O. Box 609, Fort Erie, Ontario L2A 5X3

Not valid for current subscribers to the Paranormal Romance Collection or Harlequin® Nocturne™ books.

Want to try two free books from another line?
Call 1-800-873-8635 or visit www.ReaderService.com.

* Terms and prices subject to change without notice. Prices do not include applicable taxes. Sales tax applicable in N.Y. Canadian residents will be charged applicable taxes. Offer not valid in Quebec. This offer is limited to one order per household. All orders subject to credit approval. Credit or debit balances in a customer's account(s) may be offset by any other outstanding balance owed by or to the customer. Please allow 4 to 6 weeks for delivery. Offer available while quantities last.

Your Privacy—The Reader Service is committed to protecting your privacy. Our Privacy Policy is available online at www.ReaderService.com or upon request from the Reader Service.

We make a portion of our mailing list available to reputable third parties that offer products we believe may interest you. If you prefer that we not exchange your name with third parties, or if you wish to clarify or modify your communication preferences, please visit us at www.ReaderService.com/consumerschoice or write to us at Reader Service Preference Service, P.O. Box 9062, Buffalo, NY 14269. Include your complete name and address.

LAURIE LONDON

77586	EMBRACED BY BLOOD	___ $7.99 U.S.	___ $9.99 CAN.
77544	BONDED BY BLOOD	___ $7.99 U.S.	___ $9.99 CAN.

(limited quantities available)

TOTAL AMOUNT	$ _____
POSTAGE & HANDLING	$ _____
($1.00 FOR 1 BOOK, 50¢ for each additional)	
APPLICABLE TAXES*	$ _____
TOTAL PAYABLE	$ _____

(check or money order—please do not send cash)

To order, complete this form and send it, along with a check or money order for the total above, payable to HQN Books, to: **In the U.S.:** 3010 Walden Avenue, P.O. Box 9077, Buffalo, NY 14269-9077; **In Canada:** P.O. Box 636, Fort Erie, Ontario, L2A 5X3.

Name: _____
Address: _____ City: _____
State/Prov.: _____ Zip/Postal Code: _____
Account Number (if applicable): _____

075 CSAS

*New York residents remit applicable sales taxes.
*Canadian residents remit applicable GST and provincial taxes.

HQN™ | HARLEQUIN® www.Harlequin.com

PHLL0312BL